I0668746

ONEIROI

THE ICHOR SERIES
BOOK FOUR

TRISH D. W.

TRIGGER WARNING

This story contains mature topics that may trigger some readers and can be inappropriate for a younger audience. These triggers include excessive gore that results in characters' deaths, suicidal ideations, an off-scene suicide attempt, discussions about mental health (i.e. grief, depression, guilt), and betrayal by loved ones.

Dedicated to the people in my life who inspired the seer and the savior, the heart and the hammer, the singer and the seeker, and the hero and the huntress. You shaped this story. Your presence in my life was the ink on the parchment. Thank you.

THE PROPHECY

On the eighty-eighth night of the
    eighty-eighth year
When crimson shifts to gold,
A prophecy will unfold.
From the ashes of time,
Eight figures will rise.

Eight, the sacred number of
    immortality,
Seals the destiny of a seer and a
    savior,
A heart and a hammer,
A singer and a seeker,
And a hero and a huntress.

A river of black will cease to exist,
Unless the one with sight sees
    through the mist.

THE PROPHECY

A world of hatred and oaths will
    prevail,
Unless the oracle can see the truth
    and can derail.

The ultimate fate is decided when
    the heart twice fails,
And from the savior, a terrible
    scream will wail.
The sound will echo forevermore,
And from the scream, spawns a war.

Hatred and Sight,
Oh, how they will fight.
The winner is untold,
But one thing is known.

Whichever side has the hammer
    which swings,
The hero who knows he must bleed,
The muse who no longer sings,
The seer, who sees the future with
    great speed,
The huntress who clips the
    monster's life strings,
The heart whose life will cede.
The savior with death she brings,
The seeker with life he leads,
Will be gifted the role of eternal
    queens or kings.

The world will crumble like
    Pompeii,

But the seeker will guide fallen
friends away.
To safety, the seeker will find the
ashes he will revive.
The world will be unlike any other
and will eternally thrive.

Unless the hatred wins,
Then the seeker and the seer, the
hero and the hammer will
surely die.

ONE

HART SOMMERS

It has been five days since Styx won the first round in a game nobody else knew they were playing. Torrents of Zeus's rage strike the ground, ceaselessly searching for Styx behind any hidden rock or grassy terrain. Poseidon's seas rise to furious lengths, threatening to part in hopes of finding Saffron hidden beneath its endless depths. All humans who have died since Saffron's capture mutter the word a grief-stricken Hades says the most.

"Ogygia."

But where am I in the fight beside the gods?

I am a lowly human, yet destined to unfurl Styx's cruel destiny. Moments after the disheartening truth came out on Mt. Olympus, Zeus sent me back to Earth where I belong, but I descended with a single job. As the last remaining oracle, I must be the one who finds Saffron's location. Then, I must find the way to defeat Styx.

I have granted myself two improbabilities, even though

a part of me still struggles to believe the path the Fates have aligned my life with. I sit in Apollo's art room, an unblemished pencil in my hand, staring at an empty canvas. There should be a story upon this canvas. A clue to where Ogygia is, which is Calypso's island, that is deemed impossible to find.

I settle the tip of the pencil to the canvas, but nothing happens.

Each time I have used my powers, it was a surge that pushed through my lungs. Burrowed its way into my bloodstream and restricted my vision until it consumed me. For so long, I feared the power roaring and thrashing inside of me, sent down from generations of powerful oracles, but in the moments when I treasure it the most, my premonitions fail me. In the five days since Zeus told me to find his daughter, with a terrible crack in his voice that spoke his fear, I have failed him.

I have failed Saffron, who protected me from Styx and saved the world from the prophecy unfurling in the villainess's favor.

The art room's door creaks open, ever so softly. He takes one step into the room, and the scent of him envelops the space. He hasn't spoken a word yet, but he has already consumed me. Electricity gently glides down my skin, bringing every hair on my arm to attention. I turn around, and although I have seen his face many times before, my heart skips a beat. My mind, dented with self-consciousness, still stares in awe that he wants me.

Apollo holds a tray of fruits, cheeses, and bread. There is a small smile on his face as he pads across the room and sets the food on the stool beside me. I cannot think of the last time I ate, perhaps early yesterday; when Apollo is this close to me, smelling of sunshine and hope, I do not hunger for food. I thirst for his touch. The warmth that he exudes.

I drop the pencil, unblemished from work, and I reach for him.

He circles his arms around me, nestling against my back, and the stress weighing on my shoulders momentarily dissipates. I am encompassed in his touch and warmth. Pleasantly distracted by the tickle of the ends of his blonde hair against the curve of my neck and the softness of his kiss against the skin behind my ear.

He says nothing, but in the comfort of his silence, my own omissions come to life. "I can't do it. I can't find her, and I hate myself for it." He places a hand on the curve of my jaw and tilts my head back so I can meet with his face. "Am I good enough for…"

He doesn't let me finish my sentence. His mouth is upon mine, coaxing away the doubt with each gentle nip of his teeth against my bottom lip. His touch is ginger, but demanding, too. Forcing me to forget, at least for a few seconds, about my despairing thoughts. I open my mouth, and I let him help me focus on something other than defeat.

When he pulls away from the kiss, he stays close. Presses his forehead against mine and lets me breath him in. "You have only started your journey as an oracle. It is only sensible that you take time for something this big." Another kiss lands on the tip of my nose. "One of my oracles struggled with premonitions for almost six months, and all she was trying to discover were weather forecasts."

My eyes meet with his. "Really?"

"Really." He takes both of my hands in his, further wrapping me in his embrace. "You are magnificent, μέλι, and a few days of stilted magic should not make you feel

3

any less. And if I must remind you every hour of every day that you are everything perfect in my world, then I will without hesitation."

"I love you."

Apollo's smile consumes his face as the words register in his ears. "And I love you."

My vision spots, blurring the image of Apollo in front of me. His scent evaporates, too. Instead of his sunshine, the faintest aroma of sand and saltwater tickles my nose. It's a feather-like touch that brushes along my septum, and I cling to the first feeling of a premonition since Dionysus's party.

My vision is completely black, obscured from Apollo and the room, but my hands know the scene in front of me. Saltwater lands on the tip of my tongue, and smooth, hot sand nestles in between my toes. I am moving, jostling towards this premonition that brings us all closer to Styx's ruination.

Towards Saffron, the hero of the prophecy.

Time is limitless in the void between present and future. I only know my premonition has ended when the soft clatter of a pencil drops to the floor and the scent of saltwater evaporates. When I feel the cold tile floor beneath my feet instead of hot sand. When I hear his voice once again, beautiful like a hymn.

"Holy gods," he mutters.

I draw my gaze towards my canvas, which was empty only moments ago, and now bursts with life. Saffron sits on an island, still wearing the tattered gown from Dionysus's party. With ripped sleeves and a shortened hem created by feverish hands. Her elbows rest in the sand, as Saffron tilts her head up towards the sky and stars at the crescent moon.

4

A few feet behind her, a crow sits with its eyes closed. Blood pools in the surrounding sand; the tattered pieces of Saffron's gown drapes over its tiny build. The island is expansive, threatening to swallow the crow and Saffron whole, but there is nobody else there. Not Styx, Calypso, or Hecate. Only two occupants sit in their pretty cage, waiting to be released.

"It's impossible." Apollo stumbles back, hand moving to his mouth.

"What are you talking about?" I follow his shocked gaze, and I land on the sleeping crow. "It's just a bird."

"Epiales."

He says the name nearly expunged from history, and my mind reverts to the first drawing I made for Saffron. They hired me to create a portrait of Saffron, but when the fog of premonitions faded, Saffron was not alone in the artwork. She stood with a god I had never seen before, and carnage surrounded them. Epiales, the personification of nightmares, was that mysterious male with a mop of curly black hair, who feared the mass deaths around them as much as Saffron.

"But he's dead."

Apollo hesitantly moves towards the drawing and me. He places his hand on my shoulder, suddenly cold to the touch, and we both stare at the truth that settles upon us like the beginning of an illness.

"I'm not so sure anymore."

Apollo presses a kiss to my head, but it is an unspoken farewell. A terrible omen that starts with the personification of nightmares, but the end is unclear. Death awaits, but whose? Styx or ours?

"I have to go." He presses another kiss to the top of my head. "But I'll be back as soon as I can."

5

I know where he goes- Mt. Olympus. The place I am forbidden from entering, but he flees to with news about Epiales. He doesn't take the drawing with him, but leaves me alone with the dreaded truth.

There are almost no remaining stories about Epiales, the personification of nightmares, but he is the gods' proclaimed traitor. In the final Titanomachy War between Zeus and Kronos, Epiales fought for the king of Titans. And just like so many who chose Kronos, Saffron executed him. While there are famous paintings that depict Saffron executing Kronos and the Mother of Monsters, Echidna, no artwork depicts Epiales. All who bleed red forgot him.

But not for long.

I lean forward, finger outstretched, and I trace the curve of his wings. Coldness erupts in my veins, chilling my blood, but I cannot move my hand away. I let my finger drag around the outline of him, and then my vision fogs. Dark spots obscure the scene, while another one unfurls.

There is a scream, so feminine and heart aching. It threatens to rupture my eardrums, and with the sound of true agony, glass shatters. The bellow becomes a part of the wind, immortally echoing its horror. I know it is Saffron who screams, but for who? The re-animated god on the beach with her, or for somebody else?

Images form in my mind, appearing like ink blots.

"Apollo was right."

A male voice shatters the vision, and all the darkness ebbs away. I hate the god who brings me back to the present because I know that version of a future was important. Possibly the most vital part of the impending war, but it is gone. The ink blots have dried. The fog has dispersed.

I turn around, and Hermes stands in the doorway.

A part of me wants to yell at him. To curse him for

distracting me from my sole purpose in this world. I want to find Saffron, and all the others who are destined to destroy Styx, but then I look at him. Truly stare at the boyish face, distraught with mistakes. My tongue dries, the anger gone, too.

Gods are always beautiful, and Hermes is one of the more handsome immortals. But not today.

Today, Hermes is a mere mortal, burdened with the weight of too many mistakes. Deep bags are heavy under his lids. His hair, typically both messy and organized, is in disarray. I can see the indent of his hands rummaging through the locks like fingerprints on glass.

He doesn't stare at me, though. His haunted green eyes lock on the drawing behind me. I follow his gaze, and it is a new canvas sitting on my easel. The previous drawing of Saffron and a crow sitting on the beach is gone. Now, it is a male's face that I instantly know is Epiales. Glass surrounds him, and several figures cast shadows around him, but his face is the only decipherable one.

His eyes are the brightest shade of silver, like gunmetal glinting in the sunlight. The dark mess of curls hanging over his forehead, dusting the top of his eyelashes, illuminates them. He is handsome, just as Hermes is, but they are complete opposites. Where Hermes's face is soft curves, Epiales is all sharp angles.

Hermes takes a hesitant step forward, his eyes never moving from Epiales's sketched face. The closer he nears me, the more harrowing his appearance becomes. Saffron has been missing for five days, but Hermes looks like he lost his wife decades ago and still has not survived the casualty. He has always been a naturally slim male, but now he is skeletal. I can make out his spine poking through his shirt.

In high school, my teachers taught me that gods can alter their appearances based upon their mood and preference. It is why Aphrodite's form is ever-changing and never settles on a single body. Hermes chooses to look malnourished and on the brink of death. He chooses to wither away because of guilt, for his choices or heartbreak. Perhaps both.

He stands to my right, towering over me as he peruses Epiales's face. I did not have the chance to finish drawing him, so I cut him off at the shoulders, but Hermes does not care. He stares at this image like Epiales is truly in front of him, as real as him and me.

"The monster has returned," Hermes whispers, lips curling with barely kempt rage. "That monstrosity is with my wife?" He poses the words as a question, but I do not need to answer him. He already knows.

For days, I could not see a vision, but they roar through me now. Strike me in the chest with the severity of one of Zeus's bolts. Hermes's words knock me off my stool, and as my body smacks onto the ground, darkness envelops me.

I hear my voice, but I do not associate it with myself. Something else thrives inside of me, spewing a prophecy I have never heard before today. But it's the unwavering truth. It is a truth Hermes must hear.

A monster, some call him.
A nightmare, other hymn.
But when the scars fade,
And the old bones decayed,
A monster, he is no more.

He is the truth the Savior must see,
He is the crow the world must free.

Gold becomes red,
Mistakes are now dead.

He is the restored.
The one who wields the final sword.

He is the revival.
The one who must bleed for survival.

I open my eyes, the prophecy fading from my mind, but Hermes is gone. And where he once stood lays paper shards. The rest of the canvas is intact, but where Epiales's face was, there are only tatters.

TWO

SAFFRON

If you stare at anything long enough, it can become lethal.

It can twist your mind, turning rational thoughts into creations of destruction. Worse, if the object of your fastidious observation should be dead. If the sight you can't deviate from was a sight you were never supposed to see again, except in your most haunted nightmares.

I have been on this island for five days, ever since Styx and Hecate left me here with him. Zeus designed Ogygia to be undiscoverable, and I wonder how much he regrets that decision now that I'm gone. Or does my absentee father care at all?

Nobody is going to find me, which means nobody will know the truth that Epiales is alive. Brought back to life by the same hands that killed him. I stare at those hands for longer than I should, equally condemning and thanking them for the powers they gift me with.

There is nothing on this barren island, except for a

dozen fruitless trees and endless white sand. There is nothing for me to stare at except these hands that brought him back to life and him, my beautiful storyteller.

I almost miss the scars, which used to litter his flesh in varying cuts and slashes. The multitude of tattoos remains on his milky skin, but the severity behind them is gone. The stories I once loved left with those scars, leaving behind only the black ink.

He should be dead, but the slow rise and fall of his chest contradicts the truth I have continuously told myself for eighty-eight years. Everything, except for the scars, is exactly as I remember. The perfectly coiled black hair still frames sharp cheekbones and an even sharper jawline. And if he ever opens his eyes, I know the magnitude of his stare will still send electricity throughout my body.

I fear nearing him, as if he is a mirage, and if I get too close, he will disappear. I stay close enough to ensure he is still breathing, but I'm far enough away that I cannot touch him. Cannot let myself believe this is anything but a long, excruciating dream.

The only time I touched him was on the first day of our captivity. In a daze, underneath the sun's merciless rays, I tore parts of my dress fabric and draped them over his naked body. My dress sleeves became a cover for his face and neck. The long train became an oversized shirt that fell a little past his knees. I used a few strips to cover his feet, too. He is burning faster than I would like, which brings my gaze to the unforgiving sun.

"I know you're trying to find me, Po, but you're killing him. Cover the sun, please."

I say this every day, and nothing ever changes. Po can't hear me on Ogygia, and his sun never leaves Epiales alone. I repeat this same line every day, but pretend not to care after the words leave my lips. Pretend that I am not worried about Epiales, who does not have the strength to open his eyes or fend off the heat. But that is all it is. Pretend. A farce I am trying to convince myself is the truth.

On the sixth day, I build him shelter.

All my rage and the overwhelming sense of helplessness come alive. I rip three out of the thirteen trees out by the roots with my bare hands. My screams make the remaining trees tremble as I slam the trunks against my knees and shatter the bark into scattered pieces. I pull apart the branches, staining the rough material in gilded blood.

By the time I am finished with his makeshift home, the sun has begun its descension from the sky. Pinks and reds bleed onto the white sand, dancing a deceiving tale of elation for only my eyes. It is then, as I curse the sky and the sun and its pretty colors, that she manifests.

Hecate.

My bones hum for her death. Sing a tune I cannot exact because of Styx and the oath I made to her. Still, Hecate keeps her distance. She stands at the edge between sand and water. The waves lap at her ankles, staining the hem of her gray gown.

"I come with gifts."

She holds folded clothes in her arms, but dangling from her index and middle finger is a bag of fruits. Crisp green apples peak out of the top, sitting beside matching grapes. I do not need food for sustenance, but my stomach growls with unmatched hunger. It is the only sound, along with the lapping water, on this barren island.

Her round eyes flick to my curling fists. "I see you're

13

still mad." Her gaze drifts. It roams around the expansive island and lands on Epiales. "Has he woken yet?"

"Why?"

The word that croaks out of my lips, the first I have spoken in six days, has nothing to do with her question. And she knows it. Hecate drops the pile of clothes between us. A stray peach rolls out of the bag. It lands by my foot, daring me to take a bite.

"Because love is both the greatest addiction and the worst weakness."

Green smoke covers the island once again. Her magic lifts the peach from the ground, cleans the sand from its skin, and drops it into my hand. I do not remember opening my palms and accepting her offer, but here it is. This damned peach serving as Hecate's olive branch.

I curl my fingers into the peach, breaking the skin. Juice slips down my fingers, sliding down my forearm. For a delusional moment, the liquid mirrors red blood.

"Tell me when he wakes," Hecate orders. "I have errands to run until then."

I glare at her, a death threat poised on the tip of my tongue, but she is gone. Off to complete errands that undoubtedly have dastardly consequences.

And she leaves the clothes and the bag full of food.

I scream as I chuck the peach into the ocean. It sprouts wings as it flies across the air, and it could stretch miles if magic did not interfere. A green shield materializes a few hundred feet outside of the island, and the peach bounces off it and drops into the ocean.

"Curse you!"

She hears me because the sun winks out as soon as the second word leaves my lips.

I collapse onto the ground. My knees sink into the

warm sand, and with the rage come tears I have held back for six days. Tears I have associated with weakness and desperation, but why lie about my feelings? What is the point?

In a land without time, I cannot tell how long I cry or how many times I pick at my cuticles until they are a bleeding, miserable mess. They always heal, and I always harm them once again. A cruel cycle that joins the sobs and the helplessness. Only the stars and Hecate's remnants are my company in my sorrow.

Until a whispered, uncertain voice stalls my heart.

"My queen."

THREE

HERMES

It is irrational, but I hate Hart Sommers.

Our conversation, if the oddity of it all can make up as a conversation, plays a haunting tune in my ears. A full day has come and gone since I saw her standing next to her drawing of Epiales. Guarding over it like he deserves to be protected. He stole Saffron from me once again. He chose the wrong side and still gets a second chance.

I can still feel the pieces of paper underneath my fingertips from when I shredded the drawing. It coats them like blood only I can see, and when I am not trying to rub myself clean from its carnage, I am cursed with an echo of her prophecy. The prophecy that surrounds him, the gods' forsaken Epiales, and my wife.

My ex-wife.

The truth that she is gone, both from my life and the world's, is worse than any blade. Harsher than any curse.

But it's true. Even when we find Saffron, she isn't returning to me.

Voices shout all around me as we sit in Poseidon's throne room and strategize, but I can only hear Hart Sommer's cryptic promise. ***But when the scars fade, and the old bones decayed, a monster, he is no more.***

Why must I suffer more torture? Why does he get to be with her, in a slice of land I cannot find, while I wallow in a pool of my mistakes? I am not faultless. I should have told her everything. Shouldn't have lied about an affair with Hecate. But in the scope of mistakes, Epiales' is worse.

Right?

He deceived her, and while I did too, mine was with selfless intentions. I only wanted to protect her. Save her from Styx and the looming prophecy hanging over her head like a storm. I love her, but Epiales can't get past his own selfish desires to truly comprehend the magnitude of love. He chose revenge. He was a willing villain alongside Kronos. I chose my wife first, and I suffered Typhon and Kronos's punishments for her. He didn't choose my wife until Kronos tried to take her from both of us.

My ex-wife.

Tears blur my vision so often that I scarcely remember what it is like to see without the blur of sadness. Voices rise around me, building in anguish and convalesces, but I only hear Hart Sommers eerily whisper. ***He is the truth the Savior must see; he is the crow the world must free.***

Dark mist possesses the room. It shrouds the arguing voices, blanketing the table and its guest in its obsidian magic. The only visible deities are Hades and Persephone, who sit at the end of the expansive table where we strate-gize. Hades' magic drowns out Poseidon's insults to Athena, swallowing any rebuttal Athena says next. In the bane of this silence, Hart's voice finally ceases its torment.

"Enough bickering." When Hades speaks, it is rare, and it is powerful. He commands a room with a mere syllable without ever raising his voice. "We are on day six of searching for Saffron through the oceans, and it has been unsuccessful. Tell me, brother. Who is out there right now searching for my daughter?"

The shadow obscuring Poseidon lifts. "Asopus and three of his daughters are swimming with my son, Triton. They will find her today. I'm certain."

I am not the only one who hears the doubt in his voice. If he believed Asopus, his daughters, and Triton would find Saffron today, then a joke would lace his words. He would have made a sexual innuendo while simultaneously answering Hades's question and insulting Athena. Gods, if he thought we were on our way to find Saffron, he would be blissfully drunk right now. But in the six days since her capture, he hasn't had a drop of alcohol.

That is the truth of this grave situation.

"When we faced Kronos, he had less than two decades to manipulate Saffron into killing us all. He thought with his ego and his manipulation skills, he could convince her to destroy us. While we were all concerned, we subcon-sciously knew we were going to win that war. With Saffron, the most powerful of us all, on our side, we knew Kronos would fall."

Hades eliminates his shadows, ensuring we can each see the mirrored expression of dismay on everyone's faces.

He waits to finish his statement until we all feel the gravity of this situation, like an acidic taste in our mouth;

TRISH D. W.

then, he says. "Kronos was an enemy we knew well. We understood his strengths and his weaknesses. We knew who was on his side and what his objectives were. He was an opponent we faced before and knew how to defeat. Many of you sat here ninety years ago, and you laughed and drank and trained to prepare for winning a war against him."

"But Styx is not Kronos," Persephone begins where her husband ends. Her voice is as grave as his, as if, in this moment, they share the same mind. Feel the same aches. "Styx is a power we thought we contained in a river. A fear we all forgot after eons of her docile actions. We know her aim is to become an eternal queen, but we know little else. We do not know the magnitude of her powers. She hides her weaknesses behind insurmountable power that we barely understand."

A sole tear slides down Persephone's face, and she does not wipe it away. She lets us see her sorrow.

"Styx has Saffron prisoner, but we do not know why," Hades says. "She brought Epiales back to life, and we do not know why. It's been six days, and Styx has not attacked; again, we do not know why."

Persephone reaches for her husband's hand, and he readily takes it. They squeeze tightly, and their eyes lock. We are audience to their unwavering love, as they lean against each other in fear for their daughter's wellbeing.

"We know some people she has aligned with," Hades says. "But we do not know if the missing gods are friends or foes."

They are talking about Ares.

On the same day of the ball, Hecate guided Ares away from the huntresses, and we have not seen him since. Sika, one of Artemis's most loyal huntresses, swears Hecate

20

tricked Ares, but there is still lingering uncertainty. He has tried to kill Saffron before, and though he did not join Kronos, Hecate didn't either. Styx lures gods and goddesses who never would have sided with Kronos. Another twine of fear knots inside us all. Immortals we believed we could trust have deceived us, and now nobody knows how to trust.

Is everybody in this room an ally for us, or are they an informant for Styx? The question plays in everybody's head, but it is a voice none of us wishes to say aloud.

"Kronos had sixteen years, after finding out Saffron existed, to hatch a plan of domination." Persephone looks at all of us, cementing our fear into memory. "But Styx has had thousands of years. Ever since she heard that prophecy, she has plotted and planned for our demise. She stored away every bit of information about us, using it for artillery before we understood the gravity of her malice. We are going into this war knowing there is a good chance we will lose it unless we find my daughter."

Her bottom lip wobbles at the last two words.

The other roles in the prophecy remain shrouded in mystery. Nobody knows who the huntress and the hero are supposed to be, nor do we understand who will be the hammer, the seeker, the singer, or the heart. Only two women, Hart and Saffron, are unequivocally the seer and the savior. And without the savior, without Saffron, we are dead. A pile of rubble underneath the ruins of Styx's eternal reign.

And we can't find her.

Neither can Hart.

Perhaps that is why I hate Hart. Because there was a kernel of hope, withering away inside of me, that believed Hart would fix my mistakes. I fondly remember the oracles of the Delphi. I remember her ancestor, Aashritha. She was not only beautiful, but her ability of foresight was unparalleled. She knew everything that occurred in the world and everything that came thousands of years later. I see Aashritha in Hart, and I keep waiting for her to tap into that magic. When she finally did, and I saw a glimpse of Aasritha's magic come alive in Hart, she told me the worst news yet.

That Epiales is alive.

"What do you suggest?" Athena asks.

Athena, the goddess of wisdom and battle strategies, is asking for advice for the first time in eons. First time, ever. Poseidon's sobriety and lack of jokes are alarming, but Athena not having an answer is worse.

Gods, are we really going to die?

"We need to separate," Hades says. The answer comes so swiftly, I am certain he and Persephone discussed this plan before today. "Into four groups, preferably. Poseidon, Amphitrite, and a group of lesser water gods stay in the castle. They continue to search the water."

Poseidon and Amphitrite nod their heads, and the latter says. "We will send half of our castle out every day, while the other stays on guard in case there is an attack."

"Another group needs to retrace Artemis and the huntresses' footsteps that led them to Ogygia the first time," Persephone says.

Artemis frowns. "It was a portal. We didn't stumble on Ogygia, they tricked us into entering it."

"I may not know Styx well, but I know Hecate." Persephone's voice takes a grave tone, the betrayal of her friend still wielding a heavy blow. "And Hecate frequently forgets to close her portals. Retrace your footsteps and try to find that portal if it is still there."

"I watched the portal close," Artemis says. "It's gone."

Persephone shakes her head. "No, it closed, but it's not gone. The only way portals truly close is if the witch goes back to stitch the air back together. Go back to where it was and pry it open with your hands. It'll be there." Under her breath, she adds. "It has to be."

None of us believed Styx was working on her own in her crusade for the throne, but none of us guessed Hecate's deceit. How quickly would we have found Artemis and the huntresses if we had known Hecate worked with Styx? We could have stomped this looming war to embers if we knew Hecate's role in it, but we trusted a goddess who never deserved that gratitude, and now Saffron is gone.

"We will leave as soon as Lamb wakes."

"It has been six days, and she hasn't-" Hades begins.

"When she wakes," Artemis interrupts, jaw hardened. "We will go, but I do not leave her behind."

Lamb is her eldest huntress, but more than that, she is the rope that tethers them all together. For the many who do not know Lamb well, they see what she wants them to, which is her meekness. She uses her mundane appearance and quiet demeanor like a sword and shield, but many gods haven't realized this truth about her. They see a mouse amongst felines, but Lamb is so much more than that. She is one of the best fighters in the huntress clan, and she is the greatest friend Artemis has ever had.

Artemis can survive many losses, but not Lamb's.

Nobody argues with Artemis; instead, Hades turns his attention to me. "We need another group to search for the missing gods."

The ones who aren't Saffron.

"You want me to focus on somebody else?" Anger

23

rushes through me, fast and brutal. "She's my wife. I should be out there, searching for her with everybody else!"

Ex-wife, my self-deprecating brain reminds me.

"Nobody is as fast as you," he continues, like I did not interrupt him. "And we need to know how many people are in her army. We know about the few who fought against us at the ball, but that is it. We only know the tiniest truth, and there are a lot of missing gods. A missing Olympian, too."

Realization dawns on me. "You want me to find Ares?"

"We want you to discover if he is still on our side, or if he is working with Styx."

As soon as the words leave Hades's lips, Athena glares at him. "My brother is not a traitor."

"And I did not believe Hecate would ever betray me," Persephone rises to her feet, eyes unwavering on Athena. "This time around, our greatest sin is to trust anybody. We could be sitting with enemies right now."

Artemis's huntresses have silently sat at the table with us, but as the silence rages between Persephone and Athena, Sika speaks up. "And where will you go, King Hades?"

While Lamb is one of the strongest huntresses, Sika is the strongest. She always has been, even when Willow was alive. She might be one of the wisest, too, because while Persephone is answering her question, Sika leans towards Dýnami and whispers in her ear. Beneath the projection of Persephone's voice, I cannot hear Sika's murmur, but whatever it is sends the hairs of my arm to attention.

What does she know that I don't?

"Hades and I will separate. Hypnos, Thanatos, and I will return to the Underworld. We will continue to interrogate any humans who have entered Ogygia, and we will maintain the mania ensuing down there."

"And I will go see Hart Sommers," Hades answers.

"Why?" Athena asks. "And where do you plan on sending me into this illustrious plan? Because if you tell me to stay down in this underwater cesspool a minute longer-"

"Gross," Poseidon interrupts.

"When my daughter first received her powers, she did not know how to harness them. She needed somebody like Poseidon, who has abilities himself, to learn her craft. Hart Sommers needs me to train her. She needs the dead oracles to teach her how to become the best one yet."

"And where are you sending this owl-face?" Poseidon asks. "Timbuktu? Antarctica? Tartarus? The Dagger of Chains, maybe? I am a fan of the last option."

Athena narrows her eyes at him. "If you think I want to stay here, with you and your filth, then-"

"Back to Mt. Olympus," Hades says, interrupting their endless bickers.

"Why?"

"Zeus's focus is on finding Saffron right now. He's scouring the world from his place on the clouds, but his attention fleets too quickly. I need you to go back to Mt. Olympus and make sure he stays focused on his task. I need you to help him find my daughter from the skies."

"And me?" a soft voice inquires.

Jamila sits next to me, looking so much like her ancestor, Hattie, that my heart sinks a little each time our eyes lock. I love her, the way any father would love their daughter, but the sight of her reminds me of too much. The deaths of Saffron's closest friends, which changed her forever. She stopped being the girl who loved strawberries and laughed at the moon. And my sweet, kind daughter is always the dead memory of my favorite times with Saffron.

"Where will I go?" she asks Hades.

Before Hades can answer, when the room is perfectly silent, there are three knocks on the door. In the nearly empty castle, the three knocks echo for miles. It slithers through the open door of the battle room, and it promises sinisterness.

"Now," Sika says.

Dýnami jumps to her feet, and she runs out of the room from the opposite door. Artemis stares confusedly at Dýnami's actions, but I stare at Sika. I watch her calm expression shift as she produces an arrow, levels it on her bow, and points it at Kymopoleia. Poseidon and Amphitrite's daughter barely flinches with the weapon in her face, but she is the only one.

Poseidon and Amphitrite jump to their feet, and his trident materializes in his hand. He points the three prongs in Sika's direction, and he sneers. "What is the meaning of this? Lower your weapon!"

Artemis produces a bow and arrow, too, but she points hers at Poseidon. "You will not harm her, or I swear to the gods-"

"What?" Amphitrite interrupts. She has a sword made of coral pointed at Artemis. "You will what?"

I look back at Sika as chaos whirls. At the determined slit of her eyes, the unwavering grip on her bowstring, and the poison tipped on the arrowhead. She has planned for this moment, cloaking her weapon in magic that can incapacitate an immortal. But why?

For a flickering second, I wonder if she is a traitor, but why would a traitor choose to attack Kymopoleia, a low-level goddess, first? And if she was a traitor, wouldn't she have pulled the trigger already?

I look back at Kymopoleia. She rarely ever speaks, or shows any inkling of amusement, but today is different. Her full, red lips curve into an amused smirk, and she asks Sika. "How did you find out?"

Poseidon's grip on his trident trembles. "What?"

Amphitrite stares at her daughter, who looks so much like her, and asks. "What are you talking about, Kymo?"

Sika doesn't respond to Kymopoleia, as her words were omission enough. The arrow flies faster than Kymopoleia can deflect, and it sinks into her chest. The poison worms its way through her bloodstream, and after she rips the arrow out of her body, she collapses onto the tabletop.

A scream ricochets through the air, and for a moment, I look expectedly at Amphitrite. But when I stare at the red-haired goddess, her mouth is open in shock as she stares toward the huntresses. Artemis is the one who screams as she runs towards one of the blonde huntresses, Akita, and rips her head from her shoulders with her bare hands. She throws the decapitated head across the room, and before Akita's corpse can drop, Artemis rushes towards another huntress, who has an arrow through her throat.

Sika.

FOUR

LAMB

I count the days of my agony as I wade in and out of consciousness by the huntress at my side.

On the first day, it is Artemis who sits beside my bed. Her hands are always cold as ice as they claim mine, squeezing my fingers a little too tightly. I'm too disoriented to tell her to lessen her hold, but even if I could, I don't think I will ever tell Artemis. I let the pain mix in with my goddess's grief as she clings to me.

"We're in Poseidon's castle," Artemis says. Her voice is scratchy from tears, and through the fog of pain and partial consciousness, I find myself baffled at how my near death has rattled her. She is a goddess who has witnessed death more than life, yet she whispers with a raw throat. "Asclepius is with us, and he says you're healing quick. Soon, you'll be able to open your eyes." She pauses. "Please open your eyes, Lamb. I need you."

I cannot open my eyes, and I slip into the dreamless slumber once again.

On the second day, it is not Artemis at my side, but Sika.

When I wake up, she lies on the bed with me, her shoulder bumping against mine. I still cannot tell anybody that I am awake. My mouth will not open, and neither will my eyes, but I hear the distinct crunch of teeth biting into an apple. Rare splatters of juice cross my neck.

"Ready for your monologue of the day?" Sika asks. She is wise enough not to wait for a response. "I had a dream last night. The first time I have dreamed since Saffron killed Morpheus and Epiales. I know it's asinine to think it's possible to dream again, but I know I am. They are as real as me and you. I feel crazy admitting it out loud and haven't even told Dýnami about the dreams. I'm fearful she would laugh off my worries and call me insane. Check my forehead for a fever in true Dýnami fashion."

Sika lets out a laugh, but there is no mirth behind it.

She's terrified.

"It's why I'm telling you, I guess. It's easier to admit what should not exist to a person who can't respond." She lets out a shallow breath. "Don't get me wrong, Lamb. I want you to wake up. Gods, I want it so badly. More than I want anything in this world. But I need to say what I saw to somebody who might not actually hear my words. The last thing I want is for everybody to know I'm going mad."

I want to reach out my hand for her. She's so close. I can feel her hand near mine, only a few centimeters apart, but I cannot extend my hand. The only part of me alert are my ears; they can hear every haggard breath, every twist of her fingers in her hair, and the alarming thump, thump, thump of her heart.

"I think it was a nightmare," Sika says at least. "But it felt like a warning."

A warning for what? I want to ask, and I hate that I do not have the strength to speak. To be there for my friend.

Sika continues, "I was back in the prisons. The same one we burned down during the fight against Kronos. I was alone, but at the same time, I wasn't. There was a monster there, with a laugh so loud it splintered the ground. I held onto my bow and arrow, but I could not lift my arms." She sounds so devastated and broken as she adds. "I couldn't do anything but listen to the laugh until my ears bled. Twelve arrows flew above my head and hit the ceiling, and that damned laugh continued as the ceiling fell on top of me and I died."

Open your eyes, I command myself.

Move your hand to hers, I demand.

But I can't.

I'm not strong enough yet.

"I died, and he lived." Sika's voice is so hollow, I'm uncertain if she's even real and in this room with me. "And while I could not see his face, could not identify who this monster was, I knew only I could kill him. Only I could defeat him, but I failed."

The mattress softly squeaks underneath her weight as she stands, and the warmth of her shoulder against mine dissipates. I want to open my mouth and beg her to stay, but I hear the door open and shut behind her. I try to rise to a sitting position, or even open my mouth, but I slip into oblivion once more.

On the third day, it is Vee who sits on the corner of my bed, reading from a book. Since Vee joined the huntress clan a few years ago, I always find her with a book in her hand. Now, in a castle, she receives literary gift after literary gift. I do not recognize the story she reads from, but one quote snags my attention.

"The tyrant is the child of Pride, who drinks from his sickening cup. Recklessness and vanity, until from his high crest headlong, he plummets to the dust of hope."

It is the last thought in my head as I slip into unconsciousness once again.

Dýnami wakes me on the fourth day, slurping on some drink. "It may not be rocky road ice cream," she says. "But gods, Amphitrite makes some yummy smoothies. You need to wake up already so you can try it. It's green, so it looks gross, but just wait until you try it." There is a long slurp. "It's delicious. A true delicacy."

I slip into unconsciousness as Dýnami tries to land smoothie droplets into my mouth, swearing it will heal me better than Asclepius's medicines.

Shikari is with me on the fifth day, but she is not alone. Hound is there, too. They barely focus on me; instead, they bicker about nothing and everything in between. Hound complains about the humidity in Poseidon's castle, but Shikari calls Hound stupid for believing the bottom of the ocean has humidity. Then, Shikari mentions she is hungry, and Hound brings up the fact that twenty years ago, Shikari ate one of Hound's desserts without permission. They go back-and-forth for hours, and I forgot how much I missed them. Flaws and all.

Akita is here on the sixth day, with one hand wrapped in mine. Her index finger anxiously taps, taps, taps on the top of my hand. Gods, I want her to stop doing that, but I still am too weak.

For most of the sixth day, I am in and out of consciousness, but Akita is never silent. If she is not tapping on my hand, she is rambling to herself. Or, maybe, to me. I'm not sure. I catch snippets in the moments of consciousness.

"Copperhead never hated the gods for our enslavement. She said that revenge was a sword without a blade. Pointless to hold on to. But she-"

I fall asleep before hearing the rest.

When I awake again, Akita is in the middle of a sentence. "-her fault. I have waited almost ninety years for this, but what if I fail? What if she does not die and all of this is for nothing?"

Excuse me?

What in the gods is she talking about?

Akita's hand falls from mine, and I force my eyes open. She stands in the doorway, hand on the doorknob, and our eyes lock. Her eyes fill with tears. It is a harrowing look. Guilt. It is immediately identifiable and always disastrous. They slip down her pretty face, and they are the gravest warning of what is coming next.

I open my mouth, but she slams the door shut behind her. The little croak I let out is unheard, and as valiantly as I try to stay awake, my eyes flutter close once again.

On day seven, it's Frigate, who does not speak, but the familiar scent of jasmine identifies her. She does not hold my hand like Artemis, confide in me like Sika, or read me her favorite story like Vee; Frigate sits there like it is her obligation and nothing more. She sits there like we have not ridden together for centuries, becoming sisters in arms.

Twice, I open my eyes. Both times, she stoically stares back.

"Akita." I force out the single word, and despite my weak state, the word comes out clean.

Yet, Frigate looks away. "Go back to bed." There is nothing gentle in her tone, but I listen.

I do not stay asleep for long.

I fell into a dreamless slumber until suddenly, in the

blackness of my unconsciousness, Willow's voice screams down a tunnel. "Wake up!"

I open my eyes, but I cannot see anything. Frigate has a pillow pressed against my face. I know it is her because of the smell of jasmine that strangles me as efficiently as this pillow. Her knees are on my chest, forcing me to stay down. I scream, but when the sound leaves my lips, I realize I am not the only one.

Outside of this room, the sound partially obscured by the pillow, I hear the war drums. I recognize the echo of death. The dropping of bodies that will never rise again.

I reach my hands out for something, anything, but there is only a bed and Frigate. Frigate, who I have ridden beside for centuries. A sister, who I have slept beside in the wilderness. Fought alongside in the most harrowing battles. She has betrayed me in the worst way possible, and I do not understand why.

I dig my claws into her hands, but she swats me away with ease.

Frigate and I have fought together while training millions of times. We have faced each other with weapons and bare fists, and almost every time, I win. The only times she has defeated me is when she gets her hands around my throat. Her grip is a vice I can never shake.

Now, on the brink of exhaustion, I wonder if Frigate let me win so many times. Perhaps I can't fight her because of my weak state, or perhaps she has plotted my murder for years. Decades or centuries, even. In the thickening level of hatred, did Frigate lose those fights on purpose? Did she want me to underestimate her strength, so I never saw my murder coming from her hands?

Death holds an inviting hand for me, the second time in the past week, but I cannot reach for him. His black gloved hand is too far away, and it disappears altogether when Frigate lets out a scream. The pillow no longer presses down on my face, obscuring my airway. It delicately rests there, but I am quick to swat it away.

My body aches with pain as I sit up. Instead of the scream that wants to erupt, I let out a chorus of coughs. I heave and gasp and try to cling to the fabric of life that is tattered, nearly in ruins. I take too long to find the strength to stop coughing and open my eyes.

Frigate lies on the floor, her unblemished knife sitting beside her. Her eyes are open and stare at the ceiling as thick rivulets of crimson blood spill from her. Three arrows stick out of her chest. All three lay directly over her heart, laid with perfect precision. I draw my gaze up to Frigate's murderer, to my hero, and Dýnami stands in the doorway.

Time shows a person's every angle. The beautiful and the ugly. The vulnerable and the venerable. But as the soft cerulean ocean shines through the glass wall and hits Dýnami's tawny cheeks, a new angle presents itself.

Anguish, in its rawest form, paints over her harsh features. Plentiful tears stream down her cheeks, sliding over raised, healed scars and new slashes. They slip between her lips as she asks a single question. "Can you walk?"

I have never been the strongest or fastest huntress, but I have never been weak. Too weak to walk or talk or function. Helpless is a new, harrowing ailment that I have not faced since I was a child in the prisons. I want to tell Dýnami that I can run with her and fight with her, but the false words clog in my throat.

Instead, I shake my head. "No." Simply saying that word brings me pain, my throat still raw from the unforgiving sun.

"Hold on tight."

Dýnami, normally all laughter and smiles, is now a warrior of twisted rage. She lifts me and throws me onto her back. I wrap my arms around her neck, and she rushes out of the bedroom door and into a thrush of violence.

The last time I was in Poseidon's castle, death fell from the sky like rain droplets. As I take in the scene of fighting bodies and vicious battle cries, a sense of déjà vu crashes into me. They are new villains, but for a delirious moment, they are Kronos and his army again. Fighting us and killing us in ways we never reanimate from.

Kerria rushes towards us, a bloodied sword in her hand. Bloodshed mars her dark complexion, from the cut on her forehead to the splatters of others' deaths upon her exposed arms. In my discombobulated state, I see Kerria the same way I once saw Frigate- as a sister. I do not realize her raised sword and vicious snarl until Dýnami hurriedly pulls two bows out and flings them towards Kerria with the same strength as a bowstring. Kerria dodges one arrow, but the other sinks into her shoulder.

A curse spews out of her thin lips, and then she is upon us. Her sword is swinging down toward Dýnami's neck, but before the blade can reach its mark, Dýnami blocks it with a battleaxe. She has always kept that weapon holstered at her hip, but in the two hundred years we have ridden together, she has never used it. Never needed to use it, even in the Battle of the Labyrinth against Kronos and Typhon.

There are no words between Kerria, one of our newer huntresses, and Dýnami. There are no questions about why Kerria betrayed us. No screams of disbelief or betrayal. Kerria never explains why she chose Styx's side instead of riding beside Artemis and us for all of eternity. They fight like strangers, and before Kerria's sword can touch Dýnami, the latter has her battle axe lodged in the side of the former's head.

Kerria falls to her knees first, then crumbles face-first into the ground.

"Careful," Dýnami says before bending forward and plucking her axe out of Kerria's skull.

She wipes it across her pant leg and charges forward in the fight, not bothering to spare our former sister another glance. I do, though. I stare at Kerria on the floor, who now has a halo of blood around her head, until Dýnami's silhouette obscures her from view. My eyes that grow with unshed tears stare at Kerria until Dýnami's rushed movements. They bring me back to the present, where she faces another enemy.

It is a cyclops this time.

A gargantuan, twelve-foot-tall cyclops looms over us with a cracked smile that shows all his razor-sharp teeth. Blood stains their mottled flesh. Crimson colors his sickly pale green flesh, and when my gaze wanders, I find a half-eaten Gigiana a few feet away. Her arms are gone, along with her legs and part of her neck.

Another huntress dead. How many is that now?

Three that I have seen.

"Slide off," Dýnami tilts her head back, but she doesn't look at me. Her focus stays rooted on the nameless cyclops. "I'll pick you up when I'm done."

The cyclops roars with laughter. "I'll eat her in front of you, *prósopo choírou.*"

He calls Dýnami a pig face, but she doesn't react. She glowers at him, unwavering in her confidence, as she moves into a squatting position so I can easily slide off her back. He waits for their fight, his confidence in his fighting abilities bordering on cockiness. I take three steps back before their fight begins.

And it ends on my fourth retreating step.

The cyclops opens his mouth, a retort ready on his lips, but Dýnami has already begun the fight. She holsters her axe, then removes her bow and four arrows from their place on her back. Before he can speak, all four arrows are on the bowstring and fly towards him. They land, one after another, in quick succession across his chest. The beast roars loud enough to shake the paintings off the nearest wall, and he charges towards Dýnami.

His long legs give him a slight advantage, but he only makes it halfway towards her before Dýnami's battle axe is out of its holster again. She uses both hands to throw the weapon, and with the same precision she has with her arrows, the sharp blade meets its mark. Almost the entire axe slides into the cyclops's one eye, and more than rage stresses his scream.

Pure agony wracks through the monster, and just like Kerria before him, he crumbles to his knees. In this position, he is still taller than Dýnami by a few inches, but she remains unscathed. She prowls towards him, rips her axe out of his bloodied eye socket, and swings her weapon back. The muscles in her biceps are prominent enough to see from a mile away before she exerts all her strength into wielding this axe once more.

It slides into the center of his neck. Thick, green and gold blood oozes out of his neck. It careens down his chest, but he still lets out little moans. Still lives with half his neck cut off, a ruined eye, and three arrows in the chest. Dýnami swings her axe again, and again, and again.

Dýnami has always been an efficient warrior, but today, she is a ruthless killer. His body has already stopped moving, and I am certain he is dead, but her axe does not stop wielding deadly blow after deadly blow. She paints her sorrowful face with blood. I can barely stand upright, but I never feel vulnerable. For I have a beast in my corner, and oh, how she bellows.

After the tenth or eleventh strike, the cyclops's decapitated head bounces on the floor and lands a foot away from Gigiana's corpse.

Dýnami is always one to make jokes. When others have insulted her appearance, she has beaten them to a bloody pulp and made them bite back their words. She adds salt to every wound she inflicts, so I wait for the punchline. But today differs from any other day for Dýnami. Agonizing circumstances strip Dýnami of her humor. Her jubilance is a shield she has sheathed herself with since the dawn of time.

Instead of saying one last line to the fallen corpse of her mighty enemy, she walks to me and asks. "Can you walk?"

"Probably not."

"That's a better answer than before." She holds out her hand. "Let's try walking a little. We must leave fast, and I do not know how much longer I can fight and carry you."

I take her hand and let her wrap our arms together. Our movements are slower now, as my legs quiver with each advancing step. We pace by another huntress corpse, Mercia this time. She lies on the ground with a gaping wound in her chest. Her discarded heart lays a few feet away from her body, and I bite back my emotions. Force them to hide in the deepest pits of myself until I have time to process it all.

Poseidon is within eyesight, along with his wife. He and Amphitrite are back-to-back, fighting four different cyclops at the same time. Poseidon's face twists in anguish, and I doubt it is because he is in physical pain. Every cyclops is his child, and they have all betrayed him. Turned their back on him in favor of a war against him.

I do not dwell for long because a male blocks Dýnami and my path towards the castle's exit. He is both lean and muscular, with a face drawn out in wrinkles that are rare to find on a god's face. I recognize him instantly as Atlas; the titan cursed to hold the world on his shoulders forever, but why is he here? How did he escape the Atlas Mountains?

He rushes towards us, stepping over corpses of fallen monsters and huntresses without sparing his deceased comrades a second glance. He focuses solely on us. Narrowed eyes flicker between Dýnami and me, and while his inner question is silent, his expression screams it aloud.

Who shall I kill first?

Dýnami uses her grip on my arm to tug me behind her, answering his unspoken question.

She removes one arrow from its pouch, but she doesn't produce her bow. She holds both her bloodied axe and arrow with tight grips. Atlas strolls towards us rather than running. His confidence bleeds onto the drenched floor, but unlike the cyclops, Dýnami's right hand trembles with uncertainty. She can face a cyclops without fear and defeat him before he can reach her, but this is a titan prowling towards us now.

With any immortal's directed ire, they remind us of our fragility.

She waits patiently for him to approach her. The rest of the battles soar past us, but time has slowed, as if Kronos is alive once more, taunting us with his presence. Alive once more with the slowly ticking clock. Atlas's movements slows, giving me too much time to dwell on the probability of my death.

When Atlas stands in front of Dýnami, a sword materializes in his hand. The blade itself is almost six feet tall, and he proudly raises it into the air. She stands there, with only a battle axe and a dainty arrow, but she does not balk. Dýnami glares up at him and dares him to end her life.

It is then that I realize Sika is dead.

She must be, if Dýnami is ready to die. Her tears and rage all lead to the harrowing truth that I never expected. Sika, my dearest friend beside Artemis, is gone. She, just like Willow, has left to join our sisters in Elysium. She promised to never leave, but the truth in her absence now sits on my chest with the weight of an anvil.

And Dýnami wants to join her in Elysium.

I want to join her, too.

Atlas screams as he swings his blade downward, and I desperately search the battleground for a weapon. I can barely keep myself on two feet, but I can't lose Dýnami, too. I look around at the corpses, hoping to find a sword or spear, but there is nothing. It is as if all the weapons disappear the moment they touch the ground.

I am helpless once more as his blade touches her axe. The impact shatters the material into a dozen shards.

Dýnami slides backwards, causing me to fall onto the ground. I smack my behind, which is only cushioned by the thick lumps of blood on the hardwood floor.

With a throat that feels like it is on fire, I whisper. "Please fight."

Don't die, too.

They are the words that I do not say, but she hears. Corpses lay scattered around us, and decades or centuries of comradery die with them. She is one of the few that I

41

have left. Frigate, Sika, Willow, they are all gone, but not Dýnami. I cannot lose Dýnami, too.

Dýnami walks back towards Atlas, and he laughs at her. It's a full body, uncontrollable kind of laugh. "You have a death wish, girl," he says between the bouts of guffawing.

"Only a little." She slings her bowstring off her shoulder and places the arrow on the bowstring. "But not enough to let some wrinkly ball sack kill me."

I didn't realize I started crying until a bubble of laughter came out.

Atlas sneers and pulls back his sword again. She sends an arrow towards him, and it sinks into his neck. He barely reacts, only hisses a little, but the arrow doesn't stop his trajectory towards Dýnami's neck. The blade is an inch away, ready to cut her head clean off her shoulders, when a tall figure tackles Atlas to the ground.

Hermes is thinner, but at six and a half feet tall, he swallows Atlas's much shorter frame. The impact on the ground sends his massive sword across the ground, landing right at Dýnami's feet. She bends down and picks it up as Hermes puts Atlas in a headlock. His knees pin Atlas's legs onto the ground, and no matter how much the titan thrashes, he cannot escape Hermes's clutches.

He glares back at us. "Get Artemis and the remaining huntress and leave! Run!"

Atlas roars. "Get off me!"

"Go now!" Hermes snarls at us. "They are here for you!"

Us? There are gods as mighty as Poseidon and Hades, who fight in this battle, but they are here for the huntresses. Why? It makes sense now why the strongest enemy, Atlas, would choose to fight Dýnami and me instead of a god. I understand Sika is dead, and both Frigate and Kerria tried to murder me.

But why?

Dýnami reaches a hand for me, face strewn with worry. "Lamb! Take my hand. We have to go!"

Once our hands clasp, we run as fast as my tired body will allow. Three cyclops run for us, bloodied blades ready for our necks, but an immortal always distracts them. Poseidon throws a trident at one's neck, the skeletal forms of Achilles and Atalanta tackle another, and Athena chucks a spear at the last one's skull.

We find Artemis in the battle room, the room to the exit's direct right, but she is not alone. Jamila, Saffron and Hermes's adopted daughter, stand to Artemis's right. Her hand rests on Artemis's shoulder, but the latter does not respond to the touch. Artemis only stares down at the corpse in her arms.

On an instinctual level, I knew Sika was dead before now, but having an idea and seeing the reality are two very novel experiences. A fist-shaped punch of grief slams into my stomach, threatening to expel everything inside of me. She was the strongest of us, even stronger than Willow, and now she is so fragile in Artemis's arms. I never realized how thin Sika was, or how human she was, until this moment as blood creates a bubble around her.

Dýnami makes a sound that is a terrible mixture of a sob and a hiccup, but there is no disbelief on her face. She stares down at her soulmate's body, with tears sliding down her cheeks. She does not ask how it happened, not with a broken arrow lying on the floor beside Sika and Artemis. Somehow, Dýnami knew Sika was going to die, and she could not save her in time.

Artemis has one arm draped over Sika's body, but the

other delicately pushes aside Sika's wayward curls. They continuously fall over her forehead, and each time, Artemis tucks them behind her ear. Every few seconds, one of Artemis's tears tumbles down on Sika, hitting her cheek or forehead or chin.

"Artemis, we have to go," Jamila says, but by the defeated vibrato of her tone, I know this isn't the first time she has uttered those words.

Artemis does not respond.

Other feet pound into the room; Dýnami and I spin our bodies in anticipation of a fight. My body screams in outrage, begging for more sleep. More time to rejuvenate. But there is no time when a battle roars and friends fall. I grab a fallen case of arrows, and the bow sitting beside them, and I prepare for another cyclops or Atlas.

I prepare for my death.

But it is just the remaining huntresses who barrel into the room.

Shikari leans against Hound's body, her face covered in blood. The closer she gets, the clearer I can make out the source of the blood. A long, jagged scar starts at her temple and harshly falls to the jut of her chin. One eye remains closed, where the cut is especially sharp, and I wonder if it will ever open again. Shikari has almost her entire body pressed against Hound, but at six-foot-two, she easily handles the additional weight.

They are accompanied by June, Vee, Laconia, Iris, and Daphne, but that's it. Out of the sixteen huntresses that once stood proudly, there are only eight remaining. Iris strides into the room, but when she locks eyes on Artemis, her steps falter. She glances at Sika's body, and her eyes shift colors. They become the darkest shade of blue, and the tips of her hair shift from orange to that same color blue.

"Artie," Iris lets out a sigh, but just like when Jamila spoke, Artemis does not respond. She continues to tuck that same stubborn piece of Sika's hair behind her ear.

As soon as everybody is inside, Vee shuts the double doors behind her. Hound gingerly places Shikari in a chair, then she and the mostly unscathed others pile furniture against the door. We shove chairs, dressers, and side tables forward, but these are mundane trinkets against gods and cyclops. It will take seconds to break down the door, push aside the furniture, and swallow us whole.

The roars of battle are loud outside, but in this room, we are deathly silent. My thoughts are mirrors of everybody else's, or so, so much worse. Many of us have died, including Akita, whose decapitated body lays a few feet away, but none is as gut-wrenching as Sika.

"Who killed Akita?" I ask and watch as every face darkens with unbridled rage.

Artemis finally lifts her head, hitting me with her fierce glare. "Me, and if I could, I would kill her over and over again for all of eternity."

Akita's harrowing words the day before. *I have waited almost ninety years for this, but what if I fail? What if she does not die and all of this is for nothing?* Have a deeper meaning today.

It has been decades since Copperhead's death, but like a tidal wave, memories crash into me. Akita blamed Sika for Copperhead dying, but after days of condemning Sika's life, Akita acted like nothing happened. She laughed and drank and rode with Sika, without ever threatening her again. I thought she realized Sika was not to blame for Copperhead dying, but it was Kronos and Raven who deserve Akita's wrath.

But I guess not.

I walk on unsure footing towards Artemis. With each step I take, a sense of déjà vu reanimates, and I am in Apollo's kitchen ninety years ago. Approaching him as he cradles his dead love in his arms, repeatedly chanting the same words. Artemis doesn't chant or rock Sika's corpse back and forth like Apollo did for Gaillardia, but their grief-stricken face is identical. I rarely see the physical similarities between her and her twin, but today, it is blinding.

I sit down beside Artemis, and I grab her hand before she can tuck that piece of hair behind Sika's ear again. "When I was dying on that island, you promised me something."

Artemis stares at me as I put our joined hands on my lap. "I promised a lot of things." Her voice is a hollow shell of its former glory.

Iris's presence becomes more prominent than ever. The declarations of love Artemis made on that island echo in my ears, but louder than that is a promise I need her to remember now.

"You promised that if I opened my eyes and lived, then you would stop being afraid. Well, my eyes are open, and I am alive, so you must hold on to that promise." I can't look at Sika's corpse, which looks too peaceful except for the wound in the center of her throat. "I know it's easier to be afraid when all those around you are dying, but you have to let Sika go. We have to run so we can fight another day."

Iris chimes in. "Kymopoleia, Frigate, Kerria, and Akita snuck Atlas and an army into the castle. They're outside this room right now, killing every huntress they see, so the prophecy does not come true. Poseidon plans on breaking the barrier and drowning the castle whole, so we need to leave now or all the huntresses will drown with the cyclops."

What prophecy? The question whirls through my head, but I do not have the time to get answers. Right now, all that matters is convincing Artemis to let Sika go so the rest of us can live. Iris has a hand extended, inviting us to run in a portal of rainbows.

I take her hand, then hold Artemis's tight. "There are at least two hundred cyclops outside this room, and they are here for us. We need your help to get out of here, but we can't take her with us." The last words crack, but she hears them all the same.

"I..." Artemis begins.

"Poseidon will give her a proper burial," Shikari says, but her fight with consciousness makes her words muffled. "And we will visit her for a proper funeral after we survive."

"But we need to survive," I add.

Artemis stares down at Sika's body just as the first pound hits the door. With one punch, a cyclops splinters the door. It won't be long until he breaks the door down, pushes the furniture aside, and comes for us all.

"You must let her go," I say, but Artemis won't look at me.

She can only stare at Sika, the greatest huntress of us all. "I thought the prophecy was about her," Artemis whispers, still brushing aside the curls. "When you were asleep and didn't look like you would wake, I thought it would be Sika."

I still do not know what the prophecy is, and there is no time to ask. Dýnami steps into view, blocking Artemis from my view. She lowers herself to a crouch, and while I can only see her back, I hear her sadness.

She leans forward and presses a kiss to Sika's forehead. "Tell Willow I say hi when you join her in Elysium. I will visit you both soon."

Then she looks at me, so vulnerable and destroyed, and I help her up to her feet. Sika's body rolls off her lap, landing delicately on the floor. Dýnami steps towards Sika and bends over to whisper something in her ear. I cannot hear the words, but I don't want to, either. Those are the last farewells between two soulmates.

One by one, we all take each other's hands. Jamila takes my other one, joining our clan of huntresses as the war crumbles Poseidon's castle. Once all our hands lock, Iris creates the largest rainbow in every shade of blue, and we leave the castle.

We leave Sika one last time.

FIVE

HERMES

The moment we witness a rainbow, with only streaks of blue, shoot across the ocean, I lower my caduceus. Atlas grins, cracked teeth bringing bile to my throat. He believes he won this battle, but with his back towards Poseidon, he doesn't see the powerful god's hands rise high in the air.

Poseidon's face contorts with rage, betrayal, and determination, and the water obeys his monumental demand. It is rare to see Poseidon irate, and when it comes, it is always rooted in heartache. He does not cry, but his face contorts with every emotion possible. He loves all his children, and today, almost all of them chose Styx instead of him. A fallen army of his cyclops sons is the backdrop to an unconscious Kymopoleia, his favored daughter.

It is too much for him, and now the world will drown in his fury.

Thick ropes of water slam through the windows, break down every door, and consume the mansion. We have

49

fought many battles here, lost many loved ones, but today's fight ruins it all. Water envelops this entire castle, bringing it to rubble around us.

The cyclops know how to swim, but they require oxygen to live. They move their enormous arms in frantic movements, trying to push themselves to the top of the water's surface so they may survive another day, but they are traitors of the worst kind. They turned on their father, and Poseidon stares at his sons with a cruel curl of his lips. He raises his arms higher in the sky.

Many forget that Poseidon is a ruthless god, who does not take betrayal lightly. Beneath the debaucheries and lackadaisical quips, a rare few underestimate him. His sons, included, but the cyclops are about to learn this invaluable lesson.

Thousands of sharks rush through the water, their jaws opening with a particular desire to taste cyclops meat. Amphitrite beckons her dolphins and a school of every poisonous fish comes to their disposal. Eels and stingrays and killer whales surround the cyclops in a tornado of carnage.

It isn't long before the cerulean blue sea is stained red and green with monster blood.

I swim to the shore before the last muffled scream stops, and once I break through the surface, I fly in search of Ares.

SIX

SAFFRON

The night following my first full day as a goddess, when nightmares should have ceased forevermore, I suffered my worst one. Epiales ensured that each night I closed my eyes that it would be an escape instead of torment, but he was no longer around to protect me. I killed him, and as a result, a creature worse than any monster crept from the shadows of my unconsciousness and came for me.

It has been eighty-eight years since I heard his slithery voice and felt the chill of fear in his touch, but I have not forgotten. It is impossible to forget an incomparable, mind-numbing fear. Hermes was gone that night, off delivering messages as soon as I drifted off to sleep. I felt his absence in the lack of snores and the coldness on his side of the bed. Worse, the barbarous thing knew he left because that was when he advanced.

I have only been to Tartarus once, the immortal prism

in the Underworld, but I instantly recognize the abysmal land within the dark crevices of my nightmare. There is nowhere else in this world as cold as Tartarus while still scorching hot at the same time. My silk nightgown now gave a sudden feeling of nakedness. I wanted to run. Sprint far, far away from the land of unforgiveness, but my nightmare refused my request.

Against my own wishes, my bare feet grazed the ground of the abyss, and all I felt was death. My toes sunk into stilled hearts and crushed dreams. A sob threatened to leave my lips as the sadness of this prison consumed me, body and soul. The wicked touch of decay threatened to graze my skin, and the putrid stench of defeat burned my nostrils.

Then the creature laughed.

No matter how many years have passed, I still remembered his laugh. It was cruel, unforgiving, and sharper than any whip. It struck its mark on a part of me that would reveal no wound, but it hurt with an excruciating intensity. I knew I was strong enough to kill this immortal being, but for a staggering moment, I was weak enough to collapse to my knees. The sound of my collapse echoed in the prison, and that sinister guffaw bounced off the walls. This man laughed as if the world was crumbling under his might.

Suddenly, the feeling of death wasn't as frightening as him.

"Saffron."

A foreign voice, one that I have never heard before, or since, this horrific nightmare, spilled like acid into my bloodstream. I slammed my palms against my ears, futilely attempting to staunch the sound, but it was as impossible.

He penetrated every sense.

My sight was his because I could see nothing but the grin that peeled over yellow teeth. Touch was his because no matter how desperately I tried to cling to a semblance of sanity, all I felt was the floor vibrating beneath me as he prowled forward. My ability to hear anything but his laugh and the chains he wore around his wrists and ankles, clamoring with each step. As he neared, I could no longer smell my perfume or the lingering scent of Hermes on my skin. He leans close enough for our noses to touch, and his vile breath and the stench of his rotting flesh invade every sense.

His proximity was a disease.

I could taste the mixture of red and gold blood in my mouth and feel it falling out of my ears and sliding down my neck. He was killing me, and I tried to open my mouth and scream for help. Thanatos was always near Tartarus, the ever-faithful guard, and I hoped he could hear me if I was loud enough. My mouth hung open, but my fear of him clogged the scream in my throat. I could barely breathe, the power within me being sapped out and replaced with chilling despair and scorching vulnerability.

I slammed my eyes shut the moment I tasted the rancid acridity of his breath, which fanned over my lips with each exhalation. His stare was an inferno that scorched me from the inside out, but I never opened my eyes. I could not gaze at this creature, whose mere presence stole the strength from my bones.

He clasped my chin, and my heart slammed to a complete stop.

He was ginger with his touch, but his nails were longer than that of a wolf. His thumb grazed the skin, and a jagged part of the nail tore my skin. It was a minor cut, only a few centimeters, but the pain of my bleeding ears was mundane compared to the agony that ransacked my body. My skin turned to ice, while a volcano erupted in the pit of my stomach and oozed out thousands and thousands of miles of lava. The scream could never leave my throat, and I only whimpered as agony rippled through my entire body.

In the decades since this nightmare, I have never felt such pain. Even after I killed hundreds of titans, monsters, and gods in the fall of the final Titanomachy war, and it did not hurt as much as this. There was nothing more catastrophic than this male's touch, and a whimpered *please stop*, wanted to leave my quivering lips.

"Such a beautiful poison." His thumb fell from the cut, and his tongue quickly replaced it. He licked the laceration, his touch rough like sandpaper. I begged my arms to lift, so I could push him off me, but I was a statue, and he was my admirer. "A belladonna in the flesh."

Full lips pressed a kiss on the wound, and I could feel my blood staining his mouth. I managed a whimper, but that was it. No other sound.

"But you made a grave mistake, sweet Belladonna." His hands drifted and moved from my chin to my hair. He twirled a piece repeatedly on his finger until it tugged at my scalp. "Open your eyes and see the mistake you made."

I did not want to, and he knew it. He taunted me, spinning that one tuft of hair until strands slowly and painfully ripped. I have had my hair pulled before, but this felt nothing like it had before. This was agony. Each time he pulled a strand from my scalp, it felt like a blade inched into my skull.

It sucked the strength out of me, and finally, I opened my eyes.

His eyes were the same shade as Kronos's, Zeus's, and Poseidon's. That startling shade of blue, like if lightning struck a clear sky. He was handsome and grotesque, a nightmare and a hymn. I could not look away, but gods, all I wanted was to scratch this image from my memory.

"You left too many alive in your deadly wake, and they will bring me to you. One day, when your shields are down and your poison is less lethal, I will be there. Those who you spared will save me, and now you don't have your nightmare to protect you."

I do not need protecting, I wanted to say.

But then his lips crashed against mine, and all I could do was scream.

The moment I screamed, forceful hands plucked me out of the nightmare.

It was Hattie, looming over me and yelling my name over and over and over. I was too scared to open my eyes, but I knew it was Hattie who woke me. It was Hattie who laid in bed beside me, curled my body into hers, and calmed me until I could finally look at her.

"Did I make a mistake killing Epiales?" I asked. It was the one and only time I uttered this question.

There was no judgement on her face. "You did the only thing you could. He was a bad immortal, even if you loved him."

However, the next day, I found a cut right below my chin from where the creature scratched me. When I searched my scalp, I found a bald spot right where he pulled out several strands of hair.

Epiales stares at me from where he lays, and it is impossible to look at the personification of nightmares without the haunting memory of that night returning, too. A miniscule part of me is grateful. I think of that jagged scar, which still inks my flesh, instead of the fateful day I murdered him. I never forgot about the fateful night in Tartarus, but seeing Epiales makes it a fresh wound again.

Seeing him answers the question I asked long ago.

Did I make a mistake killing Epiales? Yes, yes, I did.

But that does not change the emotions roaring through me. I never thought I would see him again. He was dead days ago, but here he is, alive and looking at me like no time has passed at all. I hurry to my feet, creating as much distance as possible between us without completely leaving him.

He sits up, and the torn slips of my gown fall off his chest. "Hi." His voice is rough, but tender, too. Rough from the lack of use and tender because he always is with me.

Almost always, anyway.

"Hi."

We are stuck on this island together, and although I knew he would eventually wake up, I didn't plan on what I was going to do in that eventual moment. I thought it would be obvious to me when he woke up, but here I am, clueless how to approach the man I killed, then resurrected. We used to talk about anything and everything. There weren't empty spaces where words should be, but that was a long time ago, and heartbreak does terrible things to one's psyche.

"Do you mind telling me how I'm alive?" He glances down at his body, fingers grazing his tattoos that once hid the most prominent scars. "How I'm healed?" his voice cracks at the end of the question.

While I loved those scars, he abhorred them. They were the reminders of his sordid past with Morpheus and Zeus. He risked his immortality to help his nephew flee with a mortal woman, who was Heracles's slave in a time of human strife. Those scars were the punishment he bore, which Zeus mercilessly gave before throwing him into Tartarus to be forgotten forever.

But now they are gone, and I do not miss the slight twitch in his lip as he represses a smile.

"Here are some clothes." I point to the pile Hecate left. "There's food, too, but I should probably look for more. I'm sure you're hungry."

Before another word can escape his lips, I run into the woods. Sand kicks behind me as I scurry off to hide from my problems. He asks a question I thought would be easy enough to answer, but the words clogged in my throat. It's difficult enough to look at him, but to hear his voice and communicate with him is a bladed reminder of everything we suffered together.

I willingly came to the island to exchange my life for Artemis's and the nymphs, and I knew they were going to use my powers for their own malevolent purpose. But I did not expect he would return until they laid his bones at my feet. I did not expect them to leave me here with him, forcing me to remember just how beautiful he is and how warm those silver eyes are.

It's a coward's way out, but I hide in the woods behind the comfort of a tree. My feet remain planted on the ground, unmoving for hours. I lean my head against the tree's trunk, and I let the night's serenity calm my racing thoughts. Not a single cloud hides the magnificence of the night sky, and although I am a prisoner on this island, at least I can still experience beauty.

"Did you see Selene yet?"

He joins me in the woods, but each step he takes towards me is hesitant. Like a hunter around a skittish deer. I keep my gaze on the moon, but I don't retreat. It's a terrible idea, but I let him get closer.

I shake my head. "Nobody has heard from her in centuries. If she was there, she was too fast to see."

"She doesn't like the new gods." He strides closer and leans his body on the tree to the right of mine. "She prefers the old world and busying herself with nothing but the moon's grace."

"It must be a relaxing life. Up in the sky."

"Did I ever tell you about Selene and Helios?"

Selene and her brother, Helios, are the personification of the moon and the sun. While Apollo and Artemis also hold dominion over them, it is Selene and Helios that protect its beauty and radiance every single day. It is said that Helios drives a golden sun chariot every morning, bringing the sun into the sky. Then, at night, Selene drives a white chariot across the sky to paint the moon beside the stars.

It is their only importance in this world. When this world became too much, they stayed up in the sky just waiting for their moment to ride their chariot. To gift the world with the beauty that the sun and moon provide.

I shake my head, words unable to leave my lips as memories of every story he has ever told me replay in my head.

"I used to envy the constellations," he admits but doesn't elaborate.

It has been decades since I have seen him, but he

forgets nothing about me. He knows my curiosity, and in the silence that ticks behind his words, I tilt my head towards him. There is a soft smile curling over his lips, knowing he won the first of his many battles. He wanted me to look at him, to acknowledge him instead of running far and fast.

"Why?" I ask.

His smile grows ever so slightly, and I quickly stare back at the sky with sudden heat on my cheeks.

"Because there is nothing more peaceful than a starry night sky, and they get to experience it for all of eternity. There's no grander death than that."

I do not realize he moved until he is all I can see. He leans against the same tree as me, with his shoulder dangerously close to mine. "What are you doing?" I whisper.

His index finger brushes against the top of my hand. "Why did you do it?"

He isn't asking why I killed him. He knows that answer as well as I do. Epiales wants to know why I brought him back to life. There is so much hope in his eyes, which burns so bright they threaten to steal the moon's vibrancy. He wants to hear that I brought him back to life because I miss and love him. That life without him was as pointless as a night without its stars.

"I missed you, and gods, I loved you."

The hope dims when the word *loved* is past tense.

"Loved," he echoes the word.

"I loved you more than I thought it could love somebody."

The love I had for him was all-consuming. I thought it would kill me, that level of affection. It nearly did, when I had to rip his bones out of his flesh and end his life. With that one word spoken in the air, years of conversations and touches swarm back. Our kisses, our arguments, our laughter, our cries, they all play on endless repetition in my mind until my eyes blur with so many tears.

He stands in front of me, caging me in with one hand on the tree trunk beside my head. The other cups my face. He collects each tear on the pad of his thumb, except one. That sole tear falls onto my lips, and he stares transfixed at the sight. Slowly, he moves down towards me, and I do not move. I know what he is about to do, and I have time to push him away. To tell him he shouldn't, but I don't.

His kiss is so gentle as his lips wipe away that one tear. "Gods, even when you cry, you're the most beautiful creature this world has ever seen."

Electricity consumes my body, sending me spiraling towards an old version of myself I thought died. My heart beats at twice its normal speed, and I lean towards him for another kiss. Yet, it is when our lips collide again; I hear Styx's voice in my head. I finally understand the words she said on the fateful day I resurrected Epiales.

"Return him to our world so that my prophecy may come true. Let my war begin with his resurrection."

"Bring your heart back to life."

I thought she wanted my compliance, to convince me to join her side by granting me a chance to bring Epiales back to life, but I was wrong. There is more here at stake, and it starts with Epiales and me falling in love again. It centers on those pesky, two words spoken in between a rueful command.

Your heart.

His teeth nip my bottom lip when I place my hands on his chest and push. It doesn't take too much force to move him, and he stumbles back a few steps. Tears obscure most of my vision, but I can see the realization on his face as clear as the cloudless sky. I place my hand on my lips, which still tingle with his touch, but he stares at something else.

"You didn't want to resurrect me, did you?"

SEVEN

HART SOMMERS

I need to sleep, but I can't bring myself to move from my blank canvas. There's too much at stake if I step away. Each time I blink, my eyelids grow heavier, and it becomes arduous to raise them again. I place the tip of my pencil on the canvas.

"Please," comes a drowsy plead. To who? I'm not sure. Perhaps I am begging the Fates to tilt their favor in my direction. Or, I am praying to the oracles of the past who started this sordid rivalry with Styx. I'm too tired to ponder the direction of my words. I simply speak. "Just give me something. Anything. Please."

Whoever I speak to doesn't answer. I'm left in this expansive, quiet room with only the night as my company. The opened curtains allow the stars to trickle in. It has been so long since I have slumbered that I fear I'm going mad because I sense the stars' judgements. Their impatience as I sit on this stool, hand perched in front of the easel, with no progress.

This isn't a commission piece with money at the end of the tunnel. No, it is so much more than that. Whatever I create can help us defeat Styx, who nobody can find. We do not know if she is on that island with Saffron, or if she hides in another location plotting and scheming her way to Mt. Olympus. Many search for her, but I can find her fastest if my clairvoyant abilities listen to me.

If I can make my powers work, then I can find her. I can find all the members of the prophecy who must complete their role for us to win. The entire world rests on my shoulders, and I am not as strong as Atlas. I cannot hold on to the world. I'm too weak, and the weight is too heavy.

A soft knock raps against the door. "Can I come in?"

Lowell stands in the doorway with two steaming mugs in each hand. He looks healthier than the first day I came into Apollo's mansion and found him with Argus. The pale pallor is gone, and his skin is once more the rich brown that compliments him so well. His eyes are no longer rimmed red with tears and pain. They sparkle with rejuvenation. It has only been a few days, but he seems to have gained some weight back, too.

It is the first smile I have mustered all day. "Of course, especially if you're bringing me some coffee."

His advancing steps falter. "I brought hot chocolate with peppermints, but if you want me to get you coffee instead…"

"No, it's fine. That sounds delicious."

He strides towards me and sets the hot chocolate in my awaiting hands. "I'll always remember your favorite drink, H."

Hot chocolate with peppermints was my favorite drink in high school, back when I didn't enjoy coffee, but that changed years ago. I haven't had a cup of hot chocolate since my senior year of high school after discovering the combination of hazelnut creamer and coffee. Still, I smile and accept the drink, warming my frigid hands.

"I'm surprised Apollo isn't in here. You two have been inseparable lately." Lowell lifts his drink to his lips.

"Zeus requested to see him."

To report on my discoveries. Or lack thereof. That reminder, as miniscule as it is, disintegrates my thinly veiled hunger. I set my hot chocolate onto the stool in front of me, where my art supplies rest.

"I think Argus went with him."

"Not thirsty?" He takes another sip of his drink.

"I guess not." I try to smile, but the effort fails.

Lowell's attention drifts behind my head, where an untouched canvas mocks me. "Growing up, every time I would walk into your house, it always smelled like paint. Instead of candle scents, your father would sit in the living room with a circlet of paint cans and brushes."

I might have received my looks and oracle ancestry from my mom, but my artistic side has always been born of my father's love. He was an accountant, but on the weekends, he was the world's clumsiest artist. He always insisted on sitting in the living room where the light was best, and no matter how many precautions my mom tried to make, Dad always ruined every nearby piece of furniture.

Eventually, my mom gave up trying to put tarps on the couches and rugs. She embraced his insanely chaotic nature. Our tan-and-blue rug became an array of colors that would make Iris proud, and our single-colored couch received splattered polka dots from the immeasurable amount of times Dad would fling his paintbrush backwards.

His artwork differed from mine. While I enjoy shading pencils and the beauty of a person's appearance, Dad liked to create landscapes. He was talented, and whatever artwork he didn't sell became décor throughout our house. The older I got, the more pieces on the wall became my creations.

Reminders of those times brings a soreness, but fondness, too.

"I swear, each color had a specific smell." Lowell's gaze wanders around the room, jumping from piece to piece that scatter the wall. They are all Apollo's art, but soon, I hope I can join mine on these walls. "I knew when your dad was drawing a desert because of the sour yellow paint."

"Sour?" I hide back my laugh.

Lowell cracks a small smile, but he still doesn't look at me. "The blue smelled best, in my opinion. It almost smelled like waffles."

This time, I can't stop myself. A bubble of laughter flows out, and Lowell finds his attention back on me. "What is wrong with your sense of smell?"

His smile widens, and soon we both sit in my art room, laughing about nothing and everything. The past and present blending together into a situation concocted by our most inane imagination. Somehow, I lay on the floor beside Lowell as our laughter dies down. Apollo created a multitude of suns on the ceiling, and it's a beautiful reminder that no matter where I am, a part of him will be there, too.

"Are you not having visions?" Lowell asks, his voice softer than usual.

"No, and I don't understand it. When I was just in our apartment, scribbling away on a notepad, I had visions almost every day. Now, when the world needs me to see the future, there's nothing. It's defeating, to not succeed when there's so much pressure, and the longer I sit here, staring at that empty canvas, the worse I feel."

"Maybe you lost your ability."

I shake my head. "No, it's an extension of me. Without that ability…" I can't finish my sentence.

Who would I be without my gift of foresight?

I wouldn't have found Apollo without being an oracle, and a world without him is akin to suffering in the Fields of Punishment. If I did not have this ability, then Lowell and I would still pretend to love each other the way lovers should. We would not lay here underneath painted suns, laughing like genuine friends. Without being the oracle, my life would not exist the way it should.

"Without that ability, you wouldn't have people hunting you down. Nobody would want you dead, H."

I turn my head to face Lowell. "Without that ability, Styx gets the throne. I know that as much as I know how to breathe. A goddess created of hatred only knows how to do one thing, and that is turning the world into cinders beneath her vengeful feet. We can't let her become queen. *I* can't let her become queen."

"But why does that have to be you? Why can't some-body else be the hero? Why can't someone else be a goddess's shooting target?" The last question comes with a hardened edge. Any semblance of a smile is long gone.

"Because that's what the Fates decided for me, and who am I to turn down the chance to save the world?"

He looks away from me, staring up at the ceiling once more. Minutes pass as we lay on this uncomfortable floor, an awkward silence settling between us. He has more he wants to say, but he won't, and my exhaustion has stolen any words from my lungs.

"Well, if I can't change your mind about this, then at least let me help." Lowell stands up, picks the hot chocolate off my stool, and sits down where he once laid. He passes me the mug. "Your dad always said the best cure for artistic blocks was lots and lots of chocolate. So drink up, H. Get your inspiration."

It's true.

Dad always said that chocolate was the cure for any mind block. Whenever he wanted to work on the week-ends, but he lacked the motivation, he would beg my mom to make his favorite chocolate chip cookies. We all joked that it was Dad's excuse to pig out on cookies, but Mom always made them for him.

And he always finished his artwork.

I run my finger along the rim of the now mostly cold "hot" chocolate. "I love how much you remember about my family. You're the only person left who even remembers them with me. Do you remember my mom's chocolate chip cookies?"

"I couldn't forget those for as long as I live." Lowell's laugh is soft and devoid of the earlier tension. "Do you remember the time I tried to use her recipe and make them for you a few days after the funeral?"

"Oh my Gods, they tasted like cement. How did you mess that up so monumentally?"

"Hey!" He outcries. "You tried making them, too, remember? For your birthday, you tried to make a batch with that recipe, and we were sick the rest of the night."

"I'm half convinced she tricked us with that recipe and laughed at our attempts at her place in the Underworld."

"Your mom was always too sneaky for her own good," Lowell looks at me with a teasing glint in his eyes.

"I want one of her cookies right now. It was always the cure for an overactive mind." I wrap my hand around my feather necklace and trace the wing's outline. "She'd know exactly what to do right now."

Lowell wraps an arm around my shoulder, and he opens his mouth to speak. I will never know what he wanted to say because the room becomes black as night. Not even the artificial suns on the ceiling can illuminate the black smoke covering the room with the god of the Underworld's arrival.

Hades stands in the art room in black armor and an onyx helmet under his armpit. He shakes his head, and a splatter of saltwater hits me in the face. All the gods are regal in their own right, but Hades doesn't embellish his excellence. He stands before me, drenched from head to toe, and smiles like we are long-lost friends meeting again.

Even though an army of a dozen undead soldiers stands behind him. They are creatures out of a nightmare. Rotting flesh hangs off their bones and there are empty sockets where their eyes once rested.

Two stand nearest him.

One is a man of prominent height. He is easily six and a half feet tall, with a helmet concealing most of his face, except for his rotted grin and eyeless sockets; somehow, I feel them staring at me.

The second soldier is a woman, as recognized by a long ponytail and a detailed breastplate that depicts her story of heroism. She is Atalanta, one of the most infamous female heroes in history that was not a part of the huntress clan. She stands at nearly six feet; with a spear she has pointed an inch away from Lowell's jugular.

"Um, hi?" Lowell gulps. His Adam's apple grazes the tip of the spearhead.

I jump to my feet. "Put away your weapon. He's a friend!"

Atalanta makes an odd noise that almost sounds like a scoff, but she listens. She stands straight along with the rest of the soldiers, with her spear placed at her side. Lowell stands up beside me, and his shaky hands take the hot chocolate from me.

"I'm going to, um, go heat this up for you. See you in a second, H." He takes his own mug and rushes out of the room.

Once the door is closed, Hades says. "I do not believe we will see your human friend again."

"What are you doing here?"

I can't take the star-struck tone out of my voice. One of the greatest gods in existence stands in my art room with an army looking at me. Their distorted faces hide human emotions, but Hades's expression is easily readable. I see the hope that rains down on his face like a storm.

Then, his eyes drift to the empty canvas.

"I'm here to train you to wield your powers, and it looks like we have some work to do."

"I'm flattered, Lord Hades, but-"

A dark eyebrow raises. "But?"

"Apollo is the god of prophecies, and he has-"

Again, he interrupts me. "Apollo is your soulmate, your third destined love. Do you truly believe he can be impartial while training you?"

Hades steps forward, and a cloud of dark mist follows each advancing foot. He doesn't always trail behind a steam of obsidian. No, the god is showcasing one of his many abilities. He reminds me with each step that he is a master with his magic, and with a little training, he can hone my gift, too.

"We do not know one another, but I have met each of your ancestors. From Aashritha to your mother. I know the power that courses through your veins and the magnitude of all your untapped magic. Apollo's love for you will make him always want to protect you, but I do not want to protect you. I want to train you so that nobody will ever have to protect you. I want you to be the one others fear too much to attack."

He looms over me, his army of the dead circling around us. I should fear this moment. Hades is synonymous with death, although he is not the god of it. Instead, hope finds its way to the center of my chest.

"So that Styx can fear me?"

"Styx already fears you," he says. "But we will make sure she knows exactly why she should fear you."

"When can we start?"

EIGHT

LAMB

How can a person sleep as long as I have? Hypnos kept me prisoner in his slumber for days; despite that, my exhausted body yearns for more rest. I fall with the others on an unforgiving dirt floor, and my bones rattle with its force. I lay there, surrounded by a significantly smaller group of huntresses, and I want to close my eyes. Slip away from the pain radiating throughout my body and piercing a more fragile part of myself that has grown weary of immortality.

The sun sets over an array of woodland trees, setting the ground alight with oranges and magenta streaks. It is a beautiful, yet cruel reminder that when I wake tomorrow to the sight of the sunrise, Sika will not be there with me. Instead of seeing her hand outstretched with an apple and a wry smile, I will remember the blood that gushed from her neck as Artemis cradled her corpse.

The others stand, dusting the dirt from their pants and smearing the crimson blood with the movement, but I stay stagnant. I lay on this floor, surrounded by trees and mourning souls, as the first of an infinite amount of tears tumble down my cheeks. Iris wraps an arm around Artemis's shoulders and leads her away. Others hug each other with a mixture of relief that they are alive and sorrow that a loved one is dead.

Dýnami makes it a few steps before her knees buckle and she collapses onto the floor. Her sobs are the loudest. Many cry, like myself, but mine is the sound of soft rain patters; Dýnami is the storm that threatens to smite everyone who made her suffer. Nobody looks at the sunset because the pink is too similar to the color of blood, and when death still taints the air, beauty is never beholden.

"Why?"

My question sounds like cracked glass tumbling on the floor, but nobody hears the word. My voice is too quiet. Asked by a person who usually blends into the background and rarely speaks. I forget the question comes from my lips until the word repeats itself over and over again in my head, the torturous sound of a hammer.

"Why?!"

This time, I am heard by everyone. Dýnami does not look up from the floor, but everybody else does. They swivel their shocked expressions towards me. I cannot remember the last time I raised my voice, or if I have ever spoken above a hushed whisper, but I can barely think beyond this one horrid question I have no answer for.

Rage, so swift and foreign, enters my bloodstream until all I can see is the redness of my ire. I stand to my feet and furiously wipe at the tears with the backs of my hands, but nobody answers my question. I glare at each person, god and huntress alike, but even the birds in the trees have silenced.

"Why *her*?"

Dýnami flinches from where she kneels.

"Why do my friends fall at my feet every time an arrow flies across a room?!" I throw my hand through my hair, pulling at the wheat-blonde tresses just as Sika always did when she was nervous. "Why did death have to steal lives that still wanted to live? Why do you all speak about a prophecy that I do not know about, and why does that prophecy mean Sika had to die?" Tufts of my hair fall from clawed fingers as one cursed word keeps finding the wind and listening ears. "Why, why, why, why, WHY?!"

My tears have made it impossible to see anything. I can make out the silhouettes of several huntresses, but I can't see their faces. This only makes me cry harder because even once the tears subside, and I can look at everyone around me, Sika won't be there. Willow won't, either. Reaper and Copperhead are dead, too. Even Akita and Frigate, who betrayed us, have been my family for centuries.

When I can see again, it will be a sea of faces I recognize, but most of the huntresses remaining are new. They did not bleed alongside me in the Battle of the Labyrinth. They did not exist during the enslavements, and they do not understand me.

"Why must I live while all the rest die?" I whisper my last question, hoping the wind washes it away before Artemis can hear.

A warm hand rests on my shoulder, but I do not look at who it is. I only hear her voice, sweet and woodsy like cinnamon. "On the eighty-eighth night of the eighty-eighth year, when crimson shifts to gold, a prophecy will unfold. From the ashes of time, eight figures will rise." Iris's free hand wipes away my tears as they slip from my eyes.

"The eight figures are called the seer, the savior, the seeker, the singer, the hero, the hammer, the heart...." There is a pause, then, "And the huntress."

The woods are silent, allowing me time to process her words. "What is the prophecy?"

"The prophecy states that on the eighty-eighth day of the eighty-eighth year, after Saffron turns into a goddess, Styx has a chance to steal the throne from Zeus and become the eternal queen. Nobody will steal her throne or usurp her. She will be omnipotent unless the eight figures can complete their part of the prophecy and defeat her."

To a person oblivious to who Styx is, they will not understand the magnitude of terror that will ransack the world if Styx is queen forevermore. She is the personification of hatred, and from that hatred, she spawns apocalyptic mayhem. Styx feasts off the suffering of others within her river, siphoning all their terror until their screams are the last remnants of their souls. If she becomes queen of Mt. Olympus and reigns over the world, then the humans are her hunting ground, and nobody will be safe.

"In order for us to defeat Styx, all eight must complete their task before dying, or else she wins. The oracle must see the truth and stop Styx's plans, the heart must die for a second time, the savior must scream, the hammer's first swing must start the final battle, the hero must bleed, the muse must lose the ability to sing, the seeker must lead lives away from danger in the final battle, but the huntress must clip the greatest monster's life strings."

I do not have to ponder long to determine who the greatest monster is. "Typhon," his name comes out like a plague that threatens to infect us all. "The prophesied huntress must kill Typhon."

Typhon has been the one monster throughout history that is unvanquishable. The world has declared him the Father of Monsters, creating children almost as frightening as him. Yet, none compared to the child of Gaia, who almost defeated Zeus thousands of years ago. I faced him long ago in the Battle of the Labyrinth, and death would have seized me if Saffron did not scare Typhon away. It is the only reason Dýnami, Shikari, Hound, and I are alive today. Not because we could defeat him, but because he fled.

Nobody has seen Typhon since the Battle of the Labyrinth, but his destiny intertwines with ours and Styx's. He will re-emerge, and it is the prophesied job of one of us to kill him. His taunting laugh during our last battle still sends unwanted chills down my spine. How can any of us defeat him?

"Yes," Iris says.

"But who is it?" I ask.

Now that the tears have died down, Iris's vibrant face comes into view. I watch the moment her dark hair, streaked with the orange hue of the sunset, shift to the darkest shade of somber blue. The color of her eyes shifts with her emotions, too. She paints a morbid picture, and I almost want to take back my question.

"We don't know yet, and I don't think Styx and her army know, either."

"Then why-"

"Rather than guessing who will kill Styx's mightiest weapon, she sent Atlas to kill us all. Better no huntress than underestimating the ones you let live." It is Dýnami who answers. She has risen to a standing position, and while she does not move closer, we only stare at one another. Undoubtedly, I look as decimated as Dýnami. Her hair is wayward, and her eyes are rimmed red with heartache. "Sika thought the prophesied huntress was you. You're the oldest."

"But I wasn't the best."

Sika was.

Dýnami nods her head, not trying to deny my claim. "Hopefully you are wrong, and Sika and I were right because here you stand. You're now the strongest, and you're the eldest. It must be you because..." Dýnami points to the water in the distance behind a thrush of trees. "The only other person who could have been the prophesied huntress rots in the ocean."

She turns her back to me and walks away.

Nobody asks me if I think I am the huntress from the prophecy because they know I will say no. Instead, Iris inquires. "Do you have any more questions?"

"Why did she send Atlas after us instead of Hecate?"

"Because nobody saw him coming, and if there is anybody who can find the remaining fragments of Kronos's rebellion, it's him. He will find any monster or god who holds any bitterness towards the Olympians as he has done for eons, and that is what Styx needs. A soldier who wants us all to suffer."

NOBODY SLEEPS THROUGHOUT THE NIGHT, BUT THE NEXT day, we have a funeral for all who died the day before. Artemis, the remaining huntresses, and I stand around a circle of fire. The flames wildly dance with the billowing winds, growing ever so slightly in the company of our sorrow. We do not have the bodies of those we have lost, but the visceral melancholy on all our sullen faces tells the winds and the flames and the trees exactly what we are doing.

Tonight is the fallen huntresses' funerals. We do not mourn the traitors, even if Frigate and Akita's absences are gaping, festering wounds, but we stand around the pyre and remember the others who fell the night before.

Daphne, who was closest to Gigianna, steps forward. Her hands tremble as she holds an arrow with green feathers at the back. Gigianna's signature. Daphne speaks about her friendship with Gigianna and reminisces about her fondest memories with her before lowering the arrow into the flames. I try to cling to Daphne's words, to process Gigianna's death with the same ferocity that I do for many others, but it is too difficult. Each word Daphne says flitters in one ear and escapes the other. My mind is too fuzzy with deathly thoughts, too muddled by centuries of memories of the now-dead.

Daphne takes a step back, and Vee moves forward. She holds one of Xiomara's knives, which she always preferred over arrows, and talks about her friend. Yet, just like Daphne and her speech about Gigianna, I cannot process the words. I hear them and understand the sorrow that wrecks Vee as she discusses their time together, but I only hear Sika's laugh in the forefront of my thoughts. I want to mourn Xiomara, but I hear Akita in my ears and all the clues that lead to her deceit that I was too oblivious to notice.

Vee drops Xiomara's knife into the flames. It does not burn like Gigianna's arrowhead, which has already turned to cinder at the bottom, but it persists. Vee takes steps back, and June moves forward with tears glistening her hooded eyes. She lifts Mercia's bow. Mercia was a talented artist who created designs all around the wooden weapon. Now, June's tears join the artwork.

"She hated when the attention was on her," June sniffles in an attempt to push back her tears, but her attempt is futile. Steady streams flow down her rounded cheeks as she inhales a heavy breath. As she heartily exhales, she hurriedly says. "So I won't talk long. She'd hate it." June tries to laugh, but just like her attempt not to cry, she fails.

I must look away.

And I lock eyes on Artemis.

Iris and Dýnami stand in between us, but with all their focus on June, it feels like it is just Artemis and me. June continues to talk about Mercia, about her talent as an artist and her affinity for finding the most docile animal to ride, but I focus on Artemis. Nobody notices us gravitating towards each other. We meander to the back of our campsite, between a thicket of trees, and distance ourselves from the roaring flames and sobbing bodies.

We lean against the nearest tree, so we can still see the funeral arrangements, but not bear witness to the words that give us no solace. Artemis digs into her satchel and pulls out an apple.

"There's no way that was in your satchel this whole time."

Artemis extends it towards me. "One of the rare sides of being a goddess."

I take the apple, and I know what should follow next. I should speak to her. Tell her everything. I should poise my worries as inspirational quotes and finally explain how defeated I feel. Honesty should pour out of my lips as my broken body accepts Sika is dead, and two huntresses I trusted with my life killed her. The world repeats itself in my suffering, and I should admit that I am sick and tired of the Fates' cruelty.

"I trusted Raven." I run my thumb along the groove of the unblemished apple, my stare fixated on this movement rather than Artemis's probing focus. The bright green fruit tastes my tears as they fall. "And she killed Willow in Poseidon's castle."

Out of the corner of my eye, I see June throw the bow into the fire and retreat. This time, it is Dýnami who steps forward. Suddenly, all my focus is on that damn pyre and the woman who stumbles toward it. She holds nothing in her hands. Everything that was Sika's died in the castle with her. Instead of something of Sika's, Dýnami pulls at her necklace until it comes undone.

She holds her necklace, a tied piece of leather she has worn for almost two hundred years, and curls that hand into a tight fist. "I knew Sika was my third great love the moment I met her. She didn't know, of course, but I did. The moment I saw her, I knew the Fates put her in my life for one reason, and that was to love her unconditionally until..."

Dýnami abruptly stops. She places her fisted hand to her lips and chokes back a heart wrenching sob. Not even the fire crackles, fearful to interrupt such a delicate moment between a grieving love and her last goodbye. Dýnami has always been a strong woman, and today is no exception, but her worst nightmare has come to fruition. She lost the extension of her soul, and a pang of guilt pierces my chest with the harshness of a blade.

Dýnami falls to her knees in front of the flames, and Vee rushes towards her. She places her hands on Dýnami's shoulders, but she pushes them off. There, in the silence of her grief, comes the sound I never wanted to hear.

Dýnami, uncontrollably sobbing in front of the flames, bidding her soulmate farewell.

I stare down at the apple once more. "I trusted Akita."

"We all did," Artemis says.

I shake my head. "But we didn't listen to her. She tried to tell us she hated Sika. That she blamed her for Copperhead's death, but we didn't listen." I can barely see the apple in front of me beneath all my tears I refuse to shed. "We didn't listen when she sobbed for her friend and vowed to avenge her. I didn't listen, no matter how many times Akita laid the clues in front of me."

I do not say the words, but they are read in between my lines.

It's my fault that Sika is dead.

Before Artemis can attempt condolement, Dýnami speaks from her place upon the ground. "The day I knew, I wanted to immortalize it. It's rare to find that third great love, especially with a world as ruined as mine. I was as a human slave, so I ripped off a piece of my leather armor." Dýnami stares down at her fist, where her makeshift necklace sits. "I have worn a piece of the day I found Sika around my neck every day since, thanking the fates for intertwining our paths for many centuries. I got two hundred and fifty years with her as my friend, and for seventy of those, she was my everything."

Dýnami presses a kiss on the leather necklace, and plentiful tears stream down her cheeks. She has her last kiss with Sika, and I can hear her crumbling heart with the final motion.

"Who can say they were as lucky as me?"

She throws the necklace into the flames, and this time when Vee comes to hug an inconsolable Dýnami, she hugs back. Her sobs fill the woods, reminding every roaming deer and critter that the world is a little less warm without Sika in our lives.

"I didn't listen." I place the uneaten, tear-ruined apple back in Artemis's hand.

Dýnami calls herself lucky, but when the funeral has ended and the circle passes around food, Dýnami turns it down. She has never turned down a grilled squirrel, and the entire group knows it. The woods grow quiet with Dýnami's rejection, and she pointedly looks away.

When night falls, many do not sleep, but nighttime claims me with violent fastness.

Morpheus and Epiales are both dead, gone into another realm that Saffron sent their souls to, and I have not dreamed in that time since their departure.

Until today.

I think I have stumbled awake by my mistake and ingested a mysterious mushroom or two, but then realization takes its toll. I am dreaming once more.

It is a nightmarish version of the woods my actual body is in. The tall grass does not darken because of the night. Magic dips the grass in death and tar. The trees are all dead, their bark milky white and their limbs wilted. I roam through the ominous woods without a destination in mind, in an endless search for momentary escape.

Many huntresses can find an escape from their sadness, but I have never had an addiction I could focus all my morose rage on. Every-body, either human or God, finds something. A particular fix that devi-ates their minds away from their own debilitating thoughts.

Zeus beds anybody- male or female- to hide the fact that he is in a loveless marriage; Dionysus drinks himself into oblivion to forget that he believes himself otherwise worthless; Ares covers the world with the blood of casualties to stop himself from wallowing in his own loneliness. Even Artemis has found an escape through conversa-tion, yet I have found nothing to relieve my sadness and anger.

It's worse today, when the guilt worms its way into my blood-stream and taints everything inside.

I scour the woods until I find a lone white horse. It stands in the middle of woods, where I rationally know it does not belong, and it stares at me. I must truly be going mad because I think this horse understands I need to run. To escape, just for a little, and he is here for the ride. With every passing year, the huntresses' faces become more and more unfamiliar. Death has stolen all my friends, leaving behind only Artemis and Dýnami, but how long will it be until Dýnami joins Death? And if she is gone, then will I ever truly try comradery with the other huntresses?

I move towards the white horse, and I let the tears consume me. I sob with each step until I can scarcely see my footprints in the mud.

When I first became a huntress, Artemis told me I would become immortal, and I was excited. Gods, who wouldn't want to live forever? Immortality is a gift, so few receive, and everyone wants. Then I received the promise of forever. I am older than many of the surrounding trees. I am older than Saffron, the most powerful goddess in the world. Many of the huntresses who cried at the bonfire are not old enough to remember the last Titanomachy War. Their ancestors suffered in the battles with me, not them.

My dead friends fought in that battle with me.

And gods, I miss them.

The horse never looks away from my advancing form, and when I am close enough to run my hand through his porcelain mane, he lets out a soft neigh. This animal, not native to these woods, offers an escape from guilt and sorrow. I eagerly reach out my hand when the sound of a twig cracking stops my movement.

I whirl my head back, but there is nothing in the abyss of my dream.

Another twig crackles from outside my dream world. In my waking existence, somebody approaches who is not a huntress. Artemis trained all huntresses to have light feet in the wilderness. We are not clumsy enough to step on multiple twigs and alert others of our presence.

Which means….

"Maybe another day," I say to the horse.

I retract my advancing hand, and just as I do, he changes. His white fur becomes as black as night. His mane turns black, too, with silver tips at the ends. But most startling are his eyes, which were once a soft hue. Now, they are bright as blood and burn with a fire that comes at a deadly cost.

"Another day," the horse says in a voice that is too much like Hades's.

I jolt my eyes open and hastily reach for the bow and arrows I keep to my immediate left. I spin my body behind me, my arrow placed on my bowstring, and I stare at cat-like yellow eyes. At nearly sixty feet tall, I face one of the most frightening monsters in history, one who should still be dead after its ordeal with Oedipus.

There, personified once more, is the Sphinx.

NINE

HERMES

My winged sandals propel me out of the watery depths of Poseidon's rage, and they allow me to hide in the depths of the clouds. I am one with the birds, witnessing the aftermath of Poseidon destroying his castle and all his traitorous children. The ocean around his rage bubbles like boiling water, while the surrounding area has waves as tall as a skyscraper. Anyone who is within a fifty-mile radius of the water will surely die, drowned by Poseidon's acute desire for retribution.

Neither me nor my sandals leave the aquatic destruction's rueful sight. From this angle, I see ships surrender their life to the gaping jaws of vengeful waves. I am too far away to hear the screams of the fallen, but I know it does not sate the rage of the seas. It clamors for more bloodshed, but the sinking ships will not sedate Poseidon. Only the death of Atlas, Styx, and Hecate will satiate him.

It is because of these waves, and remembering Atlas's role in the cyclops' deception, that I discover where to search for Ares. It was not Atlas who the huntresses saw Ares with, but they both bend the knee to the same wicked female. A hurricane whistles at my backside, the closest to a scream the victims will ever make, as I fly across the world to Mt. Atlas.

The wind is as angry as the seas, slowing my typically quickened movements. Everyone and everything revolts against the brewing war Styx brings, and I am one of many who suffer its touch. A storm brews above my head, further stressed by the wintry winds and the rising hurricane lapping at my ankles. There is no escape from the gods' rages, which I fear will only grow worse with each passing day without Saffron.

The world tentatively survived without Saffron for eons, but after one century with her guidance, the gods dissemble without her. Styx fights for the throne, but it is Saffron who is most deserving of usurpation. Zeus is a mediocre monarch, and while I will never vocalize the thoughts aloud, we need more than mediocrity against Styx.

We need the world-hailed savior.

We need my wife.

Ex-wife, comes the hissing voice within my ear. The same wretched sound that reminds me that everything happening is partially my fault. If only I had told her sooner. If only I had lied better.

The long distance between Mt. Atlas and the oceans gives me far too much time within the chasm of my self-deprecating thoughts. It provides me with too many minutes of wallowing and games of *what if* that leads nowhere but misery.

A strike of lightning shines a light upon Mt. Atlas, and all my thoughts freeze with the frigid winds. I soar high into the air until I camouflage my body behind a dark gray cumulonimbus cloud. Zeus must be watching my movements because two small holes, no bigger than a quarter, opens in the center of the cloud where my eyes are.

The cave within Mt. Atlas has a half-circle of candles providing limited illumination, but it is enough to see the monsters lurking within.

Ares is there, holding the Earth on his shoulders while Atlas hunts for the huntresses. I am too far away to see his expression, but I notice the way his arms tremble and hear the crumbling mountains each time his grip falters. Hecate sits in the cave with him, with an orb of green magic levitating off her palm.

Five other immortals are there with them.

Calypso, whose island captured my wife and her ex. Seeing her reminds me that Saffron and a newly alive Epiales are there, with no one else, while I cannot find her. The huntresses are going back to Hecate's portal site, hoping to find Ogygia. But as I stare at Calypso's lithe build, I see a kernel of hope that I can save Saffron myself.

Two of the traitorous muses, Erato and Urania, sit on either side of Hecate. The former appears to be sleeping, but the latter has a hand on Ares's leg. That's why the Earth keeps shaking in his grasp. He is simultaneously trying to keep the world on his shoulders and knock Urania's hand off his leg.

All who sit around the cave are enemies we knew from the ball, except the last two, who sit on the other side of the cage. They almost obscure themselves from view, like they still teeter between loyalty and betrayal.

The first is one of Ares's sons with Aphrodite, Hedylogos, the god of sweet talk and flattery. How can a god, whose divinity is words, can be so easily tricked by them?

He refuses to look in his father's direction, but Ares's neck cranes towards his son when he isn't flinching away from Urania's grasp.

Next to him sits Apate, the goddess of deceit. It's befitting that she sits here amongst traitors. I can blame her no more than I can blame Zeus for storms or Dionysus for wine consumption. I could have expected her presence amongst them. But just like Hedylogos, there is a speck of doubt in her decision. Deceit and fraud can always switch at any second.

Styx isn't present in the cave, though. Hecate is her second-in-command, and she sits in a mountain most didn't know held a miniature army, but where is the true mastermind? Where is Styx?

I want the answers to the questions nibbling at the base of my neck, but that does not free Saffron as quickly as the plan formulating in my head right now. My gaze flickers back to Calypso, and I know how to steal the answers from her lips.

I will find Ogygia.

I will find Saffron.

With the promise on my tongue, I fly towards Mt. Olympus in search of a few friends eager for retribution.

TEN

HART SOMMERS

Since I was a child, Hades has scared me.

Every tale about Hades had death's hand reaching for an embrace. I, like so many others, fear death. It's inescapable for humans, but it is an unknown entity, and change scares many; death is life's biggest change. I know Hades is not the god of death, but he wears the onyx crown. He reigns over the corpses and wandering souls. My family is in his domain, and while I miss them, their destination frightens me.

Hades has been here for two days, and my discomfort hasn't lessened. I should feel better in his company because, except for sleep, we have been inseparable. He and I stay in the art room from the moment the sun rises until Apollo insists we end for dinner. Yet I cannot shake the heightened sense of fear in his proximity.

We sit cross-legged on the floor, bodies angled towards each other, and he extends his hands to me. I falter.

"Why are we on the floor?"

"I would like to try something different. Take my hands, please." Hades's hands remain outstretched, suspended in the air, while I nervously tuck mine underneath my legs.

The first day Hades started training me, he only observed my current schedule. I sat in front of my easel, staring at an empty canvas until inspiration arose, while he sat a few feet away. On the second day, he taught me about his magic and asked me to draw my interpretation of his explanation. His voice is deep and smooth like velvet, but when his words caressed the air, an icy chill scattered up my arms.

Throughout his explanation, I never received a surge of magic that guided my artwork. I mundanely drew shadowy figures, which heavily mirrored the undead Achilles and Atalanta, who guarded the art room doors. His helm of invisibility levitated in the air between the corporeal, shadowy beings, but that was it. There wasn't a powerful force driving me to further conclusions. I didn't receive a single vision.

Hades's face never fell with disappointment, but I felt it in the humid air.

The multitude of jewels on his fingers glint off the natural light shining through the opened windows. He wears six rings, all with black bands, but different gems bespeckle each one. Rubies, sapphires, emeralds, diamonds, topaz, and amethyst create a rainbow of opulence in the otherwise morbid scenery.

I stare at the amethyst ring on his pinky finger as I accept his hands with my trembling ones. His touch is surprisingly warm. I expected frigidness with his touch, a temperature that corelates with his Underworld, but only the rings are cold against my skin.

"Close your eyes," Hades says.

I hesitate. "Why?"

"Miss. Sommers, do I scare you?"

"Yes," the word comes out quicker than I can curb it.

His expression does not change with the revelation. There is no shock or disappointment or surprise. He merely sighs.

"I never wanted to be the God of the Underworld. When we first defeated my father in the original Titanomachy War, my siblings and I argued for days over our dominions. Our father, and his father, were rulers of the skies. All of us wanted that coveted affinity, but Poseidon knew he would not win against Zeus and me. I was the eldest brother, and Zeus was the more powerful, so Poseidon quickly grabbed the seas and abdicated."

I stop myself from asking him for an explanation behind this story. He understands why I fear him. It is his title as ruler of the dead that makes many, like me, scurry from his company. How many times has he had to tell this story to another frightened human, so they'd stop flinching from his touch and averting their gazes?

"When Zeus corralled our siblings together and received the majority vote as ruler of the sky, he assigned me the role of the King of the Underworld. I did not want to be surrounded by death because with death always comes fear. Fear that cannot dissolve, no matter how kind or patient I can be. I hated my brother when he told me what my role will be in our eternal future, but then he reminded me I will eventually be ruler of all humans because there is only one direction a human's life goes."

His attention drifts away from our locked hands, and they find Achilles and Atalanta. Their backs are facing us as they guard the doorway, so they miss the tentative smile

93

Hades gives them. They miss the pride that exudes off of Hades in plentiful waves as he stares at his soldiers, his subjects, but most importantly, his friends.

"I knew Zeus was a fighter first, a wise male second. He would not be a perfect king. In fact, I knew he'd eventually turn into the cowardice, lethargic ruler who currently hides on Mt. Olympus. It's why I wanted to be king of the skies, but when Zeus said that I would eventually rule them all in my Underworld, I realized that was the best decision for the humans."

"Why?" I ask, suddenly enraptured by his story.

"The king who rules over the most subjects must be vigilant in his work. There isn't a day off for the ruler of the dead, and that level of focus and determination is lost on my brother Poseidon. He has many positive traits, but his work ethic is not one of them."

Hades laughs at that, but the sound quickly falters.

"The King of the Underworld must also be patient because when many humans realize they are dead, they react with sadness, anger, or a disheartening mixture of the two. It took Zeus many centuries to have patience, then empathy for the humans, and even now, it is threadbare. He only cares for the beautiful, but I care for all humans. I always have. I did not want to rule the Underworld, but I wanted the best afterlife for the humans, and I am not too humble to admit that I am the best god for the job."

He pauses.

"And my wife is the best goddess for the job."

With death, I have only allowed myself to see it through one color. It was only dark and filled with disparity. I never opened myself to the possibility of more; instead, I closed a door on myself and threw away the key.

Hades forced the door open, and now I see more

colors. The blossoming reds of rebirth, the yellow of a new horizon, and the twinkling blues of hope that I thought would die with your mortal existence. Hades is a deliverer of a peaceful afterlife, who accepts the flickering fears of the living because eventually, all who die will realize his benevolence.

My expression must shift because Hades repeats. "Close your eyes, Miss. Sommers."

And I do without hesitation.

There isn't a sound to be heard, no lingering aromas to cling to, and the wind ebbs away. There is no sense distracting me from the darkness, only the touch of Hades's hands and the bubbling anticipation of something more. It could be seconds, minutes, or hours where I linger in the in-between, but eventually, the astral form of a sitting body forms.

I think it's Hades's form that joins me in the seclusion of my mind. The glimmer sits where he does, with outstretched hands, and its frame is a thousand sparkling diamonds, like the ring he wears. His name is on my tongue, ready to join me in the unconscious world I have created, but another form materializes.

The frame is identifiably a female's, with round hips and a full hourglass build, but she hides her identity from me. Just like the first form, she is only a border of thousands of gems. The emerald form sits to the first one's left, and she holds out her hands.

One by one, five silhouettes form, and each one shines with a color from one of Hades's rings.

I know who they are without seeing their faces, and the realization comes out as an exhalation. "The oracles of the Delphi."

The most powerful oracles of the ancient world sit in a

semi-circle around me, and when I speak their identity aloud, their anonymity disintegrates. Each one becomes corporeal once more, wearing tunics of the color they arrived in. White for the diamond, green for emeralds, red for rubies, purple for amethyst, blue for sapphire, and gold topaz for my ancestor, who sits nearest me with the same honey-colored eyes.

Aashritha says. "I've been waiting a long time for this moment, Hartika."

The oracles who surround me all vary in ages and appearances, but while Aashritha appears the youngest amongst the group, they are all thousands of years old. My ancestor sits amongst her comrades but looks the same age as me. Like, in some distant universe, we could have been sisters rather than ancestor-descendant.

They all extend a hand and wait for me to accept their touch, but I stare only at Aashritha. Too many centuries have gone, blurring our bloodline. Other than her dark complexion and colored eyes, she does not look like my mother. She does not look like my brother or me, either. I see her and know she is family. We are strangers, but not.

It's why the words come out too easily. "I'm scared."

"I was your age when I died. Even though my parents sent me to the Delphi when I was sixteen, I still had more power than any other oracle. It scared me when I was only twenty-six years old and saw three thousand years into the future. I saw this future in three hundred and twenty versions, and at only twenty-six, your age, I learned that in all the versions of a future, only three ended without Styx ruling the world and eradicating humanity."

The eldest oracle, the diamond one, places a reassuring hand on Aashritha's shoulder. Aasritha bends over and places a kiss on top of the comforting hand.

"Twenty-six is too young to receive the weight of the world. It was too young for me to die, but the Fates know the path we must take. They know the fear we have as we take the steps they meticulously planned, but we have to keep moving. We must accept that path one step at a time."

Aasritha has both her arms outstretched, palms up, and offers to teach me how to become the best oracle I can. She invites me to learn the three versions that will end this war without Styx destroying humanity and all the gods who fight to save it.

"It's funny that the same gods who enslaved humanity are the ones who are going to help us save it from Styx."

My words aren't funny. They are a stall towards the inevitable, and all the oracles understand this.

"In one version of the future, you succumb to your fear," Aasritha says. "Do you wish to know what happens in that one version where you refuse to learn and do not tell the future for others to hear?"

I clasp my feather locket, a nervous habit I can never break. Words have escaped me, so I can only nod my head.

"Epiales is the first to die, followed by every single huntress. Lamb is the last to die, but her death shatters Artemis, and she falls into a state of madness nobody can free her from. She is the first goddess who dies with Iris shortly afterwards. The goddesses' deaths were merciful compared to the rest that follow."

Iris pops into my mind. The resilient goddess, with her rainbow-colored staff, as she saved my life at the ball a few days ago. I hear Aasritha's words, and I see a mangled Iris on the floor of that ball, her bones creating a circle around her deflated and unmoving body.

I shudder. "What happens next?"

"Without the huntresses, nobody can slay Typhon. He cannot kill gods, but he can cause them unimaginable pain. Hermes does not die in the war; instead, he becomes an eternal prisoner. His screams never cease under Typhon's torture, and they never will. He will live out the rest of his immortality in suffering."

"The huntresses were the ones who find the hammer of the prophecy," the emerald oracle says. "Without the huntresses alive, the hammer never joins the gods' side of the war. The hammer wields their weapon for Styx, killing countless mortals before Styx kills them."

"And Apollo," Aashritha begins.

"Stop."

They listen.

I love Lowell as a friend and family, but my years with him shifted my perception of the world. Before him, I wanted to be a hero who stormed into battle, unafraid of the outcome. Then, he hid me away in our apartment, and I treated it like a cage. I told myself my cage was a shield that protected me from battles I could never fight, and I exchanged my fearlessness for fear.

I do not blame Lowell. He didn't force me to stay in a loveless relationship that twisted my views on everything. We both suffered by staying in a relationship for too long, but because of it, my thought process altered. I became a coward when all I wanted was to be strong.

Then she said Apollo's name after a slew of death and anguish.

And something broken in me rebuilt.

I take Aashritha's hands, and I lock eyes with her. "Teach me everything."

"We will do more than teach you, descendant of Aasritha," the elderly diamond oracle says. She places her hands on my left forearm. "We will give you more power than any oracle before you."

The emerald oracle places her hands on my right forearm. "We are the six most powerful oracles of the Delphi."

Next, the ruby oracle places both hands on my left shoulder, sharp nails grazing my necklace chain. "And while you are a powerful oracle with untapped potential."

"You are not strong enough," says the amethyst oracle as she touches my right shoulder.

Last is the sapphire oracle, who is a long-faced, middle-aged woman. She gives me a kind, small smile and places her hand on my calf nearest her. "But every day, as we imbue you with more of our abilities, you will become the strongest oracle in history."

Colors flow from their palms into my skin, burrowing into my veins until they illuminate me with their powers. My veins are no longer just blue, but they flow in reds, greens, purples, whites, and finally, gold.

"You are finished with fear. Cast it aside. Bury it in an unmarked coffin. Embrace the fright and become who the world requires."

Images flash fast and undecipherable through my mind. The oracles' stories, from beginning to fiery end, break down my thoughts until I am not just one person. I am a combination of seven strong women of foresight; we will crumble Styx's world like Pompeii together.

My eyes open of their own accord, and when I look down, my veins still gleam with the currents of their magic. The lock I placed on my mind opens, and I see its evidence around the room. I no longer hold Hades's hand; rather, we stand side-by-side in front of three canvases completely covered in artwork and words.

The first canvas is a map of the southern portion of

the world. Beneath it is a drawing of Lamb, Artemis, Iris, and the other huntresses. Artemis pulls apart the air, where invisible magic barely shimmers between two cypress trees. The veins on her biceps bulge with the movement, but it's evident what she finds.

"It's the portal to Ogygia," Hades says with wobbling hope.

"They're going to find Saffron."

I hear a sniffle, and pointedly do not look in his direction, so he may cry with relief on his own. My attention snags on the remaining canvases. The second one is mostly words, with drawings scratched onto the corners. There is a white crow on the top left corner, a raven on the top right, and palm trees sprouting from the bottom.

The words say,

> *The birds, the birds, they call to me.*
> *Birds of death and resurgence,*
> *Of nightmares and treachery.*
>
> *To win against hatred,*
> *You must claim a fallen Oneiroi,*
> *You must forgive three.*
>
> *Forgive the heart who must die twice,*
> *The hammer with deceit as their vice,*
> *And the hero whose life comes at a fright-*
> *ening price.*

The last canvas present is the place inside my mind, where I met with the past oracles of the Delphi. Their hands are on me, imbuing me with their abilities of foresight. It is the only canvas with color. I threw paint splatters across the canvas, bathing each oracle in the color I associate them with, and the sketch of myself has all six colors dragged over my body with shaky fingers.

"Holy gods," says a deep, soulful voice that reminds me why I have agreed to stop living in fear.

I turn around, and Apollo stands in the room, grinning at the evidence of my magic. He looks at me, not the canvases, and says. "You are magnificent, μέλι."

ELEVEN

LAMB

The Sphinx is both beautiful and frightening, with wings as majestic as an eagle stretching from one mile to the next. The creature of riddles takes one step forward, and the ground trembles beneath her weight. Her eyes, almost as large as my head, never look away from me. She prowls closer until her head is directly above mine. I drop my weapon, and the feline predator grins back.

"Smart choice," it coos in an inhumane, almost robotic tone.

"Lamb, duck!" A scream lets out.

Hound stands up, with an arrow placed on the bowstring. Her furious attention locks on the Sphinx, but I know this creature better than Hound. Arrows cannot defeat such a prominent monster.

I open my mouth to scream, to tell her not to release that arrow, but it is too late. She lets her weapon fly, and my brazen, hostile, kind-hearted friend realizes her mistake. The arrow bounces off the Sphinx's forehead and lands directly in her skull. Hound collapses on her back on the ground, never to get up again. Her eyes are wide and unblinking at the sky, where not even the stars can provide comfort.

The thunk of her body wakes the two slumbering nearest her. Artemis stands in an instant, along with Vee. The latter kicks the girl beside her, June. The Sphinx stays hovering above me as she patiently waits for every person to wake up and realize she is an inch away from biting my head off.

I try not to, but my attention snags on Hound's corpse, where the arrow still juts out of her forehead. Hound was a woman who would give the shirt off her back to warm another, but then grumble and complain about it the entire time. Shikari, her greatest friend and favorite person to bicker with, stumbles when she sees Hound dead on the floor. Her fingers twitch beside her bow, but she doesn't pull it free.

She stays perfectly still as the monster focuses all her attention on Artemis. The Sphinx is a daunting sight, a compilation of three creatures. Her face is human, except for her feline teeth, glinting in the moonlight. Her torso is a human woman, with bare breasts lightly covered in golden lion's fur. It's the same color as her tail, which swishes in delight for the upcoming feast. The lower portion of her body, and her arms, are that of a lion. Muscles cord every square inch of her arms, reminding me once again that she is not a monster easily thwarted. The last animal sewn into her flesh is an eagle, which provides the long, lethal wings eerily still in the air. Her nose is beak-like, but mostly mundane.

"How are you alive?" Artemis asks, unable to hide her disbelief.

"It is embarrassing how easy it was for Lady Hecate to free monsters from the Underworld when she still had the King and Queen's trust." In a full one hundred and eighty degrees, the Sphinx turns her head back to where I lay beneath her. "Little huntress." Her voice is ethereal and haunting, but I will not run again. I face the beast head on. "In order to survive morning, you must correctly answer my riddle."

"No," Artemis snarls. She takes a step towards the monster, but Iris grabs her by the biceps and keeps her at a distance.

"What would you prefer? Giving your huntresses a chance to defeat me, or should I let them fire their weapons the same way your angry one did moments earlier? Your friends have a better chance with my riddles, I assure you."

She speaks about Hound's death as if it is inconsequential. Like Hound was not a person who mattered. Like Hound's death, wrecking the lives of others creates a trickle effect and shatters the rationale of nearby friends. The Sphinx speaks about Hound the way others would discuss the weather or the wind, further inciting others' ruefulness.

"What is your riddle?" I ask.

I am not accustomed to being the center of attention. There have always been other huntresses faster than me, louder than me, better than me, but the Sphinx only focuses on where I lay. The others are inconsequential to her, compared to me.

It brings me back to Hecate on Ogygia. Hecate told me Artemis cursed me with a name that others would underestimate. I was a lamb, natural prey to any nearby predators. She failed to see the potential lethality in me. The hauntingly still monster watches me with saliva forming at her lips, hungrily waiting to consume me whole.

The Sphinx believes I'm the easiest to kill, too.

Just like Hecate.

And what I mistake that will be.

"The more you take, the more you leave behind. What am I?" The Sphinx asks.

Artemis has been an efficient teacher to all huntresses over the centuries, but the Sphinx died thousands of years ago. She did not train any of us in the art of riddles. I have known about the tales of the Sphinx and her original riddle against Oedipus, but that is the extent of my knowledge. I hear the question leave the Sphinx's lips, and I do not have an answer.

Artemis taught us how to handle weapons, how to fight. Reminded us of the importance of mercy and to only kill if absolutely necessary. She trained us on every living god and goddess, ensuring we knew the best way to speak to them or fight them, if needed. She did not teach us about the dead and defeated, though.

Artemis realizes this, too.

It is why she screamed so loudly for Hound. Just as I hold the weight of guilt with Sika's death, Artemis holds the same burden for Hound. Artemis isn't to blame, but she will always wonder if Hound would be alive if we learned riddles. If we were prepared for a monster, none of us should have ever faced.

The creature waits ever so patiently for the first huntress to walk towards her.

It is Daphne who makes the courageous move. She cranes her neck upwards and faces the beast head-on. "It is time."

The Sphinx does not answer if Daphne is correct or not. She sits perfectly still until, in the blink of an eye, her mouth chomps down on Daphne's neck. Screams echo around me, coming from all directions, as the Sphinx swallows Daphne's head whole. The rest of her body crumbles onto the floor, never to rise again.

Her skull cracks beneath the might of the Sphinx's maw. For as long as I live, that sound will never leave my ears. It will haunt me from now until my last day, and it isn't over. Other huntresses will make their guess, and other huntresses will die. From where the Sphinx stands, a few feet above me, droplets of Daphne's blood splatters on my neck. I hold in my growing nausea, and I want to move, but I fear Daphne and Hound's fate will be mine if I move too fast from a lion's paw.

The Sphinx swallows Daphne's head, bones and all, and licks away the blood on her bottom lip. "Who's next?"

Every huntress waits, mulling over the riddle and their presumptuous answer. Artemis pulls out a bow and arrow, and she fires her weapon against the Sphinx. Her throat scratches itself raw with her clamorous rage, but each arrow that should sink into the Sphinx's skin bounces off and penetrates Artemis's flesh.

Yet, she keeps firing the weapon, only to harm herself.

On the seventh arrow, which nicks Artemis in the shoulder, Iris tackles Artemis to the ground. "There is nothing we can do!" Iris screams, but in that scream, I hear the desperation. This is our fight against a wise monster who surpasses almost all gods in age. Artemis and Iris cannot save us from these riddles.

Laconia's legs tremble like a newborn deer as she moves towards the Sphinx. Everything about Laconia is uncertain. Her gait. The nervous twitch of her hands. The answer she is about to say aloud.

"It's your breath," Laconia says in a whisper.

She is the next to lose her head.

Jamila takes a step forward, but the Sphinx is quick to say. "Only the huntresses, not the pretenders."

Her tone is apathetic, devoid of any attempt to insult, but Jamila still flinches. She is ready to die alongside us, to guess and potentially die; yet, she does not have a chance. She wants to become one of us, a huntress, but she hasn't made the oath yet.

Artemis hasn't let her until Saffron is freed, and it just saved her life.

It is Vee who walks towards the Sphinx next. She does not strut forward with over-inflated confidence like Daphne, but she doesn't cower behind every step like Laconia. Vee calmly moves towards the Sphinx, stepping directly in front of the paw with the least amount of blood-shed, and faces the gargantuan creature.

Vee removes an arrow and places it on her bowstring. She says nothing as she points the weapon at the Sphinx and says one word. "Footsteps."

"What did you just say?" The Sphinx's apathetic tone waivers, and I recognize the sound in her voice all too well.

Fear.

The last time someone guessed her riddle correctly, the Sphinx died. She did not question the others' answers, but for Vee, brilliant and kind Vee, the Sphinx shows fear. I move from under the Sphinx, and she focuses solely on Vee. She does not notice I fled until I am standing beside Artemis.

She points the arrow directly at the Sphinx's heart, but she doesn't look toward her mark. Her glare stays firmly placed on the Sphinx's eyes, which brim with unmistaken disbelief. "I have studied your riddles my entire life, so it took me a while, but I remember. The answer is footsteps, just like those." She glances down to where her paws lay firmly on the ground. "Are the last ones you will ever take."

Disbelief is prevalent on the Sphinx's face, and in that moment of shock and vulnerability, Vee releases her arrow.

When Artemis tried to kill the beast, the arrows bounced off its flesh and hit her, but not this time. Vee understands the Sphinx better than us all, and when the arrow flies, it meets its mark with a cacophonous *plunk*. The Sphinx stumbles backwards, but she does not die from the wound.

That isn't Vee's intention, anyway.

She whips her head back, black ponytail swaying with the movement, as she locks eyes on Artemis. "Take your revenge," she says.

Iris removes her arms from Artemis's body, and she rises to her full height. There are rare times when I forget Artemis is a goddess, but moments like this remind me. Her deathly glare lands on the stumbling monster, who tries to flee from the scene like a wounded animal, and a sword materializes in Artemis's hand.

She runs towards the creature. The Sphinx does not flee. It stumbles and meanders backwards, but she is wounded and in the line of a goddess's fury. Artemis leaps into the air, and the tip of her sword plunges into the monster's neck.

Then she saws.

She can make this death quick, but she lets the Sphinx suffer.

The decapitated three huntresses, who were a part of Artemis. Too many have died, and now she gets a small

TRISH D. W.

part of her revenge. She drags that sword slowly and cruelly through the Sphinx's neck. Minutes pass until finally the head falls off.

Artemis turns back to us, covered with the inhuman blood of our enemy, chest heaving with rage. "This is not our last fight against these monsters, but this will be the last time huntress blood spills." Artemis looks at the reminders of the carnage in our broken and hopeless forms, and she locks her gaze on me. "Nobody else dies."

A dozen deer materialize in the space between Artemis and us. She moves towards the largest stag, whose antlers have sharpened tips, and she mounts the creature. We all move towards an animal, and Vee moves to stand beside me.

"How did you know the riddle?"

Vee takes the deer to the left of my chosen one. She doesn't answer until we mount the creatures. "My mother was a slave of Athena's at the time of the revolution. Athena taught my mother the importance of wisdom, and my mom made sure I learned that valuable lesson, too. Others grew up learning how to play sports. I learned seven languages and every riddle over the past three thousand years."

"Your mom sounds wise," Iris says. "And she just saved your lives."

"She died a few months before I became a huntress, but I never forgot her studies. Not for a single second."

"Hopefully, your mom is in Elysium. She is the mother of a hero."

Artemis turns away from Vee as soon as she finishes her statement, so she misses the redness forming on Vee's cheeks. She doesn't witness the small, imperceptible smile that grows, too. Vee has been a huntress for roughly eight, maybe nine, years, but today is the first time she finds the pride in her profession. She finally sees herself as a formidable huntress.

"We need to move faster. Ride during nighttime and sleep only in increments." Artemis's gaze snags on our fallen sisters, and her jaw clenches. "Their funerals have to be quick, and then we have to keep running."

Artemis snaps her fingers and the ground trembles. The soil rises from its imprisonment beneath the grass, turning into serpentine coils. They wrap around the ankles, wrists, waists, and necks of our fallen sisters. Shikari crumbles to her knees when Hound's body is completely covered by the dirt that claims her. She reaches a final hand out to her closest friend, but before she can touch Hound's outline, she and the two other huntresses fall into the earth.

In their place, three cypress trees start to fruition. In a matter of seconds, corpses have manifested into a sight of beauty. Laconia always loved nature more than the other huntresses. She always condemned the huntresses, who took flowers as hair accessories, because it ruined the eternal beauty of a flower by forcing it to wilt prematurely. If Laconia could see what she had become, a flourishing eighty-foot-tall cypress tree, then I'm certain she'd be smiling from ear to ear.

We do not have time for ceremonial speeches, not like we did for the women who died in Poseidon's castle. This manifestation into three trees is a wordless proclamation of love, the only one we can afford right now. Artemis lingers over the trees, cementing each one into memory.

"Let's go," she orders.

Iris takes the deer closest to Artemis, and she reaches a hand for her. Artemis doesn't look at Iris, but I know she sees the outstretched hand. Artemis sees me watching them, then she takes Iris's hand. The harshness on my goddess's face lessens when she finally meets Iris's eyes.

Shikari is the last one to get on her deer, but as soon as she sits, we ride far from the Sphinx's crime scene.

We ride towards a potential portal and the imminent promise of more monsters more terrifying than the Sphinx.

TWELVE

SAFFRON

We haven't spoken in two days, not since he learned the truth. When he realized I did not want to bring him back, he asked for the undiluted truth, so I told him everything. Not just everything with Styx, but everything that transpired since his death.

He and I sat together, our backs against parallel trees, and I started the story with my ascension into a goddess. I told him about the titles I earned with the divinity and the pleasant years that followed my primary years as the goddess of humanity. I began my story with Hattie, but my life these past ninety years includes Hermes. He was interwoven into every morning and night, and eventually, the story of my life tilted in his direction.

My marriage to Hermes, along with its divorce, came from my cracked lungs. It hurts to talk about him, especially with Epiales, but he doesn't display any judgement.

He doesn't look away from me as I admit everything we achieved together and lost.

We reversed our roles on that fateful night. I was the storyteller, and he was the devoted listener. He didn't interrupt, but when he had questions, he would wait for a natural pause in my story. He mainly asked questions about topics that brought me joy, like adopting Jamila and rebuilding the world. Wisely, he avoided any inquisitions about Hermes and Hattie.

I ended my tale with the prophecy, and how I ended up stuck on this island with him after being forced to bring him back to life. He had no questions about his resurrection, or why Styx wanted me to bring him back. The sunrise peaked from the trees by the end of my explanation, and he stood up, announced his hunger, and left.

He has not spoken to me since, and I haven't found the right words to initiate a conversation.

Until suddenly, after I make a fire in between us, Epiales asks. "Do you want to hear a story?"

He pops a grape into his mouth, then extends his hand with one for me. Our eyes lock for the first time in these two days of limbo, and I accept the grape. I have avoided eating any of the food in case Hecate never returns with more, but this is more than just a green grape. It's his way of accepting what I've told him and wanting to move past it.

My finger grazes his palm, and he lets out a soft sigh at the contact.

I pop the grape in my mouth and ignore the small electricity that came from that touch. "Have I heard this story before?"

"No, my queen, you haven't."

"I think I have some time to spare." The words are

teasing, but my tone isn't. Am I even capable of creating amusement in my voice anymore?

Epiales gives me a wry grin, but when I do not reciprocate, he looks away to face the water. "Tartarus is death."

"I remember."

Other than my nightmare, which I never told him about, I was in Tartarus with Epiales. His godly abilities were waning as he was withering away in Tartarus, so he could not create an illusion in our dream world. He brought me to him in Tartarus, where warmth was impossible to find, but death was inescapable. I spent two nights in that eternal dungeon. I still fear its frigid embrace, but Epiales was there for centuries. Suffering the cold and the despair until a part of him wilted and died.

Epiales continues. "I never knew darkness had a taste until living down there. It's pungent. Tart and acidic. Beneath the taste and the smell of decaying bones came a promise. Darkness promised that every horrible thought in your head came to fruition. That all your powers would turn on you, making you loathe them as much as you loathe the god responsible for your imprisonment."

Again, I murmur. "I remember."

Many years ago, he told me that Tartarus tortured him with his affinity of nightmares. He would suffer nightmares every single day, but they existed beyond his dreams. They taunted him every waking moment, except in our dreamworlds together. There was one nightmare in particular that chilled me to the bone. He spoke about me being the center of his terror. He said I let out a scream that echoed forevermore, which was the sound of irreparable heartbreak.

"It was easier down there once I met you," he admits.

He uses one twig to poke the fire, but it does not need

to be stoked. He just needs something to do with his hands, to distract himself from the spectral reality of the story that he spins. Or, he needs the light to remind him he is no longer in the darkness.

I am unabashedly mesmerized, staring at the way the fire dances within his eyes, until he turns his head, and I am consumed by the vibrancy of his gaze. There was fear in his voice when he explained Tartarus, but when his eyes meet mine, some of that fright melts away.

"The prison was easier when I met you, too."

I'm the first to look away, but I still feel his stare. It feels like he physically cannot look away, like I am the light he needs to see to remind himself that he is free.

"I never thought that I would escape from Tartarus, but you were witness to the reality. You know I was finally freed."

Morpheus helped him escape from the Underworld on the same day I jumped into the River Styx to avoid capture. I was a foolish girl to think I could outwit Styx, and now I pay the consequences of my idiocy.

"But you didn't see who helped Morpheus."

"What?" I jerk my head back to face Epiales. "I was there. It was just Morpheus and the humans Kronos brought to his cause. Are you talking about the titans who went after the castle?"

"No, not the titans." Epiales says, then asks. "Do you remember how he freed me from Tartarus?"

It has been decades since that war, and with another rising from its ashes, it is more difficult to search my memory. Still, I ponder until the glint of a sword rushes through my mind. "He struck Tartarus down with a sword. He broke the chains in half."

"Right, and how is that even possible?" Epiales asks. "Some of the most formidable immortals are in Tartarus. If a sword was all it took to strike down Tartarus's gates and free everyone, then would it really be as impenetrable as claimed?"

"No, I guess it wouldn't be."

In the throes of the mania, I did not ponder the possibilities of Epiales's freedom. My primary focus was Hattie, who was in a castle filled with newly escaped prisoners. I didn't wonder how a sword could strike down Tartarus, or the possibility that others could have helped Kronos without revealing their identity.

"How did he get the sword?"

I almost don't want the answer, but I need it. The only other people at the gates of Tartarus are dead. Epiales provides the last fragment of answers for a question I never thought to ask.

Epiales says. "Styx gave Morpheus a sword of her creation, forged from her river. I didn't know it then, but he told me a few days later that Styx approached him in a dream."

"What did she say?" I whisper the question, as if Styx is listening to every word.

"It was a few days after Morpheus's soulmate, Snow, died of old age. Styx was the one who told Morpheus that I was tortured and imprisoned for helping him, and if he wanted to save me, then he had to obey everything Styx said."

And so he did.

I often wondered why Morpheus joined Kronos's side. He had won against Zeus. He freed his human soulmate from enslavement and disappeared where nobody could find them. I glance around the island, wondering if this was the spot Morpheus and Snow ran to in their escape from enslavement and hatred.

"Styx told Morpheus to join Kronos's side, but to never speak about their conversations. Kronos couldn't know that Styx was Morpheus's true guide because if Kronos discovered the truth, then I would die."

"Was that true?"

"Who knows? Morpheus's guilt guided him instead of reasoning, and he obeyed every word that came out of Styx's mouth. He pretended to be on Kronos's side, following every command, but he met with Styx in secret. She gave him the sword two nights before he rescued me, and just as she promised, he freed me from certain death. Those were his first words to me." Epiales lets out a sigh and copies Morpheus's words verbatim. "She was right; I saved you."

Epiales has been dead for almost a century, and has slept for days, but he has never looked more exhausted than he does right now. I cannot stop my eyes from dancing up towards where he sits, and I'm unsurprised to see him staring back. Tired, silver eyes pierce through every shredded defense. He holds out his hand, and after several seconds of hesitation, I accept.

The electricity is just as strong as the first time we touched, and it ignites so many memories. That is who Epiales is to me, a surplus of memories I can never escape and might not want to. His eyes drift downward, to where our hands conjoin, and his thumb delicately drags across the top of my hand.

"After you killed Morpheus, I realized that I should have asked more questions, but it was too late at that point. And there was so much going on between his death and mine. Styx's involvement in my freedom felt inconsequential because she was a prisoner in her river. Many, including myself, thought she was harmless. I love stories, and yet I was a fool for forgetting hers."

He slides a finger over the discolored skin where my wedding ring once sat, and he pauses his story. I told him I was married to Hermes, but this is physical proof of my life with him. A life where Epiales died and Hermes theoretically won. Yet, instead of festering jealousy, Epiales lifts my hand and presses a kiss right where the ring once sat.

"Before I continue, can I say something?"

"Can I stop you?" I tease, but neither of us smile.

"You said you loved me past tense. Is there a chance you can love me again? His words make my heart stutter.

"What?" I let out a scoff that almost sounds like a bubble of laughter. "We are in the middle of discussing how you knew about Styx's deceit, and you want to talk about love?"

The last word comes out broken and shaky.

For so many years, I was certain that Epiales was my final great love. My beginning and my end. My one and only. Even after our arguments and our divided views on the world's future, I convinced myself that Epiales was my third great love because his love consumed me. Stole any sense of rationality until I was a puddle of emotions and desire.

But then he died, and I could survive it.

And I went searching for another chance at love.

I landed on Hermes.

Now, I know nothing. Not the love I am supposed to move towards. Not the dead love that I could re-animate. I know nothing except the pain that comes with a broken heart.

"But I am one of your great loves, and if that means I

have to share you with Hermes and whoever that third love is, then I will gladly accept whatever-"

I pull my hand out of his. "Epiales, stop." I stand to my feet, brushing the sand off, but the burn of his gaze lingers on me. It curses me with far too much desire than a person should hold within them.

"I didn't mean to upset you." I don't turn around, but I can hear the sand shift as he stands. He takes a few steps closer, and the warmth of his chest on my back disintegrates my resolve. "My queen…" he begins.

I clear my throat. "Please finish your story."

There's a long pause, as he stands so close to me without touching me. My request hangs in the balance because I know he wants to talk about us, but I know that is exactly what Styx and Hecate want. They might not know that he isn't my third great love, but when I loved him, it was all-encompassing. If I fall for him again, it will take possession of me like it once did. And that's what they want. They want me to love him, right? They want him to be the prophetic heart, and I fear they could be right.

I stare up at the stars in their multitude, counting each one as the seconds tick by in heated silence. With each star I count, I curse the Fates for my predicament. It is so easy to feel his skin lingering near mine and fall right under his spell again.

"Right after our dream together, the night before my execution." He carefully evades mentioning that I killed him. "Hecate materialized."

"What?"

I spin around to face him, and I break the last thread of distance we had. He fully presses his chest against mine, and while I don't touch him, his hand lands on my waist.

My eyes fall onto his lips, and I follow every syllable that leaves them.

"She told me I would die tomorrow, but I wouldn't stay dead. Just as Styx saved my life once before, she would again." The hand that doesn't hold my waist moves to the nape of my neck. He tilts my gaze upwards until we stare into each other's eyes again. "She said that the savior's heart was always meant to be brought back to life. Any idea what that means?"

He stares at my lips, begging me without words to end this conversation, and gods, a part of me wants to. How long has it been since someone stared at me with blanket desire? Hermes and I haven't been a genuine couple in years. Maybe even a decade or two. On a pleasantly rare occasion, Hermes would kiss me, but that was it. I haven't seen a carnal burn behind a male's eyes in so long.

Until now.

He is a drink of water after days of wandering in a desert, and I lean towards him. The taste of grapes on his breath slides across my lips, but right before we kiss, his last words reiterate in my mind. Realization comes with it. I turn my head right as his lips would have touched mine, and instead of my mouth, he kisses my cheek.

I take a step back. "You could've stopped any of this from happening with Styx if you told me this on the day of your execution. Hecate told you about their plans the night before your execution. If you told me, Zeus would have seen your change in allegiance. I might not have had to kill..."

You.

It's the last word I cannot say aloud.

"The Fates are sneaky little minxes, aren't they?" He shrugs his shoulders nonchalantly.

"Are you working with them?"

"What?" Epiales asks. "I would never betray you-"

"You have betrayed me before. Our relationship was dangerous because it was rooted in passion, not trust. You betrayed me before with a titan who promised less than what Styx delivered. She is the reason you are alive, not Kronos. Both Hecate and Styx helped you, and you kept that fact from me."

I stumble away from him, but he follows my movements. He wraps a hand around my arm, and he thrusts me back into his embrace. My body collides with his, and the hand that doesn't hold my arm grabs my chin.

He forces me to look into his eyes. "Choosing Kronos instead of you was one of my life's biggest regrets. If I could turn back the wheels of time, I would have chosen death within Tartarus instead of at Kronos's side. You almost died because of my decision, and I will have to live with the actions of my mistakes for the rest of my existence. But I would never do that again to you. Styx helped me, but I never aligned myself with her. From the moment I realized my mistake, my allegiance was only to you. You must believe that."

"But I don't."

I take a step back, then another, and his hands fall to his sides. Deceit is all I know from Epiales. Every male I have ever loved has betrayed me, and I will not be a victim to his lies again. Before Styx raged havoc on my world, Epiales was my storyteller, love, and villain. I cannot forget that, especially now that he speaks about all the ways Styx has helped him over the years.

He is the reason I have lost friends like Panda and Pyro. I lost a bit of myself when I had to execute him. I married the god of thievery, but Epiales has stolen a lot, too. My trust, for one.

"Saffron," Epiales says my name like a prayer. "Please don't pull away."

But it's too late.

He tries to talk to me for several hours, but I do not respond. Eventually, Epiales falls asleep, and my only company is the moon above. While Epiales sees Selene within the moon, I see my friend whose huntresses taught me how to fight when I was an uncertain human. When I see the moon, I see my friend who taught me my worth back when I thought so lowly about myself.

"Hey, Artemis." I whisper to the closest thing to a friend that I have on this island. "Did you ever hear the joke about the moon and the two dumb blondes? There were two blondes laying in the sand one late night, staring up the moon. One blonde asks the other which one is closer, Mt. Ida or the moon, and the second blonde says the moon. When the first blonde asks why, the second blonde says that it's because she can see the moon, duh."

A familiar male laugh cuts through the silence. "That's a terrible joke."

"Yet, you laughed." I turn around to see a wide grin on Epiales's face, hating the way the expression softens me. "Aren't you supposed to be asleep?"

"I've spent almost a hundred years without the sound of your voice. The second I heard you talking, I woke up just to hear it." He sits up, so he is resting on his elbows. "Why are you still awake?"

I see Hypnos's face, shrouded in hesitance towards me, and the reminder of my grievance against him returns with fervor. He wouldn't hate me enough to stop allowing me to sleep, but I see the way he looks at me every time he is in my proximity. I killed his son, and while he understands why I had to, the truth doesn't shed away the sadness he wears like a scar.

Since Hermes stopped sleeping in bed beside me, which was long before our divorce, Hypnos's haunted gaze joined me in bed. Every time I try to sleep, I see the personification of sleep behind my lids, and I can no longer rest.

"Sleep and I stopped being friends a long time ago." The words come out clipped and cruel, but I do not take them back.

"You're different."

I have heard these two words more than any other statement since Hattie's death, and each time they laced the words with judgement. Others wanted me to remain immortally innocent and naïve, so when I became the woman that I am today, disappointment was written on all the god's faces.

About twenty years ago, during a party at Dionysus's house, Psyche said my soul changed. It morphed into something that was the polar opposite of my human soul, and she admitted it was a terrifying sight. I was tainted. Ruined. And she hasn't spoken to me since.

The first time Hermes said that I was different, I could almost hear his heart beginning to break. He had fallen in love with the innocent human, who had a fastidious fascination with strawberries. He loved the girl, who giggled every time we danced, but she died with my friends.

As Psyche said, my soul had changed with my transformation from human to goddess, and Hermes only loved that human soul.

Hermes stayed with me regardless of how different I became, but I knew he kept hoping I would revert to the person I was when we met. But I never did. Perhaps that's why he lied about cheating on me with Hecate. He wanted a way out, and lies come easiest to him.

There was only one person who didn't state my difference with disgust, and that was Ares. We have spoken twice since I was a human, and the first time was after Psyche nearly ran from me in fright. He looked at me the same way he always had, with a mixture of indifference and reverence.

"Are you going to chime in about your disgust with me, too?"

He didn't initially answer; instead, he took his time sipping his glass of wine until it sat empty in his hand. Then, he said. "Disgust isn't the word I would ever use to describe you. You are more radiant than ever. A valiant soldier who survived the scars."

He realized the compliment came out of his lips, and he quickly left the party.

I hadn't seen him after that day until he brought the traitorous huntress to me.

"Sorry to disappoint," I say.

"You could never disappoint me, even when you hate me. Even when you hide your smile from me and the rest of the world. You are still my queen, today and every day."

I refuse to look at him, the trickle of distrust still humming against my bones.

"Please continue to talk to the moon as if it is going to respond. I'll just lay here, listening to you all night long."

THIRTEEN

HART SOMMERS

As morning light streams in through the slightly parted curtains, Apollo wakes me with the soft caress of his lips wherever the sun reaches. He starts with my cheek, placing a tender kiss along the cheekbone, then he descends to the curve of my jaw. Each pepper of his lips against my skin feels like summer and an inexplicable sense of comfort.

His hand slips underneath the covers, sliding across my hips as he kisses down the length of my neck and nibbles on my exposed collarbone. He pulls my body against his, absorbing me in his warmth, and the sigh that escapes me is derived from pure bliss.

"If I could wake up this way every day for all of eternity," he leaves another kiss on my collarbone. "Then the Fates have surely chosen their favorite god."

I turn my body, so we are chest-to-chest. "Gods, how can you look so perfect this early in the morning?"

Their appearance far surpasses humans' mundane

appeal, but Apollo continuously amazes me when I wake up every morning with lingering morning breath and dry drool around my mouth, and he looks as devastatingly handsome as the night before. His sandy blonde hair is tousled, but perfectly so, like the pillow expertly styled each strand.

"μέλι, you are the perfect one, not me." Apollo kisses the tip of my nose.

I snort. "You're a literal god. Perfection is embedded in your DNA."

"I have a present for you."

Wise male, changing the topic.

"I'm too tired for *that* kind of present this morning." I tease, and Apollo uproars with laughter.

"It's a real present."

He removes one hand from my waist and holds it, palm up, in between us. The sunlight hits his palm, and a velvet box materializes, then opens on its own. Gold invades my vision. A perfect, gleaming gold bracelet with a single charm dangling in the middle.

A honeycomb.

Apollo delicately removes the bracelet from the box, and I wobbly extend my wrist. "You always say that you play with your necklace when you're scared because it is a nervous twitch, but it reminds you of your dad, who you've told me is the bravest man you know."

He slides the bracelet on my wrist and beckons the sun to gleam over the honeycomb charm.

"I think you hold on to that necklace because it's your way of reminding yourself that you come from a family of brave people who are heroes in their own right, and you are just as brave as them. I never want to replace your family, but I wanted you to have a reminder of me, too."

He flicks the honeycomb with his finger and smiles at me like I am his sun and moon and stars and everything that comes in between.

"Why a honeycomb?" I ask, already knowing the answer.

He holds up my wrist, letting the sun bathe his present, and he murmurs. "Because for the rest of our lives, you are eternally my μέλι."

"I love you so much."

We fall into a soft kiss, but it tells the truth of our emotions, transcending words. We can tell each other that we love each other a million times, but actions speak the loudest.

Although we stop kissing, his face stays close to mine. I can taste his words as he promises. "Every year I'll add a new charm. You will be covered, wrist to shoulder, in charm bracelets, before I stop."

I lean into another kiss, but a ruckus upstairs stops us. Rationally, I know what the sound resembles, either a stool or chair falling to the ground, but when I hear the war drums, I only assume the worst. Apollo quickly gets out of bed and runs out of the room in nothing but a pair of briefs.

I sit frozen, letting irrational thoughts plague my sanity. Does Styx know the dead oracles are training me? Has she has come to kill me before I'm strong enough to defeat her? All the warnings the oracles told me, about if I fail, run together in an endless stream of despair.

Then, my eyes latch on to the honeycomb dangling from my new bracelet.

And I let out a soft exhalation.

I get dressed first in the first slip-on dress I can find in my closet, and I follow Apollo upstairs. I expect disaster behind the ajar door, but with my hand clasping my honeycomb, I walk inside. Styx is not here, waiting for me with an army and an incapacitated Apollo.

It's Zeus.

The stool he dropped still lies on the floor, but the rest of the room is intact. Zeus stands where the stool once did, with his back turned to me and his focus solely on the drawing of Artemis finding the portal to Ogygia. Apollo stands beside him, and as I walk into the room, I hear the end of their conversation.

"-should know they're going in the right direction."

"No," the growl at the end of Zeus's declination leaves no room for arguments. "Now go, I want to talk to your artist alone."

Zeus doesn't turn away from the artwork, but he knows I'm standing by the door. Apollo, however, did not. He whips his head around, sees me standing there, and shakes his head. "Absolutely not. Last time you saw her, you nearly killed her."

Zeus finally looks away from the canvas. Lightning bolts dance in his vision. He takes a menacing step towards Apollo, and while he is tall, Zeus is taller. He is an imposing creature, with shoulders as wide as Mt. Olympus, and he has a temper quicker than any flame.

"While many try to take my crown, I am still your king, and that is a gods-damn order. Leave."

The gilded glint of Zeus's crown is a stark contrast to his white-gray hair, which is shaved close to his scalp, and it's impossible to ignore.

"I'll be right outside the door," Apollo says.

Zeus ignores him.

Apollo stops in front of me before leaving the room.

Zeus's anger is a rising, boiling entity. I know Apollo wants to assuage me of my safety, but the words never come. I kiss him on the cheek, and that's it. Apollo walks out the door, but just as promised, he leans his body against the adjacent wall.

"Close the door and come here," Zeus orders.

I obey, but as I close the door shut, the last image I see is Apollo's face morphing into one of fright.

There are many aspects of life I fear, but Zeus is not one of them. Apollo fears our proximity, but I know Zeus and I are destined for an unlikely friendship. One that will tilt the war in our favor. This certainty has not been definitive in a vision, but just like a word on the tip of my tongue, I know it exists. A story that involves us, trust, and this war.

Zeus's focus is back on the first canvas, occasionally flickering to the prophecy on the second. "You're a very talented artist."

"Thank you." I walk towards him, and a sheen of green tint partially conceals my vision. "You were fond of one oracle in that drawing. The one in the green was your favorite, right?"

A flickering emotion crosses his features. "One of my children." His attention sharply focuses back on the first canvas, the only one that does not incite anger or sorrow, where Artemis has found Ogygia in between the two trees. He asks. "Will this help us find Saffron faster?"

I do not answer until I am beside Zeus, exactly where Apollo previously stood. "If I can send it to Artemis and the huntresses, yes. Argus has been asking almost every day to take-"

"I just told Apollo no, and that answer will not change just because the person asking is prettier. Unless you'd like to make a compromise on this floor, but you must be loud enough for Apollo to hear."

"Quit deflecting by pretending to seduce me." This thought should have stayed in my head, and yet I purge the command aloud.

I wince as he stares at me.

Glowers is a better word for the expression he sends my way.

"You are a beautiful human."

"But you're not interested in me," I say with the same assuredness.

"I'm interested in seducing everyone."

"Do you realize how often you lie, or does it come as naturally as breathing for you?"

Zeus grow silent.

"Why won't you let us take the map to the huntresses? It'll be the fastest way to find Saffron."

He doesn't answer for a while, and I wonder if he will tell me the truth at all. I do not think he will attempt to lie again, but silence might be his next form of escape.

"I don't want the huntresses to find Ogygia first." His admittance is muffled and barely decipherable, but I hear him.

"You want to find her first?" He doesn't immediately answer, and a different realization dawns on me. "You want to find *him* first."

Epiales.

The personification of nightmares, Epiales, was one of Kronos's most loyal soldiers in the most recent Titanomachy War until he switched sides to save Saffron's freedom. Two centuries' worth of hatred festers between Epiales and Zeus, and neither one will absolve their abhorrence for Saffron's sake. I am not entirely sure Epiales or

Zeus deserve forgiveness for their actions, but it is the only way to survive.

"He should have stayed dead. He is a festering disease, and I have no doubt he is working with Styx to turn her against us. *Against me.*"

Zeus plays a role, just like many other gods. He pretends he does not care about Saffron because the world believes it's true, but the last two words dissolve his façade. It's not fear of Saffron stealing his throne that guides his words; rather, it is fear for her safety that leaves the most powerful male god a trembling, irrational, paternal mess.

"The world thinks you hate her."

"Because I once did," he admits, then scoffs. "I don't know why I just told you that. You're just an artist."

"You're deflecting again."

"And it's gods-damn creepy how well you know me. This is the fourth time we've met, and it's the most we've ever talked."

He glares down at me, but I do not balk. "Why did you once hate her?"

Zeus wants to throw a lightning bolt. His hands clench and unclench at his sides. He continuously flickers his attention to the lightning bolt strapped to his holster, and I know he debates my death. I know him too well, and he's carefully crafted a chauvinistic guise. I scare him for knowing what lays beneath that mask.

But I know he won't kill me.

He takes several minutes to regulate his breathing, to calm the rage within him, before he surprises me with an answer. "After the titans stole the throne from me, we all swore not to have children, especially with humans. Demi-Gods were a threat we could not control, but then I met Metis."

133

Even as he says her name, there's an undertone of soft-ness that he doesn't grant to anybody else. Not even Hera.

"I knew better than to fall in love with a human. They are meant for dalliances and nothing more, but Metis looked so much like my first wife with the same name, and I loved the woman dearly. I thought I'd like the new Metis as much as the old, but where my ex-wife was crass and overly vocal, the human Metis knew the power of perfectly poised words. She was a quiet one, but so witty, too. I didn't mean to, but from the first moment she smiled at me, I knew I found my destined third love. My soulmate."

Zeus rushes his explanation. It's a jumbled mess that makes me wonder if he has ever talked about Metis before. Am I the first he's been honest with? If so, what a lonely life that must be.

He has played a role for so long, possibly his entire exis-tence, that he has forgotten his own authenticity. He stares at the second canvas, and his hand reaches for the palm trees I drew, but he doesn't touch them. Just hangs his hand in the balance between.

"Metis was an artist, too. Oil paintings." He smiles, ever so slightly, at the memory. "She once drew a shark, although she had never seen one before, and it was so detailed. For a moment, I thought I was in the ocean. She asked me what a shark was, not understanding what she drew, and after I told her, she said our future daughter would really enjoy playing with this shark."

He drops his hand before it touches the palm trees.

"It was the most insane, nonsensical sentence, but when she mentioned a daughter, the oddest thing happened. I do not need a heart to beat, but I swear to the Fates that it skipped a beat. Metis made me feel something I never had before- excitement. I wanted a child with her.

Everyone believed the pregnancy was an accident, and I let them believe it. But I wanted to have a daughter with Metis more than I ever wanted anything in my life."

"I forgot about the prophecy surrounding the second child, born of Metis and me. Perhaps it was because this Metis was human, not a titaness like the last one, or I was just too stupidly hopeful for my own good. Whatever the reason, the nine months Metis was pregnant with Saffron were the greatest in my life. I never cheated on her, not once. I wouldn't even kiss Hera when she asked, but I wish I did because that's how she discovered Metis. With her discovery, I suffered the worst day of my existence."

I try to imagine it. Finding Apollo dead, murdered by a former lover's hand, and I shudder at the thought.

Zeus's next words are a whisper. "I hated Saffron when I saw her in that arena on her eighteenth summer solstice. I hated her because she looked so much like her mother, and it was a terrible reminder that no matter how powerful I was, I couldn't bring Metis back from the Underworld. Then I found out Saffron was my daughter, and she incited the prophecy that would eventually kill me. My hatred festered. Her existence made me love Metis too much, which caused her death, and then it was going to steal the second greatest love."

Zeus reaches for his crown, his second greatest love, and plucks it off his head.

"Even gods can be fools," he says, more to the crown than me.

I move towards Zeus, confidently at first, but when I place my hands on the crown, I meet his gaze hesitantly. He doesn't push me away or remind me that only a king can touch the crown. Instead, he lets go and allows me to hold it.

"I'm training with Hades and the oracles of the Delphi, and while I haven't seen everything I need to yet, I know you have a large role in this war. You will need to be the player in the game that Styx never sees coming. You regret your decisions with Saffron, but this war will be your time to atone. I cannot see exactly what you will do, but there will be a time when you must lie to everyone to save her. Will you do that? Risk everyone's trust for hers?"

I extend my hand, offering to return his crown to him, but he doesn't reach for it. "As you said earlier, I lie as easily as I breathe. When you call, I'll do anything I need to. Until then."

Before I can ask him again for permission to show the map to the huntresses, or to ask him to ignore his vengeance against Epiales, he strikes his lightning bolt between us and leaves. His crown still sits heavy in my hand.

"Why him?" a voice, typically velvet smooth, croaks out.

I turn my head, and Hades leans against the doorway.

Typically, Hades masterfully conceals his emotions from me, but today I can see everything like ink on parchment. Hurt lays in his wake, and anger, too. Hades has been the truest father to Saffron, and he has never hated her. Only love for a daughter who isn't biologically his, but is his daughter when it truly counts.

Hades isn't able to conceive children on his own, and while Saffron is his only child, Persephone has three others and they're all with Zeus. He dotes on his children, and he loves them more than Zeus is capable, and yet he always has to share with him.

That truth burns behind his angered words. "Why him?" He repeats. "Why does Zeus get to be the father who helps save Saffron? He has thousands of children, all who could use his protection, but I have one. One." His voice wobbles. "Why can't it be me? I'm here, training with you every day to save her, so why can't it be me? Why him?"

"I'm sorry."

Hades shakes his head. "No, don't say those words because you can't find anything else to say. Just tell me why."

"Because of the same reasons you told me why you are the King of the Underworld. You are patient, and you are vigilant, and you are brave. Those traits make you a natural hero, especially when your daughter is in danger. Styx sees your bravery coming a mile away, but she only sees Zeus as a coward. If he can finally stop being the disappointment that the rest of the world sees him as, even for a few weeks for one person, then we might have a chance at tricking Styx."

He hears my words, and he understands, but his emotions cloud any rationality.

"We are taking a day off from training. I'll see you at dinner."

Hades turns around and leaves.

FOURTEEN

HERMES

My feet land on the cloudy entrance of Mt. Olympus, but no matter how many times I have returned to this spot since Kronos captured and tortured me, a wave of nausea possesses me. The rubble Kronos created was repaired and polished clean, but I can only see the destruction of the past. I force a faux smile on my lips and walk with assured confidence, but my mind wages a war of the past that only I can hear.

Typhon's malicious laugh, the rattling of cages, and Hecate's macabre echoes in my ears, like they do every time I return to Mt. Olympus. I doubt it will ever go away; the fear associated with this place. In the few years that followed the war against Kronos, I couldn't stare at a cloud without my chest constricting and my heart hammering out of my chest. The fear of those memories has improved, but they won't ever go away.

Especially when I am forced back to the site of my torment.

But I do not let the world see my struggles. To anyone looking at me, they will see the same Hermes of the past. The god who existed with an overzealous outlook. Many have forgotten the torment I suffered at Kronos and Typhon's hands almost one hundred years ago, so it is easy for them to believe I have moved past the terror. I play a convincing role, too. Even Saffron believed I no longer heard my own screams or replayed those days in my head.

Except Aphrodite.

I stroll into her home, where she and Hephaestus silently sit. Hephaestus bears a permanent frown on his face, leaving a deep crease in between his bushy brows as he reads a book on blacksmithing. Aphrodite is on the couch across from Hephaestus, her appearance ever changing. Before they realize I am in the room, I witness the truth of their relationship.

Aphrodite watches him with rapt fascination, but he believes the lies she spins about not caring for him, and he pointedly ignores her stare. They play a cycle of eternal misery, even when they love each other more ardently than many marriages on Mt. Olympus.

Aphrodite notices me first.

"Hermie!" She leaps off the couch, and her sheer pink gown flows like the wind behind her as she bolts towards me. Her arms quickly envelop me, and she hugs me tightly. "It's so good to see you." She pulls away from the hug, but doesn't remove her hands from my shoulders. Her grin is wild and beautiful. "To what do we owe this pleasure?"

Hephaestus's book is still open, but he isn't reading anymore. His attention drifts to where I stand; specifically, where Aphrodite's hands rest on my shoulders. He doesn't hate me with the same fervor as Ares, but I had an affair with her during their marriage, and he will never forgive me for the betrayal.

I remove her hands from my shoulder, and Hephaestus's eyes drift back to his book.

"I need help from you both."

"Help with what?" Aphrodite asks.

I tell them everything. The attack on Poseidon's castle, and the job Hades and Persephone tasked me with. Hephaestus's attention reverts to me when I talk about Ares's imprisonment on Mt. Atlas, where he holds the Earth on his shoulders around a crew of enemies.

I end with, "I need your help to free Ares and steal Calypso for answers."

Hephaestus snorts. "Let him rot there. You won't get my help."

Aphrodite sharply turns to face her husband. "And why not? He's your brother."

The book in his hands closes with a sharp clap. "He's your lover."

"Oh, for Zeus's sake-" she begins.

"Great, bring your other lover into this conversation," Hephaestus dryly interrupts.

Aphrodite frowns. "I haven't been with Ares in over a hundred years. Ever since…" she stops, looks at me, then sighs. "Since he ended things. Freeing him will not bring him back into my arms, and you know it."

Hephaestus looks at me, and it is like they are having a covert conversation without me. One that only they can hear. I don't like it.

Hephaestus lets out an angered sigh. "Why do you need us to help you? There are better fighters all over Mt. Olympus."

"Because you have a net that can capture Calypso." I drag my gaze to Aphrodite. "And one of your sons is on that mountain, as a traitor. I need you to convince him otherwise."

Many eons ago, when Aphrodite and Ares were still lovers, Hephaestus devised a plan to catch them in the act. He created a powerful net that can capture immortals, and when the two adulterers were in the throes of passion in her martial bed, a spring launched the net on top of them. They could not move until Hephaestus freed them, and that is a powerful tool in a surprise attack battle.

Aphrodite switches forms.

Her varying appearances are more than a way to manipulate surrounding people. They are her way of expressing herself. She shifts to her second favored form, which is a tall, leggy blonde. She wears this form when she is fighting. To her, it is a form that mirrors Athena's appearance the most, who she views as the most formidable goddess. It is also the form she wears when she's most frightened.

Her bottom lip trembles as she asks. "Which son?"

Hephaestus stands up, ready to console his wife, but he hesitates. I know why. Aphrodite has many children, but none are with him. Most are Ares's children, and that's what stalls Hephaestus's natural inclination towards comfort. He loves and abhors her. Wants to comfort and throttle her.

"Hedylogos."

"He sits there and lets his father struggle? He doesn't help?" Aphrodite's disgust for her son with Ares is clear.

"I have a plan, but I need both of your help."

Hephaestus grunts. "Let me punch Ares after we free him, and you have a deal."

"Hephaestus!" Aphrodite outcries, but he doesn't look at her. He fixes his attention on me.

"Do we have a deal?"

"Yeah." I kind of want to see Ares get punched.

"Great, I'll go get my net."

Hephaestus leaves the room to retrieve the net that he created eons ago because of Ares and Aphrodite's affair. Shortly after Hephaestus and Aphrodite wed, Aphrodite strayed from their marital bed. She slept with Ares first, which is predominantly why Hephaestus hates him more than the rest of us. Hephaestus thought he and Aphrodite were soulmates, but her betrayal solidified his naivety.

She follows every limped step he makes until his hulking form is out of view; then she turns her focus on me. "Are you doing alright?"

"You are too smart to ask a question like that."

I turn away from her, turning our silence into awkwardness, until Hephaestus comes back into the room with the golden net slung over his shoulder. He is one of the few gods taller than me, at a staggering six foot eleven, and while he doesn't care to clean his body of the soot and hard labor, it's rippled in muscles. He rarely fights, loathing Ares's proximity on the battleground, but he is a formidable opponent in any arena.

Yet, Hephaestus and Aphrodite are not enough.

We need another warrior who Zeus will not miss. "We have a few more people to grab for my plan to work," I say, but neither of them responds.

They silently follow, as we meander through the larger houses of the Olympians, moving towards the houses of the lesser gods. Nike is not inside her house, but in the backyard, kneeling over a garden of tomatoes. The gods do not need food for nourishment, but Nike loves to garden for the humans. She frequently takes the fruits and vegetables she grows to the more impoverished towns.

Long ago, I asked her why she gave food to the humans, and her face fell with grief. "Because my angel told me to never forget the starving humans."

Her angel. The human soulmate she had, who was Saffron's closest friend in the prisons. It has been almost a hundred years since he died, but Nike never forgets him. She wakes up and breathes the reminders of his death, and sleeps with his image in her head. Yet, unlike Hecate, she does not resort to villainy to get back her lost soulmate. She mourns and honors him every day without tainting her kindness.

Nike doesn't turn around when I walk into her garden, but she knows I'm here. "What do you need, Hermes?" Her tone is kind, if not impatient.

"I need your help."

"Alright." Nike stands up and brushes the dirt off her skirt.

She doesn't need me to embellish further. Since Angel's death, she never hesitates to come to Saffron's aid. I know guilt has held her captive since Angel died. She wanted to protect him from the world's strife, and when Angel died, Nike felt she owed a lifelong debt to Saffron. Saffron doesn't agree with the sentiment, but Nike is immortally loyal to Angel's best friend.

"When are we leaving?" She asks.

"We have to pick up a few more immortals, and then we can go."

Our last stop is for the remaining muses, who have not sung since their sisters' treachery. They sit in their home, which they do not illuminate with candles, and wallow in their silence. Their sisters are not dead, but they grieve them all the same. Sometimes, there are worse losses than death. When people leave your life on their own accord, it hurts more than when death forcibly whisks them away. At least with death, you know your loved one wanted to stay. When they choose a path that is without you, it is infinitely worse.

It is my job to switch their grieving process. Right now, denial and sadness wrecks the remaining muses, but I want the rage that comes with this form of betrayal. The remaining seven muses sit in their living room, staring at nothing, until I enter with Hephaestus, Aphrodite, and Nike.

Thalia, without looking up from her space of nothingness, dully says. "Leave, Hermes."

Eons ago, Thalia and I were lovers, now we are nothing more than strangers. Yet, she is the most fearless of all the muses. If I can convince any to join my cause, it is her.

I disobey Thalia's request, and I sit in the empty spot between her and her sister, Melpomene. The latter does not lift her head or acknowledge me, but Thalia's dark eyes glare at me. "I have a question for you," I say.

"And I remember telling you to leave my home."

"Funny, you used to beg me to not to leave." The flirting tone surprises me almost as much as it surprises Thalia. I miss my wife ardently, but flirting with Thalia comes as naturally as existing. Guilt surrounds me with the act, and I soberly add. "Sorry."

"Ask your question, then leave."

"What would you do if I told you I know where both your sisters are right now and that I have a perfect plan for you to get your revenge?"

As expected, all sisters raise their heads.

145

"What makes you think we want revenge?" Clio asks.

But I hear the razor-sharp tone on her tongue. Clio, the muse of history, has never concealed her emotions. Rage is a common component of all aspects of history, which guides monumental moments, both good and bad.

"They tried to trap you in the Dagger of Chains. They made you think they loved you, and then they betrayed you. Stabbed you right in the back when you thought they were the ones protecting you. If Artemis or Athena ever did that to me, I would want revenge, and I am not as close to my sisters as you are to each other. That level of deceit can only lead to revenge, and I'm here to offer to you."

Melpomene abruptly stands, her round eyes filled with tears, and storms out of the room. The muse of tragedy rarely smiles, so her reaction doesn't surprise me. Or Polymnia's, the goddess of sacred poetry and pantomime, rushes after Melpomene as she curses at me for showing up to their home.

That leaves behind five muses.

"I will go with you," Calliope, the muse of heroic poetry, says. She is the tallest muse at six foot three, and she is the best fighter amongst them.

But I want more to join my side.

I look at Thalia. "Join us, please."

Calliope can shatter a skull with one hand, and I have witnessed her single-handedly take down three gods with relative ease, but Thalia is silently lethal. Many believe that because she is the muse of comedy that she is incapable of anything else. My fleeting time with her let me see her abilities with a blade, and it is exactly what I need.

Thalia narrows her eyes but doesn't respond.

I drift my attention to Clio. "Well? What about you?"

Clio hesitates for a moment, then says. "History favors the side that remains loyal to Zeus. Bringing my traitorous sisters to him in chains would show that loyalty, so I'll join your plan."

That's not the only reason Clio wants to capture Erato and Urania, but I will not correct her when she's agreeing to help me. Her sisters' betrayals hurts Clio more than she cares to admit, but if she wants to hide behind her history books and factoids, then I won't stop her.

Terpsichore simply says. "Good luck on your journey." She doesn't talk again.

That leaves Euterpe and Thalia. The former looks at Thalia and says. "I'll go wherever you go."

"I want my golden mask back." Thalia glares at Hermes with undiluted rage, which is a complete juxtaposition to her teasing nature.

"A golden mask? I don't know what your…oh, that mask."

We ended our relationship almost an eon ago, and I forgot the reason behind our separation. I thought we simply drifted apart, but the reality is much, much worse. Thalia's sigil is a gilded comedy mask that she proudly mantled in her bedroom, and each night I would spend there, the more appealing that golden mask looked. I kept telling myself I wouldn't steal from the woman I was bedding, but I really wanted that mask.

Oops.

"Yeah." Anger clips her words. "That mask. Swear to the River…"

She stops, and realization dawns on us all. We have sworn unbreakable oaths to Styx for eons. The words have become commonality, but now inciting her name is a reminder of the looming war. Now, her name is as forbidden as the names of the titans who fought alongside Kronos.

"I swear to the gods that if you do not return my golden mask to me, I am sending Horkos after you," Thalia revises.

"Well." I clear my throat and turn to the two muses who already agreed to join me. "Clio and Calliope, you ready?"

Thalia jumps up to her feet. "You seriously won't return it?!"

I'm already backing out the door with my smaller-than-anticipated army when Thalia grabs the first item she can find, a painted vase, and chucks it in my general direction. It smacks Hephaestus in the head. Ichor dribbles down the side of his face, but he only sighs in slight aggravation.

Hephaestus has a chariot large enough to carry three people, and after a long, tense silence, Aphrodite agrees to let me carry her as the muses join Hephaestus. Clio and Calliope glower at me, but they do not vocalize their grievances. Nike flies first, and I quickly follow behind, with Hephaestus's chariot at the rear.

"You have no idea where that mask is, do you?"

My cheeks redden. "It's been an eon since I stole that thing. Of course I don't."

Aphrodite's laugh is so joyous the thick clouds part in awe. "Have you stolen from every woman, or am Thalia and I just the lucky ones?"

I stole the seashell Aphrodite sprouted from, but Hephaestus trapped me a few days later until I gave it back. Not one of my finer moments.

"No, sometimes I steal the person instead of their items," I say the words with a teasing lilt, until I remember I lost that prize, too. Saffron isn't mine anymore.

That terrible reminder jolts me into the past. I can still see the ear-splitting grin on her face when I told her that my favorite things in life are the ones that I steal, and that I'd steal her all over again if I could. I can still feel her hands, tiny compared to mine, as we danced within the gazebo. The first time she told me she loved me plays a haunting tone in my head, and gods, I want her back.

"When Saffron is freed from Ogygia, do you think there is any way I can win her back?"

"Hermie..." The sympathetic drawl of Aphrodite's nickname for me is answer enough.

"Forget I asked."

We do not talk again for over an hour, but as I fly through the sky towards Mt. Atlas, Saffron remains my only thought. We once had a great relationship. It was not chaotically passionate like mine with Hecate's, but it was simplistically perfect. We melded together friendship and a romantic relationship so intricately that I only wanted to talk to her each morning and kiss her goodnight before going to bed.

Sure, some sparks died over the years, but what relationship doesn't dilute with time? I can get back the moments where we danced in the gazebo and played Monopoly until halfway through the night. I can steal her back again, just like I had all those years ago.

Right?

Nike stops a mile away from Mt. Atlas. We can all see the mountain's formation, and the three Furies. They monitor the cave's only entrance, but we're too far away to notice, unless they already know we are here. I slow down beside Nike, and I force out every thought until all I can see is my objective. This is another heist, and if anyone can execute the rescue of a captured god, it is me.

"What's the plan?" Clio asks, as Hephaestus's chariot stops to my left.

"Can your chariot carry one more person for the last mile?" I ask Hephaestus.

His gaze flickers to Aphrodite in my arms, and his jaw tightens. "Yeah."

"Good." I set Aphrodite into the chariot, nestled between Hephaestus and Calliope, and pointedly ignore the pitiful stare she directs my way. "Nike and I will be the distraction for the Furies, so you can get inside the cave. Once inside, Hephaestus, you need to throw your net on Hecate. She must be the first one disposed of, and she's too powerful to try to defeat without the surprise attack."

"And we attack our sisters?" Clio asks.

I nod my head. "Take your revenge." I turn to face Aphrodite. "We need Hedylogos to switch places with Ares. He is the only one, other than Hecate, strong enough to hold the world on his shoulders. Find a way to put him there until we can return Atlas to his spot."

Aphrodite schools her features, refusing to show the rampant emotions raging inside of her, but it's apparent that she hates this plan. Hedylogos, although a traitor, is still her son, and no mother wants to be the source of their child's pain. Still, Aphrodite agrees with a silent nod.

"Hephaestus, once you have Hecate incapacitated, there's two other goddesses in the cave. Apate will need to be taken down fast, but Calypso must be captured. We need answers from her. Can you handle facing them both?"

Hephaestus grunts. "Two low-level immortals? Yeah, I think I can handle that."

I force an unconvincing smirk. "Then let's free Ares."

And find Ogygia.

FIFTEEN

LAMB

S leep has become a foreign entity these past two days.

We ride, we hunt, we hurriedly eat, and then we ride some more. Every shadow lurking behind a bushel of trees and every snap of a twig heightens our senses and turns our sane thoughts into ones of mania. The few moments we allot ourselves to close our eyes, monsters lay beneath our lids, and we stir awake and resume the arduous journey.

Reminders of our friends' deaths follow shortly behind us, like ghostly footsteps we cannot see but know are there. I swivel my head back several times a day, foolishly believing that Sika is somewhere behind me. Each time, I bring myself dismay because Sika is in the Underworld, along with every other friend we have lost along the way for world peace. Yet, those invisible footsteps trail behind, warning us that if we falter, they're here to drag us to the Underworld with them.

Nobody talks, unless it is Artemis giving a direct order to stop. Our breaks are for our animals, not us. We let them sleep as long as they can, and then we rouse them awake and continue.

None of us remember the portal's coordinates, where Artemis and I were tricked into Ogygia, so we can't tell Iris where to transport us. It'd be so much easier if we could use Iris's abilities and fly in a rainbow to the exact spot where we lost so much, but the Fates are cruel to those who dream. We must ride and retrace every step whilst hoping we remember the destination.

Instead of finding the destination, we all find the gnarliest, most decrepit versions of our sorrows. All minds need time to process extreme loss. People need rest and the allowance of tears. To scream and cry and beg the world to reconsider their loss.

War gives us no time; it is the thief of settling hearts.

I feel Sika's absence everywhere I turn. Her goofy laugh is no longer a part of the wind and the trees. The happiness she gave Dýnami decays with her at the bottom of the ocean. She is not the only one we have lost, and that reality is clear on everyone's faces. With Hound's death, Shikari's unwavering optimism died, too. She stole Hound's pessimism from the grave, and while she never speaks, she grunts her displeasure at every step.

It's easier to show rage than sadness.

Willow prepared me for the macabre truth: that a huntress is a warrior first, a person second. I am accustomed to suffering the loss of a best friend without time to grieve her. The others, who were not alive during the last war, have not yet learned this terrible lesson. That is why there is so much anger festering around us, building like an inferno that nobody can extinguish. We can only let it burn everything in its path.

Behind me, an anger-filled scream pauses the others from advancing forward. I turn to face the scream, and Shikari stares back. She says nothing, but that scream is vocalization enough.

"Are you alright?" Artemis asks, perusing Shikari for any visible injuries, but physical pain is not the reason behind her outrage.

"No," the single word slips out of Shikari's clenched teeth. "I am not alright."

I slide off my ride, but her angry glare halts me from advancing towards her. "How are you alright? Your closest friend died because your other closest friends betrayed her. Betrayed *you*."

Akita's and Frigate's faces flash through my mind, along with every memory of our centuries together. As memories of our conversations burn my ears and twist my thoughts, another face joins them. Raven, the huntress who killed Willow, joins them in a triad of treachery. Other than Willow and Artemis, I trusted Raven the most out of any other huntress. I rode with her for the longest. Longer than I knew Sika. She joins Akita and Frigate, and they all laugh at me within the crevices of my mind.

It takes longer than I care to admit, but I force them away.

I will have time to grieve my trust for them, to hate them, but that is not right now. After we find this portal, I can truly stop and think about Sika's death. Grieve the centuries we could have had together. The extra jokes we could have shared. The revelations we could discover. I will have time to fester in my guilt for not realizing my other friends' deceits until it was too late.

"Because right now is not the time," I say.

As so many do, I am ignored. Shikari's exclamations are louder than my soft voice, and she muffles me with her outrage. "How are any of us alright?! We lost over half our sisters! We watched as their heads were bit off by a sphinx, or their entrails were ripped from their stomachs by a cyclops or five."

Her focus never settles on one person. She bounces her rage off each of us, forcing us to come to terms with our feelings of helplessness and ire at the most inopportune time. Shikari's mind is a tomb of memories, endlessly replaying, and she forces the rest of us to see the memories, too.

"We move towards a portal that may or may not be there, but for what?" Shikari asks. "So we can walk right into another monster's trap? So I can watch more of you die?"

Nobody says anything to her, but we all hear her. Some of us might agree that going to the portal is a bad idea. Saffron is the most powerful goddess in the world. If anybody can free themselves from Ogygia, it should be her.

Right?

Shikari runs her hand through her thick, black tresses, pulling out a few strands with the erratic motion. "Why do we always have to be the heroes while Zeus sits on his ivory throne and whores his way through half of Mt. Olympus? Why do we have to be a hero for a goddess who is stronger than every other immortal? Gods should save her, not huntresses."

"Careful, Shikari," Artemis says.

Shikari ignores. "We are only shields for the gods, but they forget we are shields who bleed. We are shields who fall so they can stay safe."

"I know you're angry, but your words teeter on hubris," I say.

Hubris is one of the gravest sins a human can make, believing you are better than the gods. She does not swear her strength is better than the gods, but she cites herself braver than the king of all gods.

It is true.

There's nobody in these woods who will disagree with Shikari's claim that King Zeus is a coward, but thinking the words and speaking them aloud are two very different, very dangerous things.

The gods have killed for less, and we have lost too many already.

"I'm angry?" Shikari scoffs. "Of course I'm angry. My sisters are dead, and I think if we continue to move towards this portal, we are creating a clear direction for all the monsters to follow. Then, all of us are dead, and is it worth it?"

Jamila jumps off her stag. "You mean, is my mother worth it?"

She has been silent for most of the trip, and her sudden vocalization stuns us all. Most of us, like Artemis, Iris, and Dýnami, have known Jamila Pyro her entire life. We watched her from a chubby-cheeked baby to a toddler who always held onto Hermes's leg for safety, and now she is an adult who no longer cowers behind her godly parent.

She is almost as short as she was in primary school at barely five feet tall, but she raises her chin high in the air like she is twenty feet tall. Shikari is still on her deer, creating a considerable height difference between her and Jamila, but the latter is unperturbed. She stands in front of Shikari, her head underneath the animal's nose.

"Are you saying our bravery is not worth it for my mother?"

"Lady Saffron is the most powerful goddess in the world," Shikari says. "She can get out on her own."

"You're right about one thing. She is stronger than Zeus, Poseidon, and Hades put together, and they all know it. *She* knows it, yet instead of hiding on that ivory throne, she fights for humanity every single day. Instead of a crown and promised safety, she chose a blade and a less savory fate. Do you forget why she is on that island right now instead of Lamb and Lady Artemis? Because I don't."

Shikari's face slackens as the anger leaves her body, but a raw emotion like that always needs a vessel. Red slides into Jamila's body, coursing through her veins with a fury that she has kept hidden. In the mess of my sadness, I forgot why Jamila is with us now. She, just like us, bleeds only red while both her parents fight on the front lines of an upcoming war.

Just like Shikari, Jamila's anger mingles with her feelings of helplessness.

But she doesn't balk.

"My mom saved the nymphs, Artemis, and Lamb by trading her freedom for theirs." Jamila never looks away from Shikari, but she points in my general direction. "Lamb was minutes away from death when my mom went to Ogygia. We all saw her after Artemis brought her body to Poseidon's castle. We all nurtured her back to health after days' long coma. She had minutes left, if that."

I didn't know that. I knew I was close to death, and I felt his cold, yet inviting embrace, but I didn't realize that it was minutes that separated me from this world and the next. It's daunting to think of how close I came to returning to Willow, with an eternal place in Elysium

Fields. Would Sika be alive if Saffron was a few minutes late, or would Artemis have spiraled into a place nobody could find her without both Sika and me?

Thanks to Saffron, we will never know.

"Lamb is alive because of the same goddess who you do not want to search for, and you can say it is because you think Zeus should search for her instead. I know the truth, though. You're frightened, and when people are scared, they get angry. When people are scared, they run. That's all you are, a scared girl who wants to run instead of face death head on."

"I..." Shikari tries, but the words falter.

Jamila continues. "I will dispute nothing you said about King Zeus. He is a coward, and if I am struck down for saying it aloud, then I do not care." The sky grows cloudy with a warning, but Jamila screams to the god who listens and seethes. "Zeus is a coward who sits in the skies and waits for others to save his daughter from the immortal who wants his crown!"

Artemis takes an approaching step. "Jamila, stop. I cannot save you from him."

Jamila ignores her and glowers once more at Shikari. "But my mother is not a coward. She is the most selfless and powerful creature in this world, and right now, she cannot escape Styx. I also know huntresses are not meant to be cowards. Even when you are scared, you are supposed to be fearless. It's why I have always wanted to be a huntress. So, I could embrace my fears and be regaled a hero for it."

"The gods should-"

"*Gods* are," Jamila interrupts. "Or have you ridden beside Artemis for so long that you forget she is an Olympian who fights alongside you? Iris is here, too, instead of that ivory throne you loathe so much. I get it. Losing a loved one makes you put your anger in places where it doesn't belong. Trust me," her voice breaks ever so slightly. "I know that, but redirect it back to the goddess who started this all. Revert your anger back to Styx and all these monsters who dare to kill us."

That word, monsters, stills Shikari's defiance. She hears that word, and she pictures her friends' deaths. Sees the cyclops end Gigianna. Re-witnesses Hound's decapitated corpse beneath the Sphinx's paw. Jamila reminds Shikari about her rage, but she re-directs towards the true culprits.

Styx and the monsters.

Jamila realizes this, and she capitalizes on it. "Let's ride in the direction the monsters know we are going, and let's remind them why huntresses are meant to be feared. Remind them why their greatest mistake was killing your sisters. Remind me why I want to be a huntress so much and slay some damn beasts!"

Shikari stares at Jamila for a long while, but Jamila does not break away from the eye contact while an unspoken conversation settles in their gaze. When they eventually look away, Shikari asks Artemis. "May we ride again?"

This time, as we ride through the woods, Shikari and her stag are the fastest.

LONG AFTER THE SUN HAS SET, AND THE MOON AROSE, Artemis slows her animal down and orders us all to rest. For a few precious hours, our tired legs slide off our deer, and we build a fire and cook every animal we can hunt.

Within thirty minutes, everybody has eaten at least one squirrel and is sleeping in a semi-circle around the fire.

Except Artemis and me.

Iris sleeps on Artemis's lap, while the latter slides her hand through her curly, multi-colored tresses. I glance down at the altercation with a wry smile. "So, you talked to her?"

Artemis smiles back. "Maybe a little."

We slip into a silence that June's snores almost immediately interrupt. "How can the tiniest woman be so damn loud when she sleeps?"

Artemis lets out a huff of a laugh. "I half wonder if she is one of Zeus's kids. Her snores sound like a thunderstorm."

As soon as the words leave her lips, June snores so loudly that the woman next to her, Vee, jerks awake. She rubs at her bleary eyes, sees how close June got to her in their sleep, and moves to the other side of the fire beside Jamila. In seconds, Vee is back to sleep and far from the cacophony of noise June incites each time she slumbers.

"You know, if you let Jamila become a huntress, June won't be the tiniest anymore."

June is maybe an inch taller than Jamila, but their height is not the spawn of this conversation. We all saw a warrior within Jamila today, but I think Artemis already realized Jamila is a huntress in the making, long before today. Still, at the mention of Jamila becoming a huntress, Artemis deviates her attention toward the sky.

"Hm," is all she says.

"Why are you hesitating? She would be a great huntress."

Artemis's hand stops in the middle of Iris's hair. "In less than three days, ten *great* huntresses have died. Three

161

of them were traitors, but the rest died loyal to me. I couldn't protect them, and now they are dead."

"That wasn't your fault," I say.

"Do you believe me when I say Sika's death is not your fault?"

I grow silent.

"Jamila is Saffron and Hermes's child," Artemis says. "She can't die because I can no longer protect you all. Great or not, you are all falling faster than I can catch you."

I have no response to that. No careful rebuttal that makes Artemis think about changing her mind about Jamila. I cannot find the words because as soon as she mentions death, all I see is an array of carnage in front of my eyes.

Artemis lies on her back, with Iris still resting her head on her lap, and whispers. "Goodnight, Lamb. Get some rest."

I do not listen.

Night had befallen us, and as everyone else slumbers, I refuse to shut my eyes. Nightmares wait behind my lids. Sordid tales of slit throats, arrow-pierced hearts, and echoing screams. Reminders of the past plague my sleep, as if Epiales is back to taunt me as ruefully as Kronos's twisted time had.

My gaze stays trained on the woods surrounding our camp site with dreadful anticipation that more carnivorous enemies will strike. Our foes are always hungry, forever searching for their next meal, but the past will prepare me for tonight. I feel it in my bones, the surety that another monster will sleek out of the trees.

Especially as a new huntress is slowly forming, fearless and ready to strike down any monster who gets in our way.

Wind bristles the trees, and every noise, minute or clamorous, straightens my spine. Who will emerge next? Will it be the Minotaur, whose strength can turn every surrounding tree into cinder? A colony of birds playfully chirp, and I raise my weapon in their direction. Are these the Stymphalian Birds with beaks that are perpetually stained with human blood?

I scarcely give myself time to blink, fearful that the moment I take my eyes away from the woods, it will be too late. The dreadful anticipation of battle settles on my tongue. I perfectly poise my arrow on my bow, and when six pairs of eyes meet me from two hundred yards away, I let out a blood curling scream and release the bowstring.

My arrow spirals in its alacrity towards the three-headed Hydra. The mighty creature, who stands almost thirty feet tall, lets out an ear-piercing screech when my arrow slides into one of her six eyes. Yet, she only stumbles a few feet before one of her other heads rips the arrow out of the eye with its teeth.

Then, the creature rushes towards us, faster than ever.

Artemis and Iris are the first to wake to my scream, with weapons materializing in their hands. Iris creates an eight-formation with her multi-colored spear, while five miniature rainbows descend beside the remaining waking huntresses.

Weapons, specifically designed for each huntress, fall into their opening palms.

A blood red, Shikari's favorite color, crossbow lands first. She hasn't grinned since Hound's death, but she is now. A cruel smile peels over her lips, and she whirls her body towards the furious Hydra. Simultaneously, we release our arrows towards the creature. The Hydra deflects my arrow that aimed for another eye, but Shikari's crimson arrow meets its mark.

Blood spills out of the Hydra's neck as the arrow worms its way into the center.

Once more, she stumbles backwards.

Shikari's arrows re-materialize on their own, each a different shade of red, and she does not stop firing the arrows at the Hydra. Neither do I. Yet, we are only stalling the inevitable, hoping the other huntresses will be awake and ready enough to slay another beast.

Tiny June holds the largest weapon, which is a cyan-colored axe. The axe's staff is almost as tall as her, but she runs towards the Hydra with a massive grin. Running shortly behind her is Dýnami, holding a torch in one hand and a magenta spear in the other.

As soon as the Hydra breaks through the trees and stands at our campsite, June is ready for her. She swipes the mighty axe and slices off one of the Hydra's paws. The monster's scream is loud enough to be heard from miles away, but June's elated cry is almost as piercing. The Hydra does not have enough time to process her pain before more pain consumes her. Dýnami slams her spear into the neighboring paw, then drags her torch to the amputated one.

"Yeah, Dýnami!" June screams as her grin consumes her entire face. "We got to burn this bitch!"

I make an advancing step towards June and Dýnami, but I am quickly tackled. My shoulder takes the brunt of the fall as Shikari lays herself on top of me. I can barely see beneath her, but I can see enough. A creature almost as large as the Hydra, with golden fur bright against the contrasting night, leaps over us.

Its claws graze Shikari's back, and she smothers her scream by pressing her mouth against my shoulder blade.

Teeth break through my skin, but I scarcely notice. I can only see one of the most formidable monsters land a few feet away from us.

The Nemean Lion turns to face us once more, and a mighty roar shatters any hope I had that we would survive tonight.

SIXTEEN

HERMES

ike speeds towards the unsuspecting Furies, tucking her wings close to her body as she cuts the surrounding air in her trek towards her enemies. Her wings' edges are sharp enough to cut skin, and it is the Furies only warning of her arrival. With the edge of her wing, she slices Tisiphone's wrist, causing her to drop her weapon, but then comes to a complete halt in front of Megaera.

Megaera pales one moment before Nike rips the wings off her back in two fatal tugs. Megaera's scream is an eerie pitch before she tumbles downward onto the unforgiving ground. Her demise is a grotesque distraction, and I soar towards another Fury, Tisiphone, at the opportunity.

She doesn't see me until I am directly in front of her, with both hands on either side of her face. Her uninjured hand comes for me, and its nails rack through my hands, arms, and shoulders, but she isn't fast enough to escape her brutal fate. I rip her head off her shoulders, and Tisiphone quickly joins Alecto in a downward spiral to the bottom of the mountain.

The oldest and most destructive Fury, Alecto, whirls to face Nike and me.

A bird-like squawk escapes her snarling, blackened lips, giving us a glimpse of her rotted canines. Her nails, once a few inches, grow ten times their normal length until ten blade-length weapons form on the tips of her fingers. Her blue, almost white, eyes lock on me, and she flies forward with a death-defying screech.

Caduceus materializes in my hand, and right as the tip of her nail drags across my cheek, I swing my weapon across the side of her head. We both let out a curse and tumble away from each other. Nike advances forward before I can. Her gilded sword is bright as the sun. She matches Alecto's nails with a destructive clatter.

Without turning around, Nike screams. "Go! I got this!" Alecto doesn't spare me another glance as I fly into the cave after the others, but their blades clash together and echo in the surrounding air.

As I fly into the mountains opening, Apate flies towards the exit. Ichor decorates her face, which slowly heals from an altercation with either Hephaestus or Aphrodite. The scar starts at the top of her forehead, falling diagonally until the golden blood drips off the curve of her jaw.

She sees me, and her small eyes widen with the realization that she has nowhere to run. Apate stumbles to a stop at the edge of the cliff, eyeing *Caduceus* in my hand. An inner debate rampages her thoughts, and I know the moment she decides that fighting me is her best option. Her body tenses, and the hand closest to her holstered sword twitches.

A sword impales her stomach and sprouts out of her

ribcage, causing a bubble of ichor to spill out of her shocked, open mouth. She does not have time to turn around to face her assailant before tumbling to her knees. The sword pulls out of her body, and the muscled arm wielding the weapon aims for her neck.

In one fatal swipe, Apate's head tumbles off her neck and falls off the cliff to the unforgiving ground.

Apate cannot die because of a decapitation, so her body continuously twitches beneath the booted foot on top of her bloodied back. Her hands scratch the surrounding floor, searching for a head she will not easily find.

"Where is she?" a deep, menacing voice growls.

I follow the length of the booted foot, and lock eyes on Ares. Anger encompasses his features, now splattered in gilded blood. Some are our enemies, but there's a ring of gold blood over his quickly healing, broken nose. My gaze momentarily drifts to Hephaestus's fists, with cracked knuckles. Hephaestus grins back at me.

Ares growls, focusing my attention back on him. Except for being punched in the face by Hephaestus, he does not appear to be the one we saved from captivity. The god of war stares at me and reminds me why he is one of the most feared immortals in history. He applies pressure on Apate's back, and I can hear her decapitated head screaming in pain from the bottom of the mountain.

"Where's who?" I ask.

Ares spins his bloodied sword around his hand, aching to inflict pain, as he snarls through clenched teeth. "Where's Saffron?"

His question makes me pause.

The only desire Ares has ever had for my wife is her death. He has thirsted for her brand of carnage since she was a human girl in the arena, and that hasn't changed over the years. Since Saffron became a goddess, and the possibility of killing her became obsolete, Ares hasn't seen her. He refused to come to our wedding or any notable event she was attending for nearly ninety years. He stands in front of me, chest heaving and face racked with rage, as he asks about my wife, but why?

I fly to the edge of the mountain's cave, and the moment my feet touch the edge, the tip of *Caduceus* levels with Ares's jugular. "Why do you want to know where my wife is?"

"Ex-wife!" Aphrodite singsongs behind me.

"Shut-up, darling," Hephaestus grumbles.

There's a pause, then. "Sorry, Hermie! Continue!"

Their interruption momentarily draws my gaze away from Ares, and I survey the surrounding scene.

Hedylogos stands beneath the world, his arms already trembling with the overbearing weight. Tears track down his cheeks as his focus levels on Aphrodite, but her back is to him. She refuses to look at the son who betrayed her trust, but just like Hedylogos, she cries. Hephaestus stands beside his wife, with one arm around her shoulders. His other hand holds the net encapsulating a furious goddess.

Calypso.

Not Hecate.

The muses scream in the background, but I only care about one missing goddess. I search the small space, waiting to see green magic or wide, blue eyes, but she's nowhere in sight. Red blinds my vision, as a gnarling, twisting emotion slams into my chest and threatens to rip out my heart.

"Where is she?"

"That's why I'm asking," Ares snaps.

I ignore him and focus on Hephaestus. "Did you let Hecate get away?"

"She wasn't here," Hephaestus says.

"She left about an hour ago," Ares interjects. "But she doesn't stay gone long, so we need to leave." Ares grabs the nape of my neck before I see his hand shoot towards me. He pulls me into him, and he makes sure I can see every fragment of his rage as he snarls. "Now where is *she*?"

"Why in the gods do you care?" I snap at the same time Aphrodite answers.

"Ogygia."

Ares lets go of me, and he whirls to face Aphrodite. "Ogygia? Is she…" he stops the question from escaping his lips. Instead, his rage focuses on the captured goddess, who knows exactly where Ogygia is located. He takes one threatening step towards Calypso. "I'm going to rip every limb from your body-"

"Not the time," Hephaestus interrupts, then looks at me. "Grab one of the traitorous muses and carry her to Mt. Olympus. I'll materialize an extra chariot for Ares to ride in with the remaining muses."

Ares doesn't look away from Calypso with murder blazing in his eyes, and I don't understand it. He hates my wife. He hasn't seen her in decades, so why does he care? The room is too quiet, except for Hedylogos crying and the muses' muffled screams behind their gauze. It's quiet, with unanswered questions and secrets that threaten to expose themselves.

Ares throws the bound and gagged Urania over his shoulder and carries her into the newly materialized chariot. I pick Erato up honeymoon style as she wiggles in my arms and tries to escape. I barely register her weight in my arms as I glare at Ares until he flies back to Mt. Olympus with Clio, Calliope, and Urania.

"Why was he pretending to care about her?" I ask Aphrodite and Hephaestus the moment Ares is out of earshot.

"We don't have time for this," Hephaestus grumbles, and then throws a netted Calypso into the chariot.

"Ow," she whines.

Hephaestus glares at Calypso for daring to be hurt, but then extends a hand to help Aphrodite into his chariot. He is about to leave when Hedylogos screams. "Mom, please!" She turns to face her son, who struggles to hold Earth as he cries. "I'm sorry. Please don't leave me here!"

Tears stream down her ever-changing cheeks, but she doesn't balk as he screams, "*Mom!*" repeatedly.

"No son of mine would sit here and watch their father suffer. No son of mine would hurt me this much." She hurriedly wipes at her tears with the backs of her hands. "Come back to me when you remember who you are, but until then, I want you to suffer like you made Ares and me."

Hephaestus grants his wife reprieve and hurriedly escapes the mountain.

I wait a few more seconds, just in case a plume of green smoke materializes, and I can get my retribution. But nothing happens. Hedylogos continues to scream for his mom, and Erato continues to squirm in my arms. There is no Hecate. There is no retribution.

I fly away with anger boiling in my veins.

Nike waits for me outside the cave, her body covered in monster's blood. She glances at Erato, then falters on my face. "We won the first of many battles, yet you look worse than ever."

I do not respond. Instead, I soar towards Mt. Olympus at lightning speed.

Nike matches my strides. She periodically glances at me, gauging the truth behind the mayhem in my mind, but I never speak. Not when we drop the traitors off to Zeus and Hera, or when I follow Nike to the prison on Mt. Olympus, where Calypso still lays in a coil of golden net.

I barely process thanking Clio and Calliope, or when they leave the room.

Blind rage and mounting insecurities threaten to strangle me, and I focus all these bubbling emotions on the only goddess who knows exactly where my wife is.

Calypso's eyes meet mine, and she whimpers.

SEVENTEEN

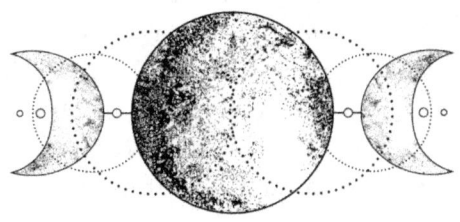

HECATE

My first warning that something went terribly awry is the muffled, yet piercing, screams of Apate. The sound does not come from the mountain, but when my foot lands on a particularly squishy rock. Apate's decapitated head sits underneath my foot, her mouth concealed beneath my heeled boot.

I hesitate before removing my foot from her mouth because what she will tell me derails heavily detailed plans, and it will not be Apate who must report this grievance to Styx. Atlas and I are the only two who know where Styx hides and waits to strike. I will have to go to Styx and explain how Apate laid decapitated at the bottom of the mountain, and whatever other stories she is about to tell.

Green fire laps at my hands, coiling around my arms like twin serpents, when I finally remove my boot. Apate's eyes widen with fear, and for the first time, she remains silent. That's another clue about how dastardly the situation in the mountain has become. Apate is never quiet for long.

"Tell me everything."

She tells me everything in quick succession, but when Hermes's name leaves her lips, she nearly trips over the word. Her gaze hesitantly drifts back to the green fire that now spins in my hair and slithers across my shoulder blades. She knows my history with Hermes, as does every god, and she waits for me to kill her.

If I had the power to do so, I would.

Out of any god to infiltrate Mt. Atlas and steal Ares and Calypso, why did it have to be him? I expected him to hunt solely for Saffron, the goddess he foolishly believes is his soulmate; instead, he steals from me. He has never stolen from me, but I suppose I deserve it. I stole his trust, only to turn it into cinder at his feet. I eliminated his chance at saving Saffron from her fate with Ogygia and Epiales.

But I hate how close he is to the upcoming war.

I regret many actions that led me to this spot, underneath the Atlas Mountain, as a decapitated head talks my ear off, but if this war hurts Hermes, that will be my greatest qualm. I love Mastiff more than I love my sanity, but I still love a piece of Hermes. He was a part of my life for centuries, and that type of bond doesn't completely dissipate with time.

Long ago, I thought I could lure him to Styx's side.

When we were on Mt. Olympus as Kronos's captives, I thought I could tell him everything. I was close to divulging everything to him one night, after I told him about soulmates. He was falling in love with the wrong woman, and I thought I could show him the truth. He has always been a power hungry immortal, who wanted to climb the ladder to the top, stealing from everyone along the way, but Saffron ruined him. Made him stop his ascension that was rightly deserved.

It's the only reason he's not with me right now, joining Styx in our fight.

But, as Apate finishes her story, she reminds me that Hermes is not fully benevolent like his comrades. There is a darkness festering inside of him, waiting for someone to crack him open. Saffron stripped him of his desire to become an Olympian, but she did not take away his inherent need to win. She did not peel away his selfishness that demands he get everything he wants, no matter the cost.

Even at the risk of starting the war.

"I'll be back later," I tell Apate.

She lets out a sigh of relief. "Oh, thank the gods. I have missed my body...wait, where are you going?!" My magic wraps around me, ready to transport me away, as Apate screams. "Reattach my head to my body first! Lady Hecate!"

I leave, with Apate still screaming at me to help her.

When I portal to Styx's hiding spot, the charred ruins I reassembled to their former excellence stare back at me. The sight reverberates me back to the past, before Styx freed herself from her river and Saffron was only a frightened human. I pretend that the sight does not make me think of Mastiff, or the threadbare moments of trust I had with the proclaimed god-killer. I raise my chin in the air, and I stroll into Styx's lair as if I do not fear her retribution.

The nearly empty halls let out an ominous echo as my heels click against the concrete slab floors. Memories, mostly atrocious, but some pleasant, return with a vengeance as I reach the spiral staircase to the far left. I turn my head back, staring at the expansive hallways filled with former screams, before returning my focus to where Styx plots.

Bellows of my past mold into the present anguish as a deep, male voice cuts through the silence with a sound derived from genuine pain. The clatter of chains becomes a symphony as I ascend the staircase, nearing the closed door where this unfortunate male suffers underneath Styx's intrusion.

I knock three times, and the screams and shaking chains abruptly stop.

Styx cracks open the door. I cannot see the male who suffers, but I know he is human because red blood paints a morbid picture across Styx's incredibly pale, sharp cheeks. "You are not supposed to be here." Styx's voice is haunting and monotone tone, sending a frigid shiver down my spine. There will never be a time when I do not fear this goddess, yet she sees me as her closest confidant.

I pretend she does not frighten me, so I force an exaggerated sense of confidence in my voice as I respond. "We need to talk."

"Good or bad news?"

"Both."

The male screams again, but this time it is a plea. "F-f-free me," the deep voice begs. "H-h-h-help."

"Ignore him," Styx steps out of the room and closes the door behind her. Now, he sobs without a morsel of hope. "My soldier just needs a bit more training. Let's leave him as you tell me how you failed me."

We walk down the spiral staircase I just ascended, and with a silent apology to Hermes, I tell her everything. I name every immortal- Hermes, Aphrodite, Hephaestus,

Nike, Clio, and Calliope- who helped free Ares, imprison Hedylogos, and capture Calypso, Erato, and Urania.

Styx's expression never changes, but that doesn't assuage my fears. She often reminds me of a viper. Both she and the snake hide themselves, either in a river of their own making or in the desert, and they wait for their prey to believe they are safe. Then, they strike with a lethality that makes them the most dangerous of all species.

She may appear docile, but all it takes is one second, where I drop my defenses and she sinks her claws into me. I may be her accomplice, but just like everyone else, I am disposable once deemed inadequate.

"You believe Hermes will aim to kill Epiales if he is the first to find Ogygia?" Styx asks after I divulge everything.

We both stand in front of the vacant, barred room which started everything.

"I do. His selfish need to steal her back will make him forget rationality."

"And now that he has Calypso, he has the potential to find her before I wanted Zeus to find her."

"That is correct. I think both gods will kill Epiales if they're the first to find him, so we must ensure Zeus or Hermes get there before the huntresses."

Styx wraps a hand around a bar, her fractured finger-nails grating the material until a screeching noise rattles the air. "Do whatever you can to stop Calypso from divulging Ogygia's location for another two or three days. Saffron and her heart need to be on the island a little while longer before he dies."

They need to truly be in love before Hermes kills him, is what Styx does not say.

I bow my head. "I'll slip into her dreams tonight. As

long as she stays silent for the rest of today, your plans should still go smoothly."

Styx doesn't respond; instead, she commands. "Leave Apate's head unattached to her body. She is useless. Now, leave. I must play with my soldier a little while longer."

EIGHTEEN

SAFFRON

Every star in the sky has a story, but once, they were merely white dots that tempted me with ideas about an escape from my jail. The other prisoners let me lay beside the window, and each night before I fell asleep, I stared at those little white dots and imagined another world. One where those dots were as warm as a hug and the jail was as far away as they looked.

I learned the truth about stars because of Epiales.

He laughed when I asked him about the white dots, and even as a young teen, my heart skipped a beat whenever I heard that joyous sound. When his laughter died down, he moved from his place on the throne and sat on the stairs with me.

I couldn't see his face that night, but I could feel him like he was an extension of my body. Felt his warmth for the first time when he wrapped an arm around me. I laid my head on his shoulder, softer than any floor, as his voice whisked around me, becoming a part of the wind.

Then he spoke about the major and minor Ursa constellations. I think, as he told me that story about the constellations, I first truly fell in love with him. I might have always loved him, from the first time I heard his voice, but the night when we spoke about stars was when I realized the feeling that consumed me in his presence.

It is the middle of the night, and I still cannot sleep. I stare at the stars that paint itself in tragedy. The stories unfurl in the darkness, forming in the eccentrics of the solar system, and it is my solace amidst the roaring fire and serene sky. But the twinkling sight is a reminder of who sleeps a few feet away. Whenever I see the stars, I hear his whispery voice.

My feet move on their own accord. I can blame the night chill, or the lack of sleep, but they are excuses to mask the truth. I'm lonely. So achingly lonely, and he can provide me a little comfort. I need it the way others need nutrients. For years, life has starved me of physical contact, and I need it just for a bit.

He wakes when I lay my head on his chest. Yet, he doesn't speak. Fearful of breaking the tentative truce, he pretends to still sleep while wrapping an arm around my waist. He does a terrible job of pretending, though. With my ear against his chest, I hear the erratic thump of his quickening heartbeat.

I do not break the silence, either. I still do not trust him. Still see him as a villain I cannot avoid, no matter the danger in his proximity. But I have missed the simple act of cuddling. How long has it been since I received something so simple, yet so treasured?

Probably since Jamila was young enough to curl her little arms around me. Before she got too old to cuddle with her mom.

I close my eyes, and for the first time in so long, I do not see Hypnos waiting for me. Unconsciousness takes my tattered soul for a momentary reprieve.

When I wake, I expect to feel the grainy caress of the sand upon my cheek, but it's still warm and soft. Epiales's hand slides through my dark tresses, gentle with every strand. I do not need to breathe to survive, but my breath hitches with his touch. We have gone through so many tribulations together, but I don't remember ever getting the chance to just lay in each other's company. This is new for us, and I like it more than I want to admit.

"Good morning, my queen."

His words, gravelly and dripped in an emotion I can't dwell on, send a shiver down my spine. "Good morning, storyteller."

I crane my head up, careful not to lift it off his chest and break our momentary illusion, but I want to see him. He is already staring at me, smiling down at where I lay in his arms. "Last night reminded me of our first conversation about stars. Do you remember when you thought the stars were food?"

I had almost forgotten, but Epiales remembers every moment we've had together. The memory almost makes me smile. "I was so hungry that I hoped I could reach far enough into the sky and grab one of the yummy white dots."

The window was so small, about the width of my hand, but I saw the sky and all its stars and played pretend. I stared forward and thought it was food, and I would imagine I was eating it. Sometimes, it would help with the hunger. Most of the time, not even the beauty could mask the gnarly truth thrashing in my hollow stomach.

One particularly hungry night, when I fell asleep and

found Epiales waiting for me, I immediately asked him about the yummy looking stars in the sky. My stomach grumbled with the same intensity in that dream as it did in the waking world.

"You listened to me rant about the stars, then taught me everything about them until I stopped seeing them as potential food."

He continues sliding his hand through my hair, carefully unknotting stubborn pieces. "I felt bad because you looked so defeated by the truth."

"I was defeated." A sudden memory returns with this story. "And the next morning, I found a basket filled with white cookies. Still, to this day, those were the best cookies I ever ate because they tasted like the stars. How did you do that from Tartarus?"

"I wish I could have baked them myself. It's a secret hobby of mine, but Tartarus has limited ovens." He lets out a huff that is supposed to be a laugh, but Tartarus isn't a laughing matter. "I still had a bit of magic down there, so I materialized the basket full of cookies and sent it to you. It took a lot more magic than I expected, which is why I couldn't join you in the dreamworld for a few days after, but it was worth it when I could see you again. I have never seen a prettier smile than yours after I gave you the cookies."

"I didn't know you baked."

"It's amazing what you find out about a person when you're not rivals." He laughs at his attempt at a joke, but his statement only reminds me of what we really are.

Rivals.

I do not realize I am moving away from him until his hand stops its descent through my hair. He holds the back of my head and uses his grip to turn my head to face him.

It does not matter how many times I have stared at him, it still sends a current through me. He freezes time with this single movement, and we are equally speechless as the realization of our proximity becomes apparent.

I feel where his eyes travel, from the strand of hair hanging over my forehead, to the freckle on the corner of my nose, and finally do my lips. I try not to, but I follow his lead, and soon, we are leaning into each other, unable to look away from anything but the other's mouth. He calls us rivals, and it's the unequivocable truth, but that harrowing truth cannot deter me.

I could easily get out of his grip, and yet I don't want to. A sick part of me both acknowledges the fact that he is the enemy, but also yearns to have him touch me. He makes my skin sizzle, and although I shouldn't, I crave him.

Epiales gives me a tentative kiss, and when I do not immediately pull away, I can taste the sigh that escapes his lips. He keeps one hand on the back of my head, while the other tightens around my waist. The first few kisses are almost hesitant, but then need possesses him. He flips us over, so I lay in the sand, and he looms above me, opening my mouth with his tongue and delving inside for more.

We are feverish in our touches, like this will be the first and last time we have a moment like this. His hand dips underneath my shirt and explores my flesh for the first time. My hand drags across the waistband of his shorts as he bites my bottom lip and a moan escapes my lips.

But that sound, one of pleasure and so much more, shatters my illusion that we can restart our story.

It forces me to remember who is on top of me. It isn't Hermes, the only other male to incite that sound, but it's Epiales. My storyteller, who once made me love him to uncontrollable levels, but betrayed me with the same ruthless precision.

I remember every battle we faced against one another, where casualties skyrocketed and my hope for his benevolent side plummeted. I hear the arguments he and I shared about Kronos's vileness, which always ended in Epiales declaring himself as vile. My body stings with the memory of Eros's arrow piercing me, and the forced affection I was giving Kronos, who was ready to take my choice away in his crusade for power. In Kronos and Epiales's crusade.

I can still feel his lips against mine, but I can also feel the outline of his hipbone beneath my fingertips. The same hipbone I ripped from his body on the fateful day when his malevolence was too much. Tears coat my cheeks, joining in with our kiss, and the normal electricity within our touch quickly replaces with fear.

"Get off me," I whisper. He doesn't hear me, and the next words come out as a screeched scream. "Get off! Get off! Get off!"

He stops kissing me, but he doesn't immediately get off me. My words are still registering in his head when I use my magic to fling him off. He flies through the air before falling onto the ground a few feet away. His elbows hit the ground, hard, and when he stands up, I see the bloom of crimson blood on the sand.

Not gold.

Red.

"What's wrong?" Epiales asks, taking a step towards me. "What happened? Did I hurt you?"

I shake my head, but my eyes cannot look away from the truth I knew when I brought him back to life. There's a difference between knowing something on an instinctual level and seeing the proof laid out in front of you. I felt his humanity, but I didn't know with utmost certainty until his elbows dripped with the truth.

"Saffron, what is the matter?"

He stands in front of me again and reaches both his hands out to cup my cheeks, but I flinch. The skin between his eyebrows creases with confusion, but eventually, he follows my line of vision. I see the moment he finds the splatter of red human blood on the floor. Then, ever so slowly, he picks up his elbow.

By now, he must realize that his injuries still hurt because when he pokes a probing finger on the cut, he lets out a hiss. Yet, the realization still hasn't hit him. He resembles one of Medusa's statues, frozen with unwavering petrification. His bottom lip trembles, trying to form words, but there is only silence.

I do not know what to say to him, to comfort him when reality comes crashing with the same intensity as these waves. I can only stand in front of him, staring at the same injury with him, as the truth thickens the air. He lifts his now-bloodied fingers and holds it in front of his face, as if the color will change the longer he observes it.

"It's mine?" Epiales asks, voice cracking.

I nod my head.

He looks up from his bloodied fingers, and he stares at me. I do not know what my expression gives him, but it's enough to shatter the illusion that he is still an immortal. Epiales, the former personification of nightmares, stumbles away from me before running into the woods.

And I, ever the fool for him, follow.

NINETEEN

LAMB

Shikari groans as she rolls off my body, but she grabs her crossbow. Blood spills from her back in steady rivulets, but in the face of certain death, she points the crossbow at the Nemean Lion. He has impenetrable skin, and only a hero as strong as Heracles had the power to kill him. Her arrows won't do anything to him. It won't even delay him, like it did with the Hydra.

But Shikari uses Jamila's earlier words as ammunition.

She does not desist from certain death. She is the hero that young children look up to when they aspire to be a huntress. I stand up beside her and grab my bow. I place an arrow on the string, and we lock eyes.

"It's been a privilege riding with my hero all these years." Shikari has tears in her eyes, but she does not let them shed. She turns to face our monster, and I follow her head.

He runs towards us, and our arrows fly in his direction.

Before they can reach him and bounce off his impenetrable fur, a goddess of shimmering colors leaps into the air behind him. Iris lands on his back, and her staff cuts off his windpipe. She has both hands on either side of her weapon, and she bellows as she pulls back against the Nemean Lion's throat.

Attraction does not come easily to me. I have never looked upon a person and felt desire the way others do, but in this wild moment, I understand why Artemis loves Iris. It is not because of her conventionally attractive looks, which is common amongst immortals; it is her fearlessness. The wind sends Iris's brown hair, streaked with every color of the rainbow, everywhere. It creates a halo around her dark complexion, and her round face appears angelic in the throes of battle, like it is her divine duty to eradicate the world of creatures like the Nemean Lion.

And gods, it is a magical sight.

The Nemean Lion screams, but it is a choked sound. One of defeat and disorder. Triumph turns Iris's eyes a shade of gold as she looks at us, but then her gaze drifts behind where we stand, and her eyes shift to the palest shade of blue. Because of all the death we have faced, I understand what blue means all too well.

"Behind you!"

Shikari and I whirl around as the Hydra's one-hundred headed brother, the Ladon, assails a razor-shaped mouth towards me. I place an arrow on my bowstring, but he is too quick. The element of surprise will be my demise, because I am not fast enough.

Shikari is, though.

For the second time today, she tackles me to the ground, but her back falls on top of mine instead of her stomach. Her bowstring faces the Ladon, and she pulls the trigger. I turn my head just in time to see the arrow enter the Ladon's open mouth.

He screams as Shikari shuffles off me. I'm sticky with Shikari's blood, but relief washes over me. I thought I wanted death, but when it came for me in the form of sharpened teeth and vengeful desires, I remembered Willow's words for me when I was dying on the island.

"Right now, you are meant to survive. You are meant to fight for our goddess and our sisters."

"Thank you." The words fall from my lips as a rainbow lands in my opened palms.

I do not know where my arrows or bow went, but it does not matter now. When the rainbow fades, a four-foot-long sword materializes. The blade is a light shade of mint green, while the magnificent handle is dark as moss. Shapes whorl around the handle, but I do not have time to investigate. Adrenaline pumps through every orifice, chanting the same word.

Fight, fight, fight.

I rarely ever fight with a sword. My chosen weapon has always been a bow and arrow, but I drag the tip of the sword across the dirt and familiarize myself with it as I turn to face my newest foe. Just as the Hydra did, the Ladon rips the arrow out of his mouth using another pair of teeth. He reminds me how easy it would have been to rupture my flesh as he bites down on the arrow and splinters the ruby-glinted arrow into a dozen shattered pieces.

I spare a glance at the space, quickly realizing that the Hydra, Nemean Lion, and the Ladon are not the only monsters thirsting for our demise. Orthrus, the two-headed dog, strides towards Vee while the Crommyonian Sow and Colchian Dragon search for their prey. Artemis meets the latter with unbridled fury, while the Crommyonian Sow chooses the last fighter.

Jamila.

Countless children of the Echidna and Typhon emerge from every crevice of the woods, gleaming with the belief that this battle is already won for them, forgetting we only pretend to be the prey. We are the predators, and they have fallen into our trap, not the other way around.

The Nemean Lion learns this truth as he collapses onto the ground. His eyes both pop out of their sockets, causing a stream of green blood to stain his gilded fur. The creature is not yet dead, but Iris's grip on her staff does not waver. She strangles the creature as blood oozes out of its ears, mouth, and sockets. She doesn't let go until his fur's vibrancy reduces to a mundane shade, and its legs give out underneath him.

Iris doesn't let go until her staff cuts through the now-penetrable skin.

The Nemean Lion's head falls to the ground with a definite plunk, and it is only then that Iris jumps off his back. She peruses the battlefield, golden hair glimmering brighter than the sun ever has, and she rushes towards Jamila's side.

The Hydra discovers the truth each time she screeches. This formidable creature, taller than all the other monsters here, has fallen onto its knees. They cut her paws off and cauterize the stumps with Dýnami's torch. Still, the creature stirs and swipes at them with her teeth. Its tail slashes through the air with deadly efficiency, but it never catches June. She climbs up the creature's back as Dýnami fights the tail with only a spear and a torch. The latter never extinguishes. It rages and yearns for more monster flesh to burn.

We are survivors through and through.

We built up our fearlessness and trained to thrive under the scrutiny of underestimations. The Nemean Lion and the Hydra are learning this invaluable lesson, and the Ladon is next.

Three of the Ladon's heads strike for me, another three destined for Shikari, but we are both ready. I spin with my sword, and a strike of green moves through the air and slices off two of the monster's heads. The third head dies last, with my sword hilt-deep in its jaw. Green blood oozes down my forearm, and I relish in the sight.

I want more.

Shikari and I rarely fight side-by-side, but we are in sync. We switch sides, duck, and strike at the same time. The Ladon's heads do not regenerate like his sister's. We do not need to cauterize the wounds. Instead, we bathe in the blood of this enemy as each head tumbles from its neck and writhes on the floor before declaring defeat.

With each decapitated head, the Ladon's screams grow quieter and quieter, until all sounds cease.

Green blood completely covers Shikari's face, except for her pearly white smile that I thought I wouldn't see again. It is vibrant against the darkness of the Ladon's blood, and it is a radiant sight. It brings a smile to my lips, too. We stand in a ringlet of ninety-nine heads. Clinking weapons ricochet throughout the battlefield; yet we stare at each other and let out a slew of laughter.

It is a laugh without origin; nonetheless, a laugh we needed. It is such a deep laugh that my stomach aches from the exertion. Neither of us can stop. It is medicine in the most asinine way, but it cures us of the anger and sorrow that has gripped us these past few days.

Shikari and I have never been close, but we laugh together like we have been friends for centuries.

"How's your back?" I finally ask.

"How's your shoulder?"

I look at my shoulder, remembering the momentary pain when she first tackled me, and the sight shocks me. It's popped out of its socket, and I did not realize until now.

We look at each other, our grins all encompassing.

Until a scream, loud and torturous, pierces my ears and gains my attention.

Across the battlefield, Orthrus has Vee pinned to the ground. The weapons Iris made her, a set of six yellow throwing knives, scatter around the battle scene. She is beneath the monster's claws without weapons, as both of its heads near her exposed throat.

There is another scream coming from a different direction, but I do not pay it any attention. I run towards Vee, my shoulder screaming in pain with every movement, but I force myself to move faster. Shikari is not behind me. She probably went to the other screaming huntress.

Orthrus nears her throat, his canines dripping with saliva, and I throw my newly created sword through the air. My aim remains true, with or without a bow and arrow, and it cuts through the back of one of its heads. Orthrus replaces his bellow with Vee's as he turns his last useful head in my direction.

I no longer have a weapon, and my dislocated shoulder makes that arm nearly useless, but I do not cease. My body collides with Orthrus's, who only stumbles from my surprise before his mouth clamps around my dislocated shoulder. I scream as my free hand wraps around the sword, impaling his head. I rip it out, and in the same motion, plunge it into his last skull.

His teeth slacken from their unrelenting hold on my shoulder.

I retreat, taking my sword with me and watching as Orthrus stumbles backwards, then falls on his backside. Blood spills out, creating a pond of green beneath him, but adrenaline keeps me on my feet. I stagger towards Vee and extend my free hand.

Her own blood, not Orthrus's, covers her face. Orthrus ruined her left shoulder with brutal slashes, and her ripped shirt undoubtedly holds identical wounds. Death nearly captured her today, so when I help her to her feet, I expect fear plaguing her features. Pain decorates her furrowed brow as she continues to drip with blood, but she grins at me, the same way Shikari did after defeating the Ladon.

"That was…." Vee pauses.

"Are you alright?" I ask at the same time Vee lands on a word.

"Superlative."

There is a pause, then.

"And that means what?" I ask.

"Incomparable to anything else." Dreamily, she adds. "Incredible."

I look at her mutilated face. It is a miracle that Orthrus's claws did not penetrate a vital organ, but the wounds are deep. Blood still spills down her body and onto the floor between our feet. Vee was moments from death, and she smiles and declares this the greatest day of her life. Incomparable to anything else.

"Are you alright?" I ask again, this time with a judging lilt.

"Of course I am. Why wouldn't I be?"

I do not state the obvious, the scar across her face, but I say. "What just happened is not incredible."

The pain in my shoulder threatens to rob my consciousness, and I stumble back a step. Vee holds me still. "How is this not incredible? These beasts have been dead for thousands of years, and it cemented all the men who slayed them in history as the greatest heroes. Heracles, Oedipus, Iolaus, Theseus, and Jason created a path of immortal praise against these monsters. Now, women will pave the future of heroism. It is truly superlative."

"Superlative isn't a word."

I lose my comment in the wind as I observe the scene surrounding me. The hydra is dead, laying in a puddle of her limbs like her brother, the Ladon. June and Dýnami run towards the Crommyonian Sow, where Iris and Jamila fight back-to-back. Artemis faces the Colchian Dragon beside Shikari. They're both bloodied and sweaty, but the infamous beast moves with staggered steps. His blood drips from multiple wounds.

Some rumors say Jason slayed this creature, but the gods know the truth. Artemis told me the true tale of the Colchian Dragon dozens of times. Jason never slayed the beast, although he received the credit. Instead, a powerful witch named Medea charmed the dragon to sleep long enough for Jason to steal the golden fleece from his guard.

Nobody has seen the Colchian Dragon in three thousand years until today. The undefeated monster fights alongside Artemis and Shikari, and I turn to face the dragon. Once more, adrenaline pumps fire through me, and I run with a battle scream towards the Colchian Dragon.

Vee sprints beside me, with all her throwing knives back in her possession. She holstered three, but two spin through the air toward our newest opponent.

Let's make history.

TWENTY

HART SOMMERS

It's strange, but the oracles, who were born thousands of years before me, are the most genuine friends I have ever had. Each morning after breakfast, Hades clasps his hands in mine, and he propels me to a world where they exist as shimmering auras and vague appearances. Aashritha's face is most prominent because a part of me calls to her as my ancestor, or it could be because she is the most powerful oracle of them all.

We sit around a darkened room, illuminated only by their shimmering gemstones, and they transform me into a weapon. My drawing pencils tell the beginning of many stories with every stroke on an empty canvas. I wield it with the same precision as Ares does his sword, and I create my own masterpieces, beginning when my weapon meets his greatest opponent: time.

Their touches, and the magic they imbue me with, guides me in the right direction, but there is still something blocking my mind. A door I cannot find the key to unlock.

When their hands leave mine and I am brought back to the real-world moments before dinnertime, I see the canvases I have created, and I know where they start. It's always Saffron and me, the savior and the seer, and the next step is the heart.

But I do not know what comes next.

I'm still not strong enough to know how to save the world from Styx's war.

Today, when I leave the oracles, Hades and I see a drawing of Saffron. She stands on an island I instantly know is Ogygia, with her hands cupping a fragile heart. It's a broken thing, with cracks that appear irreversible. Death always joins an immortal who loves a mortal, and the proof of her disarray lays in that ruinous organ.

Her heart has suffered too much strife, but the smallest black lace ribbon still holds it together. The weight of her despair is too much for the lacey ribbon to handle. It threatens to unravel, leaving her heart in pieces on the floor, but a heavily tattooed hand lies atop the black-ribboned heart, vowing to protect it from further harm.

I've drawn him so many times in the past few days that I recognize him instantly. Epiales stands beside her, the ends of his curly black hair brushing against her shoulder as he leans forward and cups his hand over her tattered heart.

But something is different this time.

A light purple string connects Epiales and Saffron. It's not a part of her ruinous heart, but it comes from within her. A part of her aura leaves the shield around her body and goes to him. The lavender string coils around his tall, lean build, protecting him the same way he protects her heart. The strand of purple leaving Saffron enters his heart, stitching his soul back together.

My drawing shows it all. The open cavity where his heart is located, and the empty spot that fills with her energy. Her humanity.

He stares down at her with unadulterated love, but she only looks at her tattered heart with the tiniest smile, daring to bloom for the first time in years.

"She hasn't smiled since her friend, Hattie, passed away," Hades says as he stares at her almost-smile in the drawing. It brings tears to his eyes, but a real smile, too. "I never thought I'd see it again. Even the tiniest version of it."

"Do you believe he is her prophesied heart?"

Everyone who knows where Saffron is, and who she is with, believe he is Saffron's destined heart. The one prophesied to die twice and incite the war. Whoever kills Saffron's heart will tilt the war in their opponent's favor, and now everyone fears killing the once exiled god of nightmares.

"I love Hermes dearly," he says. "But I was there when Saffron executed Epiales, and she never loved Hermes the way she loved Epiales. There was a moment when I thought she would not marry Hermes. Not because she didn't love him, but because she didn't love him enough."

Hades leads us away from the canvases and we sit on the loveseat pressed against the far left corner. From this vantage point, we can see every drawing I have created in the days since he and the oracles started training me. In almost all of them, Saffron almost smiles. It never comes to fruition, but it's close.

"I'm sure you are familiar with the story of how Saffron freed the humans from enslavement."

"Yeah, I am."

It is one of the most popular stories in history. Saffron

was still a Demi-god when the final Titanomachy war ended, and the gods captured everyone who worked with the already-executed Kronos. The gods feared placing all the traitors into Tartarus because Epiales, Kronos, and many other titans had already escaped from that imprisonment, and it was the best way to capture an immortal.

Zeus knew the titans and traitorous gods had to die, and Saffron was the only one with the abilities to end their lives.

For an infinitesimal moment, the halfling Saffron had all the power. She orchestrated her plan from the moment she knew how the war would end, and it was almost perfect. Saffron agreed to kill every traitor as long as all gods swore an oath to the River Styx that they would free their slaves and never again try to control the humans.

The plan was deemed as perfect in every history book, but I know the truth now. It was a nearly perfect plan, except for Saffron's love for Epiales. Zeus agreed to the plan as long as when he spoke the oath, Epiales's execution followed. The act of killing Epiales killed her humanity, too, and she died.

Only to be reborn as a goddess.

No history textbooks spoke about Epiales, except that he was one of the many gods who fought with Kronos. They never spoke about his love for Saffron, or hers for him. I never knew that Epiales had a hand in freeing Saffron from the effects of Eros's arrow when Kronos stabbed her. It wasn't until my life was interwoven with the gods that I learned the multi-layered, complicated truth about Epiales and Saffron.

Hades says. "She never wanted to kill him, but she had to make a choice. Humanity's freedom or Epiales's life. Even if she chose Epiales, Zeus would have sent Epiales back to Tartarus, and I could not free him from Zeus's constant scrutiny. And that was a fate Epiales deemed worse than death."

"Saffron saved humanity instead of him," Hades continues. "To save her friends, Hattie, Diam, and Zig, over Epiales, but the decision destroyed a part of her. Her heart gave out as soon as she killed him, and I held her in my arms and watched as she came back as a goddess. She pretended she was alright after his death, but there was a small part of her that did not return for many, many years. Hermes refused to talk about Epiales, insisting she forget he existed like the world eventually would, but she couldn't. Nobody forgets their first love, even if they're dead and gone."

I stare at the newest drawing of Epiales and Saffron, and I admit it aloud for the first time. "They both are vital to the end of the war, but there's something I'm missing, and I don't know what it is. It all starts with Saffron on this island, and I know that once we free her and Epiales from Ogygia, then the true war begins. That's when Styx comes out of hiding and the bloodbath begins, but there's more. So much more that I haven't unlocked yet, and so much of it surrounds him."

Hades leans forward, and when he kisses the top of my head, for a moment, it feels like my father is here. He always gave comforting kisses on the top of my head when I was most anxious. Hades even smells like him right now, like nutmeg and a crackling fireplace.

I tilt my head up and find Hades's knowing eyes. "He would be proud of you. It may not be today that you find the truth, but you will find it. You are strong, and you are resilient."

I know I should never underestimate the power of a

god, but his ability to speak to my father baffles me. Hades can make me feel like my father is here in the room with us, speaking through Hades, and it is the greatest gift I could ever receive.

"When this is all over, can I see them? Just for a little?"

Even as I ask aloud, I know there is something wrong with it. Like this is one of the many things I am still not privy to. I know I will never see them again, but it makes little sense. Of course, I will see them again, either through death or a visit to the Underworld.

But Hades nods his head. "Of course, but for now, let's go eat. Whatever is cooking downstairs smells delightful."

"There is the seer and the savior," Aashritha says the following day.

As she says the words, I see Saffron and I as clear as day.

We stand at a distance from the other oracles and myself, but we are side-by-side in armor I have never seen before. I clutch my feather necklace while she points an all-white sword toward our enemies. Gold blood mars her cheeks and neck.

But I'm unscathed.

Instead, little white flecks fall from the sky and land in my braided hair and shoulders. It's not snow, but I do not know what they are as they dance down on my body, showering me with ominous approval.

"There is the hero and the heart," the emerald oracle says next.

Beside me, a mess of curly black hair materializes.

Blood matted part of it, but I cannot distinguish the color until his pale forehead forms. Then, I see the mesh of red and gold blood that falls down on him like rain. I recognize the male by his hair, but before he can truly form and cement himself as a figurehead in the prophecy, a loud clatter pulls Hades's hands from mine.

The oracles disintegrate.

And the noise forces me back into the real world.

Lowell lays, stomach down, on the floor a few feet away from the opened door. A broken glass of white wine scatters across the room, staining the ground. Lowell still holds the charcuterie board he brought upstairs, but broken glass covers it and makes it inedible.

Atalanta and Achilles are on either side of him, their weapons pointing at his back. Atalanta snarls at Lowell, and I know she's trying to speak, but she cannot in this form. Her grumbles are incomprehensible to everyone but Achilles, whose already grotesque face worsens with rage. He presses the tip of his sword into Lowell's back, threatening to tear skin.

Lowell looks up at me from his place on the floor, his face in a deep grimace. "I'm sorry. I know I'm not supposed to interrupt, but I've missed you, H. Thought I'd bring us something to eat and drink so we could catch up."

"Lower your weapons," I tell Achilles and Atalanta.

Achilles listens.

Atalanta does not.

I crouch down to where Lowell lays in a puddle of white wine, and I extend my hand. I can only imagine how lonely he must be in a home with only strangers, except for me, and I've been too busy for him. Our roles have reversed in our crammed apartment since we left a few weeks ago. Now, I am the one who is letting him become a shell of his former self, and guilt worms its way through me.

Lowell takes my hand, even though Atalanta grunts with disapproval.

Hades lets out a heavy breath that almost resembles a laugh. "Lower your weapon and go back to your post. The glass shards won't harm her."

Atalanta doesn't want to, but she obeys. She and Achilles resume their post at the doors, while I help Lowell to his feet. He brushes off pieces of sliced cheese as Hades leaves the room in search of a trash bag and some cleaning supplies.

Lowell nervously smiles. "Sorry, H." The ground shakes underneath hurried feet, and Lowell's eyes widen with fear. "Oh no, he told me not to come in."

A second later, Argus stands at an intimidating height and glowers at Lowell. "I told you not to disrupt her, then you sneak in?" He takes a few steps into the room. "Are you out of your little, pea-brained mind?"

Lowell flinches. "Sorry, Argie."

"Don't call me that. I keep telling you, I don't like it." Argus heavily enunciates every syllable. "Let's go."

Argus places an arm on Lowell's arm, and I quickly say. "After dinner, we will hang out. I promise."

Argus drags Lowell out of the room as Lowell yells. "I can't wait! I'll make another charcuterie board!"

The door slams shut behind Lowell.

My eyes drift to the artwork Lowell interrupted, where I was going to learn more than I ever had before. The contributors to this war, who need to live and play out their journey so we can win against Styx, were right in my grasp before Lowell came in and accidentally intercepted.

I close my eyes and beg for Aashritha. I need her to

come back and tell me the rest of the people in the prophecy. Before his interruption, I was going to learn who both the heart and the hero were, and I know more faces were going to unearth. Aashritha needs to come back, so I can go back to that vision.

So, I can save the world.

I stay in the loneliness of my mind for too long, and the oracles do not come for me. They do not guide me back to the vision that can tell me everything. Lowell didn't mean to, but I'm so mad at him right now. The weight of my role as the oracle places on my chest almost lessened. I was about to feel victorious, and then I was shot down.

I understand Icarus, the human male from ancient tales who flew into the sun, a bit more now. He only wanted to go higher, reach great lengths, but he failed. Before he could reach the sun and all its splendor, the heat shot down him down, and he died. I understand now because I wanted to reach for my dream, and in a clatter of broken wine, my dream went into a blaze.

"Oracle," comes the deepest voice I have ever heard. Argus stands in the doorway with a hesitant stance. "May I ask a favor of you?"

"Depends on the favor."

He takes a step into the room, and most of his eyes drift to the map of Ogygia. "I know King Zeus forbade you from giving the map to the huntresses, but they need it to free Lady Saffron, and I miss my friend." He stands up straighter, even as his voice wobbles with uncertainty. "I will take the consequence he gives me, but I would like to take the artwork to the huntresses and help them find Lady Saffron. She made me promise to protect you, but you have an army at your disposal while she is all alone. So, I would like your permission before going after her."

Many immortals are hailed for their beauty, but not Argus. I am one of many who can't look at him for too long without diverting their gaze. I hate that I am afraid of him, but my admittance does not change the fact that Argus, who towers over me with a thousand eyeballs scattered across his flesh, is a terrifying sight.

Throughout history, Argus has been a bodyguard to many notable immortals. Most famously, eons ago, he guarded Hera until Hermes killed him. When Saffron needed a guard, Hades brought Argus back to life to serve one final goddess. His diligence to Hera when in her service was commendable; yet, his unwavering loyalty to Saffron is more than his duty. He called her his friend, and I doubt many give him the chance to be their friend with his appearance. It's a terrible truth, but it's a truth all the same.

"He wants to find Ogygia first," I admit.

"He wants glory, but all I want is Lady Saffron's safe return. I'll let the history books call him the hero, and I'll stay where I belong in the background. As long as I can bring her home safely, then I am happy."

"Zeus wants to kill Epiales, and if you take that from him, he might kill you."

Argus's mouth forms a deep frown. "Please close your eyes, Oracle. You can say I stole it without your knowledge."

A small part of me wants to make him reconsider, but that is the cowardly side of me trying to win every argument. So, I close my eyes. His footsteps are quieter than usual, but they still shake the surrounding floor. But I never open my eyes until Atalanta makes a grunting noise.

When I take in the room, Argus is gone, and so is the drawing.

Hades walks into the room a moment later with a trash bag in one hand and a broom in the other. "I just saw Argus leave."

"Hm, I didn't see him," I lie.

Hades kneels to the floor and drops the biggest shard of glass into the trash bag. "Now that you mention it, I don't think I saw him either. My memory isn't what it used to be."

I smile down at Hades, then join him on the floor to clean Lowell's mess.

TWENTY-ONE

SAFFRON

I should let him run, far away from me, with every bit of heat, frustration, desire, and hatred that he brings. He is a human now, and if he runs into unchartered territory in the belly of the woods, he could very well die. If he dies, then so do Styx's plans and any hope she has of conquering this world.

So why am I running after him?

Why do I care what happens?

Epiales quickly cuts through trees and jumps over branches at a speed rivaling mine. It doesn't take long for me to lose his trail, but I do not leave the surprisingly expansive woods. I should give up and run in the opposite direction. Every rational thought in my mind is telling me to return to the warmth of the beach, but I don't stop searching for the man who journeys through a possibly dangerous area, without anyway to defend himself.

He was a god for too long, and he relied on those powers more than his natural strength. If he comes across a creature, or he believes he can break through a tree stump without stopping, then he can seriously hurt himself. I should let him die, but my heart cannot allow this, even when my head is praying for this turmoil to end.

When I hid in here, I stayed in the same spot, and I hadn't heard a single movement; however, it would be naïve of me to believe that means nothing lives inside of these woods. There could be bears, doubling me in height, with their claws embedding themselves in Epiales's chest as I search aimlessly for him.

The thought makes me run faster.

I leap over fallen tree trunks, evading branches poking out in every direction, while my eyes scour for the six-foot-one man fleeing into danger because of his fear of mortality. I should've told him earlier that he was human. When we were discussing the stars in the sky, when he was so calm, that's when I should have told him. Or when we spoke about the siblings who ride their chariots in the sky, but I didn't.

Instead, I let him find out at the most inopportune time, and the truth of just how short his second chance at life is becoming entirely too clear.

In the far distance, I can make out a mop of curly, black hair, and the woods echo my relief. I run to where he leans against a tree, with his hands pressed against his hips. He breathes heavily, with so much sweat on his brow that his hair sticks against his forehead. This is the first time he hasn't been able to run miles without losing his breath, and it's further proof that he is no longer the same god I killed eighty-eight years ago.

He's human.

"How?"

"I don't know," I admit.

He doesn't flinch away when I walk towards him, which I take as a good sign, but I do not get too close, just in case. Instead, I lean against the tree next to the one he heaves against. I wait until his breathing regulates to continue.

"You're the first person I've ever brought back to life, so I don't know how it works."

"Did you know what I was before I bled?" There is hesitance in his voice as he asks this question, clearly afraid of the answer.

I give into his fear when I nod my head. "Yes, I knew, and I'm sorry I didn't tell you. You shouldn't have had to find out that way."

There's a long silence that follows this revelation until he finally asks. "Care to tell me a story, my queen?"

"It's going to be a messy story. I'm not really sure what happened."

"I have some time," he attempts to joke about his circumstance, but it doesn't land.

He lifts his head, and our eyes meet across the small space separating us. His eyes, the bright shade of silver, cannot conceal his emotions from me. He opens a chasm of fear and vulnerability, and while I shouldn't, the expression reminds me I am not the only one who suffers right now. He, just like me, is suffocating with the loneliness of the island, and the fear of what mortality brings. I never feared death, even when I was human, until Zig died. Now, I understand how Epiales looks at me, more than I wished.

I look away from him. "It was the strangest feeling, resurrecting you. You were once nothing but bones, unable to be brought back. But then our memories together started playing in my head. I could see everything we experienced together. The beautiful, the catastrophic, the devastating; I could see it all. I felt every bit of my former naivety and dependency, which I haven't felt since I was a human. When I raised my hands and started re-assembling your bones, those mundane feelings grew until I felt it leave my body."

"Your humanity left your body?" he asks.

"I think so. It's hard to explain, but it was like my humanity was dormant inside of me, waiting to come back to life, and you were *right there*. You were one of the few people who only knew me as a human, and that part of me has always belonged to you." The laugh that escapes my lips is a sorrowful sound, devoid of humor. "When I was a human, the love I had for you was unhealthy, but so raw, and all those feelings rushed back with those memories. I saw a chance to save you, and the part of me that loved you the most, my human side, went to you. It was a strand of color, this light shade of purple. It left my chest and went right into yours. Like I was-"

"Giving me a piece of your heart," Epiales finishes my thought.

"Yeah. I gave you my humanity so you could live another day. I don't know how I could do it, but I know I couldn't again. You're the one and only person I will bring back to life. You took all that I could give."

He stares at me, at my chest, which no longer has any lingering humanity, and he whispers. "You gave me a piece of your heart."

Is that what it was? Did a fragment of my heart transfer to him?

My heart, that's what starts the entire war. The heart of the savior must die twice to start the war, and if I truly gave him a piece of my heart, then that means...I don't want to say the words out loud. To actualize them. I just got him back, but if he is the prophesied heart, then that means he dies again.

Styx's words when she commanded me to resurrect Epiales surges back. *"Return him to our world, so that my prophecy may come true. Let my war begin with his resurrection."*

Epiales stands in front of me, cupping my face with both his hands. He smiles at me as he drags my eyes back to his, but I can't return the favor. He might die all over again, and Styx did this on purpose. Forced me to see him again. Left us on an island together, so I remember every explosive moment we've shared.

"What's the matter?" he asks, and his voice is so tender, my heart molds to the sound.

You're going to die again, are the words I should say.

But haven't I suffered enough death? I run into his arms and wrap mine around his waist. He quickly hugs me back, encircling me in his warmth. I know I should tell him about the prophecy. I shouldn't wait to tell him the truth until he figures it out. He deserves the truth, but in his arms, I must admit, nobody has hugged me without an ulterior motive in a long time.

So many gods and humans fear me now, and the one person I expected to always provide me with comfort chose his lies over me. Epiales deserves the truth, and I will tell him, but after I get a little more warmth from his touch. Because…

"I've missed you."

His lips are soft against the top of my head. "Those words are my waking dream come true, my queen. I've missed you so much."

Craning my neck up, he leans his head down until our lips are a breath away from one another. "I've missed you every day since I killed you. Until I had to force myself to forget you. When I married Hermes, I felt like I was cheating on him for missing you, but the feeling wouldn't subside. I buried it until the grief of others outweighed yours, but then an oracle drew you, and all those feelings rushed back. I have missed your stories and your smile and your warmth for eighty-eight years, and even if we only have-"

He doesn't let the rest of the sentence leave my lips as he claims my lips. I shouldn't, but I am quick to respond to the kiss, matching the speed of his mouth as he lowers me onto the sandy ground.

His tongue is teasing, sliding across my bottom lip, and I invitingly open my mouth for more of him. He is fire, and even if I burn, I need more. My hands scour every inch of his body as he slips his tongue into my mouth, groaning upon contact. My fingers slide down his abs, scouring over the grooves and dips of his body, before they reach the hem of his shorts.

His hands are on my hips, but as I slowly lower his shorts, his hands ignite hot lava wherever they touch. He slides up my stomach, eliciting a moan from my muffled lips, while his hands move towards the straps of my dress. His lips dip to the newly revealed flesh as I run a hand through his curly locks.

I want more. To absorb myself in him, but a sound stops us.

The crunch of a branch pulls me away from Epiales, and I stand in front of him defensively. My previous relaxed state vanishes as a creature emerges from the woods. I expect a wolf, its carnivorous canines glinting in the moonlight, or a bear with claws that are ready to cut through Epiales's stomach, but the tiniest bunny hops out from behind a tree and stares quizzically at the two of us.

Epiales chuckles. "Let's go back to camp."

Two days slip by with languid kisses, unfolding stories, and a sense of happiness I haven't experienced in years. I should search for an escape, but I continuously slip into his arms. Just a little longer, I tell myself. Let me be happy here a little while longer.

We fall into a routine.

Each morning, he wakes me with his lips careening down the length of my neck, and we fall into each other's embrace. Then, I search for food for us as he attempts to fish. Attempt is the key term. By the time I return around lunchtime with a rabbit, fox, or hawk, and a bundle of berries, I find him screaming at the ocean for its obstinance.

His anger quickly manifests into humor as we laugh at his attempts. We laugh further every time I try to make the fire, then fail, and Epiales has to build it. I haven't laughed in years, but now I cannot stop myself. Years' worth of pent-up amusement compounded until Epiales ruptured it, and I smile.

Gods, I have missed smiling.

Not the false smiles I pretended for a while. A real, genuine smile that warms the center of my chest and reminds me that this world isn't so dark. As the sun shines, we focus on our growing harmony. The first time he was alive, we were friends and lovers amid strife. There wasn't time for happy moments, and if we were fortunate enough to grasp it, it slipped like sand from our fingers.

So, in the daytime, we steal back our happiness. We

laugh and we sing, and we dance without steps. We eat, throw sand at each other, and swim in the ocean. There's limited freedom here. Hecate's gilded cage shimmers in the ocean, reminding us we cannot journey too far, but there's an abundance of warmth. I feel like a kid again, giggling when a fish caresses my leg but scurries away from Epiales in fright.

But in the nighttime, we ask the questions that we fear in the light.

Epiales lays his head on one of his arms, but the other drapes over my waist. I rest my head on his shoulder, comforted by the rhythmic thumps of his heartbeat. The multitude of stars dance above us, their calm, alabaster light shimmering down on our flesh. The stars do not have powers, but it feels like they absolve the burns the sun gives us, and take away the tension the day brought upon us.

We're most calm when night has fallen, and the stars are our friends.

"May I ask about him?"

I do not need to ask who he wants to learn more about. No matter our divorce, my name is synonymous with Hermes's. He has been a fixture in my life for almost its entirety, and although I am no longer his wife, we are still woven into one another's life strings.

I haven't wanted to talk about Hermes because the memory of him comes with a horde of lies. Secrets he expertly hides behind a quickly spoken lie and a charming smile. We were never perfect, but I thought he'd keep his promise never to lie to me. He can trick the rest of the world, but not his wife. That was the deal when I forgave him for deceiving me about my parentage.

And he lied.

Again.

I steady my mind with the calm thump, thump, thump of Epiales's heart. I forgot how much I centered my breathing on this sound when I was a human. It is a reminder that no matter how much the world falls around you, you're still alive. Your heart still beats.

"I loved him. Truly loved him. It's hard to describe it, but being with Hermes felt like jumping into a safety net. I could risk it all and know I'd land safely. When I was a human and a new goddess, I took comfort in knowing he would do anything to protect me. It's the main reason I fell in love with him. His hero complex made me feel good, but then you died and Ar-"

I don't finish my sentence. There are many truths I can divulge to Epiales, but some words clog my throat, unable to come out. He waits for me to finish, but I cannot talk about him. Not when there are too many questions that follow him, where answers scatter away before I can catch them.

I clear my throat and divert back to Hermes. "Then I grew stronger, and I didn't need him to always protect me. He got worse, then. Or maybe he was always that protective, and I just stopped liking it. He would interrupt every conversation I had with Hera and Zeus, like they would strike me down if I said the wrong words. He'd insist on going to Poseidon's castle with me every time because of what happened with Kronos and Eros's arrows. The other gods would praise him for being such an attentive husband, but I found his need to protect me suffocating. It felt like another prison, but this one kept getting smaller, and I didn't have the key. I thought because I loved him, and I knew he loved me, that it would be alright."

"Why did it bother you so much? His need to protect you."

217

"The simple answer is that I'm stronger than him. Continuously protecting me made little sense. I didn't need it, and he didn't trust me when I said that I didn't need it."

I'm stronger than them all. He kept insisting on protecting me from Hera, Zeus, and Kronos's ghost like I was still that breakable human he saved from Ares long ago, but I shed that skin and got plated armor. Still, he looked at me and saw the girl in the arena, and nothing I could do would break that image from him.

"The complicated answer is, I knew he wasn't being overly protective of me. Not fully. Every time he wanted to save me from something, it was because he wanted something, too. He would come and interrupt my conversations with Zeus and Hera so they'd dote on him, and Zeus would see that Hermes kept the promise they made when I was a newborn. Everything he said was a carefully orchestrated lie or manipulation, and I loathed it. The constant games he always had to play. I loved him, but around others when he started his trickery, I wanted to run."

Long ago, Zeus promised Hermes a spot on Mt. Olympus and my hand in marriage if he protected me. Hermes was one of the few gods who knew about my existence, but more than that, he wanted to become an Olympian. He believed he deserved it. And he does. Hermes is powerful, quick, wise, and loyal. He would be an exemplary Olympian, but he tried to get it through trickery. Hermes always reminds Zeus that he protected me when I was human, and on some instinctual level, now deserves to be an Olympian.

"My fight against Kronos was a sore wound." I look at Epiales. "*Your death* was a sore wound Hermes picked at every time he came down to Poseidon's castle with me. He always reminded me he saved me from you. Hermes wasn't trying to be malicious. I think he was trying to remind me of his version of our good times, but it just further divided us."

Epiales looks away from me.

"Poseidon noticed and started saying my trips down to his castle were 'girl's night.' He would even invite Hattie, even though he didn't like how easily she could hurt him. Hermes kept insisting it couldn't be girl's night because Poseidon wasn't a girl, but Poseidon didn't like that. Once, Hermes came down to the underwater castle without Poseidon's permission, and he dumped a squid on top of Hermes's head. By the time Hermes fled, ink covered almost his entire body."

I softly laugh at the memory now, but the reason behind the story disintegrates the humor. Those nights with Hermes at Poseidon's castle were the start of our fall.

"I could get over the fact that I hated his need to save me from danger, because I loved him. And I knew his need to save me was his form of telling me how much he loved me, too. But it wasn't enough to stop him from lying. And it wasn't enough to stop me from distancing myself from him. We tried, and I loved him dearly, but it wasn't enough."

"Were you happy with him? That's the real question, my queen. Love and happiness are not always interchangeable."

"I was in the beginning." I stared at the sky, like Hermes could somehow eavesdrop on the conversation. "But we should have never married. Adopting Jamila made our lives a little better, but we were friends who wore wedding rings and played pretend. The love started to die with my humanity. For both of us."

Those last three words are the hardest to say aloud. It

wasn't just him who drifted away with my changing personality. I drifted, too. We were both at fault for our marriage faltering. He broke a marriage made of cracked ice, but both of us held chisels. Both of us created those cracks, making it so easy for him to break it.

"He did save you from me," Epiales whispers, ashamed. His hand tightens around my waist, but he won't look at me. "I regret much in my life, but I kept thinking I was making the right decisions until the end. Until I saw what Kronos did to you. You do not belong with a male who does not make you feel the way you deserve, but he did save you from me. When I realized I was destroying you, he helped me bring you back. Hermes has many faults, but so do I, and it started when I met Kronos."

"What do you regret most?"

"Glasswing," he doesn't hesitate. "I hate what Kronos did to you, and that I aided him in his cause until that moment, but Glasswing was my plan. I visited her in her nightmares, and I told her to switch sides. Morpheus controlled many of the humans at Kronos's disposal, but I saw two people. You and Glasswing."

An infinitesimal part of myself feels jealousy that our moments in our dream world were not unique. That he shared them with Glasswing, who grew up beside me as my shower mate in the prisons. She was the most beautiful human I have ever seen, still to this day, but her time in the prisons rotted her from the inside. Her time with Psyche as her cruel master turned that rot into insanity, and Epiales capitalized on it.

"Please don't pull away," Epiales begs, and I should, but I don't.

I stay and I listen.

"I told her what Kronos wanted me to say, but I

stopped going to her nightmares a few weeks before I stopped our dream world. Tartarus made me too weak, so Morpheus took over in Glasswing's mind. He shattered what remained, and when I watched you both fall into the River Styx…"

He shakes his head as guilt consumes him.

"What did Morpheus tell her?"

"I don't know," he admits. "But if I was strong enough, she may not have died like that. I was told to go into the dreams of one of your cellmates, and I chose her. If I chose another, someone mentally stronger, then Glasswing might not have become a victim to the River Styx. It's a fate nobody deserves, and my actions led her there."

"I killed Hattie."

I have never spoken the words out loud before, and when I do, my heart ruptures. He holds me, not asking questions until the weight of my truth subsides. It was the worst day of my life, realizing what I had to do, and every day I regretted it. I love having Jamila as my daughter, but I stare at her, and I see Hattie's final moments. It's a twist of a blade, loving someone and also hating their face because of everything it symbolizes.

Tears slide down my face. "That's my biggest regret."

"Hattie was your friend, right?"

"My best friend, yeah." I close my eyes, reverberating myself back to that fateful day when she was shivering in her bed, and I tremble. "After the war with you, I promised myself I would not kill another human or an Olympian, unless there were no other options. I would not kill some-body that had no chance of defending themselves, but then time changed me. Zig had a heart attack, and I couldn't start his heart again. He died, and I felt so weak because I couldn't save him."

"That wasn't-" Epiales interjects, but I interrupt him.

"Then a doctor diagnosed Diam with colon cancer when he was in his late sixties. I am the Goddess of Bones. I can heal or break anything, but I can't control a colon. Apollo kept healing it, but Death had a time for Diam, and it came regardless of Apollo and my powers. He died at seventy, and that sense of helplessness was drowning me. Then came Hattie's dementia."

Tears build up in my eyes as I think back to a haggard, decrepit Hattie. A small part of my heart shriveled away with each forgetful look that passed over her dark eyes. I can still feel my chest searing with agony when I think of the diminished version of her.

"She lived with me so I could heal her broken bones every time that she fell, but I couldn't fix her brain. Her dementia kept worsening to where she couldn't recognize Jamila, and every day I had to remind her until she forgot who I was. One Sunday, she had a moment of clarity and looked at me with tears in her eyes. Hattie begged me to kill her quickly because this disease was eating her brain. She hated it because it kept making her forget who Diam and I were. She couldn't remember her children. I didn't want to kill her. She was my best friend. More of a sister to me than any goddess who I share a father with, but she just wanted to die, and I would do anything for her if she asked, so-"

"You ended her suffering so she and Diam could be together again," Epiales finishes my sentence.

"Since she was in her nineties and suffering with dementia, there was no autopsy, but anybody that checked would've seen a bone embedded in her heart. The day I killed her was the worst of my life, and I haven't been the same since. I became hardened, a shell of the happy woman I once was, and everybody began distancing themselves from me. I changed, as if my heart left with Hattie, and nobody liked the change. It's as if they could sense I was a monster who killed her own best friend, even though I told no one what I had done."

"My queen, you're not a monster." With ginger care, Epiales lifts my chin until my teary gaze meets his soft smile. "You changed; you're right about that. But nobody is meant to stay the same their entire life. They learn from their circumstances, and they adapt. You suffered loss after loss without truly understanding the weight of grief, and you adapted. And yes, you are different, but you still hold all the qualities that made me fall in love with you. Your power, your compassion, your selflessness. It's all still there."

He points at my chest and smiles.

"You killed her to save her from an even worse fate, and you risked your own heart so hers could reunite with her soulmate's. That doesn't make you a monster, my beautiful Saffron. That makes you a hero to the person you loved most."

"Why do you have to be you?" I whisper softly, and he responds with a soft kiss on my lips.

Hermes is the obvious choice.

He is a beloved god amongst the Olympians, and he loves me so much. I know that once I'm off this island, he will try to get back together. I could fall back into that safety net, but Epiales brings a part of me alive again. My humanity, which dreamed of peace and happiness, now lives in him. It's etched into his soul, giving me a sliver of my former happiness. I need the smiles it elicits. The warmth he emanates. I know I should avoid him because of the prophecy surrounding his death and his villainous past that nobody else will forgive.

I should fall in love with another immortal, and although one face burns through my mind, right now, I need Epiales. The Fates gave him back to me, and I don't want to lose him yet. They gave me a reincarnated human, who was once a monster, but now holds my heart gingerly in his protective hands for as long as it beats.

"Epiales, I need to tell you something."

He places another delicate kiss on my lips. "I love your stories." He kisses me again. "Tell me everything."

I pull away from his lips so I can get a clearer look at him, and I know he knows something. He has waited for me to divulge the truth, lingering on my tongue. The other shoe he's been waiting to drop since discovering his humanity. There is an absence of fear on his face, but then I begin my story about the prophecies, and my belief that he is my destined heart predicted to die again. He leans down and kisses my cheeks every time I cry, but he doesn't ask questions. Not until I finish explaining everything.

Only then, he asks. "Are you certain it's me?"

"No, but the prophecy says that my heart already died, was brought back, and will die again. Nobody else fits that description except you. I loved you, then you died, and when I brought you back to life, I fell in love with you again. Styx made me bring you back just to love you again and watch you die, so her war can begin. I don't under-stand why your death starts it, or how it will make Styx win the war, but-"

He grabs both sides of my face and pulls me into a searing kiss. He steals the words from my lungs, and I gladly let him. I climb on top of him, opening my mouth to invite more of him inside. Electricity scatters around my body, sending every hair on my arms to attention. His tongue delves inside, swirling alongside mine, and peace is just within reach.

I can almost grab it.

He pulls away from me, but he keeps me against his body. "You said I could die any day?" I nod my head. "Then let's make every moment last like it's my last." He slides his hands underneath my shirt, exploring my flesh as he layers kisses on my face. "I don't care if I am not your destined third love, or that tomorrow is my last day in this world. I got another chance with you, where I am not the villain and you are not the hero meant to slay me. We are exactly who we want to be, and I will take every second the Fates give me with you in my arms. Even if I share you with all your great loves. If I get you right here and now, then I'm the luckiest male alive."

"I love you."

"And I love you, my queen."

He slams his lips into mine, and I claim momentary euphoria.

TWENTY-TWO

LAMB

Before Ogygia, there were seventeen huntresses riding through the woods with Artemis. We were a sisterhood, following an oath we made to dutifully follow Artemis for as long as the Fates allowed us to live. Then, Ogygia happened, and when I woke up after nearly dying, war reduced my sisters to mangled corpses.

In the days that followed my freedom, I fell into a trance of despondency. Many huntresses have died either a traitor or an unsuspecting casualty in the gods' games for a crown. Before I had the chance to truly mourn the losses of Sika and the others, or wallow in the rage of Frigate and Akita's deceit, more huntresses fell like bloodied raindrops.

Now, as we stand around an army of monsters, only five of us remain.

Six, if we count Jamila.

A small piece of my heart fell with each dead huntress, both traitorous and loyal, for there is no greater loss than a

227

sister. Every swipe of my new sword towards the Colchian Dragon was my promise to the fallen huntress. I will never forget them. They are my sisters from the moment they took the oath to serve Artemis until the moment I die. Even the traitors like Frigate and Akita, whose sanity withered far before their souls. I did not see it until it was too late.

I fight for all of us who have ridden beside Artemis. My sisters who have died and stained the ground we fight on. I kill the Colchian Dragon, dragging my blade across his neck until his head falls to the ground. It is the closest I will ever get to closure for all the lives I have lost.

Because I killed the Colchian Dragon so fast, nobody else died.

The decimation of the surrounding monsters does not ease any thoughts of future goodwill. It is a stark reminder that no matter how valiantly we fight, Styx will continue to send every monster at her disposal. Until every huntress falls or Saffron disintegrates Styx. Vee claps my back with praise for decapitating the Colchian Dragon, while Dýnami quickly creates a fire. She jokes about the tastiness of dragon meat, which makes Shikari and June laugh. Iris portals the remaining corpses away, and she smiles as she places a tender kiss on the top of Artemis's head.

Only Jamila mirrors my emotions as she asks. "Wasn't Atlas guiding all these monsters to us? Where is he?"

"Quivering in his overused boots," Dýnami jokes.

But this time, Shikari and June do not join in on the laughter.

Our victory is short-lived. We peruse the surrounding trees, searching for hidden forms within the shadows of the woods. Dýnami's desire to try dragon meat has disintegrated, along with the laughter and the momentary smiles.

I raise my sword, still sticky with the dragon's blood, and I point towards a section of the woods.

"He wanted us tired and weak," Iris whispers.

"And with our guards down," Artemis continues.

"So when he strikes with the rest of the monsters," I say.

"With Typhon," Shikari adds with a wobbly voice, as she remembers our past, facing him in the Labyrinth.

"We would all die," Vee finishes the statement.

The trees ruffle to my right, and Shikari shoots an arrow in the direction. Her red crossbow arrows slash through the air, but we never hear the plunk of the weapon meeting flesh. Three of Vee's yellow throwing knives soar in the opposite direction of Shikari's arrows, crossing in a diagonal line down the length of trees.

Two knives pierce a neighboring tree, but the third elicits a roar of painful rage, confirming our harrowing theory. Our night has only just begun its tyrannical destruction. The only fact that consoles me now, as a monster thrashes in the woods in its march towards us, is that I know Typhon isn't among them. His height reaches the skies; if he were here, we would know.

And we'd already be dead.

Our next assailant barrels out of the trees. The creature has muscles protruding out of his biceps, almost unnaturally so, but nothing is as prominent as the twin horns sitting on either side of his bull-shaped skull. He rips Vee's throwing knife out of his shoulder as a mixture of monster and human blood spills down the expanse of his massive human torso.

The Minotaur, who looms over us at nearly fifteen feet, throws the knife back at its owner with unrivaled speed. Artemis tackles Vee to the ground a moment before the knife slices the air where her head previously was. Vee muffles a scream as her shoulder dislocates from the fall, but our opponent does not give time to dwell on pain.

He lets out a mighty roar as his cloven hoofs stomp onto the ground. Pit-less, black eyes peruse the scene as we point our weapons at him, and he decides his desired target will be Jamila. He kicks back his foot once, twice, and charges.

Iris and I lock eyes, and then we sprint towards the beast.

My stride is slower than both Iris and the Minotaur, so she catches him first. She spins her body as she nears him, her staff catching every color from the sunset, as she slams her weapon against one kneecap. Just as the Minotaur is about to swipe a claw across Iris's face, I reach them. I raise my sword high, and I slam it hard onto one of his hooves. Iris screams as his claws reach their intended mark, but he screams too as I pull my sword out and plunge it back in.

Jamila's arrows fly towards the Minotaur with perfect accuracy. They land in his skull, his neck, his chest, but they barely affect him. The Minotaur grunts each time an arrow slides into his flesh, but he plucks them out with as much ease as a splinter.

His clawed paw swoops down to where I stand, momentarily ignoring Iris, as she climbs up his back. I swing my sword at his fingers. A splash of blood crosses my face as I cut two fingers off. The remnants of his hand clasps around my waist, and he slams my back against the ground.

He knocks the breath out of me, but my agony is not complete. The beast still has a toy to play with. He raises me a few feet in the air, and he slams me back down. The pain scatters from the base of my head, where a concussion blots my vision, traveling from the base of my skull to my tailbone. It's a devastating warning that I cannot afford another hit of that caliber, or else I will join Willow and Sika earlier than intended.

Iris wraps her staff around his neck, and she pulls.

Hard.

The Minotaur can face over a dozen humans and emerge victorious, but he cannot defeat a goddess as strong as Iris. He falls backwards, just as Iris intended, but he takes me with him. My body propels backwards, still tight within his mutilated grasp. And this is it. I'm going to die. He can survive a seventeen-foot fall, but I cannot.

I embrace the pain that is about to come until a scream pierces the air. Artemis flies, a sword raised high in her hand, and she slices the Minotaur's hand clean off at the wrist. Artemis catches me, wrapping her arms around me, and we fall together. She takes the brunt of the pain, and I can hear her bones crack beneath my ear, but Artemis quickly gets back to her feet.

Holding a hand to me, Artemis says. "You promised not to leave me yet."

I take her hand. "How pathetic would it be to die at the hands of the Minotaur after being the first slayer of the Colchian Dragon?" I scoff, even though my lungs burn with the action. "I'm not leaving you just yet, Lady Artemis."

The hard *thud* of the Minotaur's body shakes the ground, and a group of birds flies out of the trees in fright. It's because of the birds that I deviate my attention away from the Minotaur, and I see a bustle of movement.

The great beast crumbles onto his knees, death once again coming for him. Iris stands on top of him, with her staff raised high in the air. The other huntresses surround the Minotaur, their weapons pointed towards him, and I know his death is imminent. It's the unknown force, waiting in the trees, that gathers my attention.

Artemis picks up her bow and places another arrow upon the string, her eyes locked on the same spot in the woods. Atlas is here, somewhere. I can feel his presence like a tick worming its way into my skin, but he's creating a show out of our destruction. He cowers and waits until the opportune time to shine the spotlight on him, and I refuse to let him feel so victorious.

The Minotaur squeals until Dýnami proudly holds his dismembered head for all of us to see. The creatures, who sit and wait in the woods, see her display too. It's a beacon to the others to come out of hiding and continue where the others left off. Over a hundred birds fly out of the trees, fleeing from the unavoidable massacre emerging from their home.

Arachne, the Chimera, a horde of one hundred humans, and Atlas run out of the woods with weapons unsheathed and murderous snarls.

Iris stares up at the sky, then shoots her gaze to Artemis before disappearing in an archway of color. As an army, five times the size of ours, rushes towards us, Artemis's face falls with the cry of betrayal. We do not have a chance at winning this battle, but we had a chance with two goddesses. Now, without Iris, the song of death plays a soft tune.

"I love you."

Artemis and I refuse to look at each other, but she hears me as clearly as I hear her murmur. "I love you, and I already miss you."

We let out battle cries as we run towards a battle we

cannot win. Artemis runs towards Dýnami, who fights Atlas with minimal success. I diverge towards Vee and Jamila, who are back-to-back as they fight a horde of humans. Shikari faces Arachne on her own, while June fights against the Chimera, and I want to help them all, but we are in sinking sand with no other destination but down.

I scream as I break through the group of humans. My sword tastes only death as I swing it again at one human, then another. They fall like dominos at my feet, but I do not slow down. Blood obscures my vision, as I cut off one human's head, then slice off another's leg, but I do not slow down. I become a bulldozer, destroying everyone in my path.

Then Vee screams.

She can only use one arm in a fight where she needs two. Her dislocated shoulder is still out of place. She is one of the most fearless huntresses, but now she lies on the floor by surrounding corpses, and I see the little girl that she recently outgrew. I am hundreds of years old, but she is barely an adult. She hasn't lived enough to die like this. Adonis hovers over her body with a sword, ready to impale her.

I ignore everything and everyone else, and my scream is feral as I plunge my sword into Adonis's back. I feel the moment I puncture his heart and life escapes his body. He collapses to the ground on top of Vee as I pull out my sword. Although he is immortal, he will not get up again. Aphrodite cast the same magic on him that Artemis gave every huntress. We will live forever unless deliberately killed.

I spit on his corpse right as pain blooms over my shoulder.

Vee yells my name, but I can scarcely hear her as the tip of a sword peeks out of my shoulder. The same shoulder I popped back into place the day before. It's been sore all day, but now it trashes with agony. The wielder pulls the blade back, and I twirl around and cut off the person's head. A mop of red hair falls onto the ground, but my blood is spilling down my body in fast rivulets. The concussion from the Minotaur continues to pound against my head, and I'm so gods-damned tired.

I just want to sleep.

Then Jamila screams, and I remember why I must stay awake.

I run to her, and I strike down three, maybe four, more humans before one can slit her throat. My movements are more sluggish, but I do not stop. I face a dozen humans, and I suffer their wrath with arrows in my stomach and cuts on my arms and legs. Each time I feel a new, sharp pain, I want sleep, but another huntress needing my help keeps me on my feet.

June bellows, and I whip my head around to witness the Chimera's mouth around her shoulder. In one fatal rip, he bites off her left arm. Blood spurts out of the wound, and I run-slash-stumble towards her. My own blood loss becomes more apparent with each passing minute, but I have to get to her.

She falls to the floor, and the Chimera chomps on her body part in front of her. His saliva drips onto her cheeks, neck, and shoulder, but she doesn't have the strength to move away. She bleeds out around the Chimera, and the beast opens his mouth once again. He leans into her as I reach them.

My movements aren't as clean as before, and I can barely hold up my gigantic sword, but I slice off his tail moments before his teeth sink into her face. The Chimera screeches and spins around to face me, discarding his soon-to-be dead prey.

He licks her blood off his mouth, then charges towards me.

A rainbow separates us, but it isn't Iris who materializes. It's Argus, the one-hundred eyed giant who faithfully guards Saffron. Iris reappears a moment later, and Argus pushes a piece of artwork against her chest. The Chimera's mouth is open wide as it reaches for me, but Argus grabs both sides with his hands.

With a feral scream, he rips the Chimera's jaw apart.

The beast scrambles away, but Argus charges forward.

Iris places her hand on mine, steering my gaze back to her. "I'm sorry it took me so long to come back. We struggled to find the location again."

"I thought you left us."

Iris shakes her head. "I would never leave you." Her eyes drift to where I know Artemis fights. "Any of you."

"We need to get June out of here."

We both run to where she lies on the ground, covered in her own blood.

Small clumps of muscle and skin still connect her left arm to her shoulder. Crimson red blood spills down her shoulder in endless streams, leaving June's normally tanned face white as snow. I fall beside her, picking up her head and placing it on my lap. Screams surround us, but June's eyes fill with so many tears as she stares up at me.

"I'm going to die, aren't I?"

"We…you're…it's…."

Gods, I can't even lie.

"I'll tell Sika you say hi," she can barely get the words out.

Iris takes one of June's hands, and she teleports them away. I do not ask where she takes June, but I pray to every god who listens that June survives. My legs rebel when I try to stand, but there are more who need my help. There are more monsters that must die.

I look around the space with further dismay. Argus drives his fist into the Chimera's chest, pulling out his heart, but there is still another monster. Arachne impales one of her spiked legs into Shikari's stomach. Her scream vibrates the floor, and I rush to her.

As I move, dragging my sword with my barely useful arm, I see Artemis still in a war against Atlas. They are evenly matched, meeting each movement with perfect precision, with no victor in sight. Jamila and Vee fight against the remaining humans, their numbers slowly but surely withering. But their movements are more languid.

None of us have much longer.

I bite back a scream when I reach Shikari and Arachne, when I lift my sword with both hands and slash it towards one of Arachne's legs. She sees my movement coming, and she lifts her leg a moment before I can cut it off.

Shikari staggers away, clutching her stomach. When she speaks, a bubble of blood comes out. "It's been an honor riding with you."

"See you in Elysium, my friend."

Shikari keeps one hand on her stomach, but the other grabs her crossbow. Neither can hold our weapons without a grimace of pain coloring their faces, but we raise them with the fragmented adrenaline we have left. Arachne takes a step towards us before Argus tackles her onto the ground. He roars with rage as he plucks off her legs the same way one would remove flower petals.

Iris returns once again, but she materializes in the puddle of humans fighting against Vee and Jamila. She doesn't fight alongside them, though. She grabs their arms, and she transports them away. Arachne lets out another squelch before Argus uses both hands to rip off her head.

He throws the decapitated remains behind him, then faces us with many eyes. "When I tell you to run, listen."

Argus has always been a daunting sight with his multitude of eyes, and I've struggled to match his gaze for too long, but now I see him in a new light. He stands to his full, dominating height, covered in monster blood, and I see the bravery beneath the unusual appearance. Artemis confided in me last night that Zeus wasn't allowing any immortals to help us, but here Argus stands, ready to die alongside us.

"We will," I say.

Shikari nods her head.

The horde of humans runs towards us, but Argus steps in front of us. He unsheathes two full-length axes, and while a handful of humans falter at the intimidating sight, most continue advancing towards him. The first line dies fast. Argus cuts two in half, then kicks the middle one in the chest. He flies across the space, and when he lands on the ground a few feet away, he doesn't get back up.

A shot of color illuminates my peripheral vision, and right as Artemis ducks from Atlas's sword, Iris grabs her and transports her away.

Atlas bellows in rage, then turns his gaze towards Shikari and me. He realizes at the same time as us that Iris made a mistake. Atlas is here for us, Shikari and me, not Artemis. Iris should have grabbed us first. Whisked us away to safety with the other huntresses. That realization that Iris's love for Artemis caused an err brings a vile grin on his haggard face.

Shikari takes a step forward, but I press my hand on her chest.

Gently, I push her back. "Stay behind Argus until she comes back for us."

"You can't fight him alone."

I know that. Artemis fought against Atlas and could not advance on him. Death waits for me behind his blade, but the typical fear associated with dying does not come. "I'm second in command. You have to listen to me."

"You're a stubborn woman," Shikari seethes.

"A stubborn woman you have to obey." I lock eyes with Shikari. "It was an honor riding with you, sister."

With that, I run towards Atlas. I limp with every movement, but I do not stop. My head throbs, as do the multitude of wounds scattered throughout my body, but I raise my sword and I meet him in a clamorous shock. We both stumble back, me more than him, and his grin widens.

"The invisible huntress. That's what they call you, right? The invisible one, who everyone forgets exists."

"I don't dwell on my titles." I grip my sword with both hands, facing him once more. "Only the creatures I defeat."

He languidly moves towards me and places a hand on his chest in mocked hurt. "Am I a monster you want to defeat, invisible one?"

He thrives off the banter during a fight, playing with his prey until it whimpers for the last time. I run towards him, ending the conversation before it truly began, but just like the last two monsters I have faced, Argus saves me. He pulls me away from Atlas by the back of my shirt, and I stumble a few feet away.

A pair of warm arms catches me as colors surround me in a multitude of hope. I stare forward at Argus as

Atlas pounces on him, and just as we disappear towards safety, I watch as Atlas rips Argus's head from his shoulders.

When the rainbow subsides, I collapse to my knees in a distinct set of woods. Artemis stands in front of two trees, her hands clasping a piece of the air.

I stare up at Iris, bewildered. "How did we find it?"

Iris holds the art piece Argus passed her, and the fresh reminder of his death returns with the image of a map and us. "All he wanted was to get her home."

TWENTY-THREE

SAFFRON

The next day, as I walk back to the beach with a makeshift basket filled with berries, Epiales isn't fishing. Instead, he stands in front of a make-shift hut created with twigs and leaves. It's barely four feet tall, and there are holes where the sun finds a passageway, but it's beautiful. In less than three hours, he made us a home.

His back faces me as he leans over, applying the finishing touches to the roof. His shirt is off, and his body drips with sweat as he ties two pieces of branches together. I slowly walk towards him, unable to take my eyes off his flexing muscles. His focus remains on building the hut, and he does not notice me until I place a hand on his shoulder.

"What is this?"

He spins around to face me, wearing a luminous smile on his lips. "This is our little world. Let me wash off real quick, and I'll give you a tour."

He leans forward, and when he kisses me, it tastes like salt. Epiales hurriedly runs to the ocean, submerging his entire body inside, and I can't help but laugh. I feared that by telling him the truth about the prophecy, this happy version of him would disappear. I remember the days he suffered in Tartarus, miserable, as his life disappeared before his eyes. History has repeated a deadly fate for him, but he smiles as he pops his head out of the water.

It's infectious, and I drop the basket of food and run in after him.

His arms quickly catch me, and he dips us both underwater. We kiss as a school of fish swim around us, and the moment we break through the surface, he splashes me with water. "You just got your only outfit wet."

I smirk. "I guess I just have to be naked the rest of the day."

"My queen, you remember I'm human now, right? You can't say things like unless you want me to have a heart attack."

I splash him with water. "Have you been working on that hut all day?"

His impish smile answers my question. "I got the idea last night, and I got all the supplies while you slept, then started it when you went out for food. I love our nights under the stars, but I want a place that is just ours for tonight, where we can be ourselves, with no one potentially watching."

We haven't seen Styx or Hecate since Hecate's impromptu visit the day Epiales woke up, but occasionally, we will feel a presence, like prying eyes watching our interactions. Styx trapped us on Ogygia for a reason, and we have little doubt that she has checked on us without our knowledge. Epiales granted us our first true escape with his imperfectly perfect hut.

He swims back to me and encircles me in his arms.

"When we are in there, you aren't a goddess, and I'm not a former god. We will just be Saffron and Epiales, two people inside our little world that nobody else belongs in."

"What about the prophecy? Doesn't it scare you?"

He hasn't brought it up since last night. "I have feared death before, and it changed who I was. It turned me into a monster I didn't recognize. So, no, this prophecy doesn't scare me. Being that same frightened, violent god does. Now, I want to live every second until it's my last, without fear of what comes next. Now, let's give you the tour of our temporary home."

He guides me out of the water and helps me slip off the dress clinging to me. Although I teased nudity, he has a spare shirt for me from when Hecate left a basket of clothes. It stops a few inches above my knees, and Epiales cannot steer his gaze away from my exposed legs.

Laughing, I playfully slap him on the chest. "Dear gods, give me the tour."

A long leaf serves as the door, and when he parts it, I have to duck my head to get inside. It's cramped, and there are tiny slits where the sun shines through, but it's cute. He used the remaining clothes to create a bed on the floor. Epiales has to bend his body at an awkward angle to get inside the hut, but once we lay on the makeshift pillows he created, our bodies mold together.

His arm wraps around my waist, pulling me against his body, while my head finds its home on his chest. Not even the muses could create a tune as melodic as the sound of his heartbeat against my ear. While one of his hands traces circles on my waist, the other one intertwines with mine.

"Your lunch is still outside. Want me to grab it?"

"I'm not hungry, I just want this." He's lying, but I self-ishly stay in his embrace, with no plans of moving.

A yawn falls out of my lips, followed by instant heat to my cheeks.

"Take a nap, my queen. We have all night." His hand threads through my hair as he whispers. "Would you like a story as you fall asleep?"

"Mhm."

I close my eyes.

"Kronos made me eliminate a dream between us. My second favorite day in history. I came for you, just like I did every night, and you begged me to free you from the prisons. You begged me for one night without the stories and just real freedom. I was told I couldn't do that, not just because I was imprisoned in Tartarus, but because if I gave you even a second of true happiness, then you might not fight for Kronos. You might hold hope for a better world."

He hesitates, then adds.

"But gods, Saffron, I couldn't say no to you."

Before his story, fatigue wished to claim me. Now, he has roused me with a story I never expected. I keep my head on his chest, but I tilt my head up and watch him drift to a memory stolen from me. He lays here with me, but he, too, is in the past.

"Where did we go?" I ask.

"Technically, we went nowhere. You were still in that terrible prison, and I was in Tartarus. But for a few hours, I used every bit of my magic to make us both believe we were in my old home. I had a mansion before Zeus cast me to Tartarus, with acres of land as far as the eye could see and a garden rich in fruits and vegetables. It was an all black mansion, but it was filled with laughter. When I transported our minds there and recreated my home, there was an echoed remnant of that laughter, like the happiness had never left. If I still had my powers, I would give you that memory back. Let you see my former home and all its joy."

"I can see it."

It's not a lie. Epiales has always been a magician of words. He spins his stories until they formulate through the canvases of my mind. I can see the expansive yard, with its freshly trimmed grass and the fresh smell of tomatoes and peppers. The whispered laugh plays like a song around me, and it brings a smile to my lips.

I can see a monstrously tall, gothic-styled mansion. Initially, his house has a daunting look that warns of nightmares and terror, but it isn't completely black. The stained-glass windows, some full-length, give a glimpse into the fanatical gleam of color thriving inside. I do not remember the night when Epiales whisked me away to his home, but I can see the source of Epiales's peace.

It's gorgeous.

"The first thing you asked for was food."

"I'm so shocked," I tease.

His grin grows. "I cooked you one of my favorite meals, soutzoukakia, and made bread from scratch. It was the first time I stopped being a storyteller to you, and I started being a person with hobbies and interests. We started talking about my love for cooking, and as I made meals you consumed in seconds, we talked about everything."

"Like what?"

"You had a small world that didn't let you experience much, but you knew colors and sounds. Understood the beauty of freedom and the fears that stole your breath. We talked about those. Our favorite colors and sounds. The first thing we'd do with our coveted freedom. Our worst fears. We let a chasm of honesty open, and then you tried to kiss me, but you were so nervous you missed and kissed my jaw."

I laugh. "I did not!"

His eyes twinkle as they land on me. "You did, but it was perfect."

"I missed. There's no way *that* is perfect." My laughter remains a remnant in the air as I ask. "So, you were my first kiss, and I don't even remember it?"

He laughs as well. "No, my queen, I didn't kiss you that night. I wanted you to remember the first time we kissed. I was almost your first kiss if you didn't miss, but I stopped anything from going further. You deserved to remember your first kiss."

"I wish I could remember that night."

"But that's the beauty of stories. They give you back a shard of your broken memories."

"You said this was your second favorite memory. What's your first?"

"Today." There's no hesitation. He slides his hand down the expanse of my back, treasuring the little moments and the zing of goosebumps that scatter the skin he touches. "Today is the first time in my entire life where I have finally been at peace with this wretched world, one I've made even more wicked. I do not care about my mortality, and the death coming for me. I don't care about power or revenge against Zeus for all he stole from me. Now that I have these days with you, I'm content."

"You never want to leave this island," I do not phrase it as a question, but a fact; yet Epiales nods his head.

"I don't want to escape our little world and return to one where you have an ex-husband, who we both know is a better option for you, and I am the villain, who doesn't deserve to hold you in my arms."

"Former villain."

I sling one of my legs over his waist, straddling him, and my hands grab both sides of his face. He immediately reacts to my touch. Epiales sits up, our faces a mere centimeter away from one another, and he wraps his arms around my waist. With our faces this close, I cement everything about this moment into memory. I focus on the small scar on his left eyebrow he received a few days ago from a twig. I observe high cheekbones that could cut diamonds, and then my eyes zero in on his lips.

"Epiales, this is my favorite day, too. Regardless of what else happens, know that today is perfect for me, too."

"I'll help you escape in the morning," Epiales says, while his hands trail up my back, sending goosebumps everywhere. "We will get you out of here so you can stop Styx."

"But tonight?" I ask suggestively, and a small smile blooms on his lips once more.

"But tonight, let's stay in our little world with all the perfection that comes with it. I want to spend tonight knowing every little thing about you, my queen."

"Then let's start with the most important question." I lean my lips against his, savoring the tender kiss, then pull away and ask. "What is your favorite color?"

"I've answered this before," he teases.

In the dreamworld Kronos forced me to forget.

"Refresh my memory."

He reaches forward and tucks a piece of my hair behind my ear. "My favorite color used to be white like the stars, but now they are brown. It is forever brown now."

This time, when I kiss him, I don't miss. My lips crash against his own. His hand grabs a tuff of my brown hair, tugging as his teeth drag upon my bottom lip, and our perfect day becomes electrified.

"Thank you," I murmur against his lips.

"For what?"

"For reminding me how it feels to be happy. Thank you for bringing back my ability to smile."

He lays me back down in our perfect little hut, and he crawls over me. "You are my heart, my Saffron."

He kisses me, and we both know this isn't forever. Our time on this island has always had an expiration date. It will hopefully end with our freedom, but death has stamped his name on Epiales. We both know it. It's the grotesque words we hide with pretty stories and languid touches. But for a little while longer, I let myself forget he isn't my soulmate, and he will not live long enough to fix every broken part of me.

I kiss him back, ignoring the taste of hope.

TWENTY-FOUR

HERMES

Hecate's betrayal came like a storm that emerged from a cloudless sky, but not Calypso's. Long ago, before Styx's war and Calypso's eventual imprisonment, I warned Zeus that he punished her too harshly. She was not a villain who reached for Zeus's crown. She was simply a young, immature goddess who was lonely on an island nobody could find.

Eons ago, Calypso lured Odysseus to her island, but she was not a nefarious witch like Circe. She did not want to turn his men into swine. She wasn't like Polyphemus, who wished to feast on Odysseus and his men. Her actions were not commendable, but they weren't inherently malicious, either. She was lonely on her island, and Odysseus was her chance to stop being so alone.

Zeus told me to steal Odysseus from Calypso, and I warned him that her mind was already fragile from centuries without comfort. "Five years is enough time for that hero to suffer a crazed nymph's company. Free him."

It took me two years to find her island, and I obeyed Zeus's request. In the middle of the night, as Calypso slept on his chest with a smile on her face, I stole him from her. I set him on a boat, and I told him to return to his wife, Penelope, who he never stopped missing. Forcing myself to forget about the screams.

I was back on Mt. Olympus when Calypso found her bed emptied once again, and the screams that tore at her throat were loud enough to pierce the clouds and reach my ears. Eons ago, I warned Zeus about the punishments he inflicted against Calypso. She shouldn't have been alone on that island for so long. She deserved freedom, just like Odysseus.

He ignored me.

So, I'm not surprised that Calypso joined Styx's side. She promised Calypso a simple gift, one Zeus refused- freedom. I think that's why she does not cry or yell as we chain her to the wall using Hephaestus's power-constricting cuffs. She smiles at us and suppresses a smile because, at least for a few days, she was free.

Her feet touched something other than sand. She smelled something other than salt water. Heard voices instead of the whistling winds.

I will never forgive Hecate's decision to betray us, but I understand Calypso's motive. Aphrodite and Hephaestus's silence declares their understanding, too. Only Ares, his knuckles healing after splitting against her shattered shoulder, does not care about her rationale. He was her captive for days after being forced to hold the world on his shoulders in Atlas's place. Rage dictates every step, every punch, every snarled question.

"Where is she?" He asks as he rears his elbow back and slams it into her stomach.

Calypso lets out a sound that's a mixture of a laugh and a wheeze, but that's it. She says nothing else as Ares tortures her. Night joins us; still, nothing. Calypso rests her head against the wall she's chained to, and she doesn't say a word.

"If you do not tell me where she is-" Ares begins another threat. His third in the past fifteen minutes, and it will end the same way the last ones had.

"Let's get some rest."

Ares snarls. "Are you insane? She's out there, and you want to rest?"

He won't say my wife's name. Saffron's absence guides all our decisions, but Ares hates her so much that he won't say her name aloud. He calls her *she* or *the missing goddess*. Never Saffron. He should have left the room with Nike and the muses. He doesn't belong with us, the gods who care about Saffron enough to say her name.

"Calypso isn't going anywhere," I say. "Tomorrow, we will get answers from her about where *Saffron* is located."

It's almost imperceptible, but he flinches. Ares, the violent god of war, flinches at my command. Then, as soon as he realizes his action, his jaw hardens, and he storms out of the room.

"You should be nicer to him, Hermie," Aphrodite says as soon as he is out of earshot.

"Of course you would want that," Hephaestus grumbles.

Aphrodite turns to him, opens her mouth to respond, but then she looks at me. An inner conflict whirls inside her, and her form matches her anxiety. She switches bodies every two seconds, flipping through dozens of figures. Most of them she hasn't worn in centuries, yet in the state of conflict, she doesn't know who to be.

Hephaestus storms away.

Calypso laughs.

Again, this sense that I do not know something returns. Like I am the last one in on a joke, and I hate it because it centers on Saffron. My Saffron, whose smile steals my sanity and who needs me to save her.

"What aren't you telling me?"

"Let's come back tomorrow," she says. "It's like you said. We all need rest. It's been a long day, and she'll tell us what we need to hear tomorrow."

"Sure I will." I can hear the condescension in Calypso's voice for miles. "Goodnight, Hermes."

I leave the room, but I do not sleep. Since Saffron left, I have become a stranger to sleep. Instead of finding comfort in oblivion, I replay every moment with her since we married. Every time our conversations became a little shorter and our laughter became a little rarer. I play through all the arguments, and the times when we should have argued, but we chose to stew in our silent contempt. We weren't always perfect, but I do not know when I ruined us so horribly that it cannot be fixed.

Hecate is to blame. She orchestrated our demise with an instrument she played too exquisitely. When I find Saffron, and I free her, she will understand. I will tell her everything, and she will come back to me. Everything will go back to how it was meant to, with us together and Epiales gone.

My surety should calm me to sleep, but I never close my eyes. I live in the past, where the smell of strawberries follows everywhere.

Before the sun can rise, I make sure I'm the first one back in the prisons. I don't know where Clio and Calliope took Erato and Urania, but Calypso is the only prisoner chained against the alabaster wall. Her head slumps against her shoulder as she sleeps; otherwise, she looks the same as the night before. Only her gown shows the blood she shed during her torture. The rest of her is completely unscathed.

"I always have a plan. It's what I'm known for. The god of mischief. The great god of thievery, who can trick even the wisest deities."

I walk towards her, and in the quieted room, my steps thump with portentous doom. She plays her role of a sleeping nymph, just as I pretend I am sneakier than her. Like I have a thousand ideas on how to trick her up my sleeve, ready to pull them out like ribbons in a parlor game. She doesn't gasp when I grab a tuft of her curly hair, or yank her head from its slumped position.

She grins and opens her eyes. "What gave me away?"

"You don't want to go back to Ogygia, but what else do you want? What do you want me to steal for you in exchange for Ogygia's location?"

"You found it once before."

"That was eons ago, and it took me two years to find it. It would take another two, and I don't have that kind of time."

"Don't have the time or don't want Saffron with Epiales that long?" I tug on her hair, hard, and she laughs. "Do you know what I want, Hermes? I want nothing from you. You want to be the hero so badly that you do not realize that you are inconsequential. I don't need you to steal anything for me, or try to trick me with your words. I

253

only want one thing, and that's seeing Zeus. Once he's here, then I'll tell him everything."

You want to be the hero so badly that you do not realize that you are inconsequential.

I stagger away. She is a low-level nymph, mostly known for the island she lives on rather than her own abilities. I shouldn't care what she says, but I can't stop her verbal blades from piercing my skin.

"And there's the god of the hour," she says with a growing grin.

She doesn't look at me, but at a figure behind me. I turn around, and there's Zeus. He strolls in beside Aphrodite, eyes locked on Calypso. Another blade meets its mark.

"Leave us," Zeus says without sparing a glance at Aphrodite or me.

Aphrodite places her hand on my arm, and she steers me away from a conversation I should be a part of. She's my wife.

"No, Hermie, she's not. Not anymore."

I didn't realize I spoke aloud until Aphrodite says the words I do not need to hear. "I'm going to win her back." The devastating expression on Aphrodite's many faces crumbles my resolve. "Aren't I?"

"Do you want to stay and eavesdrop for a little while?"

"Why aren't you answering my question? I'm going to win her back, right? We were so in love."

Aphrodite looks away from me and drops her hand. "You were so in love with the idea of her. Maybe you fell in love with her for a little while, but she was mainly a prize you always insisted on stealing."

"That's not true," I say through gritted teeth.

My tears are lava down my cheeks.

"I'm sorry."

A crash ignites the prison, and we both rush inside. Calypso remains in her chains, pressed up against the wall, but Zeus is nowhere in sight. A singed circle stands where Zeus once was. Calypso hums the tune of a song I have never heard before, closed-mouth, smiling the entire time.

"Did you tell him where Ogygia is?" Aphrodite asks.

Calypso nods her head, then leans against the wall and doesn't talk again. She only hums that unfamiliar tune.

TWENTY-FIVE

SAFFRON

The smallest stream of sunlight comes through the leaves surrounding our make-shift world, and a smile ebbs its way to the surface. My eyes wander up towards Epiales, sleeping peacefully with his arm wrapped around my waist; his other one intertwines with mine.

He didn't eat last night, so I escape our hut to grab the basket of berries I found the day before. Hopefully, critters didn't wander their way to our site and eat them. However, as soon as I leave the hut, food stealing critters are the least of my concerns.

There is a dark-skinned male, with a lean build and perfectly coiffed black hair, sitting cross-legged a few feet away from our depleted fire pit. He has a twig in his hand, and he pokes at the remaining embers as I hesitantly move towards him. I haven't used my powers in days, but with a stranger's presence so close to Epiales, the sizzling awareness returns.

"Good morning." His voice is a smooth baritone, whose very design is to be unsuspecting, but I raise my hands in the air.

"Are you one of Styx's?"

A deep belly laugh leaves his lips, and he turns to face me. I see his stubbled jaw first, and the perfect fade in between his beard and hair. Then, a pair of startling familiar blue eyes meet mine, and the rest of his appearance fades. I have never seen this man before, but those eyes…

He stands to his full six-foot height and brushes the sand off his black pants suit. His appearance and attire contradict the easy waves and soft winds. Everything about him is intimidating. The crisp suit he wears, the gold rings that glint off his large hands, and the smirk that plays over his full lips, telling me he knows he will win every argument.

"You have a quaint situation here." His gaze wanders to the hut I just left before focusing back on me. "Are you ready to leave it?"

Leave. I have wanted to hear freedom's voice since the moment I arrived, but I feel the hut, and the man inside it, like they are a pair of scorching eyes.

"Who are you?"

"My name is Alastor, and I would like to make a deal with you, Saffron."

"I don't make deals with Styx or her minions."

"Haven't you already? It's why you're here. Because you made a deal with Styx and she made you pay a steep cost."

"You move one more step, and I will rip your bones out of your favorite body part."

"I heard that's cartilage."

"Do you really want to test that theory?"

It is a bluff, and nothing more. If this stranger works for Styx, then my abilities will not work, but I do not know if she's told all who work with her about this stipulation. Alastor was about to move towards me, but his foot suspends in the air. Wisely, he takes a step back.

"I do not work with Styx, for I have no allegiance to anyone but myself."

"Careful, Zeus has ears everywhere."

"So he does." Alastor glances at the cloudy sky and smirks. "As titillating as a conversation about Zeus always goes, I want to focus on why I am here. I want to help you escape."

I do not trust him, this male who resembles a snake more than a human, and yet he says the words I have needed to hear. The longer I am on this island, the more helpless the rest of the world is against whatever Styx has concocted. If I am free, then I can effectively end this war before she succeeds in her plans. Yet, my eyes narrow in on his cunning smirk, as if he is hiding a bigger secret that he'll never reveal.

"Why should I believe you?"

He points behind him, where the ocean teases me with the possibility of freedom. "That electric fence around the water, which is shielding you from Poseidon's hunt, and rendering you unconscious every time you try to break the fence, is your best way out."

"You said it yourself. The surrounding magic is stopping me from escaping."

I tried many times when Epiales was asleep, but each attempt was futile. The electricity Hecate created turned my skin to ash, and eventually, the pain rendered me

259

unconscious. I always woke again on the beach, with my hands fully healed, like I never attempted to flee.

"I can stop the electricity long enough for you to escape."

"You can?" I ask.

Freedom.

The prospect makes me both elated and dismayed, and my eyes wander towards the hut. Alastor sighs as soon as I look away from him to focus on the man who makes me want to forgo my responsibilities and prioritize what I want, but this world has never desired to abide to my desires. I am the savior, not a woman who simply wants to love a man.

"That plan won't work," I state with finality, my eyes clashing against Alastor's electric blue ones. "Epiales can't make the swim."

"Because he's human now." Before I can ask how he knows, Alastor explains. "I figured he was when I found all the dead animal carcasses."

"So, find another way that gets us both off of this island."

"There is no other way, not without Styx noticing and bringing you right back. What's more important, savior?" This time, he dares to take a step forward. Then another. Then another. He looms over me, but his gaze remains locked on the hut. "Freedom and protecting humanity from a world-ending prophecy or a boy?"

When he says it like that, my hope of freeing Epiales seems so trivial. I have always had to make this decision. Him or the world, and each time, I know the direction I will take. That doesn't mean it hurts less.

"My queen."

Epiales stands in front of our hut, his hair still tossed

from sleep, but I know he heard everything. It's evident in the frown he wears and the saddened understanding in those limitless silver eyes. This man, who once unraveled my happiness in his journey towards power, has fixed a part of me that died with Hattie. It's different this time. I'm not just choosing him over humanity. With him comes my happiness, too.

"You need to escape when you can," he says. "Leave the island."

I can actually feel the seams around my put-together heart tearing, and I drop the dead rabbit as shock ripples out of me.

"You can't make the trip with me."

I will have to swim at least a hundred miles hoping to find Poseidon or someone working with him, and Epiales cannot survive that swim. Only a god can survive, and Epiales's attention snags on a particular vein in his arm with the same harrowing realization.

I didn't realize we were moving towards each other until his arms wrap around my waist, finding a home in my embrace. "We can't let Styx win. You said so last night, so you have to leave this island. Take this freedom."

"But what about you?"

There is a sad smile on his lips. "I'll be waiting here until you come back for me."

We both hear the goodbye in our words because this world hasn't been kind to us. I will come back for him, but will he still be here? He leans down to give me a chaste kiss, and then I pull away from him. I need to get off of this island, we both know this, but the pain doesn't squelch.

"I'm going to come back for you."

"I know you will, my queen," he whispers back.

Epiales turns around sharply, wandering back into our

hut. For once, I want to be selfish and run right back into that hut, but when Alastor extends his hand out for me, I choose the people of this world by accepting.

We walk in silence towards the beach, but the mysterious god continues to glance down at me. He wants to say something; it is threatening to leave his lips, but the words never escape.

Once we are on the beach, Alastor lets go of my hand and curls both of his into fists. The sea ripples with a blinding white light as Alastor's powers course through the water, and only then does he dare to speak. "The electricity is gone, so act fast."

"Thank you." Before I venture into the water, I turn back around to face him. "And Alastor?"

"Yes?"

"I think you are freeing me so you can kill him."

Alastor didn't look at Epiales for long, but I caught the simmering rage beneath his eyes. I bore witness to his hands curling into fists. Hatred has a distinct look, a mirror on everyone's face, and I saw his hatred as clearly as I see the surrounding ocean.

Alastor doesn't say a word. He doesn't deny my claim, and he doesn't lead me away with a false promise. He stares down at me, waiting for my next words, as if these are the deciding moments between Epiales's life and his death.

"You and I are strangers who do not know each other's past, and most certainly do not know Epiales the same way. I don't know why you want to kill him, or what past mistakes he made leading you on this journey towards revenge. Maybe you lost a loved one in the war, where he chose the wrong side. Maybe he killed someone close to you. Again, I do not know you or your story, but I know his, and he's changing for the better."

I take a step towards Alastor, our eyes never wavering.

"Most importantly, I know myself, and I have been falling into this terrible void for years. You might not care because, like I said, we're strangers. But I brought him back to life by giving him my humanity, and I have re-experienced the happiness I had at that time with him near me. He was once a terrible god, and I will never disagree with you on that, but he isn't that god anymore. So, if I come back to this island and Epiales, who is now human and repentant and a part of my soul, is dead."

Alastor only smiles, trying to seem unperturbed by my words, but even from this distance I can see the flash of fear in those blue eyes. I take a threatening step forward, and although there is a considerable height difference between us, it's him who, ever so subtly, flinches.

"If you kill him before I can free him, then I'm coming for you. I will kill you slowly until all you want is the aching nothingness of death."

"Have a fun swim, Lady Saffron."

I look back once more at the hut. It's my last image of Ogygia, which has been both a nightmare and a miracle, before I dive into the water and swim towards the green gate that no longer sizzles with electricity. My hands wrap around the bars. With ease, I pull the two bars apart until a human-sized hole appears. Before the bars reverberate back to their original form, I slither through.

I use my power to push my bones faster than any other sea creature through this water. My eyes continually move around the expansive space in search of Poseidon, Amphitrite, or their children. I soar past sharks, dolphins, and other fish as I search through the vast expanse for a familiar face or two. I focus solely on my hunt for Poseidon, instead of the heaviness growing on my chest with the applied distance between Epiales and me.

A colorful array of seahorses quickly surrounds me. They're some of the tiniest creatures in the ocean, their length no taller than my hand, but over three thousand corral me into a cocoon of their making. I can no longer see anything but their tiny bodies. Until a large body crashes through them and envelopes me in a suffocating hug.

"Suck that, Amphitrite! I found her first!"

A grin splits over my lips, and I hug Poseidon back.

TWENTY-SIX

LAMB

Artemis's skin blisters and rages against the portal re-opening, but she persists. For hours, she accepts the pain that accompanies Hecate's magic until the sinister shade of green erupts, and a four-foot diameter circle appears. The force sends Artemis to the ground, but Iris quickly catches her before she touches the ground.

Dýnami whoops, and she and Shikari hug with glee, but I watch Iris and Artemis. The latter turns her neck, and when she meets Iris, a smile peels over her lips. Iris lifts Artemis's hands, already healing from the wound inflicted by the portal, but her lips ghost over the center of her palm. Everyone else cheers with joy because we are the ones who found Saffron, but I smile for a different reason.

Love spawns from the smallest actions.

These details that others miss make love form for the lucky two. Artemis clasps Iris's chin with the same hand she kissed, and she turns her head to fully face her. I shouldn't be watching. This is a tender and intimate moment between two women who finally embrace the feelings that have festered for too long, but I cannot pull my gaze away.

Not until they kiss.

I turn away and meet Jamila's gaze. The others obliviously cheer amongst themselves, but Jamila and I share a hidden smile. We have watched Artemis and Iris share longed looks and hide their truth, but war ebbs away superficial fears. They stopped pretending they didn't need to be together, and I couldn't be happier.

"Let's go!" Dýnami yells.

She doesn't wait for anyone else, and she leaps into the portal. Shikari is at Dýnami's heels, ready to leap in after her, but Vee pushes her out of the way and jumps in.

"Turd," Shikari grumbles.

She jumps in right after, followed by Jamila and Iris. Artemis and I are the only ones left; neither of us eagerly move forward. This time, we are in control of the situation. Iris can portal us out as soon as we have Saffron, but that doesn't change the past haunting our present. I nearly died on this island, and Artemis witnessed my deterioration without the strength to save me. We suffered in Ogygia.

I hold out my hand. "Together."

Artemis hesitates, skirting her attention between the portal and me. "You shouldn't go. You're really injured from the last battle."

She's right. I should have followed June and received medical help. I can taste blood on my tongue and feel its steady rivulets scour down my body like rainfall, but Iris is already on that island. There's nobody who can portal me to safety, and I need to confront the island that nearly stole my life. It's a foe I need to face head on, to remind it I am stronger. That I survived.

"I'll be fine." My hand stays suspended in the air, waiting for her to accept. "I promise."

"Epiales is there."

Epiales did not fire the arrow that killed Willow and Copperhead, but he was instrumental in the war with Kronos. His decisions created a ripple effect. Because of him and Kronos, Raven became a traitor who murdered Willow and Copperhead. Because Copperhead died, Akita's sanity unraveled, and she found an unlikely source for her rage: Sika. Akita's enraged insanity led to her betrayal in this war against Styx, which caused Sika's death. Because of Epiales, tragedy has struck us more than once, and he's there on Ogygia. Alive once again. Expunged of the crimes he's inflicted on us.

That's what makes Artemis hesitate at the portal line. My near-death experience is a part of her distaste towards this portal, but Epiales's presence freezes her steps. More than sadness lives in the depths of her eyes; it's hatred, too. She hates Epiales for his part in the last Titanomachy War. She hates him for every death his decisions created.

I place my hand in hers, no longer waiting for her to accept it. "We're not here to save him. We leave him on that island and only take Saffron."

"It's not enough," she says through clenched teeth.

"You're right, it's not. He deserves to die again and join everyone else in the depths of the Fields of Punishment. He is a monster in the flesh, and I want him dead as much as you do, but we are better than him. Better than Raven and Kronos and Akita and Frigate and Atlas. We are better than the monsters, so not saving him will have to be enough."

"For once, I think you're wrong."

"They're waiting for us, Artemis."

"I'm going to kill him. If I see him, I'm going to kill him."

We both do not know enough about this prophecy, but we're certain Epiales is a part of it. Many clamor that he is the prophesied heart, and I fear the consequences of being his murderer. I've only heard the prophecy once, but I do not forget words of death. When the heart dies twice, the savior screams, and from that scream, spawns this war.

Do we want to be the reason behind Saffron's screams?

"Let him die on that island Styx has put him on. We don't need to dirty our hands."

Artemis doesn't respond. She pulls me with her into the portal, as my words hang in the balance between a war and a grieving goddess. I slam my eyes shut as the portal pulls us downward. It's too similar to the last time I was here, and I hate the memories burning through the crevices of my mind.

Artemis steadies me, so I do not crash on the ground.

"We didn't land in the same spot," Artemis says with unhidden surprise.

She's right. Last time, we fell onto the beach, where power-restricting cages waited for us. This time, we are in the woods that conceal us from the sun, and two male figures stand on the beach with their backs to us. Iris and the other huntresses are further ahead, partially hidden behind the first row of trees behind the beach.

"What's going on?" Artemis whispers as soon as we are close. "Where's Saffron?"

"Gone," Shikari whispers back. "I think the other god helped her escape in the ocean because Epiales asked the mystery man if she escaped safely. They haven't spoken since."

The mystery man.

My attention snags on the tall, lean male standing shoulder-to-shoulder with Epiales. I can barely make out his face from where he stands, facing the ocean, but he has dark brown skin and shortly cropped black hair. I do not recognize the male, but I recognize the lightning that dances across his fingertips.

"It's Zeus," I say.

"It's his epithet, Alastor," Iris corrects.

"Ep-eh-thet?" Dýnami sounds out the word; her face scrunched together. "What is that? Another word for lover cuz Zeus has a lot of those."

"No, it's one of Zeus's forms," Vee explains. "An epithet is a malevolent counterpart."

"Mah-lev-oh-lent?" Dýnami sounds out another unfamiliar word. "What does that mean?"

"Oh gods," Vee rolls her eyes as Shikari snickers. "Malevolent means evil."

"Then just say evil. It's easier."

"Or broaden your vocabulary," Vee shoots back.

"Sorry I'm not as fancy-" Dýnami begins.

"Both of you, shut-up so we can hear what they're saying," I snap.

"Sorry," they both mutter.

We all focus back on Epiales and Zeus-Alastor. They refuse to look at one another, so they stare at the ocean where Saffron escaped. She's their equalizer, the barrier that halts a war between two festering, hate-filled souls. Zeus wants to kill him. It's evident in the lightning sparking between his fingers, eager to singe flesh, but he hesitates.

Artemis glowers, unamused.

"The moment I heard your voice from in the hut, I knew I was going to die today," Epiales says. "You can never pardon a man you hate, even if they've paid for their crimes. Even if they have suffered enough under your wrath. So what are you waiting for, Zeus? Why are you toying with your prey?"

"She forgave you. You doomed her. Betrayed her. Chose Kronos over her. Yet, she forgave you. She threatened to kill me if I hurt you, and that speaks more than forgiveness. She spoke like she loved you. Why?"

I have never believed Zeus cares for his children, except his favored Athena and Heracles. The others are inconsequential, pesky gnats that he swats away when they get too close. I have been a bystander in conversations he's shared with Artemis. His voice drips with detachment, and he rarely looks in her direction.

With Saffron, it has always been worse. He has been indifferent towards Artemis and Apollo, but he's feared Saffron. Voted for her death when she was a Demi-god and other gods fought to keep her alive. He allowed another god, Hades, to raise her as his adopted daughter. Zeus has never cared for Saffron, not even with the sliver of affection he gives his non-favorite children.

Today contradicts the Zeus I know.

His voice breaks when he mentions Saffron's threat. She didn't recognize him as Alastor, and I doubt she knew she was threatening her father, but it doesn't matter. Zeus's emotions come alive with his words. He almost sounds like he cares about Saffron's feelings.

I look at Artemis, but she won't meet my gaze. She has long stopped trying to become a favorite of Zeus's, but hearing compassion in her father for a different child must affect her. He rarely shows care for his children, but

Saffron hasn't tried; despite that, Zeus cares for her. More than he cares for Artemis.

She pulls her hand out of mine.

"I don't know how she forgave me because you're right. I didn't deserve it. The Fates weren't kind enough to make her my soulmate, but I am one of her great loves. And after everything with Hermes and Hattie, she needed to be reminded she's capable of being loved. I gave her that, just like she gave me her forgiveness and a second chance at life. My blood may be red now, but she sees me the same way she had all those years ago in our dream world, as if I was still of worth in this desolate world."

"He's human now?" Iris asks in bewilderment. "How?"

Nobody answers her because nobody knows the answer, but it further proves he can be the prophesied heart in the prophecy. It is easier to kill a human than a god. Now, he can be killed twice without Saffron wielding the executioner's blade.

"I should kill you."

"It'd break her heart," he says. "But when have you ever cared about that?"

Zeus-Alastor turns to face Epiales as lightning shoots up his arms. I can only see one of his eyes from my position. It glows the same shade as the bolts. "Do not presume you know my thoughts, nightmare."

"When you die, you realize what's most important, and that's her. I've died for her once, Zeus, and I'll die for her a thousand more times. Just be careful because she will eventually realize Zeus and Alastor are the same person, and when that moment comes, you'll realize the finality of death, too."

"You truly believe you will save yourself by threatening me?"

"Save myself?" Epiales roars with laughter, but there is no happiness in his tone, only disbelief. "You have hated me from the moment Morpheus escaped with his human soulmate, and that abhorrence only multiplied over the centuries we have fought. I know that your lightning bolt is going to kill me today regardless of what I say, and now lying seems a moot point. You're the only one here to hear my last words, and I will not mince them to assuage your soul. Kill me and be done with it."

Epiales closes his eyes and invites death's sharp touch.

Two lightning bolts materialize in Zeus's hands, and he raises them with every intention of striking them down. Artemis holds her breath, anticipating her enemy's death, but I see the hesitation written across the king's face. Whether it's fear of Saffron's wrath or guilt for her broken heart, I'm not sure, but Zeus's hands waver.

"Is he going to do it?" Dýnami whisper-asks.

"Shh," Shikari places a hand on Dýnami's mouth. Then, a few seconds later, she sharply pulls her hand away and wipes it on Dýnami's back. "Gross, you licked me!"

"And you tasted disgusting."

"Shut," I glare at Shikari, then Dýnami. "Up."

They listen for a short while.

"If I must die," Epiales says as a minute, then two, go by without his execution. "Can we take it to the hut? I want to be surrounded by her when I die."

"Be quiet," Zeus snarls.

But Epiales's question jars him. It reminds him that Saffron promised his death if Epiales dies. It reminds him that a prophecy surrounds Epiales's demise and a war that Styx believes she will win. Styx made Saffron bring Epiales back to life, then left him alone on an island for a while.

There has to be a reason for her actions, and I think it's this.

She wanted Zeus to find Epiales, but only after Saffron fell back in love with him. Styx wants Zeus to strike the fatal blow, so Saffron's promise of death will ring the victory bell for hatred herself. If Zeus kills Epiales, then we die with him.

"Don't you dare," Artemis whispers.

"He can't die."

I take a step forward, and Artemis wraps her hand around my arm. "I said don't."

Placing my hand on top of hers, I meet her fiery stare. "I miss her too. I miss them all, but I won't let everyone die because my grief won't let me see past my rationality. You think I'm wrong, but I'm not. Trust me."

Her hand wavers. She wants his death, but is it worth it? Will Willow be brought back to life, or Sika? Will Epiales' dying now turn back the tables of time and save Copperhead's life? No, none of them will be alive once again. Akita's sanity will not return, along with her life and loyalty. The past is cemented, but we can change the future.

We can save everyone else.

Artemis lets go of my hand, and I run out of the woods. Epiales still closes his eyes, so it is Zeus who sees me first. Zeus keeps his bolts over Epiales's head, waiting for the strength to bring them down over his skull.

It takes Zeus a few seconds to recognize me. I'm not a huntress he's preferred over the years, not like the attractive Willow, Raven, and Akita. I haven't provided humor for him over the years, like Sika, Shikari, and Dýnami. It takes time for him to remember the wallpaper in between the huntresses he fondly knows.

The moment recognition comes in, the first question he asks me is. "You working for Styx now?"

"Never."

His eyes wander behind me, and I know Artemis, and the others have joined me. His jaw hardens. "He's betrayed before."

"I hate him, too," Artemis says. "He worked with the same people who killed my huntresses."

Epiales finally opens his eyes, and they meet the fiery rage of Artemis. "I'm-" he starts.

"Silence," she snarls. Her focus returns to Zeus. "I want him dead just as bad as you do."

Zeus smiles, but it's short-lived.

"But we can't kill him," I say.

"Gods are talking, human." Zeus brushes off my statement and focuses on his daughter. "How did you get here?"

"Found Hecate's portal. How about you?"

He hesitates. That's not a good sign, but I stay silent. I blend back into the background of huntresses. Artemis takes my spot nearest him, chin raised and shoulders stiff to prepare for a verbal battle.

"How?" she repeats.

"Hermes captured Calypso, and she told me everything."

"And why would she do that? She's working with Styx."

"Because she wants to switch back to my side to gain my loyalty. She promised to tell me everything, including how to free Saffron and how I can kill him without Saffron knowing it was me, in exchange for a pardon."

I am not the only one who can hear the deceit Calypso embedded in an oblivious Zeus. It was Calypso's voice who spoke to Zeus, but it's Styx's words. It is her plan guiding

Zeus to murder Epiales, incur Saffron's wrath, and begin a war that will inevitably end with Styx stealing the crown from his corpse.

"Saffron doesn't know that I have multiple forms. She doesn't know about Alastor, the god of evil deeds. I can kill him right here, and she will search for Alastor instead of me. He will be dead, she will be free, and we can fight against Styx. I can even convince her that Alastor works with Styx, and that hatred will go right to her."

"Oh, my gods." Epiales cuts off Zeus with a raucous laughter. "You are an imbecile for believing that. Styx told her to say all that. How can you not see it?"

"Shut-up," Artemis glares at Epiales. "Or do you really want him to kill you?"

The lightning bolts have scattered up Zeus's neck, ready to consume him whole. When that happens, no one can control his rage, which will solely focus on Epiales.

"I understand how tempting it is to kill him."

Artemis refuses to look at Epiales because all her rage will boil over, and with Zeus, they will be an instrument for Styx's war. She focuses solely on Zeus. She reaches a hand out for her father, and before she can touch his electrified forearm, he forces his lightning away.

"He's the reason for so much death, and he should be in an oblivion along with every other traitor in Kronos's army. I don't care that Saffron loves him. It's cruel, but it's true. I see him, and I see all my dead friends in his eyes. So, I understand how tempting it is to kill him. Especially now that he's a human. It would be like tearing paper in half, but someone I care about is insistent that his death will make us lose the war, and I trust her more than I hate him. Let Styx be the executioner."

"What if it won't cause the war? Then I let him live for nothing."

"But what if he is the catalyst to it all? Do we really want to be the ones who take the risk?"

He says nothing for a long while, but he hears her words. Perhaps for the first time in existence, he listens to Artemis before making a rash decision.

"Why did you tell Saffron to leave with me?" Zeus asks Epiales. "You knew who I was, and you knew once she was gone that I would kill you, so why did you let her go?"

Epiales opens his eyes for the first time since we ran onto the beach. "She wanted to save this world, and I want everything in this world for her. Even if I'm not in this world any longer, I want her to have happiness. Saving these humans gives her happiness."

He's a monster who loves only one person, and that is enough to save his life. Zeus takes a step away from Epiales, then another. He stumbles more than retreats, as if Epiales's love for Saffron truly pains him. The hatred and vengeance lessen in his gaze; it's still there, just not as severe. Instead, there is understanding.

"I'll let Styx finish him. Or maybe he'll die on this island from starvation, but I trust you more than I hate him." Zeus picks up Artemis's hand and kisses the knuckles. "And I'm sorry I haven't always shown that."

He slams a lightning bolt onto the ground, and as the ground splinters under the weight of his power, Zeus disappears, leaving us alone with Epiales. Artemis pretends like Zeus's words hold no power, but she has never been a good pretender. She turns away from us, clearing her throat and the surge of emotions before fully facing me.

"Thank you."

I face Epiales, but before I can speak, he interjects. "I

did not know he told Raven to kill the huntresses, but I'm sorry all the same."

"But you knew Raven and Diamond were traitors." Artemis storms towards him, and her fist slams into his jaw. He collapses to the ground, but she goes towards him, grabs him by the neck, and raises him in the air. "I saved your life, but that doesn't mean you get to apologize and absolve yourself of this guilt. I will never forgive you. For as long as your miserable human life lasts, I hope it is in agony, and when you finally die, I'll be waiting for you in the Fields of Punishments."

She drops him. "Get me away from him, Iris."

Iris clamps her hands together, and a gigantic rainbow forms around us. Epiales lays where Artemis dropped him, unable to get up, as we escape far from Ogygia and the god of nightmares, who now bleeds red.

TWENTY-SEVEN

HART SOMMERS

E piales was once the personification of nightmares, but Styx is the derivation of them. The ethereal, yet haunting, sight of her belongs in the deepest pits of a child's most frightening nighttime story. She should be the reason kids do not look under their bed. She should be the reason grown adults scream for their mom to come save them.

The personification of hatred lies within her blackened, frigid water. Her short, jet-black hair does not swim around her to create a halo. Even the strands fear her, and they cling to her paper white flesh, hoping to hide from her view. The black water covers her ears but cuts off at the sharp line of her jaw.

She extends her arms wide in her water as she floats above the roaming, screaming bodies begging for freedom, as her obsidian eyes stare at where I suspend a few feet above her.

I know it's a dream, or a nightmare, without questioning the lack of gravity, because we're back in the Underworld. Her river streams into her veins, and it leaves with her towards her current hiding spot. She isn't in the Underworld, wrapping herself in the wicked chill of *her river, but the dream feels too real not to question. Some fragment of this is real.*

My body levitates horizontally above her floating one, far enough that she cannot touch me, but her jagged nails are close enough to tease the ends of my hair hanging between us. She doesn't touch me, though. She watches me with the same fastidious fascination as I do with her.

"I had hoped you'd be dead already." Styx's voice feels like a cluster of spiders, sneaking underneath my skin and wiggling through my veins.

I say nothing; instead, my eyes peruse the room littered with untold secrets. Styx does not speak unless her words benefit her. It's one of the few undiluted truths I know. She does not need to tell me she wants me dead. That is a fact she has proven time and time again. Styx wants to distract me from a glimpse into her mind, because I realize that's where I am. I'm in her mind, and she doesn't want me to unfurl the secrets that lie within.

This isn't solely a dream because those died with Morpheus. It's not a prophecy, either. I lift my hands to my face, and my veins glimmer a familiar shade of green. The emerald oracle brought me here, to the depths of Styx's unconscious, and it's my job to discover why.

"Apollo is a beautiful male." She forces inflection in her voice, pretending intrigue, so my focus turns back on her.

I have never been to the Underworld before. It is a place I once feared, so I have not looked at the art pieces created of its image from the few survivors of the land of the dead. It looks as I would imagine. There's an absence of light, and billions of humans roam around the grounds, endlessly searching for the unsearchable. The Fields of Punishments blaze red, and if I listen close enough, I can hear the screams of the punished. Every river, from the Lethe to the Phlegethon, flow along the expanse of the Underworld.

Then, my gaze snags on the obsidian castle sitting miles away atop a small hill.

"I'll kill him last," Styx rushes through her words, and each one ends with clipped anger. "I'll kill everyone else first to remind you of this moment. Lowell, Argus, Aphrodite, Dionysus, Zeus, they will all fall by my hand, and you will beg me for forgiveness. You will beg to bow to me, but I'll still kill him. Burn his flesh from his bones, and make you watch as he suffers."

I find what she tries to hide from me.

In Styx's unconscious, there are bars on the castle windows. Thick-rimmed bars that look ridiculous on a window. These aren't traditional barred windows, and the longer I stare at the abnormality, the longer the bars become. They encompass an entire strip of the castle, from roof to floor. Eventually, prison bars cover every inch of the castle, and the door closes and locks with an ominous finality.

"How can you still dream?" I ask when I finally face her again.

Her jaw clenches so tightly I can hear her teeth grinding into submission. "I don't."

The emerald oracle, who is now an extension of me, did this. She, or I, created a dreamworld where dreams no longer exist. We forced our way into Styx's mind until we divulged a truth she did not want my side of the war to know. Her threats disintegrate, joining the moaning souls in the blackened depths of her water.

"I know why you fear me now."

Styx opens her mouth, and when she lets out a piercing scream, the dream erupts like shattered glass. I cover my face with my hands, blocking the glass. Her scream morphs into another's. It's female, too, but broken with sadness rather than rage.

When I drop my hands, the scene changes.

Styx remains in her river, submerged from the neck down, as she ruefully watches the new nightmare. I no longer levitate horizontally above the River Styx; instead, I stand on my two feet on the bank of the river. On the other side, Saffron's shadowy silhouette kneels on the floor.

Everyone is a shadowy silhouette except Styx and me. Styx takes *the reins on her dream world, and she freezes me to the spot, then swims towards Saffron. I scream and thrash, but I do not move an inch. My feet stay locked on the ground, unable to move, no matter how much I push at the air to obey my simple command. This is Styx's domain, one of her own creation, and I'm a small ant at her feet.*

Saffron's mouth is closed, but her screams still echo around us. They will never leave, not as a dead body lay in her arms.

Her heart.

The silhouette disintegrates the moment Styx touches Saffron's hand while remaining in the water. She leans forward, whispers words I cannot hear. Then, dozens of shadowy figures materialize. I recognize Zeus from his large beard and lightning bolt, Hera from her diadem in the shape of a peacock's backside, and Hermes from his winged sandals. Apollo stands amongst the Olympians, and with Styx's hand still on Saffron, Saffron raises her trembling, bloody hands.

Hera dies first in a tornado of blood and guts.

Then, Zeus pleadingly says. "My daughter…" before he joins his wife as a casualty to Styx and Saffron.

Every Olympian appears and Saffron's broken heart and misguided hands murders them all. That shadowy figure was her heart, and whoever kills them murders the sanity within her. She kills every immortal, blaming them as if they were the one that wielded the weapon. Hermes, Hades, Apollo, and Persephone all die by Saffron's hand before her attention turns to me.

Finally, she sees me and raises her hand up into the air.

"H!"

I take a few discombobulated seconds to recognize the voice pulling me free from my torment. It takes longer to remember that the first dream was a clue to Styx's current plans, while the second was an instrument of distraction. A fear tactic, and nothing more.

I am not in bed like I thought I was, rather; I stand in front of an easel. Black, red, and white paint covers my hands.

Lowell's hands are on my shoulders, nails digging into my skin, and I know that's how he woke me. I need pain to rouse me when I become too involved in my dreams, but why is he in my bedroom? Apollo stands away from us, but I see the dried ichor on his wrists immediately.

"What happened? What did I do to you?"

"You slept walked again, H."

Lowell lessens his hold on my shoulders, and he tries to turn before I can see the new bruise forming on his left eye.

"Oh, no, not again." Tears well up in my eyes as I gingerly raise my hand, touching the mark I left on my friend's eye. "I didn't know, I promise."

"You never do," Lowell gives me a soft smile. "Luckily, I've become a master at waking you up from them."

My gaze immediately snags on Apollo. Mainly, the dried blood on his wrists. I just watched him die in a dream, saw his shadowy silhouette erupting as bones flew across the room, but I was the real reason behind his pain. The wounds have healed, but the dried blood is proof of my attack.

"I'm so sorry."

The tears welling up spill down my cheeks as guilt finds its mark. Apollo takes a few steps closer to me, wanting to envelop me in his arms, but the closer he gets, the more clearly I can see the blood.

I flinch at the sight of the wound I caused, and he stops walking. Lowell seems to read my mind and pulls my body closer to his. I rest my head on his chest, closing my eyes as the tears burn my eyes. Eyes that have seen too much.

Lowell speaks the words that I am too afraid to. "I've

283

got her for a bit, bro. Why don't you go to sleep some-where else? My room is open."

"I'm not leaving her."

"Because she's yours?"

"No, because I'm hers, and I'm not leaving her when she's like this."

"She can't even look at you right now, bro!"

"Call me bro one more time," Apollo's voice takes a low, lethal tone.

There's a beat of silence, then Lowell says in a quieter tone. "She can't keep looking at the blood."

"What blood?" Apollo asks. Then, he says. "Oh. I didn't know it was still there."

"Yeah. Until you clean the blood off your arms, she can't look at you. If you love her, then you'll leave so I can help her."

"She doesn't need her cheating ex over me. Plus, you-"

Lowell interrupts. "Then why did you pull me out of my room to wake her up? Like it or not, I'm a part of H's life and I'm not going anywhere. We are each other's family and right now, that's exactly what she needs. Family. So, with all due respect, get out."

There is a stretch of silence, and I can practically feel the tension building in the room, but finally Apollo asks in a quieter, almost hushed, voice. "Why is she okay around you if she hurt you too?"

"Because she's hurt me before. She's never hurt you before." I flinch as Lowell speaks my truth, and more tears spill from my eyes.

Apollo says nothing more, and I realize he is gone once the heat in the room dissipates. Once I am enveloped with coldness, I open my eyes and stare up at Lowell.

"Hey." He parts a piece of my hair that covers my face. "Did you remember it this time?"

After my parents died, I sleepwalked every single night. I would scream and throw fists and kick everything in the vicinity. In a world without dreams or nightmares, nobody could understand my fits, but Lowell always woke me before I could severely harm anyone. By the time I woke up, I never knew why I was so frantic.

But they were never dreams.

They were prophecies fighting their way to the surface of my stubborn mind. Futures I refused to see trying to bleed through my unconsciousness. Now, I am strong enough to accept the visions. Now, I remember them all.

Even the one Styx didn't want me to remember.

I draw my gaze towards the painting I drew, my fingers still raw from the harshness of the painting, and Lowell follows my gaze. To him, it must look like a blur of darkness, splashes of red, little white lines on the floor, and a single zigzag black streak. Yet, to me, there is the horrific truth about Styx's first action in this war. While we all worried about Saffron and Epiales on Ogygia, she started the first attack.

"No, I remember, and we need to get Hades in here now."

"What does it mean?"

"I never understood why I was important enough to Styx. Even once I discovered I was an oracle, I couldn't understand why I was vital to Styx's downfall, but now I know."

"Do you mind cluing me in?" Lowell nervously chuckles, but I can't dare to laugh, not when I can still feel the sharp pull of my collarbone as Saffron was commanding it towards her vengeful open palms.

"Because if we're strong enough, oracles can see the future through someone else's mind, too. I'm getting stronger by the day, and now I know Styx's first plan. I know what she's doing, and I think I can stop her in time."

I stare at the shadowy figure I created on my artwork, and a chill runs down my spine as Styx's ambush blurs in quick succession in my mind.

"We need to get Hades in here because-"

"You've always been so smart, H," Lowell kisses the top of my head, interrupting me.

"Styx is about to attack-"

Before I can finish my sentence, the tip of a dagger is my only warning before Lowell brutally slams it into my stomach. My hands that are on his shoulders tighten, disbelief coursing through my freezing veins as pain erupts throughout my entire abdomen. Lowell, the person I once considered my only remaining family, yanks the dagger out of my stomach. As I feel my blood spilling down my body, he thrusts the weapon inside of me again.

"I'm so sorry," he kisses my cheek as if he loved me. "I wish you didn't learn all of this."

He pulls the dagger out again, and just when I expect the feeling of the dagger once more, a swish moves through the air. An arrow lodges itself in the middle of Lowell's forehead. My former first love, and longest friend, collapses dead on the floor and I can no longer hold myself up on my own. I tumble down onto the floor beside my traitorous friend's body, but before I land, Apollo scoops me up into his arms.

"No, no, no, no, no, no."

My eyes are tired, stinging with both tears and sleepiness, as I stare up at the man who I should've let comfort me instead. His hands press against my stab wounds, forcing pressure, as true fear captures him.

"Someone come help! Help!"

Apollo's hands tremble as they apply pressure to my wounds, but I am so cold and cannot stop shaking under his hold, no matter how much heat his touch normally provides.

"The painting," I stammer. It's so difficult to keep my eyes open or speak, but I need to tell him. If I don't survive, then he needs to know the truth of Styx's plans. "I need you to know...."

"You will not die, μέλι, even if I have to drag your soul out of the Underworld myself and bring you back to life. You are not leaving my life before ours has truly begun." His tears spill from his chin and fall on my body. "I'm the God of Medicine. I will heal you, Hart Sommers, and then I'm going to make you my wife. You can't leave me because I'm yours, today and tomorrow and for all of eternity. I swear to all the gods, I am going to marry you as soon as I heal you because you're my everything, but I can't heal the dead. So, stay awake. Stay with me, please."

I smile softly at the thought. "You're going to marry me?"

"Yes, μέλι, I'm going to marry you. There's no one else in this world for me, so please stay. I'm in ruin without you."

I want to stay awake for him, but sleep beckons for me, and I can't ignore it. Apollo's screams and the hard press of his hands are my last senses before succumbing to sleep's command.

TWENTY-EIGHT

SAFFRON

Poseidon does not take me to the ruined remains of his castle. When his arms latch around my waist and a plume of water transports us far from Ogygia's clutches, he takes me to the place I loathe the most. It is a gorgeous cage, Mt. Olympus, with gilded bars that almost appear innocent, but it's a cage all the same. I have never enjoyed my fleeting visits to Mt. Olympus. They begin with an appeasing image and wither from the inside out.

Hera always reminds me how much she yearned for my death. Zeus barely glances at me, but when he does, there's always a wariness behind his eyes. Like he waits for me to demand his throne through blood and bones. There's no comfort in this place. Aphrodite and Hephaestus argue and then she searches for a god or goddess to ease her rage. Dionysus drinks himself into oblivion, while Athena attempts to clean the irreparable wounds of the surrounding detrimental gods with gauze and stitches. Mt. Olympus's occupants are unsalvageable.

It's a beautiful ruin.

And I hate being here.

Poseidon sets us down on the clouded floor, and the dread that overtakes me every time I enter Mt. Olympus triples when I see who waits for us at the open gilded gates. Hera stands in a floor-length plum gown with a train that creates a halo around her feet. Her golden diadem twinkles brightly against her jet black hair, which is styled in an intricate, updo style. She always paints her lips the darkest shade of purple, nearing black, and perpetually pulling into a dismal frown.

"You're free." There's a pause, then unenthusiastically, she says. "Oh, yay."

"Where's Zeus?" I ask, ignoring her jabs.

"Gone, but he'll be back soon. He doesn't want you to leave Mt. Olympus until he returns."

The statement strikes me as odd.

Zeus fears Styx, possibly more than all of us, even before we knew about the war. Any time someone would swear to the River Styx, a current of fear would shudder through Zeus. I recognized the fear well because the expression of fear on his face is a mirror of my own. It's when we look most similar, when blanketed in fright.

He would not leave Mt. Olympus without a horde of gods at his disposal unless victory was on the horizon; instead, all we feel is defeat.

So, where is he?

Hera notices my hesitance because she adds. "He's been visiting the oracle a lot. Seems to like her."

"Oh, for the love of the gods. This week has royally sucked. The last thing I need to hear is you blathering away with your jealous rants." Poseidon pats my back. "Let's leave her stewing and go get a drink. Or, maybe you get a shower first, then we drink. I love you, but you're smelling more rotten than Athena's-"

"Don't finish that sentence."

Poseidon grins. "I've missed you, God-Killer."

Hera glares at us, but we pay her no further attention. She wants to complain to us, to force us to join her in her misery, but I do not have the energy for her struggles. Poseidon and I walk away from her, and only once we are out of her earshot, I comfortably think back to Ogygia.

To Epiales.

"We need to save him."

"Who? Zeus?" Poseidon scoffs. "Hera is insane, but Zeus doesn't need saving. And even if he did, why would I want to save him? They're prime entertainment."

"Not Zeus. Epiales."

Poseidon stumbles with his next step. "Gods no. Why would we do that?"

Because he brought me happiness for the first time in decades. He gave me back a glimpse of my past that I thought had died. He gifted me with laughter and smiles again when I thought they were obsolete. Epiales made me feel wanted, and I don't want to lose that yet. I don't know Alastor, but I know the anger on his face well. If I leave Epiales on that island for too long, I'm uncertain if my threat to Alastor will stop him from killing Epiales.

But it's more than my infatuation.

"Styx believes that if Epiales stays on that island, then she will win the war. I don't know if it is because he's the prophesied heart, or if there's something else we don't know, but he can't stay in Styx's domain. He can't stay where he can die and start the bloodshed we have feared will begin."

Poseidon remains silent for a long while. While I do not enjoy my time on Mt. Olympus, I have a home here, and we walk towards it as Poseidon processes what I have said. He hesitates to answer me, to shed the humor and playfulness, to talk about something more serious. His distrust for Epiales is not as potent as Zeus's, but it's there. Festering underneath the surface.

"He fought with my father against us," Poseidon finally says.

"Until he saw I was in danger. Then, he switched sides at the end. He helped us defeat Kronos."

He lets out a breath, almost resembling a laugh. "Don't pretend that he was good. You're smarter than that."

"Okay, I won't. He was a villain, even if he cared about me, but he's different now."

Poseidon scoffs. "Do you know how many women I've heard declare they've changed a man? Come on, God-Killer."

"I brought him back by giving him my humanity. It's a part of me that now lives inside of him. A human version of him," I add at the end.

"He's human?" Poseidon can't hide the disbelief in his tone.

I nod my head. "If he really is the prophesied heart, then we know how the war starts."

"The ultimate fate is decided when the heart twice fails, and from the savior, a terrible scream will wail. The sound will echo forevermore, and from the scream, spawns a war." Poseidon whispers the part of the prophecy surrounding the heart aloud, then asks. "Are you sure he's in the heart?"

"No," I admit. "I'm uncertain of anything with Styx or this prophecy, but I know I don't want to take that chance. I also know I don't want him to die again. Not yet."

Poseidon looks at me. Really looks at me now.

"You fell for him on that island."

"Please help me." My voice breaks at the plea.

"I'll set up a meeting with the Olympians for when Zeus returns to Mt. Olympus. He might demand Epiales's death, but I think I can sway him to a vote."

"And you'll vote with me? To save him?"

"Unless Athena votes with you, then I have to vote the opposite of anything owl-face chooses." He grins. "I'll always have your side. Can't lose favor with my favorite niece."

"Thank you," I say with a smile.

"I haven't seen that in twenty years. That smile. Keep grinning, God-Killer, and for the love of the gods, shower and change before meeting me at my house for some drinks."

I laugh. "Alright. I'll see you in about thirty minutes."

"Make it fifty. You really stink."

Poseidon leaves, and I open the door to my home.

Hermes sits in the living room, body angled towards me. My first thought is guilt when I see him sitting there with such sadness etched on his face. I haven't thought about him all day. Not even once. I've been so consumed with thoughts of escape, then plans on how to protect Epiales, that I never thought about Hermes being on Mt. Olympus. That he could sit in our living room, listening to my conversation with Poseidon about another male.

I freeze in the doorway.

Hermes may be a god, but his expression is so utterly weak. "I didn't cheat on you."

"I know you didn't."

Instead, you lied to me. That's what I want to say, but then I notice his defeated face, and the anger-filled words die on my lips.

"How?" He stammers.

"I believed it at first. You were so distant, and you were always gone. Leaving me so you could hangout with your ex, but then I found out about Styx. When I learned that, all the confusion I had with your adultery made sense. You weren't cheating. You were lying again when you promised to always be honest with me."

"When?"

"When what?"

Hermes's jaw tightens. "When did you know I wasn't cheating on you?"

"The day you signed the divorce papers. I knew when I went down to the Underworld, and you took me out of there and lied about the reasoning."

For a blinding moment, he doesn't understand. He doesn't realize why I divorced him, because he jolts to his feet. His sadness contorts into rage.

"Then why?!" He yells. "Why did you choose him over me? You know I didn't cheat on you, that I have always loved you and only you, so why?!" He stands in front of me, breathing heavily and hands twitching at his sides. Tears roll down his cheeks as he looks at me and sees only betrayal. "Why would you make me sign those papers if you knew I just wanted to protect you? I love you more than he ever will."

"This isn't about Epiales."

Hermes flinches at his name. "I heard you and Poseidon. You love him. Of course he's the reason."

"I didn't know Epiales would be brought back to life when I divorced you."

His eyes lock with mine as soon as the word leaves my lips. Divorced. It's the reminder he needs. We are no longer husband and wife. He and I ruined the past we once built together, but he doesn't see his own faults. I realize where I faltered, but he doesn't.

"Our relationship ending had nothing to do with him. It was because you didn't trust me enough to make my decisions, so you tried to trick me when you promised you never would again. You broke my heart with lies about infidelity to stop me from a fate you tried to hide from me. That's all you do, Hermes. Trick and lie and steal from me, and I told you what would happen if you did it again."

Eighty-six years ago, almost an entire lifetime ago, we stood together as he asked for my hand in marriage. I told him yes, as long as he promised he would never lie to me again. Not like he did when I was a human in his castle. If he lied again, then all that we rebuilt would fall. It wouldn't be rebuilt a third time.

He promised never to trick me again, and we married.

There were a dozen errors in our decision to marry, and hurdles we could not pass, but that was the moment I knew I couldn't stay. The moment he tricked me again, I gave him the divorce papers.

"I was just trying to protect you."

Every part of my body wants to comfort him. We were married for eighty-five years. I've been there for him, comforting him during every saddening moment in his life. Yet, I cannot coddle him now. I can't wipe away the tears or hold him close to my chest because I cause this sadness.

"I know you were, but I don't need your protection anymore." My hand reaches to wipe away his tears, but I let my hand drop without caressing his tear-stained cheek. "I'm the most powerful goddess in the world, and yet you still think I am that human you fell in love with. The girl who always needs you to protect her."

"I'll always want to protect you. How could you expect that to change?"

"I know, but I didn't need a protector, Hermes. All I needed was a husband I could trust who wouldn't lie to me. Even if you believe the reasons were good, all I wanted was honesty, and you couldn't do that."

I cannot stop myself, and I touch him. My hands fall onto him, one moving to his cheek and the other on his hip. I wipe away his tears, now rapidly flowing down, while pulling him into a hug. It's cowardly, hugging him now. It gives me the warmth I've always loved, but it also stops me from seeing his devastated face.

He thought we were going to get back together when he admitted he didn't cheat. I see that now, but I never gave him the illusion we could be fixed. We were broken before the lies, but I only paid attention to the shatters when light illuminated them.

"I love you, Saffron."

"I know you do, and I love you too. So much. But I do not love you how a wife should love her husband. Not after this, and maybe not for a while." I swear I can hear his heart break. "If I was still human, and I was as helpless and naïve as I once was, then I might've been grateful for what you did. Maybe. But I would never have been grateful for the lies. Lies you knew I hated and knew hurt me. Those tricks were always going to ruin us, but I think we ruined our marriage far before these lies. They were just the final catalyst."

He shakes his head. "Our marriage isn't ruined. We

296

used to be so good, Saffron. Our nights playing Monopoly, and dancing without music, and the way we used to laugh-"

I cut him off. "You're only naming times when I was a human, but I'm not the human girl that you fell in love with anymore. She died the moment I became a goddess. I became your equal in every conceivable way, and we changed because of it. I became somebody that was no longer compatible with you, and we didn't know to react. So, the lies eventually ended this because Hermes, our marriage *is* ruined. It's done, but it started to fall when I changed. When I became a goddess."

"No, no, no, no," Hermes grabs my face desperately, pulling me to look at his face. "No, don't say that. I love you, whether you're a goddess or a human. It changed nothing for me."

But it did.

I took a long time to realize why our relationship was falling into depths we could not recover from, but I figured it out. It was because of my humanity. My humanity is fully gone now, moved into Epiales, but when I became a goddess, the human side of me became dormant. It hid itself beneath the weight of the new, immortal woman I became.

"What is your fondest memory of the two of us, Hermes? And after all the lies you've spun these past few months, please be truthful right now."

He replies immediately. "My favorite memory was the first night you slept in my bed." His tears momentarily disappear as he thinks of the fonder times between us. "You were so serene, sleeping beside me, as if that was where you were meant to be for the rest of our lives."

I smile at the memory. Hermes was so nervous when he

asked me to sleep in the same bed as him, and fear claimed me for a few fleeting seconds. Then, we curled up together, and it made sense. I trusted him on that night, regardless of what my dreams told me about the dangers of Olympians.

"What's your second favorite memory?" I ask, and he actually smiles.

"When I taught you how to dance in the gazebo. I don't think you've ever looked more beautiful than that day."

I remember the flowers and happiness that stemmed from every corner of the backyard. He was a vision that night, and regardless of anything that has transpired between us since then, this was also my favorite memory of each other. That was the night that I realized I loved Hermes.

"That was my favorite memory of ours," I say with a soft smile. "Now tell me your third favorite memory."

"When we were in Poseidon's castle, reunited after you saved me in the Labyrinth."

Memories of the Battle of the Labyrinth return with his statement. We faced Kronos, Typhon, Circe, and a massive army within the depths of the Labyrinth Poseidon hid in his basement. Circe transformed Hermes, Hecate, Ares, and Hephaestus into her dogs and forced them to fight on the opposite side, but I recognized Ares's eyes. I saw him beneath the mutt, and I killed Circe.

Saving Hermes along the way.

We forgave each other the following day, when he promised to always protect Hattie and my friends. We kissed with passion for the first time, and I learned what a hickey was that night, too. Terrible situations arose following that kiss, but it has always been our best one. It was one of the few that had such passion; it radiated throughout my entire body.

With my hands on both sides of his face, I lean him forward until my lips just barely graze his own. I do not deepen the kiss as I normally do, and the realization etches itself on Hermes's face. I pull away from the kiss, but I keep my hands on both sides of his face and stare at him. He won't die with our departure, but something is wilting, so I cement every part of him to memory. The boyish charm on his face. The thick eyelashes overlooking forest green eyes. I will always love him, but not in the way either of us deserves.

Not anymore.

"We were married for eighty-five years, and yet all your fondest memories of us are when I was human. Eighty-eight years have come and gone, but our best times were in the first two months. After that, we were just trying to chase what we once had, but we'll never get it back. We will never be the happy couple we once were because I have changed. When I died and came back as a goddess, I essentially became a new person. Someone you had never imagined spending the rest of your life with."

"Saffron..." his voice breaks but I shake my head.

"We married hoping it'd fix our relationship, but it didn't. I kept changing, and you kept trying to act as if I hadn't. We've been content, but never truly happy. Not since I turned into a goddess, and you can try to deny that fact, but you know it's the truth. Even if it takes a while for you to realize."

Tears build up in my eyes as his stream plentifully down his sunken cheeks. He shakes his head, trying to object to the truth I am saying, but no words come out. He doesn't want to lie, not right now, so he can't speak.

Hermes is once again speechless as the weight of our conversation sinks us into the watery abyss.

"I love you."

He knows we're over.

"And I will always love you, but we aren't meant to be."

"Because you're with Epiales?" When he says these words, my tears tumble down my face.

"This isn't about him at all. Right now, this is about us."

"I've known," he hiccups. "I've always known it was him over me."

Hermes brings me close to him, sharing our last kiss as husband and wife. I can hear the tearing of our hearts as our lips glide across one another's. I can feel the softness of his lips. Taste the saltiness of our sadness. When we pull away and I open my eyes, I can see the end of our marriage as if the Fates held up the string of our relationship.

The Fates pull out their scissors, cutting the string of our deceased marriage, victims of a cruel world.

TWENTY-NINE

APOLLO

I am well acquainted with fear.

It has been by my side for as long as I have existed, re-emerging at the most inopportune times, but it has never seized my heart, soul, mind, and body until two nights ago. Until I found Lowell thrusting a blade into my Hart's stomach. Until I heard the little gasp of pain she made. I didn't know the gravity of fear's power until Hart closed her eyes and stopped moving in my arms.

"Can you tell me if she's going to live?" My fists tremble.

My son, Asclepius, impassively sits beside my soul-mate's hospital bed. "Father, why don't you go get some ambrosia and rest for a while? I will take care of her; I swear on the River-"

"Don't you dare finish that sentence," I snarl, interrupting my eldest son, and he wisely closes his mouth.

"You need to sleep though, Father."

"I don't need to rest."

It's a lie. I need to sleep. Since I killed Lowell, I haven't been able to close my eyes for more than a second. What if that's the time she opens her eyes when I close mine? What if that's the moment her heart stops beating and mine forever freezes?

I should've never left her with Lowell. I should've known not to trust a man that called a god *"bro"* on multiple occasions. He was a mongrel who never deserved Hart's trust, and I should've known not to believe a man who dared to lie to Hart for years about his feelings towards her. I shouldn't have trusted him.

Now, my Hart could die for my mistake.

It was a momentary lapse of judgement. I didn't know what to do, especially while my blood was sliding down my fingertips, but Lowell swore he knew how to help her. For less than two minutes, I trusted a man that I wish I could kill over-and-over again. I ran to the closest bathroom, thoroughly cleaned all the blood off my skin, and went right back to her.

Gods, I shouldn't have left.

I killed him too quickly. An arrow to the head was too merciful compared to the retribution he deserved. But I didn't kill him quickly enough, either. If I had let him die from the plague caused by the Nosoi birds, then he wouldn't have killed my Hart. If I had killed him the moment he healed and smiled in her direction, then I would have her safely in my arms right now.

Who would've known that the greatest way to take down an Olympian was a soft-faced mortal human with a heart of gold and a barely beating heart?

I cannot stomach the thought of going into our art room, not when the stained remains of her assassination won't come off the floor. Sleep evades me because if she dies while I am finally away from my waking nightmare, then my heart will never stitch itself back together. I cannot even eat because each time something touches my lips, I fear Hart will taste nothing ever again.

"Father," Asclepius softly murmurs, sympathy thick in his tone, but I only shake my head.

"I don't want to hear it."

"But…" Asclepius says.

A grating voice interrupts.

"Brother!"

I whip my head around at the familiar sound. Dionysus walks into the room, then leans against the doorway of the room with a bottle of wine in each hand. There is a small smirk on his face, but when his eyes migrate towards Hart's comatose body, the happiness falters. I must truly be hallucinating from sleep deprivation because I swear Dionysus stares at me with understanding rather than blanketed sympathy.

"Let's get away and drink, yes?" Dionysus wiggles the wine glasses in my direction.

"No."

"It wasn't an option. Let Asclepius do this magic in peace. It's the best option for Hart."

"You do not know what's best for my wife!" I scream at him, although he has done nothing wrong. A weapon materializes in my hand, but I'm too disoriented to know which weapon I created from nothingness. "Get out!"

"I hate to do this," Dionysus says.

Vines seep from the cracks in the floor, cracks that did not exist thirty seconds ago, and they reach for me. A sword swipes down and cuts off the first vine, but the rest surge towards me. The decision to leave isn't my choice anymore, and aggravation claws up my throat as I grit out one word.

"Fine."

"Goodie!" Dionysus exclaims.

"But just one drink."

"Just one bottle, got it."

The vines disperse.

My hands tremble as I lean forward, tucking a lock of her brown hair behind her ear. Her skin is cold, too cold. Normally, she is the warmth I need in the coldness, but now I recoil from her touch as if I have made contact with a corpse. Tears immediately build in my eyes, and my only son places his hand on my shoulder.

"I'm going to do everything in my power to save her," Asclepius promises. "She will be fine while you are away."

"Thank you." The words emerge from a clogged throat before I turn from the room and storm towards Dionysus. Each step feels like a betrayal. I should not be drinking when she is dying. I should stay right next to her, my hand never leaving hers.

Dionysus leads me away from the room and towards the garden in my backyard. The same backyard where so many humans were buried during Kronos's war. Gaillardia flowers bloom in all directions, painfully reminding me of the woman I once loved who died in my arms. Is that what I'm cursed with? Forever having the women I love die in my embrace?

"Let's drink somewhere else," I say.

"Why? It's beautiful out here."

I can hear my own shattered voice all those years ago, chanting the same words in endless repetition. What will those words be when Hart dies? Or will it just be the shattering of my heart on endless repetition in my mind? Echoing forevermore.

"I said no."

My eyes snag on the eternal gaillardia flower that sprung on its namesake's burial ground. It has never died or wilted since the huntresses buried her. It has remained the same for eighty-eight years and served as an immortal reminder of who I lost; worse, of who I might lose next.

Dionysus ignores my request. I removed all the furniture in the backyard, so Dionysus makes a bench out of vines. He taps three times on the empty spot beside him, and with my eyes still on that damned flower, I take a seat.

"Did I ever tell you there was somebody before Ariadne?" Dionysus passes me my favorite bottle of wine, and while I take the alcohol, I shake my head.

"No, you haven't."

I barely pay attention to my brother. My focus drifts between the gaillardia flower and the window where Hart lays.

"Yeah, his name was Claudius, and I think he was the love of my life." I can hear the smile as the words filter out of his lips. "No, not think. I know he was."

Dionysus chugs the contents of his wine bottle, drifting the space into silence.

"He lived in Athens during the reign of King Aegeus," Dionysus mournfully adds.

"Theseus's human father?"

"That very king. I met Claudius in a brothel in Athens, and it was love at first sight. He was the most beautiful creature I had ever seen, my glorious Claudius, and I freed him from the brothel. I placed him in my house in Athens, and he was mine just as I was his, until it came time for King Aegeus to sacrifice seven men and seven women for

Crete. For the Labyrinth and the Minotaur's bloodthirsty appetite."

With grave realization, I now know why Dionysus is not with Claudius.

"I told Claudius I would make sure he didn't have to go. After all, I'm a god, and I am more powerful than any king ever will be. I can make sure another man goes in Claudius's place without guilt because I never ask for anything. I only wanted him, but Claudius refused my help. He said it would be an honor to go to the Labyrinth to fight the Minotaur with the mighty hero Theseus."

As he says the hero's name, nothing but hatred laces his tongue.

"What happened, brother?" I inquire after a sip of my wine, and Dionysus pops off the cork of his second.

"What do you think?"

Death. It's why Claudius isn't wearing a wedding band, but Ariadne is. It's why their relationship is not perfect because he had perfection, and he lost it. Dionysus gave me a look of understanding because he knows what it is like to fear the loss of your soulmate. The only difference is that my fear has not been actualized yet; his has.

"I was powerless for the first time in my life, but I had to trust that Poseidon's Demi-God son could protect my Claudius. It was dim-witted to trust a son of Poseidon's, or anyone other than myself, but I did. I trusted Theseus when I should've gone into the Labyrinth myself and kill that wretched bull. Theseus didn't care about the other human sacrifices in the maze, because Theseus only cared about saving himself and slaying a powerful beast. The Minotaur killed the love of my life just like all the other maidens and men who had a blind faith that Theseus would save them."

He is silent for some time, chugging the wine bottle's contents until he throws the second bottle across the garden. I expect him to materialize a third bottle, but my baby brother sighs in defeat as he rummages his hand through his light blonde hair. For the first time in our entire existence, I finally see Dionysus as something more than an outrageous partier; he is a man with a broken heart.

"I saved her from the island and married her because Theseus is just as responsible for Claudius's death as the Minotaur, and I refused to let him kill another person who blindly trusted him. When I saw Theseus leave Ariadne on that island to starve to death, I didn't hesitate. I had to save her, even though I couldn't save Claudius, and I married her. I wanted Theseus to see that I won something in a match he didn't know we were playing, but every time that I am with Ariadne, all I see is my Claudius."

"Do you two even love each other?" I ask Dionysus this question and he scoffs, materializing another wine bottle for him to guzzle down.

"Of course I love my wife, brother, but not how a husband should love his wife. I love her like a friend, one that I can talk to about anything, and the feeling is mutual. We are the closest of allies, and I would even call her my best friend because she sees me as who I really am. But my heart belongs to Claudius and hers Theseus. her heart still tethers to Theseus. No amount of love that we have for one another will change that. There's a reason she and I have no children."

"Dionysus, I'm so sorry."

"I don't want pity, brother. I just wanted you to know that I know what it's like to feel powerless when the one person you love more than anything is hurt. We are invincible, us gods, but when our soulmates are fragile humans, suddenly we are the weakest species in the world. No stronger than a gnat."

I clink my wine bottle with his in response. Together, we drink in silence. We do not need to say anymore words or pretend that we are alright because that would be a lie. Both Dionysus and I try to survive in a world that'll never end for us, while our soulmates continue to slip from our fingers.

"Do you think you'd ever find somebody else?" I ask.

"If Hart dies, would you be able to find somebody else?"

"No," my answer is immediate. "I've met all three of my great loves, and the pain of losing one of them was enough. I cannot lose my soulmate without my heart leaving the world with her."

"Exactly." He drinks his bottle. "Once your soulmate dies, so does the part of your heart that can adequately love another. So, no, I'll never find somebody else for more than a night. Nobody compares to Claudius."

"And nobody compares to Hart."

"Yeah, she has a really nice rack." I glare at my brother, who is smirking mischievously. "What, I can't give your girl a compliment about her girls?"

I chuck my wine bottle at his head.

THIRTY

LAMB

Iris took June to Mt. Olympus, and by some miracle, Hera didn't send her back to Earth. So, we followed her. It's been two days since we arrived on Mt. Olympus, with a warning that we aren't allowed to stay for long. Humans do not belong in the home of the gods, and it might be because of the events on Ogygia, but Zeus has calmed Hera until June wakes.

If June wakes.

After the battle with Atlas and his horde of monsters, only five of us remain. Four, if June gets an infection. Four, if June never wakes.

My hospital bed sits next to June's, and after convincing Paean, I'm close enough to wrap my hand around her remaining one. Her chest rises and falls, but her eyes never open. Paean, the god of healing, said she fell unconscious when he amputated the remnants of her arm. I understand the fear Artemis had when I would not wake as I hold June's hand and will her to open her eyes.

As each day comes and goes without her awakening, I fear she never will. That she will die before knowing we succeeded. We found Ogygia. I must continuously remind myself that June's strength supersedes many others. She is a fighter sheathed for battle, and this is one of her many fights.

To an unsuspecting bystander, June doesn't exude strength. She is barely five feet tall, with short, blonde hair that further stresses the round, youthfulness of her face. Yet, the moment this tiny blonde's mouth opens, a warrior takes possession. She is the defeater of the Hydra, and she wore the title with pride and an absence of fear.

June was the first human Artemis invited to the huntress clan after the last Titanomachy War. Artemis was hesitant to add new women to our group, especially as she mourned Willow's death, but three years later, we stumbled upon a brazen, seventeen-year-old girl who just punched a boy in the face. He tried advancing on her without her permission, and we moved forward to save her, but she saved herself.

She beat that boy to a bloody pulp, until he was little more than a puddle of tears, and then she spat in his face. "I will not marry some pimply boy when I could be so much more than a greedy man's wife."

She kicked him once more in between his legs, spun around, and skipped back to her house. Not walked, skipped. He screamed profanities her way, threatened her because of his own deflated ego, but she didn't even bother to turn and face him. She had an elated smile on her face, one that showed her victory in her stride towards independence.

Artemis and I looked at one another, mirroring identical grins, and we followed behind her. It didn't take June long to hear the pattering of feet a few paces behind her. She spun around, hair wild around face.

"I'm not above castration, Frederick!"

June thought Frederick was still following her, but as soon as her gaze met Artemis's, she bowed with instant recognition. Fell to her knees after threatening castration and cried at Artemis's feet. Before Artemis could get a word in, June stared up at the sky.

"Thank you, Fates, for finally having my world meet hers."

She became a huntress that night, and after June admitted she prayed to the Fates and Artemis every night. It was the same prayer, never deviated. Not even one word changed. She prayed she would meet Artemis and become a huntress. Both the Fates and Artemis answered her prayers, and for eighty-five years, she prayed to the Fates every night with one word.

"Thanks."

Now, I hold her comatose hand and wonder if she ever regretted her prayers. They had a funny way of twisting her wish into a travesty.

"How is she?" Jamila stands in the doorway, one hand resting on the door, and she hesitates entering. She flits her attention between June, me, and our intertwined hands. Redness blooms on her cheeks, and she takes one step out of the room. "I'm sorry, I'll come later."

I didn't think I could as I ponder June's life, but I let out a raucous laugh. It stalls Jamila. She once again bounces her attention from June, me, and our hands. Her nose, which is identical to Hattie's, scrunches with unmistakable confusion.

"Do you think we're dating?"

Her attention fixates on our hands. "I don't judge."

"I'm aromantic asexual."

There didn't use to be a term for how I felt. When I was first turned into a huntress, the world was in such turmoil that discussions about the broadness of sexuality didn't exist. I understood bisexuality, homosexuality, and heterosexuality, but that was it. In the chaos of war, nobody discussed the variety that a person can feel.

It made me feel like I didn't belong anywhere. There were three boxes, and you had to check one, but I fit in none of them. I wasn't attracted to males or females. There wasn't a spot for me, so I slipped into the background. I became the invisible huntress that everyone jokingly monikered.

Then, the war ended, the world grew, and I learned more about my sexuality. I discovered the multitude of boxes, all with different titles and explanations. I found the term aromantic, and I finally felt seen. Finally, I could check a box. I didn't feel like I had to be the invisible one any more. Some people who are aroace can form relationships, but I have never had that desire in my nearly six hundred years alive, and I do not see myself changing.

I don't want to change.

And that took a long time to realize.

"Oh, good. I was worried I was interrupting a declaration of love or something. That would have been awkward."

Jamila walks into the room, more comfortably this time, but there's still a nervousness in her gait. It's not because of June's amputated arm. She glances down at the wrapped stump and barely pauses; it's something else. She sits in the empty chair on June's other side and gives me a strained expression that I think she thinks is a smile.

"What can I do for you, Jamila?"

"Straight to the point, I like that."

But it doesn't appear she likes my forwardness. Her hands nervously run across the top of her thighs once, twice, and probably fifteen more times. She won't look me in the eye, and she keeps biting her bottom lip. After riding alongside her for almost a week, I know when she bites her lip; she wants to say something she's afraid to admit.

"Just out with it."

The words spill out of her lips too fast. "Ihave-grownupwithgodsmyentirelifeandI-"

"I didn't understand a single word you just said. Slower, Jamila. Please."

"Okay." Jamila takes a long breath, and when she exhales, the words come out slower. "I have grown up with the gods as my parents, my friends, and my bosses. I know the danger that comes with associating with them, and I know that it's most dangerous for humans to be in the huntress clan."

We both valiantly look away from June, who lays in between us as proof of her words.

"But all I've wanted since I was a little girl is to be just like you. Mom used to read me stories about you and the other huntresses. Your fight against Typhon in the Labyrinth, when you slayed the Echidna three times, and I was so impressed. More than impressed, you and Artemis became my idols. I wanted to be just like you."

"Jamila-"

"Please let me finish? If I don't get the words out, I'm afraid I never will." She interrupts.

"Go ahead."

"Thanks." She lets out a shaky breath, then continues. "As I grew up, Aunt Athena taught me how to fight, and I would imagine that I wasn't fighting alongside her, but I was slaying the Echidna or fighting against Typhon. Ever since I was a child, all I've ever wanted was to be a huntress. I even begged my mom to buy me a bow and arrow the day after my eleventh birthday. The day I met you and the other huntresses."

Jamila looks down at her hands, which continue to run alongside the tops of her thighs, and the same crimson blush returns. "Since I was ten years old, Aunt Athena has trained me on a bow and arrow. It was the only weapon I would choose, even if she wanted me to try a spear. So, I wanted to ask you if you could talk to Artemis about letting join her group of huntresses."

"Jamila, you're Saffron and Hermes's daughter. It's a bigger risk than a traditional human. Do you even think your parents would allow it?"

"Why should their opinion matter? I'm nineteen years old, and I'm an adult who can make her own decisions. Plus, your numbers are too low for an upcoming war. You need more huntresses, and you will not find somebody more devoted to the gods than the one that was raised by the Goddess of Bones herself."

"You've trained since you were nine?" She nods her head and my gaze drops to June. "June said she started training herself to be a huntress when she was thirteen. She started making sword with branches and used a sling-shot as arrow practice."

"Saffron has always wanted me to find my passion. This is my passion. I will be faithful to Lady Artemis for all eternity until the battle that eventually takes my life. I will be abstinent from any men, and I will devote myself solely to her and our ride. My aim will be true, and I will be immortally a huntress."

A figure moves in the background, and my eyes move

towards the eavesdropper. Hermes leans against the doorway of the hospital room, watching my conversation with Jamila with a sad smile on his face. He has raised this girl, just as Saffron had, and is watching her wish to become something that is not entirely human.

"What do you think, Hermes? Think you can talk to Artemis for her?"

Jamila turns around sharply, taken by surprise by the god of mischief's arrival, and his sorrowful smile falters. "I was going to tell you."

He has been in a sullen mood since his divorce, worse now that Saffron has returned from Ogygia, but he smiles at Jamila. The hardness in his expression softens in her company. "When were you going to tell me? After it was done?"

"Well, yeah."

"I've raised you to be just like me."

He says it with such fondness, but sadness weighs down his shoulders for an unrelated reason. Jamila notices it, too. Her grin morphs into a look of concentration as she bounces her attention from his slouched stance, red-rimmed eyes, and furrowed brow.

"What happened?" Jamila asks.

"They found Saffron. She's here now."

That doesn't answer the question fully, but Jamila does not care. Glee envelops her. She runs and hugs Hermes, kissing him on the cheek, and then she's gone. Searching for Saffron while Hermes stays here without a desire to follow.

We have known each other for many centuries, Hermes and me, but we rarely speak. He doesn't expect it now, either. Sullenly, he closes the door behind Jamila and sits against it. His eyes close shut, and he doesn't say a word.

His reunion with Saffron went as everyone but him assumed.

Terribly.

I don't know what to say at this moment, and sometimes, when words do not come easily, it's better to say nothing at all. That's what happens. For a long time, Hermes sits against the closed door with his eyes shut and his mind in chaos, and I silently sit beside June. I do not look at him, or ask if he is okay, but I'm a presence he needs. A steady sword as an internal battle rages.

He cries loud enough for me to hear, but I pretend I can't. I pointedly make June my entire attention so Hermes can feel both alone and in company. We stay like this for over an hour until his cries have subsided and his breathing regulates again.

Hermes stands on unsteady feet, and our eyes meet. "You think Jamila will make a good huntress?"

This isn't what he wants to speak about, not really, but it's a distraction that he needs. So, I nod my head. "She fought well with us and helped slay the Crommyonian Sow. With time, she could be a formidable huntress."

"Alright, I'll talk to Artemis and Saf..." he stops, lets out a shallow breath, then amends. "Jamila's mom. Have a good night, Lamb."

"You too."

His footsteps are the only sound for the longest time. Then, a croaky voice rasps. "That was awkward."

I look down and June smiles back up at me.

THIRTY-ONE

SAFFRON

I rarely ever drink, but the sounds of the Fates snipping the thread of life that tied Hermes and me together play in a repetitive loop, and I need the sound to cease. I shower, scrubbing away the grime from the island. To stop thinking about Epiales alone on Ogygia, I force a wall in my mind, blocking out all intrusive thoughts. While putting on clean clothes, officially ridding myself of that cursed dress, I stand in the bedroom I once shared with Hermes. My thoughts bounce between the two males. It never ends.

So, I walk to Poseidon's home on Mt. Olympus.

He's already drunk when I join him and Amphitrite, and only now I see the heaviness he wears in the bags under his eyes. The war blooms like a ripening belladonna berry, and not even the strongest gods are pervious to its tart taste. Poseidon and Amphitrite equally slump in their seats, holding drinks close to their chest.

Amphitrite's orange and red hair create a waterfall over

her long, sullen, yet still beautiful face. "Welcome to the pity party. Care for a drink?"

They're one of the few gods who have a bar in their living room. Dionysus does, too, but he brightly lights his corner of the room with grape vines and humor. This bar in Poseidon and Amphitrite's home does not derive from happiness or celebration. It's a shovel for the depressive hole they dig themselves deeper in.

I walk to the bar, picking up any bottle without a care of what lays inside. I join their macabre company, drinking away the memories of Hermes's forlorn expression, Epiales's words dripped in an eternal goodbye, and Alastor's raged glances. Amphitrite sniffles every minute or two, but she never cries. She collects her sorrow and places it in a hidden crevice of her mind she refuses to open.

"I'm sorry about your home."

Amphitrite shakes her head, but it's Poseidon who replies. "That's not why we're drinking, although I'll miss my labyrinth."

I don't ask, but they know the question. Amphitrite answers with a single word. "Kymopoleia."

"And my cyclops sons," Poseidon adds.

Neither need to clarify.

Traitors have emerged from every shadow in every room, and they learned this morbid truth with their children. I want to be surprised that their children would betray them, but after Hecate, nothing raises shock. Styx is a master manipulator, spinning her words into gold, lining the pockets of everyone who listens.

Kymopoleia has always been a quiet, sullen goddess, her gaze continuously wandering around the castle in hopes of something new. I do not know what Styx offered her, but the sad become desperate for a sliver of happiness.

If Styx showed her a wayward direction, promising her a chance at a smile again, Kymopoleia will take it.

And, it seems, she did.

As for the cyclops, I did not know them. They rarely visited Poseidon in his underwater castle, and if they did, I was not there. I met none of them, so I do not know their motivations behind turning on Poseidon. All I know is that when Poseidon loves, he gives all his heart, then some. He had dozens of cyclops children, and they all turned on him, stabbing the heart he whole heartedly gave.

"I'm sorry."

"You did nothing, God-Killer." Poseidon tilts back his drink, and he gulps his coppery liquid.

Amphitrite and I follow suit.

I periodically glance at the doorway, waiting for Zeus to reappear, until my mind becomes too foggy with alcohol to remember my primary concerns. Epiales's sullen goodbye and Hermes's tear stricken face fall into obscurity.

So, this is why Poseidon drinks.

He wants to forget the memories his mind refuses to ignore. Happiness can only ease the sadness for so long; alcohol promises oblivion. We rarely talk, the three of us, because what would we say? How sad we are that Styx's war has brought alive all the inner monsters? How much we wish time would rewind, so we knew our last times with someone would really be the last time?

Snores join the room, and when I glance over, Poseidon and Amphitrite are curled together. They drape one arm over each other, but the other remains fast around the neck of the bottle. Even in their unconscious, they do not remove themselves from their fix.

I should leave, but I don't. I lean back, and I drink and drink and drink.

A chorus of footsteps alert me to a new presence, but I do not look up. I know who stands at the doorway, panting as if he's run a thousand miles to get to me. His presence has always been a thousand needles pricking my skin. An electrical current going straight to my spine. His eyes burn a trail of fire wherever they touch, when no one else can, so I know who stands at the doorway.

"You're okay."

"You almost sound relieved." I tilt back the drink, finishing the last gulp.

Ares walks into the room, but he hesitates with each step. He treats me like I'm broken glass. Too careful. Too afraid to cut himself. Ares doesn't look at the now-empty bottle in my hand. He only stares at me, and I want him to look elsewhere. Anywhere else. Because when he looks at me, all my emotions force themselves to the surface, and I drank to forget.

He sits in the empty spot on the loveseat. "When did you escape?"

"This morning around sunrise."

He says nothing after, but he reaches for the empty bottle. I tighten my grip, but when his index finger grazes the top of my hand, all my strength dissipates. I let him take the bottle and set it on the ground next to his feet, and then I fall into his chest. He freezes in shock, but when the unmistakable sound of my sobs hits the air, he wraps his arms around me.

I know better than to believe he cares, but I need this moment right now. I need a little sliver of the peace that only he can provide, even if he ignores me for another eighty years. Ares rests his cheek against the top of my head as I curl myself further into him. I don't know if it's him or me who puts my legs on his lap, but we tangle up in each other.

It helps. His presence helps the tears finally escape, and he lets me explode with sadness for my failed marriage, fear for Epiales's life, and apprehension for what the future entails. I need him, and at this moment, he doesn't push me away. He allows me to need him.

I blame my inebriation because I repeat one of the last statements I said to him before Ogygia. "I tried to see you before my wedding."

Last time I said this, he closed himself off. Said two words and disappeared from my life again. It's what he does best, disappears. I have always wanted to know why, with everything that has transpired between us, but he doesn't let the words come alive. He hides before the conversation can exist.

I close my eyes, ready for his silence, but at least I get this moment. His arms are around me so I can freely cry.

"I know." His voice cracks with those two words, the same ones he said weeks ago in my office. He clears his throat. "I heard you when you asked to see me, but I couldn't. I stood a few feet away from my door, and I almost answered. Almost. Always almost."

"You had your sons turn me away."

"Yeah, I did."

"Why?"

The first time I have gotten the chance to ask one of my many "whys" aloud, and I don't think he will answer. He hasn't been honest since that night in the Labyrinth eighty-eight years ago, no matter how often I go searching for them. He reaches out a hesitant hand, always so hesitant with me, and he brushes away one stubborn, wet tear.

"Hermes will always sacrifice himself time and time

again for you. It's what you deserve. Someone who will put you first, always."

But Hermes wasn't right for me. I knew that then, when I went to Ares before my marriage, and I knew that on the day of my nuptials. Hermes knew, deep down, too. We weren't the perfect fit, even if it appeared that way to anyone looking in.

"Like Epiales," I say.

"Where you happy on Ogygia? With him?" His voice is scratchier now, displaying emotions that his stoic appearance doesn't give way to.

"Yes, I was happy. Now, I'm left with only fear that he is dead on that island. Killed before ever living his new life."

"So that's why you cry? Because you fear what will happen to him?"

I shake my head. "It's not the only reason. Hermes and I had *the* talk. The one we were eighty years late having."

"I'm sorry," he says, and it might be my inebriation, but I believe him. He wanted my marriage to work. It's why he didn't answer the door when I went searching for him.

"I don't belong with someone who only wants to protect me. That's not a relationship. A back-and-forth game of lies masqueraded as heroism. But I loved him. A lot."

"It's better than being with ruination."

"Is that how you see yourself? Ruination?"

The smile he gives me is a sad one. "Are you always this honest when drunk?"

"No, just this honest around you." The bubble of laughter that leaves me shows my intoxication. It's garbled and foolish, and makes that sad smile on his face grow a

322

little wider. "It makes no sense. Always being honest with you. You hate me, yet it's easiest to cry in your company. You hate me, yet I always find peace around you."

Ares leans forward and I'm so drunk, I almost don't realize his lips press against my forehead until he pulls away. "Go to bed, Saffron. I'll see you in the morning."

He slides off the couch, delicately putting my legs back on the cushion that's cold without him. He leaves the room without looking back.

THIRTY-TWO

HART SOMMERS

My father loved the beach, particularly the ones that few people have trekked before. So, it's only fitting that I see my father again on a barren island.

When I was a child, he would always take my brother and me to a beach he created with his own hands. He purchased sand from a hardware store to create the beach, and our ocean was a small little stream at the bottom of the woods in our neighborhood, but it was perfect.

The first day of spring every year, Dad, Suraj, and I would travel down the hill in our backyard, trek through the mile-long trail of woods behind our fence, until we arrived at our little beach. Dad made sure that it remained prestigious, even through the treacherous winter, because he wanted our beach to be perfect.

Now, he and I stand on a beach that puts our little, man-made one to shame. Not a single cloud darkens the sky's powder blue excellence. Sand smoother than I've ever seen before finds solace between my toes. There is a flourish of trees behind us, but my focus is on my *father. The man who I haven't seen in many years, and at the sight of him, I immediately clutch the feather locket around my neck.*

He looks exactly how I remember him. Peppered gray hair. Blue eyes that neither my brother nor I inherited. Long yet thin lips accessorized by wrinkles from smiling too wide and too often. Pale skin differing from the rest of the family's tawny complexion. There's a line of red across his cheeks from the sun; most importantly, he's happy.

His arms open wide, and he chokes out. "My special Hart. Oh, how I've missed you."

The tears come instantaneously at the sight of my father, surrounded by a blinding white light, and I rush towards him. It's been too long since I've had one of his hugs; it always smells like his aftershave and Mom's cooking. I want to feel the warmth and protection that comes from his arms wrapped around me, and I know when I hug him, the pain in my stomach will cease to exist.

I am so close to reaching him, but before I can touch him, he places his hand out and stops me. The simple movement creates an invisible barrier between us that halts me. I am so close to him, a single foot away, and yet I cannot move forward. I cannot feel the protection only he has brought me, but I watch my father stare back at me as if he is in a different dimension.

"Why won't you let me come to you?"

"Because the book of your life isn't over yet. There's still so many stories you get to make in this world."

"But I miss you and Mom and Suraj. I want to come home."

"We're not home, though. You know where we are, and it's not where you're meant to be yet."

The Underworld. They are dead, and their souls roam through Elysium Fields. Hades and Apollo ensured they were in the field of heroes shortly after my relationship with Apollo started. It's why he's so happy here, because he stands on an island amongst the world's greatest heroes. Mom and Suraj are somewhere there, too, and I want to be where the pain in my stomach will go away. I want to be where I get to hug him.

I've missed his hugs so much.

"Think of all the stories you have yet to make on this journey, my special Hart, and you know how much I love stories." He smiles, but it still brims with sadness. He misses me as much as I miss him, and I hate how I can't go to him. "Your time is not today. It's once the story ends, and the book closes, and you are far from being finished."

"Why not? I miss you, and Mom, and Suraj. I…I just want my family back."

When was the last time I saw Mom's timid smile, or heard one of Suraj's pun jokes? When was the last time I tasted my mom's cooking, or bickered with Suraj about nothing and everything? It's been too long since I've heard Mom and Dad argue about the greatest immortals, or walked through one of Dad's makeshift beaches. I always miss them, but seeing Dad so close, yet so far away. The pain of my grief grows tenfold.

"You have a family on Earth."

"Lowell, he-"

Dad cuts me off with a shake of his head. "Not Lowell, darling. Apollo has become your family the same way your mother and I created a family. We miss you every day, but we do not need you right now. Apollo does, and all who he calls family. One day, we will be together again, but don't let it be today. Once your story is complete, I know you will become my new favorite hero. I'll sing your praise from the rooftops."

He reaches a hand for me, or I thought he did, but he goes for the space in between us. His fingertips shimmer with multi-colored glitter. They dig into the barrier, like it is pliant skin, and our eyes lock. My dad smiles at me, and I know he's about to leave. I race forward, but he creates jagged scars with his fingers through the colorful illusion.

He dissipates, but the gaping wound remains. The scars open a new world, one I know I need to walk through. Another figure stands *in the new image, with a hand outstretched. She wears a floor-length topaz gown that instantly identifies her, even if the mirage covers her face. I take a hesitant step, then another, and accept the hand pulling me away from the island and my father.*

She tugs me through the new world, and the stories I must continue to tell.

I stumble into the new portal, where broken, unsteady concrete freezes my bare feet. The huntresses, Thanatos, Athena, and a few others stand on this battlefield, with their weapons raised in the same general direction. Typhon's leviathan height breaks through the ceiling, taller than the clouds, and he rains down thunderous fists.

But the huntresses have their own prophecy to complete.

Arrows and spears fly towards the greatest monster in the world, but it's the huntress prophesied to kill Typhon, who stands in the middle with a wild expression on her face. It's not fear. It's rueful determination. She's certain death awaits her, but she knows he will fall with her.

Her voice, always sharpened like a blade, joins Aashritha's, as they say. "All will crumble like Pompeii."

The roof above them falls, and with it, Typhon and the mirage.

Aashritha takes me away from the first of many stories and brings me to the last battle between Styx and me. Endless miles of grass surround Aashritha and me. A shimmering topaz veil covers most of Aashritha's face, but her honey-colored eyes break through the anonymity. Our hands remain intertwined as she leads me deeper into the new scenery.

"All will crumble like Pompeii," Aashritha says, but it isn't just her voice. The huntress's voice stays, even if she is not here in the ultimate battle, but another joins them.

Saffron's unmistakable cadence ripples with Aashritha's, joining her in repeating these five haunted words. She materializes far from Aashritha and me, wielding a white sword made entirely from bones. Green magic swirls around Saffron, as she locks herself in a battle against Hecate. Hecate's voice joins Aashritha's and Saffron's as soon as she materializes on the battlefield.

"All will crumble like Pompeii."

Thick, red blood creates a rivulet around the two dueling women. It encircles them, then careens away like a newly formed river. It swirls and twirls through the grass, over the hill, and more voices join the endless repeated phrase.

With the blood comes the soft whistle of Saffron's screams. It's startling. Hearing Saffron's screams becomes a part of the wind, slashing through all my resolve. Saffron continues to repeat the phrase, "All will crumble like Pompeii" as she fights Hecate, but I know she hears her screams. They are eternal, joining the Earth in its rotation.

Which means the blood creating a river around me is her heart's, who died twice to start this war.

Their voice, unfamiliar to my ears, joins the others. "All will crumble like Pompeii."

The hammer, wielded by a fiery woman of rage and beauty, falls from thin air. She screams as her hammer hits the sunlight, then crashes upon the ground. The floor rumbles, brewing with mayhem, then a volcano erupts. The female, who is the prophesied hammer, runs and swings her hammer against a horde of Styx's army as a volcano twice the size of Mt. Vesuvius rises from the fixture she created with her weapon.

Her voice, sharp with rage and heartlessness, joins the others. "All will crumble with Pompeii."

The volcano growls in rage, connecting this war to the catastrophe of Pompeii, but the prophecy is not over. Another figure materializes on the battlefield. Then another. And another. All the faces of the eight prophesied come to me, murmuring the same words with Aashritha.

Three hundred and twenty versions of the last battle play through this dream world. All but three end with Styx standing atop the volcano, victorious with a crown on her head and an army cheering at her feet. In three hundred and seventeen iterations of this war, Styx succeeds and a battleground of dead gods and humans lay scattered around her new, distorted world, but there are three where we defeat her.

Where the hammer wields her deadly blow, creating a volcano destined to crumble Styx's reign.

And the hero, with his back against a warped tree, bleeds more red into the river of death, as he eternally defeats some of the most formidable creatures on Styx's side.

We win because the muse, with her blade the same color as the sky, sings her final song before losing her voice forevermore. At the loss of her own chords, she stops the person who would kill the hero before he could bleed.

Victory greets us when Saffron the Savior rips the bones from all the immortals who foolishly chose Styx's tirade, and I, the seer, stand against Styx as Pompeii crumbles around us.

We only win when the seeker survives the battle and guides all the humans away from the erupting volcano, away from the bloodshed, and away from a world almost decimated by Styx.

I see the only way we can survive, in every brutal detail. Every step must be perfect, no line blurred, if we want victory. I must open my eyes, keep turning the pages of my story, because it will end with me. If I succumb to Lowell's betrayal, and the wounds he inflicted, then the huntress will die before Typhon. He will join Styx in the final battle and then kill the hero and the hammer. Rip out the muse's vocal chords before she can sing out her last song.

He will overpower them all, and destruction comes in his wake.

I must open my eyes, and I must save this world. Aashritha's hand remains warm in mine, contradictory to the corpse she turned into during this prophecy. She is nothing but bones in a pretty topaz gown, except for the hand I hold.

"You know what you must do now."

Aashritha lets go of my hand, and the final battlefield burns away like paper on fire.

330

I open my eyes, and I'm not in the hospital bed sitting a few feet away.

I have splayed my body out on the floor, my fingers stained with gold, red, black, and brown paint. It covers the expanse of the hardwood floor, telling the story of the prophecy I just witnessed in undecipherable slashes, semi-circles, and squiggles. I understand its message, can see the volcano and the hammer in the brown, misshapen dashes. The red river creates snake-like shapes around the expanse of the floor, reminding me of the two humans who *must* die to ensure the war is won.

But many, many more humans will die with them.

There's only one part of this painting that others can understand. It's the only one painted in black. Five words, created with harsh, poignant strokes, warning the others of the catastrophe awaiting them in a few short weeks.

All will crumble like Pompeii.

"The young oracle finally awakens."

I spin around, and a handsome male stands in the doorway. He is a few inches taller than five feet, but his short stature does not eliminate his gorgeous face or how much he resembles his father, Apollo. Both have long, golden hair that falls to their shoulders, and feline-like smirks on angular faces.

Asclepius walks into the room, glances at the surrounding mayhem, but merely asks. "How does your stomach feel?"

"Like I got stabbed two times."

He chuckles, then extends his hand. "Let's get you back in bed before I get my father. He will be quite mad if I let my patient lay on the floor after nearly dying."

Nearly dying. Lowell almost killed me. The prophecies sent my mind whirling with other thoughts, more important thoughts, but my best friend tried to kill me. That fact, no matter its level of importance compared to the looming war, still jars me. I've known Lowell most of my life, have laughed with him, loved him, cried with him, and fell out of love with him. He has been the epicenter of my existence, and he was quick to kill me.

I was a fool for trusting him.

"Lowell, is he-"

I don't finish my question aloud, but he understands.

"Yes. Apollo killed him before he could stab you again."

Asclepius doesn't mince his words for my emotional state, which I appreciate more than I thought I would. He tells me what I need to hear, not what he thinks I can handle. Lowell's betrayal hurts, but now I know he wouldn't have stopped until my heart ceased. It's a painful truth I needed to hear, but also know Apollo might have minced for my sake.

"Can I see Apollo?"

As soon as I ask, a desperate scream breaks through the room. "μέλι!"

Regardless of the pain in both my stomach and my palm, and the sadness weighing heavily on my chest, I smile at the sound of his voice. My beautiful god rushes towards me, tears of relief building up in his eyes, until he is by my side, pulling me into a bone-crushing kiss.

I want to be upset, to wallow in my sadness, but his kisses electrify me. For the few seconds, I am not the girl who almost died by the traitorous blade of her longest companion, or the oracle vital to the war's success. Right now, I am happily Apollo's.

Then, he pulls away, and the sadness washes over me once again.

There is so much he wants to say, the words begging to escape from his lips, but I silence them by raising my hand up into the air for his blue eyes to focus on. "I know where Calypso's Island is."

It's where my dad and I were, on Calypso's island. The coordinates whisper in my head, and I'm certain that almost any question I ask will be answered within my mind. My power has tripled, or maybe I stopped fearing it. Death is most feared by those who have never experienced its caress. I know its touch and its calm, and I no longer fear it.

Maybe that's why my powers have exploded, answering questions I scarcely remember asking.

"We found her, but none of that matters right now. You're alright." Apollo kisses me again, this time on the cheeks, and he cries. "I didn't know if you would wake. If you'd be alright, but you're here and...thanks the gods."

I grab his face with both my hands, smearing the paint from my fingers onto his skin, but he doesn't care. He doesn't even notice the paint on my fingers, the floor, or its remnants rubbing on his face. He only sees me, alive and well, and he slams his lips against mine again. I taste all his desperation and hope, and I rejuvenate myself in him.

When we pull away, I say against his lips. "No, it still matters. Get Ares here. He needs to know where the coordinates are."

Again, I don't know why Ares needs to know, but as soon as the request leaves my lips, several futures jump through my mind. All of our success centers on Ares's self-lessness and the human who remains on Ogygia.

Apollo doesn't question me; he looks back at his son. "Get Ares here immediately."

Asclepius bows his head and dutifully leaves the room

to summon Ares. Once the door curtains close behind us, Apollo and I are finally alone. He opens his mouth to say something. To ask me how I'm feeling. To learn what happened between Lowell and me. Or, to envelop me in sympathetic gazes and apologies, as if it were his fault that my best friend betrayed me.

Gods, he could ask me to marry him, as he promised he would, before I fell into the darkness of death.

I stop him before he speaks.

"I'm tired," I lie through my teeth. "Do you mind if I get some rest alone?"

I am drowning, unable to exhale a single breath without feeling a pinch of pain. The world has become too overbearing, with blurs of the past, present choices, and future consequences, and I want to be alone to submerge.

But Apollo shakes his head. "No, if you suffer, I suffer with you."

He knows what I need before I know it myself. He climbs into the hospital bed, positioning himself until my head rests on his chest and his arms are fast around me. I wanted to drown in the depths of my new, distorted mind, but Apollo refuses to let me suffer alone. He forces me to find the peace in his touch, and I love him more today than any other day.

THIRTY-THREE

SAFFRON

Zeus doesn't return the next morning, or the morning after. Hera refuses to let me leave Mt. Olympus until he comes back, and we cannot convene about Epiales without Zeus. I don't know where Ogygia is, even after living there for days, and I'm forbidden from searching for it until Zeus returns. They trap me here, in the same place as my ex-husband, who I run into at every turn in this cursed place.

I pace in Poseidon's home, glancing at the doorway every few minutes as my impatience intensifies. Poseidon threatens to drown me in a puddle if I keep endlessly walking around the house because my steps, in his consistently hungover state, are too loud to stomach. I only stop when the doorway I continually study fills with a looming figure.

Hephaestus blocks the sunlight, consuming the entire doorway with his hulking frame, and Poseidon groans.

"Thank the gods. That sun was giving me a headache. Do me a favor and do not move until sunset."

Immediately, Hephaestus walks inside the house and away from the sun. The sun hits Poseidon in the eyes from where he lies on the couch, and he groans.

"This is why I don't have a favorite nephew. You're all terrible."

Hephaestus ignores him. "Can we talk?"

"Yeah, sure."

He leads me out of the house, but we don't wander far. Hephaestus's cane taps against the floor with every step.

"It's hurting more than usual today?"

He grunts, and that's the best answer I will get. Hephaestus rarely uses his cane, except on days when the pain in his leg and hip are most prominent. I never understand why Hephaestus lives on Mt. Olympus after Hera and this cursed place caused his injury. Others forget Hera threw a baby, Hephaestus, off Mt. Olympus to kill him, but I won't. Every time I see him limp, I'm reminded why Hera will never shed her villainous shade for me.

Hephaestus tries to forget when he plays niceties with his mom, but on days when he must use his cane, he can't forget. Hermes always said he's angriest on days when he must use the cane. He leans against Poseidon's house, a white-knuckling grip on his cane, but his other hand goes to his pocket.

It retrieves an all-white dagger.

"This was going to be your present at your anniversary party, but clearly that night didn't go according to plan."

My eighty-fifth wedding anniversary was the same night Hecate revealed herself as a traitor, and Styx left me on Ogygia to revive Epiales. Others celebrated Hermes and my union, but we had already divorced. Our love was already severed, so it's appropriate that Hephaestus's present for me was a dagger. Something violent, a symbol to shatter the illusion that we were actually happy.

He holds the dagger out towards me, and I take it. I grasp the dagger; the weapon created solely from bones. I can feel its powers radiating from the blade, threatening to annihilate anybody who has deceived its owner. It's a radiant work of art, crafted by harsh, yet delicate hands.

"I named her Οστά, but if you don't like that…"

"It's perfect," I say, interrupting him.

Οστά means bones in Greek, and it's aptly named. At least two dozen bones make up the fabric of this weapon, which weighs only a pound. I test the feel along my hand, and it's perfect. So clearly designed for me, with an engraved S in the center of the handle.

"She'll respond to nobody's touch but yours, and when you press the S." Hephaestus points towards the center of the handle, where the bones intertwine to create an S. "Οστά will turn into a sword. The weapon will serve as a boomerang, answering to your magic, while the blade slices through any flesh. Immortals, monsters, and humans alike. An extension of your powers."

The smallest smile forms on my lips, and my thumb slides across the S. I apply light pressure, and a majestic sword blossoms from a miniature dagger. My grin widens. "I've always wanted a sigil weapon, like Artemis with her arrows, Zeus with his bolt, and Hermes with *Caduceus*."

Saying his name, as easily as breathing, brings a sharp stab of pain, but it doesn't diminish the joy of holding this weapon. One individualized just for me.

"Thank you, Hephaestus. It's amazing."

He bows his head. "I'm glad you like it." He starts to leave, walks a few paces, then stops. He turns back to face me. "I'm sorry about you and Hermes. Regardless of what anyone says, I know that decision wasn't easy for you, but that doesn't mean it was the wrong decision to make. It took courage to leave an unhappy marriage."

Like his and Aphrodite's.

There's love between them, a toxic and destructive one, but love all the same. He stays because he loves her, even if Aphrodite's love tears him apart, but he thinks about leaving constantly. To escape her and find a love that does not hurt as much. It's clear in the slightly envious tone in his voice.

I take a step towards him, a question on my tongue, but we're interrupted. Artemis runs up to us, her hair unkempt and clothes wrinkled. "I'm sorry, I should've been here sooner, but June just woke up and-"

"What are you talking about?" I ask. Both her and Hephaestus's faces fall, and my previous confusion rises with concern. "What happened?"

"Nobody told you yet?" Artemis asks. "Gods, if I knew, I would've gotten here sooner. Saffron-"

"Out with it. What happened?"

Artemis shares a look with Hephaestus, and it's him who responds. "It's Argus."

Lately, when we say a name with no further elaboration, it's because they became a traitor on Styx's side. That can't be Argus. My dear friend, who stayed with me during my darkest moments when I terrified everyone else. He has been one of my only anchors when the waves grew too high. There's no way he is a traitor, not when he gave up so much of his time to me with nothing in return except my friendship. I shake my head, refusing to believe their claim of his deceit.

"He's not a traitor. Where is he? I'll prove to you he would never join Styx and betray-"

"He's not a traitor," Artemis agrees, but her sorrowful expression doesn't lessen, which only means one thing.

"No." I shake my head. "No, no, no. He's fine. I told him to stay with Hart in Apollo's mansion. He's there right now. We can see him right after Zeus lets me leave Mt. Olympus. He's fine."

"Saffron."

"No!" I yell at Artemis, refusing to believe the words she hasn't yet said. "No, he's alive. He's on Earth, with Hart."

"He was on Earth with Hart," she says. "Until Hart drew a map of where we'd find Ogygia. Where we'd find you. He asked Hart if he could leave, so he could bring us that map and find you."

Tears build in my eyes, but I keep shaking my head. "No. No, he's fine."

"He called for Iris, then came to my rescue when Styx's army was defeating all my huntresses. My huntresses were bleeding out, and he told Iris to transport everyone away to find you while he fended them off."

"No."

"Lamb saw it happen. He saved her from Atlas, and he gave us the map, but Atlas-"

"I said no!" I scream, but it doesn't change the truth.

"He's dead, Saffron. He died a hero-"

I shake my head. "He died trying to find me. To protect me, and I got him killed."

"I'm sure we can bring him back from Underworld."

"So, someone else can kill him for being associated with me? No. Now, my friend gets to join Elysium with my

339

other fallen loved ones, because that's where they all go. All my friends go to Elysium while I'm here." A single, anger-filled tear falls, but I swipe it away before it can descend. "Who killed him? Atlas?"

Artemis nods her head, and I run toward the edge of Mt. Olympus. I grip the new sword in my hand and I sprint away from them. They both yell out my name, but I can only see Atlas's traitorous face. Red blurs my vision, and I dare Hera to keep me on this cursed hideaway while Atlas freely exists.

"Saffron, wait!" Hephaestus screams.

But they do not stop me.

Someone does, though.

Zeus stands at the gates of Mt. Olympus with his hand wrapped around Epiales's throat. He pins his body against the gate, strangling him before Ares tackles Zeus to the ground. Epiales gasps, clutching his throat as Ares and Zeus match, fist for fist.

"What in the Underworld is going on here?!"

Athena runs out of her home, followed by Hermes, Demeter, and Dionysus. Hephaestus and Artemis rush past me, and all of them use their combined strength to separate Ares and Zeus. I stay perfectly still. Epiales, kneeling on the ground, looks up at me completely unscathed, except for new bruises forming around his neck. Mayhem brews around us, but after hearing about Argus's death, the sight of one person surviving my company lessens the rage.

Until Zeus breaks apart from them, materializes a lightning bolt, and points it at Epiales.

My power comes swiftly, freezing Zeus's hand before he can strike Epiales down. Zeus glares at me, but there's fear, too. I have never used my abilities against him until now, and it's because of the former traitor kneeling on the floor.

"Let me go," he orders through clenched teeth.

I don't; instead, I freeze his entire body. Every bone is under my command, and Zeus can do nothing to stop me. He easily broke away from six immortals, but against me, he's subdued.

Everyone stares at me, as I easily restrain the king of all gods, but nobody tells me to let him go. The fear I've become accustomed to over the years threatens to strangle me, but I stifle it as I focus on Epiales.

"Go to Poseidon's home. *Now*."

He clambers to his feet and runs. Zeus wants to scream. I feel his jaw twitching under my control, but he can't use it. The silence is deafening, and a small part of me hates how easy this is, defeating him.

"I have asked you for nothing except humanity's freedom, which I gave my mortality for, and in return, I have given you everything in me. You wanted Kronos's death, so I gave you it. You wanted to keep the crown on your head, so I didn't demand it or even ask. Even a prophecy said it was mine by birthright and strength, but I said nothing. Did nothing to take it away from you; still, all you do is take from me. Don't take him from me." The last word comes out so broken, I'm surprised it's my voice. "Please."

I release his vocal chords and jaw so he can let out one word. "No."

I freeze them again.

"Saffron, you need to let him go." Athena steps in between Zeus and me, but she has no power here. She knows it. I know it. And the extremely furious Zeus knows it. Still, Athena moves towards me. "We will meet with all the Olympians and make a just decision, but you have to let him go if you don't want repercussions for your actions."

The lightning bolt drops from Zeus's hand, clamoring to the ground. It is without its electricity, mirroring a child's toy, rather than his formidable weapon.

I caused that.

"Epiales doesn't deserve to die," I say. Still sounding too broken.

Athena takes another step. "Let him go so we can discuss this as a unit. We can vote on the best step."

I don't plan on listening to her. She doesn't agree with my claim that Epiales should live. Even with the prophecy looming over our heads. Even with Styx's belief that Epiales will die because of us, therefore helping her win the war. I won't let Zeus's rage kill him, stealing away the last remnants of my humanity and our chance of survival.

But a hand rests on my shoulder, eliciting a thousand goosebumps, and I draw my gaze up to Ares.

Zeus's lightning bolt mars his face. A clear zigzag crosses the left side, from forehead to chin, and it doesn't immediately heal. The wound stitches together slowly, yet he doesn't grimace with pain.

"You freed Epiales from Ogygia," I say with surprise clear in my voice.

"You said he made you happy there." Ares drops his hand from my shoulder, and he looks back at Zeus. "Let him go, and I promise I won't let anything happen to Epiales. I didn't save him from Ogygia just for him to die now."

I let go of Zeus's bones immediately.

Zeus storms towards me, rage reddening his face. "How dare you?"

I stare at him, the god who looks so much like me, but I do not recognize him. We bear physical similarities, but he is not my father. No, a true father would be this cruel. Hades is, today and every day, the only father I truly have.

"How dare you?" I say back to him. "I killed him once for you, and you expect me to suffer that way twice? Do you truly hate me that much?"

The redness on his face lessens, but before he can say more, we're encapsulated in a rainbow and pulled away.

When the colors diminish, we sit in the marble seats inside the counsel room. Zeus rests at the helm as king, with Hera and Poseidon on either side of him. All Olympians are in attendance, and other high-ranking immortals like Hermes. Hart Sommers stands in the door-way, teetering between belonging amongst the gods and still being a human.

Then, right in the middle, is Epiales in chains.

THIRTY-FOUR

HART SOMMERS

God and goddesses, all bristling with barely kempt power, surround the twelve-seated table. The Olympians take their divine places, with Zeus at the helm wearing a newly materialized crown that over-embellishes his authority. It's almost larger than his head, with enough gems to cure world human poverty, and it tricks no one.

Even I, who was not present for the fight, understand the shift created by Saffron and Zeus's rage. He fears his daughter, who has more power than she dares to show. We've only received a glimpse of her capabilities. She hides the true magnitude, compacting it so nobody else can witness how volatile she can become.

Now, Zeus understands he does not have his throne because he is the greatest; he has it because the greatest does not want it. We've all known she is stronger than him, but her startling amount of power has recently been revealed.

And I know it's only a tenth of what lies within her.

"We're here to decide the fate of Epiales," Zeus announces, eyes refusing to meet Saffron's. "The former personification of nightmares. A traitor who chose Kronos's battle against our own, killing our kind-"

"Who already died for that decision," Hades interjects.

Saffron says nothing, but Hades speaking for her echoes her power. The Olympians have the final vote, but the other gods stand around the table, listening and processing the seriousness of this conversation. The room shatters into three segments: those with unwavering loyalty to Zeus, those who pledge resolute fealty to Saffron, and the few who cannot choose between them.

Zeus glowers at his brother. "Who killed those loyal to us in the name of Kronos and led a rebellion with Morpheus centuries before that."

"We can all agree that what Epiales did, helping Morpheus free his soulmate from enslavement, is not condemnable. It never should have been," Ares speaks up next.

"I disagree," Heracles says. His frown is most prominent, and his muscular arms cross over his chest like a petulant child.

Athena glares back at the standing Heracles. "Why are you even here?"

"You tortured Morpheus's soulmate," Saffron says through clenched teeth, speaking up for the first time. "You and Hebe."

She nods towards Heracles's wife, who stands beside him. Hebe flinches at the glance.

"Of course you wanted another to be blamed because you were the monster in that story," Saffron finishes.

346

Heracles takes a step towards her, his chest inflating. "How dare-"

"Silence," Zeus commands

The king casts his favored son a seething glare, and Heracles quiets. The king lets out a hallowed breath, composing himself before facing Epiales again. He sits chained in the center of the table, mirroring a pig before the slaughter. Confinements cover almost every inch of visible skin. There are cuffs on each wrist and ankle, a collar on his neck holding a weighted bell, and a chain circles his waist. There's a set of chains on his thighs, so he has no choice but to stay kneeling on the table. If the surplus of confinements were not humiliating enough, there's tape over his lips.

His wrists dribble with crimson red blood from the cuffs' tightness. Yet, he doesn't wear the look of pain on his face. His chin raises as high as the collar will allow, and he refuses to deign Zeus any attention. Epiales focuses solely on Saffron, who periodically locks eyes with him. Each time they stare at each other, I see them both on the battlefield in the last war, as soot from the volcano falls on their heads like rainfall.

I look away.

"If you want to truly discuss this, Zeus," Saffron says. "Then excuse those who are unneeded."

She pointedly glares at Heracles and Hebe.

Again, Hebe flinches.

This, like so many other moments, decides the fate of the war. Styx will win if the events of today do not tilt in the exact direction they need to. Without Epiales's fate falling in the right hands, we will never find the seeker. Without this conversation leading in its intended direction, Styx can win the war.

"King Zeus." All eyes whip to me, many visibly surprised I deigned to speak, but I only focus on Zeus.

He and I have formed an unlikely alliance these following weeks, and I hope that's enough to guide him to reason. If I can't get him to listen to me, and actually obey, then we might as well give Styx the throne.

"We need eighteen immortals to stay. The Olympians, Saffron, Hermes, and four others." I wait with bated breath for Zeus's response.

There are three ways this can go.

First, he can consume himself with his need to prove his power, and he will condemn me for trying to command him. If that happens, then Epiales dies tonight, and we lose the war.

Next, he can acquiesce, but choose the remaining four. It will lead us in the right direction, but Epiales will not become who needs to be for this war. He won't play his role; therefore, we will lose the war.

The last option is what I need from Zeus. Correction: what the world needs.

He thinks about my words for a while, hesitation lining his white brows, and each second feels like a blade against my skin. Ultimately, he asks. "Which four?"

I let out a breath of relief. We can still win this war.

"Heracles." Both Athena and Saffron groan. "Nike, Thalia, and Hestia."

The mention of the muse, who hides with her sisters in the back of the room, incites the most surprise, but Zeus does not question me. Hebe opens her mouth, ready to complain, but Zeus tilts his head towards Iris.

"Send them all away and do not return."

Iris bows her head, and dozens of rainbows materialize

in the room. One second, almost a hundred immortals covered the room; now, there are only eighteen and me.

Poseidon glowers at me. "Why couldn't my wife stay?"

"Or mine?" Heracles barks.

I do not answer aloud, but Amphitrite remains loyal to Saffron, just as her husband is, and Heracles's wife fights for Zeus. In order for the correct outcome, we need more neutral votes, like Nike, Thalia, and Hestia. Nike and Thalia, usually in the background of the gods' minds, step closer to the center. Thalia's eyes dart between me and the doorway behind me, but she doesn't move away from her spot next to Nike.

"Now, let's discuss his fate with a modicum of propriety," Hera says.

Saffron stands directly behind Hades's seat, stewing with tightly clenched fists. "There is nothing civil about chaining a human up, especially to this capacity, for crimes he hasn't committed in this lifetime."

Zeus scoffs. "Don't defend this monster's actions. He started wars with our kind, killing thousands of those humans you love so ardently without a second thought. Still, you dare to justify his crimes. He's a murderer of thousands. Just because the first death didn't stick doesn't mean we shouldn't try again."

"She's not justifying what he did in the past," Poseidon says.

"Gods, you're on her side, too?" Hera purses her lips. "You're incorrigible."

"Might take offense to that if I knew what it meant." Poseidon focuses on Zeus. "As I was saying, she's not justifying the past. She's trying to tell you that this human form might be worth redemption."

"Do you actually believe that?" Athena asks, genuine curiosity in her tone.

But the question came from Athena, so Poseidon rolls his eyes. "Oh great, the owl-face has something to say."

"I believe that since he's been human, he's done nothing but show me he's changed," Saffron answers her sister. "I also know that Styx wanted him to die with my freedom. Do we truly want to give her what she wants?"

Hera cries out. "You are mad if you believe he's changed!"

But Zeus looks at me.

He waits for my objection to Saffron's claim or my belief that Epiales has truly manifested into a man of good intentions. I want to give him the answer, and one day, I will, but I can't right now. Right now, his instincts must guide him in the direction Epiales's story must go. He will have time to regret his decisions later.

"Does it make you that angry to think a human-form of Epiales could be good?" Saffron asks.

"Yes."

Demeter rises to her feet. Her short black hair, cut just below her ears, sways with her sudden movement, giving way to alabaster smooth skin and sunken cheekbones. According to Apollo, Demeter's one of the quietest Olympians. She rarely vocalizes her opinions unless it involves her daughter, or a grievance made by a human against her sacred divinity. If the rest of the gods are vengeful storms, then she's the soft rainfall that follows. The calm that survives the mayhem. Even as she speaks, there isn't an inflection of anger.

She speaks like a teacher who must teach Saffron, a reckless child, how the world works. "You may feel ancient like us, but you haven't lived for even a splinter of the time we have. You've experienced war and heartache, but do you know what it feels like to be eaten alive? To have your first memory be a father looking upon you with such rage, before he rips your limbs apart? You have never experienced the unwavering betrayal and pain of teeth chomping down on your body parts from the father who created you."

In the slight pause in Demeter's story, Saffron says. "I understand all too well what it feels like for a father to hate you enough to want to kill you."

She won't look at Zeus, but the rest of the room does. It is no secret that when Saffron was a demi-god, the first in centuries, there was a vote on her life. On whether she'd live or die, Zeus was one of two gods who voted for her execution. Zeus, the god who fell in love with her human mother, disobeyed his own decree about halfling children, wanted her dead.

I know him well enough now to understand the bone-shattering regret he has for that moment, when fear over-rode love; now, regret fills the atmosphere. The gods remember the decision Zeus made at this very table to kill his own daughter. Saffron refuses to look at him because if she did, her face would hold the same unmasked betrayal Demeter does when she mentions Kronos.

"So you do," Demeter says. "But I was barely out of my mother's womb before he tore my body apart. Because we are gods, I remember that day. The way my ichor spilled everywhere, and pieces of my newly created body slid down his throat, nestling in the pool of his stomach. Your father may dislike you las mine had, but Zeus has never eaten you alive. You did not grow up in his belly, thrashing for freedom."

351

Demeter sets her hands on top of the table, and they tremble with the memories of a past she can never escape.

"Eons have passed since Zeus freed me from that dungeon, but there are still nights when I wake up to the feeling of my bones crunching under hungry teeth. I lie in my bed, paralyzed, as I feel a hand pulling my eyes out of my sockets. I can always hear the slurping sound he makes as he eats them whole."

Finally, Demeter looks at Epiales. The tremor in her hand has taken over her entire body.

"Epiales is from my time. He knew what Kronos did to my siblings and me; even so, he fought alongside him. Killed for him. I do not deny you saw good within him, but a single grain of rice does not feed millions. It does not alleviate the gnawing feeling that wakes me from my sleep. Steals my rationale and my peace."

A sniffle drives the attention away from Demeter. Epiales sits on the ground, chained from top to bottom, and he cries for the sins he ignored during Kronos's reign. His head remains bowed, his dark hair conceals his tear-struck face, but I see the tears drop, drop, drop onto the table. Demeter does, too.

She grabs her hands, forcing them to stop shaking.

"Dear sister." Hades stands from his seat. "I know your pain acutely, and I understand your hatred towards Epiales. Try as I might, I still hold it, too, but that's not why we sit here. We should not vote on the sins of the past, choosing to condemn him for crimes already sentenced."

"Then why are we here?" she asks.

"We all know about the prophecy looming over us, with Styx at its helm. We know the only way we can survive is if eight members of the prophecy- the heart, the hammer, the hero, the huntress, the seeker, the seer, the savior, and the singer- exist and play their part. It's my belief that Epiales is the heart of the prophecy."

"There's no definitive proof of this claim." Zeus locks eyes with me. "Correct?"

I know who the heart is, but I cannot say. I've seen what happens when I divulge the truth too early, and it ends with mass graves. All truths will come to the surface when the recipients are ready, and nobody in this room can process the level of truths this prophecy demands. I want to help them, but in doing so, I must stay silent.

"I haven't seen who the heart is yet in my prophecies," I lie, hating myself for this deceit.

Zeus believes me and turns to face Hades. "Why should we believe your claim and spare him when it isn't certain Epiales is her heart? For all we know, he could be working with Styx, and that's why she forced Saffron to bring him back to life."

"It's a possibility," Artemis adds but doesn't elaborate.

Hades shakes his head. "My daughter's humanity stayed inside her when she was a goddess, and when Styx forced her to bring him back to life, she unintentionally gave her humanity to him. That's why he kneels here, crying because of his past decisions. That's a part of my daughter's heart, which bleeds for everyone. He feels compassion, not because he is pretending for Styx's grand plan, but because a part of my daughter lives in him."

Saffron adds. "I'm not excusing what he used to be. Don't forget that I killed him without complaint because I understood the necessity. But if we kill him now, without certainty his death won't cause a trickle effect, then we give Styx the upper hand in this war. Do we really want to do that?"

"Do we really want to lose the human side of Saffron,

either?" Apollo asks, vocalizing his support for Saffron. "The same human side of her that saved us all from Kronos."

"Enough of this," Zeus says, but he isn't booming with authority; instead, his voice cracks. "Let us put this to a vote. Majority rules. I say he should die. What do you say, wife?"

"I vote-" Hera begins.

"Before you start, I propose a third option."

Hermes steps forward, surprising all but me and the few who worked with him to create this third proposal. He refuses to glance in Epiales's general vicinity, or Saffron's. His attention locks on Zeus and Hera.

"Which would be?" Zeus asks.

"It's Saffron's humanity living inside him. I vote we treat him as we treated a young Saffron. We put him in the arena, and whichever god here wins gets to decide his fate. Just as we did with Saffron."

"Before you stole her, you sneaky thief." Poseidon winks.

Hermes ignores him. "It's the fairest option."

"Fair?" Apollo scoffs at the word. "We should focus on finding Styx, not arguing about Epiales. He's a human now. In the grand scheme of things, he's inconsequential. Yet, you're focusing on his life or death, like it matters more than finding where Styx hides and stopping her before she does more harm."

Apollo's right, and there are a handful of immortals in the room who agree with him, but they have not seen every iteration of the future centering on this conversation. They do not see the fragmented events that follow every state-ment, counter, and conclusion. I understand Apollo's point of view, and if I did not see what I know, then I might agree with him. Styx is the larger foe because Epiales is no foe at all, but that doesn't devalue this moment.

It's essential to his story.

And how the former god of nightmares loves his stories.

"Deal," I say first.

Zeus doesn't care to hear Saffron or the other's views. He hears the path that I pave, and he obeys. A lightning bolt materializes in his hand, and before Saffron can use her magic to stop him, he slams it to the ground, transporting us all to the arena where everything began.

I materialize in a pew seated next to a wheat-haired, long-faced huntress, who I only know from stories. The spot to my left is empty, but Lamb observes me on my right. Every god, goddess, and huntress who weren't in the meeting, but were living on Mt. Olympus, sits in the surrounding pews. Most murmur to each other with confusion, but the ever-wise Lamb looks around the arena and quickly realizes why we're here.

"Why did you orchestrate this?" Lamb asks.

"I didn't. Hermes and a few other gods did."

Lamb doesn't look at me; she stares straight ahead at the arena. "I've never met an oracle before, but I've met a lot of liars. So why did you orchestrate it?"

Despite myself, I smile. It's only been a day since I woke up and knew everything, from when the prophecy was first spoken by Aashritha eons ago, to the moment the volcano erupts, and crumbles Styx's plans. Every lie has been torture.

Lamb stays silent, in every version of the future, when I honestly answer. "Epiales needs to leave Saffron long enough to discover who he is without her. This was the only way that he neither dies, nor stays with her."

"Just how much of the future do you know?"

I wait, making sure it is a safe step, then answer in vague spurts. "Enough to know that he must follow a path that takes us to victory."

The gods below in the arena materialize their weapons and sharpen their blades before the battle begins, and Lamb silently stews on her last question for several seconds.

Then, the typically soft-spoken huntress asks. "Will I die in this war?"

A horn sounds, starting the battle, and I do not respond.

She doesn't ask again.

THIRTY-FIVE

SAFFRON

I haven't returned to this arena since I was a human, captured beneath the heated gaze of a thousand gods. It's disorientating, standing on the dirt ground once again, watching as more and more immortals materialize in the pews. They observe the eighteen of us, and they make bets on who will take ownership of the captured human.

The first time I stood on the arena floor, Epiales was a voice in my head that promised eventual freedom. I was the human who gods fought to possess. Now, the once powerful god of nightmares is the human, and I yearn to promise his eventual freedom. As long as I defeat everyone who stands in the battlefield, then he will be alright.

I tilt my head towards the pews, where huntresses sit amongst gods, but a few are missing from the group. Hades moves towards me, standing almost shoulder-to-shoulder, and he realizes the absences at the same time.

"Where's my wife?"

"Thanatos and Hypnos aren't here, either."

I warned everyone on Mt. Olympus that this fight for Epiales isn't worth the distraction. Styx hides and waits to strike, but we are uncertain of when she will attack. She should be our primary concern, not a human who has made no mistakes in his second life. Their absence from the arena sends an unwanted shiver down my spine. It brings a sense of foreboding that feels like Styx's jagged nails.

The other gods obliviously materialize their weapons. Heracles sharpens the spikes on his club. Artemis tests the weight of her bowstring against the arrow's pull. Zeus holsters seven lightning bolts, as two more gleam in his hands. Hera twirls two daggers in each hand, and Thalia produces a scythe that looks almost identical to Thanatos's.

"I should go." Hades takes a step back, but I put my hand around his wrist and stop him.

"Zeus won't let any of us go until a victor wins and decides Epiales's fate." I look over the gods' faces in the pews, and when I do not see a newly familiarized immortal, I ask Hades. "How well do you know Alastor?"

Hades's brow crinkles. "Alastor?"

"He was the one who helped me escape Ogygia, but I don't trust him. Could he be working for-"

"Saffron. He's not working with Styx."

"How are you certain? He left Epiales to die on that island. He's-"

"Zeus," Hades says through clenched teeth.

"What?"

"Each Olympian has an epithet. An alter-ego, if you will. We can take another's name, with a concentration of only one of our powers, and unless you know the epithet's name, you won't know we're the same. Zeus's epithet is Alastor. He was the one who freed you from Ogygia."

Zeus?

He stands in the arena's epicenter, illuminated by his circlet of lightning bolts. His long, shoulder-length white hair is in a ponytail, further showcasing his face. He saved me the moment he could, but only under a shroud of lies.

Hermes is the god of trickery, but Zeus plays the role well.

Lies are as easy as storms to the father who votes for my death one second, then risks his own hide to save me the next. He doesn't kill Epiales under the guise of Alastor, but then stands here with a murderous scowl, condemning Epiales to death.

Nothing makes sense with Zeus, but when I make a step towards him, trying to find the rationale behind his actions, Hermes's voice begins the fight.

"The rules are not the same as the past arena events!"

Hermes incites a sense of déjà vu. I stand back in the arena eighty-eight years ago, cowering beside Angel as Hermes introduces the arena rules, then initiates its descent to bloodshed.

"Even if you wish to fight for this human." Hermes motions towards Epiales, who lays chained on the floor in the far southern edge of the arena. "If you are not already down on the arena floor, then you cannot challenge for his possession. For the eighteen who stand here, ready to fight to decide Epiales's fate, you will be disqualified as soon as your blood is spilled. The last god or goddess unscathed in the arena will win their possession."

Hermes's head tilts towards me. There's almost a hundred feet separating him and me, but I see his hesitation clearly. He bites back confessions with a bite of his bottom lip, then swiftly looks away.

He faces the pews, straightens his shoulders, and stoically adds. "Powers will not be used to draw blood, only to further access your fighting abilities. No bones will fly out of the fighters' skin. No storms will strike down the fighters. An earthquake will not open and swallow fighters whole."

"Boring," Poseidon grumbles at the end.

Hermes ignores him. "You may start the battles once my caduceus materializes in my hand, and it will not end until the final unscathed immortal stands victorious."

Silence awaits the calamitous storm. The eighteen of us stand around the arena, facing one another in tense anticipation for the gilded caduceus. I spare a final glance at Epiales. Unsurprisingly, he's already watching me. He looks little more than trapped prey, but he smiles. Beneath the fear and uncertainty, he smiles at me.

I smile back.

Half the arena gravitates towards the immortal they ally with. Hades stands to my left, Poseidon to my right, as Apollo, Ares, and Dionysus walk to my side. If Ares's stance surprises anyone, nobody shows it. He spares me a fleeting glance before facing Zeus's side of the arena, where Hera, Demeter, Heracles, and Hephaestus stand.

The latter wields two hammers as I unsheathe the bone sword he gifted me hours earlier.

The remaining fighters- Thalia, Hestia, Artemis, Aphrodite, Nike, and Athena- stay in the middle with Hermes. Their allegiance wavers between Zeus and me. I silently urge Artemis to look at me, to explain why she isn't on my side, just as Zeus glares daggers in Athena's direction. We all unsheathe our weapons, their blades dancing along the sunlight, and we wait.

Once that glimmering caduceus manifests in Hermes's hand, I do not hesitate.

With possession of my bones, I lift myself up into the air and bring the bones buried around the arena floor with me. I feel them fight through feet of dirt, yearning to beckon to my command. Thousands of sharpened bones, as small as an incus to the largest, rip through their burial spots, following me into the sky. I spin them in the air, turning the sharpened points towards my enemies.

The pointed edges of several lightning bolts course through the air towards me, just as the bones strike the ground. Several bones slice flesh, taking Hestia and Aphrodite out of the fight with wounds to the neck and thigh. Most deflect the weapons, either with shields or speed. Zeus incinerates the bones that near him, just as I dispose of his lightning bolts with a shield made of bones.

Miles-long wings conceal Zeus as they skyrocket towards me. The briery edges of her wings near my neck, threatening to spill blood, but I lean back just in time to miss Nike's swipe. She hovers in the air in front of me, with a throwing knife between each finger like elongated nails. The normally confident goddess of victory does not wear her typical smirk.

"He is part of the reason Angel is dead."

She does not allow me a chance to convince her otherwise; she attacks. Knife after knife cuts through the air towards me, and I flip backwards to avoid them. I kick one with the heel of my foot, watch another skid past my face, and catch the last by the golden handle. I throw the knife right back, then rush towards her with Οστά clasped in both hands.

Nike blocks the knife's merciless blade with her golden wing, shielding herself from elimination, but the moment she unfurls her wings, I'm there. My blade clashes against one of her knives, our faces less than an inch apart. Her focus is solely on me, so she does not see the spear Ares throws at her exposed back.

The spearhead pierces out of her chest, and her eyes widen with surprise before she tumbles downward. She creates a spiral on her journey to the ground, but she never crashes. A rainbow catches her, transporting her away from the arena and into the pews as a defeated player. She sits, nearly healed, beside Aphrodite, Hestia, and Dionysus. The latter, who I did not see get defeated, holds a broken arrow in his hands.

I glare down at Artemis, just as one of her arrows nears me. A split second separates my defeat and hers. I turn my head just as the arrow whisks past my nose, narrowly avoiding the skin, and I throw Οστά down at her. With a blade made from bones, it's impossible to miss my mark, and Artemis falls with my sword embedded in her shoulder.

I lower to the ground just as Iris transports Artemis off the arena ground. My sword remains where Artemis's ichor stains the ground. I land on my feet just as an arrow slashes near my face. I whip around, ready to fight whoever tried to disqualify me, only to see Apollo in a fight against Heracles.

Apollo expels dozens of arrows, trying to hit Heracles anywhere, but the latter's strength shatters every attempt. He incinerates every arrow with his bulbous club, never missing an advancing step towards Apollo. I run towards them, bones rising to the surface to join me in defeating Heracles, but his weapon is quicker.

He slams his spiked club against Apollo's head, and a mixture of ichor and brains splatter across the ground. Just as the fallen before him, Iris takes Apollo out of the arena. When he re-materializes, his wound is gone. I turn all my attention to Heracles, who spins that blood-splattered club with a vicious grin.

"When I win," he says. "I'll send you his decapitated head. Unless there's a part of his body you-"

I never let him finish the sentence. My blade becomes an extension of me, and I send it flying across the space between us. I unearth more bones from the ground, which are nearly dust after decades of decomposition, sending them towards Heracles. He deflects most of the bones, but not my sword. Οστά slides into his skull like butter, and he collapses.

Before Iris can take him away, I spit at him. "You are a disgrace of a hero."

I grab Οστά once more, gleaming in victory, as Hephaestus runs towards me. Behind him, Thalia's defeated form leaves in an archway of rainbows, while one of his hammers drinks gilded blood. Although Hephaestus fights against me, I do not mistake the proud smile fluttering over his lips at the sight of his newest creation- my sword.

He roars as he swings both hammers towards my head. I barely duck in time, just as one blade cuts a lock of my hair. I somersault beneath him, then drive my sword down towards his good foot. He jumps away in time, and my sword embeds deep in the ground.

Hephaestus already strikes down again, and I must leave my sword behind as I drop to the floor and roll away. My hand reaches for Οστά, and the bones adhere. She covers my palm once again, and I hasten to a kneeling position as I thrust the blade forward. Hephaestus freezes, both hammers raised, as the tip slides into his thigh.

"It really is some of my best work," he says about the sword inside his thigh before he disappears.

I have a second to observe the surrounding scene, and it is as gruesome as I expected.

Ares duels against his mother, Hera. She fights on the defensive, twirling and jumping away from his advances, but her movements are slow. Soon, she will fall to his blade, irreparably changing their relationship. Neither stop their assaults, but Hera's expression shows her angered betrayal.

Poseidon and Demeter fight against each other. Poseidon has drenched the ground in water, turning the dirt into mud, slowing their steps. Demeter continuously trips and stumbles, but she doesn't cease the fight against her brother.

Hades and Zeus remind the audience that they're near equals. Zeus is only slightly stronger than Hades, and every swipe of their blades and parry of their movements embellishes this truth. Zeus's lightning bolts meet the air as Hades's helm of invisibility lets him disappear then reappear at a moment's notice.

Then, there's Hermes and Athena.

The latter runs away from Hermes without defeating him, with her focus on Poseidon's fight with Demeter. He stands in the arena, searching for a figure before landing on me. I look back at Athena, and the decision to leave Hermes unscathed, and I know there's more to this battle. I married the god of trickery, and he plays the role well.

I step towards him, but he runs after Athena.

My movements are close behind him.

Athena's sword slashes through the air, aiming for the back of Poseidon's neck. He moves just in time to see her, and his trident strikes. Athena slices across his throat, nearly decapitating him, as the three prongs of his trident pierce through her armor, embedding it deep in her stomach. Their golden blood simultaneously spills, and the two enemies defeat one another.

Demeter stumbles away from the mud, which still cakes her ankles and shins, and faces Hermes. She screams as she runs towards him, her weapon raised high in the air. They fall into a battle that will end in each other's deaths, for that I'm certain.

So, I focus my attention towards the only god who can defeat me and kill Epiales.

Zeus.

I run towards Zeus, and even as he fights Hades, he sees me coming. He throws a dozen lightning bolts out into the arena. I duck in time, but Ares does not. A lightning bolt strikes him in the chest and he collapses to the ground. I'm so close to Zeus, I can taste the charred bolts, but Hera is closer.

She has thirsted for the moment she could kill me since the first time she heard of my existence, but I've hated her too. Persephone is my mother through love, but I lost the chance to be raised by Metis because of Hera. She killed my birth mother and tried to kill me before I was born. I've tried to curb my rage towards her, as I've learned how insanity claims the children of Zeus, who try to fight against Hera's vengeance. I refuse to be like Heracles, a murderous shell of who I once was, but I hate her.

And now, genuine hatred can emerge.

As soon as we stand across from one another, I swing my sword towards the diadem perfectly poised atop her head. She jumps back a step, but I follow her lead. She's not a natural fighter, and it's an undeniable fact we both know. The only reason she has lasted this long is because Ares was going easy on her, but I refuse to lessen my rage. I've waited almost a century for this moment, and I can hear the tunes of vengeance play the prettiest melody.

We dance to the tune of repressed loathing, until I slice off the diadem, and a tuft of brown hair, then cut off her head. Her body collapses to its knees, then she falls stomach-first into the ground. Her head rolls a few feet before she's transported away.

The Ichor of my opponents spills from the blade and coats my hand, while their blood smears my face, but I feel more powerful than ever before. I am hyper aware of every bone in everyone in the arena's body as I run towards Zeus and Hades. I want to use the power coursing through my veins.

Οστά flies across the arena at my command.

While Zeus deflects Hades's attacks with his lightning bolt, my weapon moves towards Zeus's head. Yet, before the weapon can pierce his skin, he catches the blade by the handle and smiles my way. My sword boomerangs back towards me, but before Οστά can touch my skin, I reach my hand forward. Using my power over the bone-made handle, I halt its advance an inch away from my right eye.

"Saffron!" Hades screams, and just like the last arena we shared, his love is his demise.

The moment Hades's attention drifts to me, fearful I lost, Zeus's lightning bolt smashes into his chest. Hades flies across the arena in defeat. I do not make the same mistakes. I know he has lost, so I focus all my attention on Zeus, who materializes two more lightning bolts. He doesn't throw them; instead, he waits for me to walk towards him.

Only two feet separate him and me as I ask. "Why didn't you kill him on Ogygia, *Alastor*?"

Zeus's jaw clenches, but he says nothing.

I wipe my sword's blade across my hip, cleaning off the blood with my clothing. "You had your chance to kill him on Ogygia. You had anonymity with Alastor's face, but still you wait until now to try to murder him. Why?"

"If I killed him on that island, you would hate me. At least here, with the vote of the other gods, if I kill him, you could forgive me."

"What makes you think I don't hate you already?"

"Because you're having this discussion with me instead of fighting first."

But I do hate Zeus. I'm his biological daughter, and he didn't choose me when I need him to. He opted for another god to raise me as his child because he didn't want me. That decision deserves my hatred, which should never falter. It doesn't matter that Hades is a great dad, because what if he wasn't? Zeus stole the chance for me to view him as a father, then he tried to vote for my death the same way he voted for Epiales's.

I scream as I run towards Zeus, my partially cleaned sword nearing him, but he drops his lightning bolts. He doesn't throw them. He drops them. His arms open wide, accepting my sword's mercilessness as it plunges into his chest.

Blood bubbles out of the corner of his mouth as he says, "Epiales is not meant for you. He is meant to be the death of you, if you let him live."

He says this with such unwavering assuredness before he dissipates in a rainbow.

I turn around, ready to defeat anybody else coming my way, but there is nobody left in the arena. Nobody but

Hermes. He is right in front of me, those green eyes that I've loved for so many decades, and then there is nothing but pain.

A blade digs itself into my stomach, searing my skin with the cruel touch of defeat, and tears instantly build in my eyes. Hermes yanks the blade out of my stomach, covered with my ichor. I collapse onto my knees just as the tears tumble down my cheeks.

Looking over at Epiales, who stares back at me, I mouth two simple words that announce my defeat.

'I'm sorry.'

THIRTY-SIX

HERMES

I won.

I didn't want to jump into that arena. To fight for the man my wife chose over me. When the idea of what to do with Epiales blossomed while talking with Nike and Athena the night after Saffron's return, I wanted to ignore the righteous choice.

I almost ignored it all and let Zeus and Saffron settle the Epiales dispute amongst themselves, but that would not work. One, or both, of them would incite a war that would divide the gods. Exactly what Styx wanted.

When I had told Athena and Nike my plan, the two goddesses filtered the plan across Mt. Olympus to anyone whose opinion could be swayed. Hephaestus and Aphrodite agreed first, followed by Demeter, Hestia, the Muses, Artemis, and Dionysus. We brought the conversation to Poseidon, but he adamantly refused to be a part of any plan that involved Athena.

He agreed to help ensure Zeus didn't kill Epiales, but insisted it was for Saffron's sake.

Other than Poseidon and the few gods, like Heracles and Hera, that we chose not to tell, there were no objections. For once, a group of Immortals all agreed on an important topic, such as Epiales's fate. It gave me flickering hopes that this war could be salvageable.

So, when the fight ensued, Athena pretended to fight me, so that there was no attention on us. Many Olympians, especially Zeus and Hera, underestimate my abilities because I am not one of the chosen twelve. They see me as a messenger. A schemer. A nuisance. Yet, those traits have formed me into a harrowing opponent.

It's how Saffron did not expect our plan. Any moment she had to think on the arena floor, Hephaestus, Nike, or Artemis distracted her with an attack. Almost, she suspected my plans, when Athena left our fight to disqualify Poseidon, but Demeter quickly distracted Saffron. Except for that one moment, Saffron hadn't looked in my direction. The few gods on her side of the battle glanced towards my fake duels and ignored me.

Nobody saw the victory befalling me until Demeter let me stab her, and Zeus dropped his lightning bolts.

I had to wait until she defeated Zeus. Only she had the power to cause Zeus to bleed, but I was the only one who could distract Saffron long enough to stab her.

The moment Saffron turned around to face me, I stared into those brown eyes, and I saw our past together. I saw every kiss, every embrace, every laugh that left her lips, and I drove the knife into her stomach. Just like our relationship, I watched the memories flutter away as betrayal covered her face.

I stumbled away from her with the certainty that I had done the right thing.

Even if she will not see it that way.

"Hermes." Aphrodite leans against the arched doorway to her home, where I hide from the one question I must answer. Even as her form changes every second, the sympathetic half-smile on her lips does not waver. "They're ready for you to make your decision about Epiales."

"Of course they are," I sigh as I stand up to my full height. "We live forever and yet they cannot let a man rest."

Aphrodite places her hand on my arm and stops me before I can leave the room. "You did the right thing." She squeezes my arm before lowering her hand and intertwining it with mine. "She'll understand one day."

No, she won't.

My decision protects the majority, but not her. Why must all my choices hurt the woman I love the most? I don't have the strength to speak to Aphrodite, and I let her guide me away from her home and towards the throne room. A dozen expecting immortals wait for us there, greedy for my words and the trickle effect they'll create.

Aphrodite and I walk into the throne room, and the first person my eyes go to is Saffron. She stands beside Hades's seat, talking in hushed whispers with him, as her nails dig into the top of the chair. To most, she appears stoic in the face of uncertainty, but I know Saffron too well. I see the newly healing cuticles around her thumbs from where she scraped them raw with nervousness. I see the way she refuses to look in Epiales's direction, like staring at him will force all her emotions to be visible enough for everyone to see.

Her compassion for him. Gods, her love for him,

conjures an inferno of rage. I want to kill him. To slide a blade into his chest and end his miserable life. Not just because he stole my wife from me. And not just because he makes my wife smile for the first time in years, even when I couldn't. I still hate him for the events that happened here on Mt. Olympus during the last Titanomachy war.

Epiales tortured me. He watched as Typhon peeled my skin off and ripped out my organs. Epiales aided in my suffering, and that form of torment has followed me for decades. I haven't etched the screams from my ears or erased the sight of my mangled limbs from my mind. Those events still plague me, and Epiales did nothing to stop the agony.

He condemned me, just like Typhon, Kronos, and Circe.

So, I hate him. I want to kill him. Want to watch his eyes glisten in immeasurable pain, just like he did when I suffered as Kronos's prisoner. I want to mutilate him until his pathetic human heart stops beating, then carry his soul down to the Underworld and into the Fields of Punishments. I want to be the one wielding the instrument that tortures him every second of his miserable existence.

But I can't.

I can't because I love her too much.

And no matter how small the chance is, there's still a chance he is a part of the prophecy that will bring Styx down. If he dies and he was essential to our success, I do not want to be the executioner. I will not be the one others blame for Styx's success, not after everything I did to stop this war before it began. Making the death of my marriage a casualty.

Phobos and Deimos stand on both sides of Epiales, who is still cuffed from head to toe, as if Zeus expects

Epiales to escape and overpower all the immortals. I almost want to laugh at Zeus's paranoia, but when my eyes wander towards Epiales, I remember the monster he had been. The nightmares he wielded left long-lasting effects that I never want to relive.

"How great you finally joined us, Hermes." Hera sneers.

I force a fake smile back at my stepmother. "Is that a white hair I see, Hera? No wonder Paris chose Aphrodite's beauty over yours." I keep my smile on my face while Hera glowers at me with all the hatred she can muster.

Aphrodite giggles beside me.

She kisses my cheek and glides over to her spot beside Hephaestus at her throne. Suddenly, every immortal has their eyes on me. Amidst the jokes and parlor tricks, this is a serious moment for the world. In my hands, I hold the power to kill a man who has caused wars for our kind and killed many, but his death would also cause the fall of the woman I love the most in this world. Perhaps more than the world itself.

"Phobos and Deimos, free him of the cuffs. He cannot cause harm in a room full of immortals."

"But-" Phobos tries to say, looking up at Zeus.

"Did Zeus win possession of Epiales in the arena? Or did I?"

Deimos smacks the back of his twin brother's head and murmurs. "Just listen to him, doofus."

Within seconds, Epiales's cuffs disappear, and the weakened human crumbles to the ground. Saffron flinches at the sight of him falling, but she cannot run to him, as she yearns. She stands up a little straighter and averts her gaze. The rest of us watch as Epiales tries to rise to a sitting position, only to fall back to the ground.

She still won't look at Epiales, or me, as she grinds out one word. "Please."

"Go fetch him food and a cup of water." I order Deimos, and unlike his brother, he doesn't look to Zeus for reassurance. He runs to obey my wishes.

"Why are you feeding him?" Zeus angrily quips. "He's a prisoner."

"A human prisoner who needs food and water to survive," I say.

Ever so slightly, Saffron's grip on Hades's throne lessens.

"You will not kill him?" Hera asks with a mixture of confusion and annoyance. "He stole your wife from you. He tortured you on this very mountain! I always knew you were an insipid-"

A scream erupts from Hera's lips, curbing her slanderous words. Her jawbone flies from her skin, falling to the center of the table. Zeus jolts to his feet, glowering at Saffron. Her focus remains fixed on Hera.

"Nobody stole me. You may see yourself as lesser than the surrounding men, but I do not. Do not speak about me as if I am property to be passed around. And he is not insipid because he has a conscious."

That's the last time she will ever defend me.

I break the silence. "The prophecy detailed the importance of keeping Saffron and her heart alive. We don't know who that heart is for sure, but I won't be the one who tests that theory through bloodshed. Epiales won't die today."

I hate saying these words. They're poison on my tongue. Saffron has been my wife for decades, and now I must accept this dreaded version of a life where Epiales could own her heart. That his role in a prophecy tethers him to Saffron forever. I am the god of trickery, who can deceive anyone, so I let my audience believe my words hold no negative effect on my wellbeing.

I'm an excellent liar.

"Epiales needs to live because if he dies, then Styx gets what she wants. I hate him as much as many of you, but I hate Styx more. More than that, I fear Styx more than a human version of Epiales."

I can't stay immobile. My feet need to move. My mind needs to pace as the realization that Epiales will not die settles in my mind that only wants revenge. He stole my wife, but he also tortured me. Both crimes deserve a deadly punishment, but I can't do it to her. I can't kill him in front of her.

Before I can admit the second part of my plan to the woman who listens with a rising hope that I will have to shatter into a thousand irreparable pieces. "Epiales is alive because Saffron gave him her humanity. The same humanity that saved us from the last Titanomachy War. That saved us from Kronos."

Zeus bellows. "The same war Epiales fought with Kronos!"

"Which is why he will still have a punishment. Just not one that ends in death."

The room becomes so silent that the thudding of Epiales's, the only human in the room, heart echoes.

"Explain yourself," Ares says, his words clipped.

I steel my shoulders, but I don't stop moving. I must keep walking, to keep pacing the space where too many eyes follow my every movement. Aphrodite's reminder that I'm making the right decision is the smallest whisper in my head against the roars of rage that will ensue.

The words come out jumbled, but they exist. Everyone

375

hears me as I say. "He cannot die, but he cannot be a part of our world either."

Deimos chooses this time to run back into the throne room with a tray full of bread and fruits. There's no noise. No screams or explanations. There is only the sound of the metal tray clinking and clacking as it lowers beside Epiales's sprawled body. He needs to eat, or at least drink the water beside the bread, but he doesn't move towards it.

"What are you proposing to do with him?" Saffron can't hide the fear in her voice, or in the way she picks at her thumb cuticles again.

"After the plague caused by the Nosoi destroyed towns, Asclepius told me about a serum he created. It can erase the human mind of all memories. He created it to give the sufferers of the plague a mental reprieve from all they lost, but I-"

"No."

I expect the person to speak out to be Saffron, but all of us grow silent at the sound of Epiales's guttural groan from his spot on the floor. All of us turn our attention to Epiales, who has forgotten about his food and water as he kneels on the floor. His focus is solely on me, pain clear in his bloodshot eyes.

"Don't make me forget her." I didn't realize why his eyes were so bloodshot until he turns his attention away from me and stares at Saffron, tears falling down his cheeks. "Please don't make me forget who she is. I'd prefer death."

I have to tear my gaze away from them when I see tears pooling up in Saffron's eyes as well. Sharply, I look over at Zeus, but he is still staring at the two of them. The clear love they have for one another.

"Father." My voice cracks when I speak. "I have

decided that the human Epiales deserves a life. Tomorrow morning, we will inject him with the medicine, and I will take him to Earth only I know the location of. If we discover definitive proof that he is a part of the prophecy, then I will retrieve him from his new life. We will do what we must. But if we are wrong and he is just a human, then he will live out his life in the place I chose for him."

Epiales's sobs join my explanation, and a few gods flinch at the sound. Aphrodite lays her head on Hephaestus's shoulder so she can press her ear hard enough to block out some of the sound of a man's heart rupturing.

"As long as he is in our world, Styx's army will use him as a pawn, and there are too many traitors we haven't unearthed. He is a weak human now, one anybody smart enough could use against Saffron, and I will let nothing bad happen to her. Not because of him."

I meet Saffron's gaze, and I see the heartache beneath those perfect, tear-swum brown eyes. She's beautiful, even as I break her heart twice in one week. I hope she will forgive me one day, but that is a fool's wish.

"This is the only option," I say only to her. Begging her with my eyes alone to understand why I have made this decision.

"And you are certain you wish to do this?" Zeus asks.

Epiales tries to stand again, to fight the fate I have forced upon him, but he falls to the ground once again. "Please, don't do this!" Epiales exclaims from the floor, his throat raw from dehydration. "Anything else. Please!"

"I am certain. By the time the sun rises tomorrow morning, we will wipe Epiales's memory clean. He will not remember his past life as a god, or the past month since he was brought back to life. He will start life anew, and he will no longer be a part of our lives."

Saffron storms out of the room, but not out of rage. The moment the door closes behind her, I hear it. The sound of her heartbreaking sobs. She tried to run out of earshot, so none of us could hear her sobbing for him, but the sound pierces my ears. I hate making her cry.

Apollo runs after her while Hades jolts to his feet.

"May I go to the Underworld now? I need to see my wife."

Zeus nods his head.

Hades disappears, followed shortly by Poseidon, Artemis, and the rest of the Olympians. In less than a minute, everyone but Zeus, Hera, Epiales, Phobos, Deimos, and I are gone. The twin gods stay as the unbiased guards, ensuring nobody kills him until the morning, when I take him far from Mt. Olympus and Saffron in the morning.

"Please." Epiales's voice is barely audible beneath the sobs.

"Your decision was ruthless," Zeus finally says. "But it was the wisest decision."

"It was a deceitful one," I admit.

Zeus nods his head, not denying my claim. "Wisdom and deceit are close friends. I will see you in the morning to see his punishment exacted."

He holds out his arm for Hera, but she scoffs and walks away without accepting his chivalry. They leave the room, then Phobos and Deimos grab Epiales. They hoist him up to his feet as the latter asks. "Where do you want him?"

I lead them towards his prison, and the entire journey, he repeats the same broken, "*please.*"

THIRTY-SEVEN

HART SOMMERS

"We Sommers have a curse. We can't hold liquor to save our lives."

Mom told me one night as we watched Suraj trying to corral our inebriated father on his fiftieth birthday. He continued to stumble while dancing to Dolly Parton, while singing at the top of his lungs. Suraj was miserable, but he didn't complain as he continuously reminded our dad that the floor was, in fact, not lava.

With that memory engraved in my mind, I am on a mission to drink as much wine as possible until I am just as inebriated as my father was at his fiftieth birthday party. Every time I close my eyes, even to blink, all I see is Lowell. How the sympathy in his dark eyes washes away and replaces itself with determination to end my life. Then, the pain from my stab wounds inflames with the searing pain of betrayal.

The moment I stop thinking about Lowell, I'm

submerged in the visions detailing every horrific death that awaits this looming war. It starts in the Underworld, then fissures into the rest of the world. Death's pungent stench will fill every road in every country until the casualties multiply.

I know the truth that dares to spill from my lips, but I can't tell anyone. Admitting the truth too early leads to death. Divulging too late leads to death. Everything I do leads to another demise that presents the throne and crown to Styx. I must play the cards exactly as the prophecy needs them dealt, or else we lose.

I can barely handle Lowell's betrayal, and the looming loneliness that comes without a friend, but more weight lies on my shoulders. It's too much to suffer alone, so I make a new friend in the form of a pearly white bottle of wine.

I tilt my head back, chugging the wine until the images fade. Until I can no longer see Lowell. Or the blade that emerged out of nowhere. Or the visions of all those instrumental in the coming war.

I chug the contents of the alcohol until the Sommers' curse emerges, and I sway from side to side. My bottle is my medicine, and I chug the contents until the curse leaves my fingers unreliable, allowing the half-finished wine bottle to leave my grasp. I do not catch the wine, but I watch as it falls to the ground with a crash.

The bottle turns into sharp shards, and the fragments scatter across the room. The remaining white wine stains the floor, shifting from white to red until it mirrors blood, and I see my dying body on the ground beside it. I stare down at the mess that I have created with awe, transfixed upon the disaster until a laugh bubbles up to the surface.

That is when Apollo walks in.

I sit on his bed in Mt. Olympus, laughing in disbelief as I stare down at shards of glass and spilled wine. "It's my blood," I say with a laugh.

"You're hurt?!"

Fear from the past few days re-surges with a vengeance, and he runs. A little black box falls out of his pants pocket as he rushes over towards me, but he doesn't notice. All he sees is me. He steps on the glass; the ends poking into his skin, but he doesn't care. Apollo hurriedly sits in front of me and checks my body for any obvious wounds, while I am still laughing and pointing down at the wine.

Apollo looks down at the glass and red liquid, finally realizing that I am unscathed, before he draws his attention back up to me. "Are you drunk?"

"Yup," I pop the 'p' at the end.

"How about you rest, and I'll clean up the mess, hmm?" He leans forward, placing a soft kiss on the top of my head, before he gets off the bed to clean up my mess.

But I can't rest. It's been difficult to find sleep amid the mania, so I peruse the room again. I've stared at the lifeless, pale walls of Apollo's home on Mt. Olympus for hours now, but the little black box on the floor is new.

"What's that box?" He picks up the glass, oblivious to the missing object, and I slide off of the bed. I am careful not to step on any of the glass as I stumble towards the black box. I pick up the velvety material, then ask. "What is this, Apollo?"

"Don't open it, μέλι."

Too late.

I flip open the box, and inside is the most beautiful engagement ring my eyes have ever gazed upon. The gem on the ring isn't a conventional diamond, but is a dazzling amber. The dark golden red hue is perfect, reminding me of a piece of a sun's ray shining down on the ground. It's perfect.

I strain to tear my gaze away from the engagement ring, but once I do, I am consumed by his shockingly blue eyes that brim with hope and fear. He is kneeling in one patch of the floor unscathed from any glass, holding out his hands for the jewelry box.

"I wanted to wait until you were sober." He shoots me a sweet smile, devoid of judgement. "But give me the box, Hart."

I obey.

Once the jewelry box is in his hand, I wait for the words. I wait for him to ask me to be his wife. Yet, there is only silence. For almost five minutes, quiet tension fills the room. Sweat dribbles down the corners of Apollo's hairline, and his teeth bite down on his bottom lip.

"Are you nervous?" I ask, breaking the silence, and Apollo responds with a nervous chuckle.

"I may have existed for eons, and yet I've never been more terrified in my entire life."

"Why? It's just me."

"Exactly, it's you." Apollo lets out a shaky breath. "I thought I experienced everything life offered. I met the humans others proclaimed as the grandest. Explored every inch of the world's monuments and climbed every mountain. I thought I saw and did it all until I met you. My beautiful, honey-eyed soulmate. You gave me a taste of a world I never truly experienced. You gave me peace in a world of chaos, and I fear that one day you will realize I'm not good enough for you. Then, the peace and the smiles and the happiness will die with your absence."

Tears build in my eyes, but I stay silent.

I can't speak.

Apollo stares up at me with unwavering reverence, like I am the goddess and he the mortal, rather than the other way around. "You're my everything, and I'm scared that you'll say no when I beg you to be mine forever. By marrying me, you will become an immortal. You'll eternally be my wife, the mother of my children, and my world. I even chose a gem that mirrors your eyes, those honey-colored eyes I love so much. I'm afraid that I'll never see you wear this ring on your finger. That you don't want forever."

I move towards Apollo and wordlessly pluck the ring out of the box. The ring is a perfect fit for my finger, sliding on effortlessly. Only then do I look down at Apollo, whose eyes shine with elated tears, and I murmur the two words I've wanted to say since he and I met.

"I want forever with you. The peace and the happiness and the laughter. I want it all, as long as you're there with me until the fiery end."

He is up within a blink of an eye, his arms wrapping around my waist. He hoists me up into the air, and before I can react, his lips crash down on my own. The effects of the wine have subsided; yet, when I close my eyes and kiss Apollo back, I am not marred by the sight of Lowell. My nightmare has dispersed, and it is because Apollo has always been my remedy.

With that thought, I kiss him back.

We fall into the bed, celebrating the moment he will tell our children about with an ear-splitting grin. It's the perfect night, and I delve into his embrace with no desire to let go. Styx comes out of hiding tomorrow, and a rainstorm of terror joins her. But for now, I want to kiss my future husband and forget it all.

Just a few more hours of harmony.

Then, I'll let the storm take my happiness.

THIRTY-EIGHT

SAFFRON

Since the verdict, I have been in my room, hiding away from the rest of occupants of Mt. Olympus. I do not want to meet their sympathetic or fuming expressions or hear them attempt conversations that will lead nowhere. For one night, I want to be upset without an audience.

Tears continue to brandish my face, and as much as I want to hate Hermes for this, I am thankful. When Hermes thrust that blade into my stomach, I was certain that Epiales was going to be executed. I thought I was going to have to experience heartbreak twice in one week.

Yet, he showed mercy.

He didn't think I noticed, but I know Hermes wanted to kill Epiales. He wanted to drive a blade into his heart and end his life, but he didn't because of me. I had broken Hermes's heart, and he saved what remained of mine.

Hermes made the right choice. Even if I hate it, he was right. If Epiales is in my world, he will be in harm's way,

TRISH D. W.

and I cannot ever escape my life as a goddess. No more can I escape the role I play in the upcoming war. The moment we met, the world fought to separate us, and just like last time, the Fates succeed.

I have been crying for at least two hours, unable to let the tears stop streaming down my face, although I know this is the best chance for Epiales to have a real life. Even if it is a life that I can never be a part of with him. I will yearn for him from a great distance, knowing he exists but not where, while he has completely forgotten about me.

He will most likely find a beautiful wife, who knows the romantic side of him only I have witnessed, and they will have children with his glimmering silver irises. Epiales will find a life on Earth that surpasses anything I could ever give him. He could become a chef, finally showing the world his culinary skills.

Whatever he will become, I'll never get to witness it. I'll continue to live my life with an aching emptiness inside of me, giving a piece of myself to everybody, only to watch them disappear. I will mourn Epiales with Zig, Diam, Hattie, and Argus, for he has a piece of my heart inside of him.

With him gone, I will forever lose a piece of myself.

But at least he will be safe.

"Even when you're a mess, you're gorgeous." Ares leans against the wall of my home on Mt. Olympus. A rusty key dangles from his left index finger. "Let's go. You have a nightmare to say goodbye to."

He extends his free hand to me, but I don't understand. "Why do you keep helping me?"

He doesn't answer, and I don't pry.

I don't take his hand, but I let him lead me away from where the gods drink and rejoice in the end to

Epiales. We are silent throughout most of our trip to the other side of Mt. Olympus, but every so often, the feeling of somebody staring at me brings my gaze up towards him. By the time I look up at him, he focuses on something else. For nearly five minutes, we play this game, until I finally catch him staring before he looks away.

"What is it?"

"You need new bodyguards." he clears his throat, almost awkwardly. "Especially with, uh, you know, Styx, still out there."

I haven't forgotten about Argus's death at Atlas's hands. The moment I can leave Mt. Olympus, I will search for Atlas until I find him and exact my revenge. I will make sure that he spends the rest of his miserable, immortal existence regretting the decision he made to kill my friend, who only wanted to free me from harm.

Argus's death has spread around Mt. Olympus, his name synonymous with heroism, but his well-deserved accolades aren't enough. Atlas still roams the world, searching for the huntresses, instead of suffering on Mt. Atlas with the world on his shoulders. I will return him there, but not without delivering him my retribution first.

"What are you getting at, Ares?"

"My sons." Ares stops in front of the prison and unlocks the front door. "Will you take them as guards until we find Styx?"

"I don't need a body-"

"But you'll need backup when you go after Atlas." Ares interrupts as unlocks the door and holds it open for me. "You'll need someone to wake you if there's an army coming for you while you sleep. You'll need company when the war gets too lonely." He clenches his jaw and says so quietly, I almost don't hear him. "And it'll give me a peace of mind, knowing you aren't alone."

I don't walk inside immediately; instead, I glare up at him. "Why do you care?"

"Fine. Never mind, then."

"Just tell me why."

"Because hate is not the word I feel towards you, and you're a fool for thinking so. Now get inside before anyone sees us."

He places his hand on the shell of my back and gently pushes me forward. Frigid gusts of air freezes all the skin on my arms. With his hand still against my lower back, Ares leads me deeper into the prison.

"Is there any way to make it warmer in here?" I whisper to Ares and he shakes his head. "He's going to freeze to death in here."

"That would finally shut Zeus up."

"Ares," I snap.

We walk forward until the sight of Ares's twin sons, Phobos and Deimos, meets my gaze. "Open the door," Ares says beside me.

Phobos and Deimos obey, and the cell doors swing open. I waste no time, and I run inside, falling upon the floor where Epiales's body is curled up. His skin is as cold as ice, and his lips are a dark purple hue. Coldness threatens to take his life before the morning. He has yet to notice my presence, but once I lay myself behind him, wrapping my arms comfortably around him, he stirs awake.

The sound of his teeth chattering echoes throughout the empty jail as he forces out two words. "M-My q-queen."

I place a kiss on his shoulder and rub my hands up and down his arms. "Get him a blanket."

"But Lord Hermes didn't tell us we-" Phobos says.

"Get the blanket," Ares growls.

"I'll go get that, Lady Saffron." Deimos is gone in a flash.

Epiales tilts his head up so he can see the gods on the other side of the prison cell. "T-Thank y-you."

Ares holds up his hand, silencing him. "I…" he lets out an aggravated sigh. "I will be right outside keeping watch. You two have fifteen, maybe twenty, minutes before Hermes comes back to check on him."

Ares storms out of the room, leaving Epiales and me with Phobos. The last remaining god leans against the cell and smiles down at me without realizing just how unwanted his presence is. Epiales cannot speak, incapacitated because of the cold, but his chattering teeth echo down the hallway. I move my hands up and down his frigid arms. Meanwhile, Phobos continues to stare with an eerie smile.

"So, how's your day going?" Phobos asks.

"Can we have a few minutes alone, please?"

"But I am not permitted to leave the prisoner."

I frown. "Then turn around, please."

He clears his throat as the smile disappears from his face. "Mhm, right."

Phobos finally looks away from us just as Deimos runs forward with a wool blanket. He throws the blanket towards me, and I immediately wrap the material around Epiales. Deimos doesn't need a reminder like Phobos, and the twins station themselves on both sides of the cell with their backs to us. I am given a sliver of seclusion, and I use this limited time holding Epiales.

For almost fifteen minutes, the cold renders him speechless. He can only cling to the fragments of warmth the blanket and I provide, until the sound of his chattering teeth lessens, and he relaxes more comfortably in my arms.

"You're not here to help me escape, are you?" I hate the fear in his voice as he asks.

I place a tender kiss on the top of his dark head of hair. "No, I'm not. You deserve a life filled with people who see you how I do. You deserve to be around people who see you as the man with compassion. A man who thinks of himself last and the people he loves first. A man who is completely changed from his past. My world can't provide that."

He turns himself around, so we face one another, and while his hand is cold, I let him cup my cheek. He pulls me in for a small kiss. It hurts so much. Feels achingly like a goodbye. "I'd rather die than lose you," he says against my lips.

"As long as you are the former Titan Epiales, vengeful gods will hunt you down until you die in my arms. I don't know if you are the heart of the prophecy, but if you are, then fate says I will kill those responsible for your death. That my scream will join the wind forever. If you are the heart of this prophecy, then we need to stay as far away from each other as possible. We need to keep you away from me because together, we are danger incarnate."

Epiales leans forward, kissing away a lone tear streaming down my face, and he murmurs. "I don't want to lose you."

"You must." I take a piece of his curly, dark hair and place it behind his ear. "Twice, you've told me you would share me, as long as I was happy. I will share you with the rest of the world, too, just so you are safe and at peace.

You'll be safe in a world far from gods and prophecies, and one day, you'll find someone who makes you just as happy."

He swallows back his own tears, and I watch as his Adam's apple bobs up and down in a futile attempt at seeming unfazed. He moves his hands, placing both on my face. His thumbs are gingerly caressing my cheeks, while his eyes engrave everything into memory. He stares with such intensity, as if he is trying to fight the power of the potion that will leave me as a godly stranger rather than the love of his life.

"I will never forget those eyes," he murmurs lovingly. "Brown became my favorite color because of those eyes."

He leans forward, placing a kiss in between my eyes, and I close them to stop the tears from brandishing my cheeks.

"I will never forget that button nose you scrunch up every time you're confused." He places a delicate kiss on the tip of my nose. "Or these lips..." his index finger grazes across my bottom lip, eliciting a surge of electricity that causes my toes to curl. "The greatest Grecian authors could write epics beginning and ending with these lips."

His lips are soft against my own, and hesitant. He kisses me as if I will disintegrate from his embrace at any moment, and I wrap my arms around the back of his neck, forcing him to deepen the kiss. I open my mouth, happily awaiting his tongue, and while we kiss, I can see everything.

Every dream he and I shared, every argument, every heated kiss that shouldn't have happened, every bit of pain that having him in my life has caused, and every moment that he made this insufferable loneliness bearable.

Epiales pulls away, while his eyes scour down towards

my body. "I'm going to miss that little freckle on the top of your lip. It is my favorite thing to look at."

He lowers his lips, caressing the freckle, and tears once again emerge.

"I'm going to find you again," he lowers his lips down to my neck and murmurs into the curve of my neck in between kisses. "I may not remember you, but I'm going to be in your life again. There will be nobody else because you are more powerful than any medicine that they give me, and I'll never forget bits of you. I'll never forget this freckle, or the way your eyes crinkle past recognition when you laugh. Nothing could make me forget these things."

"I love you," I softly whisper, fearful of the words because they are the last ones I'll ever say to him, but he smiles.

"My Queen, love doesn't even adequately describe just how much I care for you."

I knew it was time, but when Ares clears his throat, Epiales's face falls. He presses his lips against my own with the certainty that this is our last kiss, and I silently pull myself out of his embrace. I wrap him up tightly in the blankets, place a last kiss on his forehead, and then I take Ares's hand and leave.

I do not talk as Ares leads me out of the cell, steering me through the darkness with ease, but it isn't long until Epiales lets out a blood curling scream. Ares squeezes my hand tighter when I want to turn around and run back to him. He leads me out of the prisons, not slowing down until it's out of our line of vision.

"I feel like I keep having to thank you lately."

"You don't need to thank me," he says.

"Yes, I do. You saved him from Ogygia at the risk of

Zeus's wrath, and you fought alongside me in the arena. Then, you steal the key to the prisons and-"

"I don't deserve your thanks. Trust me."

"Why?"

He won't look at me as he smirks. "You don't always find the answers to the riddles of life. Just accept it."

I barely pay attention to my surroundings as Ares guides me away from the prisons. We meander away from the houses and buildings, where others celebrate his imprisonment, and stand at the edge of Mt. Olympus. A sword materializes in Ares's free hand, the other remains tightly in mine.

"Do you have the sword Hephaestus made for you?"

Οστά sits sheathed on my hip, and I roam my free hand down to its handle. "Yes, why?" I ask.

"It's pathetic how quickly I found Atlas's hiding spot." Ares blinds me with a widespread smile, sending a thousand electrical shocks through my body. "Let's go distract ourselves in some bloodshed, gorgeous."

He knows exactly what I need, an escape from Mt. Olympus, so I do not need to see Hermes force the memory-extracting medicine down Epiales's throat. I need to release the aggression threatening to swallow me whole.

I grin back up at Ares. "Zeus told us to stay put."

We both leap off Mt. Olympus.

THIRTY-NINE

HERMES

S affron isn't here to watch Epiales's last moments in our world, and it's a small mercy. Ares and many of the gods from the Underworld are absent, too, in solidarity of their allegiance to Saffron. I'm not sure when Ares decided his loyalty fell with Saffron, but I do not care as long as it means she doesn't witness this moment.

Phobos and Deimos drag Epiales out of the prisons. A wool blanket falls off his body when he trips over his chains. He can't stop shivering, his lips almost purple, and I glare at Zeus. I refused to go to the prisons last night, but Zeus assured me they were hospitable. He pointedly doesn't look in my direction, but it's a miracle Epiales survived the night.

Aphrodite picks up the wool blanket, jogging after Epiales and her sons. When I raise my hand in the air, they drop him onto the ground, and Aphrodite wraps him in the wool blanket. He flinches at her touch, but he allows her to give him a fraction of warmth before she scurries away from him.

"Do you have any last words?"

I hate the sound of my voice, the lack of emotion even as my heart swells with jealousy towards the man, who will soon have no memory of the most unforgettable woman in existence. His eyes are closed, as if he is content with this decision. We both know that's not the case.

"There's nothing I wish to say to any of you."

"Give him the medicine."

Epiales scoffs at the term medicine, because it is a poison that infects the brain until nothing remains. It is the thief of memories and treasured moments. Epiales has always cherished stories, and now, they leave with any reminder of his past life.

Apollo and Asclepius walk towards Epiales, who gives no fight. They take both sides of his shoulders and hold him still as I unearth the vial from my pocket. I pull the cork off the vile, and Epiales flinches, but he doesn't look away from me. He glowers at me, condemning me with his gaze alone, as I motion for Apollo to grab his hair. He obeys and tilts his head back.

I expected Epiales to keep his mouth closed, to prolong this fate, but he doesn't fight us. He opens his mouth, and I do not hesitate. I let the golden liquid slide down his throat, and I watch as Epiales ingests every drop.

The bottle falls from my fingers and crashes to the ground. Our audience watches with amazement at what unfurls. Epiales appears fine initially, but then his left eye twitches. Then, his right. Soon, his entire body convulses and foam blooms out of his mouth.

"What is happening to him?" I snarl, glaring at Asclepius, but he doesn't respond.

Instead, Hart does.

"He will survive the medicine." Her voice is softer than a whisper. "His story ends with blood and tears. Not poison and apathy."

Eventually, the seizing stops and Epiales lies on the floor unconscious, with the steady beat of his heart calming the fear I had when I believed he was going to die. There are several minutes when everybody merely watches him, just in case something extraordinary will occur. As if he will wake up an immortal once again, ready to strike us all down.

"Get him out of my sight," Zeus finally snarls, breaking the silence on Mt. Olympus, and he storms back into his throne room.

Those who did not want to be witnesses to Epiales's fate, but Zeus forced them to attend, like Hestia and Poseidon, leave with Zeus. A few more curious immortals stay around, wishing for more, but their hope slashes when I pick up Epiales without a fight. His long body drapes over my arms, unstirring, even as my winged sandals lift us into the air.

We soar through the air, moving farther from Mt. Olympus until it is a blip in my periphery. Only then do I glare down at the male who has caused me endless suffering. He looks like he is at peace, with his eyes closed and face dissolved of rage. I hate it. He should show his anguish on his face like a prison tattoo.

"I want to drop you." My words have a sharpened edge, giving way to all the hatred I feel for him. "I want to watch as your head splatters against the cement and you're beyond recognition, but I can't. This prophecy forces me to let you live. My love for Saffron forces me to let you live long enough for her not to hate me. But I am the god of mischief, and once Styx is dead, I will kill you in a way that looks like an accident. I promise you that."

I land on the apartment's balcony I had purchased for him, and I walk into the opened window. This is a quaint apartment, with a window-door that leads to a balcony view of the city he will now call home. It is small, a simple one-bedroom, but it'll do. I lay him down on the bed gingerly, and then pull out his new identification.

I throw the wallet on top of his stomach as he silently slumbers.

He doesn't even snore.

"If you see a photograph of Saffron, you will see her as nothing but the Goddess of Deliverance, Bones, and Humanity. She is nothing to you now." I lean in close to him, staring at him for hopefully the last time before I kill him, and I snarl. "Have a miserable life, Erik Oneiroi."

FORTY

HART SOMMERS

"What in the Underworld?"

Zeus stands in my art room, a deprived place no one else has seen. It hides in the crevices of my mind, where no one can journey without my permission. If anyone walks into my bedroom on Mt. Olympus, they will see Zeus and I silently sitting together around a plate of food, but we are far from that quaint table. We just barely touch, his pinky knuckle caressing mine, but with that small contact, I brought him with me into my mind.

That's where our consciousnesses are at, in the depths of my mind, where the other oracles join us. My mind is an art room, where every variation of the war's story unfolds. The other oracles, in their signature gem-colored gowns, do not speak. They silently sit in a circle and watch Zeus walk around the room, taking in what could have happened if I did not control the strings of every occurrence.

"This is what would have happened if you killed Epiales on Ogygia," I say, but the voice doesn't sound fully like mine.

It's a mixture of my voice, Aashritha's, and every oracle who sits among us. Because I'm not just myself anymore. I am all of us, conjoined together to create an oracle unlike ever before. We are seven minds mottled together, combining only the most powerful fragments.

Zeus stands in front of the eight drawings I created, displaying the path of destruction that would have befallen the world if Zeus killed Epiales on Ogygia. It begins with Saffron ripping the bones out of Zeus's body. Half his build is Alastor, his alter-ego, but the other half is Zeus. She realizes too late that Alastor and Zeus are the same god, and she kills her father.

Killing Zeus after he murdered Epiales shatters the tattered remains of Saffron's sanity. The break in her resolve leaves an opening in her mind that Hecate's magic worms through, and death erupts at her fingertips. Saffron raises her hands on a battlefield, and she reduces all the gods she loves to blood and skin around her. Hades, Persephone, Apollo, Hermes, and many more are dead as Styx laughs with glee.

I point to the next images. "This would have been the world's fate if Saffron won in the arena."

Again, a symphony of death and destruction.

I explain each sequence of events to Zeus, answering every question behind the images, so he can understand why he must follow my lead. He wears the crown, but I must be his voice from this moment until the war finishes. Zeus crumbles to his knees when he witnesses the fourth drawing of Saffron murdering him.

In some drawings, Epiales hangs from his entrails, and

Saffron falls at his feet with tears covering her face. Others show Hermes captured in a green cocoon of Hecate's magic. Sometimes, the huntresses die by Atlas's hands. Others, they fall to Typhon's rage while he still lives. Artemis spirals towards insanity in a few, joining Styx and Hecate instead of Saffron through magic-induced manipulation.

There are thousands of outcomes, all bleeding through the canvases, and Zeus can scarcely survive the onslaught of information. I had to nearly die to experience it all, to draw each sequence with a steady hand and unwavering belief.

I don't walk towards Zeus; instead, I glide with inhuman effortlessness. I am not yet immortal, not until I marry Apollo, but I am not fully human either. Lowell had to nearly kill me for me to embrace this version of myself, one that does not fear death or the war's repercussions. I place a hand on either side of his face, and I turn him to the one outcome that will save everyone he loves, with only a few deadly costs.

I force him to see who the singer and the seeker are, why the hammer must wield her mighty weapon, and why the huntress must defeat the greatest monster. My paintings foretell the hero's destiny, and the identity of the savior's heart, who must die twice to incite the final battle. The scent of salty tears overwhelms the room, but I do not search for its source. I stare at the ultimate outcome that ends with a volcano forming in the middle of the battlefield.

I stare at myself in the last picture and whisper. "Crumble like Pompeii."

"That's why Epiales couldn't die," Zeus hiccups, past his own staggering emotions. "I understand now, but…"

He turns his head to face me, but before he can speak, eight clocks chime a haunting tune. His face pales beneath my inquisition. "What was that?"

"It's time," the emerald oracle says.

"It's time," the ruby oracle repeats.

"It's time," they all say in perfect succession.

Finally, I look down at Zeus, and I say with all our voices meshed. "It's time for the war to truly begin."

FORTY-ONE

SAFFRON

Ares is right. It's almost too easy to find Atlas. The titan hasn't stopped his search for Artemis and her huntresses. Atlas still searches to eliminate them all from existence, so their part of the prophecy doesn't come true. Or he's too afraid to go back empty-handed to Styx. Atlas remains in the woods where the huntresses last saw them. He's a few miles south of where he killed Argus, sitting at a campsite with his daughter, Calypso.

I glance at Ares when I see Calypso, then whisper. "I thought we imprisoned her on Mt. Olympus?"

"Someone must have let her go. Another traitor we must kill." Ares's sword glints off the sunlight, illuminating his face with a silvery sheen. "I'm ready when you are, gorgeous."

A raucous laugh cuts through the words coming from Atlas. The titan dares to smile after the carnage he's created, but not for long.

Ares and I quietly approach the campsite, where they laugh and joke while planning their next steps to find the huntresses. Both our weapons glint against the sunrise, but we do not attack yet. We wait for the moment Atlas senses us and turns around to realize he is about to die.

We are ten feet away from them when Atlas tenses ever so slightly, then cranes his head. His eyes clash with mine first, and the smug titan dares to shoot me a wicked grin. "You're just as pretty as I remember."

Calypso wisely jumps to her feet and runs in the opposite direction. Her father, however, plays the fool. He takes in my curves and blatantly feminine appearance and devalues my abilities as a goddess. He witnessed my powers when I was a human who did not know how to wield them, and he lost to me then. How does he expect today to go when I am stronger than that demi-god from long ago?

"You moved onto a new god, I see. Can't be a good girl, huh?" Atlas's grin grows as his gaze focuses on Ares. "Bit of advice, buddy. When you keep choosing loose women, you-"

Ares glances down at me. "Are you going to shut him up, or do I get the privilege?"

I hate comparing them, but Ares's question reminds me of how different he is from Hermes. Hermes would hear the derogatory statement and the slurs against me, and he would blindly attack. He would always assume I needed him to be the hero, slashing away my problems, but not Ares. It's nearly impossible not to realize that Ares is giving me the choice to be protected or to be the fighter.

And I needed that today.

I grin at the unfamiliar, bubbling friendship between Ares and me. "I got it."

My gaze wanders back to Atlas, who still hasn't unsheathed his sword in his ignorance, but I hold out my hand and beckon another forward. With Calypso's immortal speed, she's miles away, but I pull at her bones with relative ease. She's too far away to hear her screams, but it won't be long until Atlas realizes.

"You killed my friend," I say with a snarl at the end of my statement.

"Who? The disgusting giant?" Atlas laughs. "You bet I did. It was almost too easy to kill your *other* boyfriend."

I take one step towards him, but he doesn't flinch. "Insinuate I'm a whore one more time."

"Oh, honey, I'm not insinuating anything. You and that pretty face have all the gods and giants and humans spun around-"

He stops as Calypso falls into the bonfire, pulled back to the fighting ground with my magic over her bones. He whirls around to face his daughter as the flames accept the feast I offer. She cannot move as I hold her body down. Calypso thrashes in the fire as it eats away at her skin and chars her bones. Atlas sprints to his daughter and tries to pull her out of the fire, but it's futile. As long as I hold her bones in my grasp, anything he does won't alter Calypso's outcome.

He takes a minute to realize this, then he whirls around to face me. "You stupid-"

I interrupt him, facing Ares. "You can deal with him now."

Ares mirrors his sigil animal, the boar, as he turns to face Atlas. He charges towards Atlas with a battle cry escaping his lips. Calypso cannot die by the flames because of her divinity, so her skin continues to heal, then catches aflame again and again. Nothing frees her from the torment, and as Ares tackles Atlas to the ground, her screams are their background music.

Ares raises his sword in the air and strikes it down before Atlas can unsheathe his sword. The titan's over-inflated confidence crashes down when the sword slides into the center of his throat and pierces the ground beneath. In three rapid successions, Ares removes two knives, then slams both over Atlas's hands, so he cannot move.

Atlas tries to push his hands free, but he doesn't risk unbearable pain by ripping them free. He thrashes, then groans, fighting to look anywhere but at his burning daughter. I walk towards him, languid in my movements, and he spews barely comprehensible curses. I ignore them all until I crouch down beside his face. He tries to bite me, but I'm not close enough, and that causes him to scream almost as loud as his daughter.

"You killed my friend," I say. "A man who did nothing wrong but try to save me. A man who didn't deserve to die. Yet, you mocked me when I said what you had done. You mocked his appearance when he can no longer defend himself. Then, you mocked my gender, my relationships, and my abilities, and that sealed not only your fate, but your daughter's."

Right now, I am not a person with compassion; I am on a warpath. I think of Argus, a man with more compassion on his pinky finger than anybody on this island, and how he never received a chance at life without judgement or prejudice.

Now, Atlas's fate no longer matters.

"I was always going to make you suffer, Atlas, but when

I saw Calypso with you, I almost thought about letting her go. She's not much of a fighter, and now that we know Ogygia's whereabouts, she's pretty useless to Styx. But then you had to insult my friend. Now, I'm feeling a bit mean."

I use my power over her bones to pull Calypso away from the fire. I lay her a few feet away from Atlas, so he can see the moment he loses her. Realization dawns on his face, and he tries to scream, but the sound muffles with the sword lodged in his throat. He finally rips one of his hands in half to free it from the knife, but it's too late.

I pull on her bones, and they obey.

She becomes confetti of blood and organs, raining down on Ares, Atlas, and me. Atlas screams so loud that blood erupts from his mouth, but he doesn't care. I turn to Ares, expecting him to judge my bloodlust like so many others, but he grins. Ares sees my rage, and how much I have changed over the years, and he still approves.

"Can I pull the sword out of his neck now?" Ares asks, amused.

"Please."

The moment Ares pulls the sword out of Atlas neck, he takes a few steps back and watches with me as Atlas heals, then screams. "You are a monster!"

"I don't think monster is the correct term," Ares says.

"What I am, Atlas, is a scorned goddess, who you foolishly underestimated. You should've thought about your actions before now, but you didn't, so now you must suffer."

With the same powers that stole his daughter's life, I levitate him, Ares, and me into the air. There's a paralyzing moment when Atlas believes this is his last moment alive. That I will rip every bone from his body like I did his daughter seconds earlier, but he does not deserve my mercy. I fly us far away from the woods he tried to kill the huntresses in, and I let him stew in the possibilities of where I am taking him.

When his familiar mountain comes into view, he screams until I freeze his jawbone.

We land inside Mt. Atlas easily, but the moment our feet touch the ground, the current god holding the earth, Hedylogos, sighs in relief. "Dad, you came back for me."

Ares turns his back to Hedylogos, who betrayed him long before this moment. "Don't kill him," is all he says to me.

"Never," I promise. "But what do you want me to do with him?"

"I'll behave, I swear!" Hedylogos quickly sobs. "I just want to go home. Dad, please let me come home."

"I never want to see you again," Ares snarls, still refusing to look at his son. "The moment you're freed, you are gone. You will not come to Mt. Olympus, you will not visit your mother, and you will certainly never see me again. You are a ghost after today. Am I understood?"

There's a long pause, and in this suspended moment, Ares shows a crack in his demeanor. A tear rolls down his cheek, but Hedylogos cannot see it. Only I can, and my hand itches to wipe it away, but I know he doesn't want me to witness this, so I pretend my focus is on Atlas.

Finally, Hedylogos whimpers. "Okay."

In one fluid motion, I throw Hedylogos off the mountain and place Atlas back at his place beneath the earth. He grunts as he takes the weight of the world again, but as I let go of his bones, his momentary fear of me leaves, too.

The foolish titan glowers at me. "One day, I'll come back to kill you."

"Once you trick another immortal into taking your post here, of course."

The moron cynically laughs. "You're damn right."

"Except what would happen if you could never leave this post again?" The question gives him pause, so I elaborate. "I thought about killing you, but what is a worse fate than this? Eternally bound to hold the weight of the world upon your shoulders?"

"I need you to splinter the ground below Atlas's feet."

"Where's my please?" Ares grunts.

I look back at Ares and smirk. "Please."

He stalls as his eyes capture the small, amused expression on my lips. Atlas screams profanities at us both, but I can barely hear him as Ares takes a step towards me. As he stares at me like that.

"As you wish, gorgeous."

An axe materializes in Ares's hand and, just as I request, he smacks into the ground below Atlas's feet. There is only a few inches of open ground, and that is perfect. Ares takes several steps back, already knowing my plan, and I raise my hands in the air.

There are many bones in the feet, ready to move to my command, and I force Atlas's to elongate. They pierce out of his skin, slither like tree roots down into the crack into the ground, and weld with the rocks. Atlas's scream threatens to shatter the surrounding mountain, but I do not stop my creation. Once all the bones in his feet are both inside his body and molded into the ground, I migrate my attention to his legs.

The bones in his legs shoot out, then curve downward into the ground. He quickly resembles a tree more than a titan. Atlas's bellows never cease. He begs for mercy, for death, for retribution against me, but none of them come to fruition. There's no freedom for him as I meld all the bones in his legs to the ground. Every bone in his body, from the waist down, branches out clinging to the walls or the floor, making him forever intertwined to the mountain.

Unable to escape again.

He can barely keep his head up from the overwhelming pain, but he wisely flinches when I walk towards him. Atlas sobs the moment my hand curls around his jaw, forcing him to lock eyes with me. "I can't wait to see how you'll get out of this."

ARES AND I DECIDE TO GO TO MY HOUSE ON EARTH. WE pick up hot dogs at a nearby stand, then walk the mile separating the stand from my mansion. We grab two each, lather them in all the fixings, then quietly stroll as we consume the first one.

"Thank you for not judging me." I bite into my second hot dog.

Ares rolls his eyes. "You need to stop thanking me for things that don't involve gratitude. I'm the god of bloodshed. Of course, I will not judge you at the sight of it."

I laugh a little at that. "Just got used to apologizing, I guess."

"Don't." He bites into his hot dog, relishing the ridiculous amounts of ketchup on top, before elaborating. "You're perfect, and perfection doesn't deserve apologies. Only reverence."

"When you talk like that, it almost sounds like you like me."

I eat more of my hot dog as I suppress a smile. Ares glances down at me, and the corner of his lip twitches slightly. "Almost," he whispers.

The rest of our walk remains mostly quiet, but pleasant. His company refreshes me more than I thought I could after the recent events, even if I know he will run from me the moment fear settles in. It's how it always works with us, but I enjoy the few moments. It will have to be enough.

We walk past the gate towards my home, and only then does Ares look away from me. "Until my sons come down, can I stay? I want to make you're…"

He stops talking.

"That I'm what?"

He stops walking.

"Ares?" I follow his line of vision, and I drop the last bite of my hot dog.

A woman sits on my front step, appearing to be in her early thirties, with a three-headed dog resting its tired heads on her lap. She looks completely different from the elderly version of her I last saw all those years ago; now, she looks how I will always remember as. Fearless, brazen, and beautiful.

"Hattie?"

Upon hearing her name, my deceased friend's head lifts. She rises to her feet, with Cerberus following her movements. The normal white tunic, which all the deceased wear in the Underworld, has blood splatters covering its entirety. Some are crimson like humans, but there's ichor, too. She leans her weight on Cerberus, and only then do I realize how pale she is and the way she presses her hand to her stomach.

Ares and I run to Hattie. "What happened?!" I yell.

Once I'm at arm's length, Hattie collapses into me. We both fall onto the ground, my arms still wrapped around my once-dead best friend, as she stares up at me with teary, dark eyes. "The Underworld," Hattie murmurs, disbelief lacing her tone. "It's gone."

FORTY-TWO

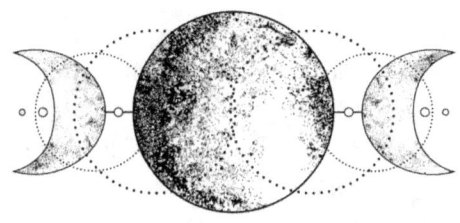

HECATE

Before me, Styx has her army.

Millions have joined our side towards Styx's eternal reign. Humans, gods, goddesses, and monsters alike stand on the prison floor, staring up at Styx and me from our place at the upper level. They cheer for her victory, but I can't focus on anything but the prison we stand in, where Saffron's story began all those years ago.

The huntresses burned it to the ground almost a hundred years ago, but the cinders remained, and that's all I needed to bring it back to life. It all looks the same, just as I left it long ago. The walls still cry with the unheard screams of the dead prisoners. The hallways still echo with the running, desperate feet of those who tried to escape and failed.

Styx, who stands beside me, stares at eons worth of murderous humans, who she freed when we destroyed the Underworld, and who are intent on the crumble of the Olympians. I, however, latch onto the sight of former slaves who died in Kronos's feeble plans for success. China and Glasswing, who turned insane because of the events of the past, stare back at me.

Styx fearfully refused many huntresses to our cause, except for the rare few who tricked Artemis enough to kill another huntress. Raven, who murdered Willow, and Akita, who ended Sika's life, stand ruefully in the crowd. Lowell stands beside them, bouncing on his heels with excitement.

On Styx's other side stands her mutilated creation, who was once Gareth French.

Once upon a time, Gareth French was a human male, who found his wife and daughter murdered in our crusade towards the crown, and he blamed Saffron. Correction: we framed Saffron. He orchestrated riots outside her home, claiming she became a monster. His abhorrence for Saffron rattled her. Later, he realized Nemesis murdered his family under Styx's command. Saffron killed Nemesis in front of Gareth, to give him peace.

It didn't.

The night after Nemesis's death and Saffron's imprisonment on Ogygia, Styx ordered me to find Gareth French. I found him foaming at the mouth in his bed with an empty pill bottle in his hand. His mental psyche was so fractured, it took almost no effort to heal him, then bring him to Styx to be truly destroyed.

It was easy enough to slip into his mind, to tilt the glimpse of insanity into a gnarling beast waiting to be released. In the weeks since Saffron left Gareth, Styx created him into a vision of her own monstrosity. A part of him is still human, with a human heart and blood that spills red, but the rest of him is something else.

Not a god or a titan, but a monster made of whirling

mechanics, blades for arms, and an absence of conscious. Now, he looks upon the room with a deadness in his eyes that can never be undone. Styx ruined many humans with her malignant inventions, but Gareth is her proudest creation because Saffron knew him before his mutilation.

Gareth, like the millions on the floor beneath us, ready themselves for a war they could die once again fighting, and they do not care. Fearlessness casts the faces of every monster, from centuries ago to modern day, who wants to thrive in a world of mayhem of Styx's creation.

While some of these murderers mean nothing to Styx and me, inconsequential humans who are too idiotic to see the true evil in front of them- they mean everything to our opponents. They were once friends, lovers, and family. They were people that the gods or the oracle sympathized with, knew, or possibly loved.

The heart is a fickle thing; I had learned from my time with Mastiff, and it is the downfall of all. Myself especially. I stand with deplorable monsters, immortals, and humans, and I hate myself a little more each day for my decisions, but this is the only version where Mastiff lives with me forever. He stands a few feet away, looking only at me, and I know that if I could rewind time, I would still choose this path.

I would still choose villainy with Mastiff.

Amongst the cheering humans, there is a litter of monsters who chose Styx's fight. The monsters, who were not killed by Saffron but by a hero or huntress, are alive once again. All who spent their afterlife in the Fields of Punishments or Tartarus are alive once more, letting out mighty roars as the war drums reach our enemies' ears.

Uranus, Kronos's father and Zeus's grandfather, stands in the center of the monsters with Typhon. I can practically feel the crown leaving Zeus's head and landing permanently on Styx's.

Behind us, sitting behind a locked door with no windows, are our prisoners from the Underworld. Those who will join the opposing side if freed. The moment we captured them, I wanted to kill those who could die- all the humans and huntresses- but Styx wants the carnage. She wants Saffron to suffer, one scream at a time. Soon, all the mortals Saffron cared for will become mindless creations like Gareth French, created to destroy her.

All the previously dead souls in the Underworld, and the unfortunate gods who lived in the Underworld at the time of our ransack, will suffer unimaginable pain within that small, windowless prison.

Willow and Sika, two of the most formidable huntresses, sit in chains beside a few other huntresses who died loyal to their sigil goddess. Beside them, Queen Perse-phone and her loyal twin gods, Thanatos and Hypnos, thrash in their chains in the room behind me. Diam, Zig, Angel, Pyro, Panda, and when we find Hattie, will regret every decision that led them to that room.

Styx raises a hand in the air, and the room filled with millions goes silent.

"Let's bathe the world in red and gold. Shall we?"

ACKNOWLEDGMENTS

The sequel curse struck me with this book. While it is the fourth book in the installment, I always separate the Ichor Series into two categories. The first two books are the Kronos duology, while books 3, 4, and 5 are Styx's trilogy. This is the sequel to Styx's story, and it was really difficult to write. I have never had so many existential crises as I did with this book. Imposter syndrome was strong this time around, and every time I would write a paragraph, I would convince myself it wasn't good enough. After many deletions, curses, and tears, Oneiroi is here. This was the toughest book for me to write in my career, and it would not be here if I didn't have such amazing people in my corner.

Thank you, Anne Dehler, for being the greatest editor in the world. You kept motivating me with your kind words. I love you more than words can say.

Thank you to amazing fans like Jess and Em. Any time I would feel discouraged with my many moments of writer's block, you would make another video about my book, and it would lift my spirits. You both got me out of a lot of writing slumps.

Thank you to my husband, Mat. You dealt with my rants about quitting it all and not being good enough, and you reminded me that writing is a part of who I am. It's in my blood. Regardless of if one person reads this, or five thousand, I will never stop writing. Thank you for being my motivation, my muse, and my soulmate.

GLOSSARY IN ALPHABETICAL ORDER

Achilles: Infamous hero in the Trojan War. Demi-God, son of a sea nymph named Thetis.

Adonis: Human male notorious for his beauty. Lover of Aphrodite and Persephone. Slain by Ares as a boar.

Aeetes: Husband of Hecate & king of Colchis.

Aegeus: King of Athens. Father of Theseus.

Alastor: (Slight Spoilers: Read with Caution). An epithet of Zeus. Avenger of Evil Deeds.

Alecto: One of the 3 Furies, who live in the Underworld.

Ambrosia: Food of the Gods.

Amphitrite: Wife of Poseidon and Queen of the Seas. One of the 50 Nereids. Daughter of Oceanus & Tethys.

Anchises: Famous Lover of Aphrodite. Father of Aphrodite's son, Aeneas.

Apate: Personification of Fraud, Deceit, Deception, and Guile.

Apollo: God of Prophecies, Music, Poetry, Art, Truth,

Healing, Sun, and Light. Twin Brother of Artemis. Son of Zeus and Leto. One of the 12 Olympians.

Aphrodite: Goddess of Sexual Love and Beauty. Wife of Hephaestus. One of the 12 Olympians.

Ares: God of War and Bloodshed. Son of Zeus and Hera. One of the 12 Olympians.

Argus: Many-Eyed Giant. Slain by Hermes. Hera's guard in most stories.

Ariadne: Wife of Dionysus. Once a human princess, who helped Theseus defeat the Labyrinth. Daughter of Minos.

Aristaeus: God of Beekeeping, Honey, Shepherds, and Cheese-making.

Artemis: Goddess of the Hunt, Wild Animals, Vegetation, Chastity, and Childbirth. Twin Sisters of Apollo. Daughter of Zeus and Leto. One of the 12 Olympians.

Asclepius: God of Medicine. Son of Apollo.

Asphodel Meadows: Largest segment of the Underworld. This is where almost all the dead are placed.

Atalanta: Famous Female Hero. Member of the Argonauts.

Athena: Goddess of Wisdom, Crafts, and Battle Strategies. Favorite Daughter of Zeus. First-born child between Metis and Zeus. One of the 12 Olympians.

Atlas: Titan condemned to hold the skies for eternity after the first Titanomachy War. Father of Calypso.

Asopus: God of Four Rivers. Famously known for his 20 nymph daughters.

Calliope: One of the Muses. Goddess of Heroic Poetry.

Calypso: A nymph who was exiled to the island of Ogygia. Captured Odysseus on his way home from the Trojan War. Daughter of Atlas.

Cerberus: 3-Headed Dog of the Underworld. Child of

the Echidna and Typhon. Guards the gates of the Underworld.

Circe: Witch Goddess. Daughter of Hecate and Aeetes.

Clio: One of the Muses. Goddess of History.

Daedalus: Creator of the Labyrinth. One of the wisest men in Greek Mythology.

Dagger of Chains: Fictional dagger created by the author. "Created" by Daedalus to imprison immortals. Inspired by the Tibetan Phurba Dagger.

Deimos: God of Terror and Dread. Twin Brother of Phobos. Son of Ares and Aphrodite.

Delphi: Delphi is a town on Mount Parnassus in the south of mainland Greece. It's the site of the 4th-century-B.C. Temple of Apollo, once home to a legendary oracle.

Demeter: Goddess of the Harvest. Daughter of Kronos and Rhea. Mother of Persephone.

Dionysus: God of Wine, Partying, Fertility, Insanity, Festivity, Orgies, and Theater. Son of Zeus and Semele. One of the 12 Olympians after Hestia gave up her spot for him.

Echo: Famous Lover of Zeus. Hera cursed her to only speak in others' echoes.

Elysium Fields: The Underworld's version of heaven. Most gods and scholars are sent here.

Epiales: Personified Spirit (Daemon) of Nightmares. Almost completely forgotten in mythology. Brother of Hypnos and Thanatos. Son of Nyx.

Erato: Muse of Lyric, Erotic Poetry, and Hymns. One of the 9 Muses.

Eros: God of Love and Sex. Son of Ares and Aphrodite. Husband of Psyche. Has arrows that, once shot, can either turn you deliriously in love with the first person you see. Or it will make you hate them.

Elysium Fields: The "heaven" in the Underworld. Heroes live there for eternity.

Euterpe: One of the Muses. Goddess of Music & Flutes.

The Fates: Three weaving goddesses, who represent the inescapable destiny of humanity.

Fields of Punishment: A land in the Underworld, where the worst humans are sent to suffer for all of eternity.

Hades: God of the Underworld and Jewels. The eldest son of Kronos and Rhea. Husband of Persephone. One of the 12 Olympians.

Hebe: Goddess of Youth. Daughter of Zeus and Hera. Wife of Heracles. Cupbearer to the Gods.

Hecate: Goddess of Witchcraft and Necromancy. Wife of Aeetes.

Hedylogos: God of Sweet-Talk and Flattery. Son of Ares and Aphrodite.

Hephaestus: God of Blacksmithing, Metalworking, Sculptures, and Fire. Son of Hera. Husband of Aphrodite. One of the 12 Olympians.

Hera: Queen of the Olympians. Wife/Sister of Zeus. Daughter of Kronos and Rhea. Goddess of Marriage and Childbirth. Notoriously hates all of Zeus's children outside of wedlock.

Hermes: God of Thievery, Trade, Wealth, Luck, and Travel. Son of Zeus and Maia. Messenger of the Gods.

Hermaphroditus: God of Effeminates. Son of Hermes and Aphrodite.

Hestia: Goddess of the Hearth. The eldest daughter of

Kronos and Rhea. Gave up her role as an Olympian for Dionysus.

Horkos: The Personification of Curses and Avenger of Perjury. If you disobey an oath you swore, Horkos will come for you on the 5th day of the 5th month and curse you.

Hyacinth: Famous Lover of Apollo. Killed by another god, Zephyrus, out of jealousy.

Hypnos: Personified Spirit (Daemon) of Sleep. Son of Nyx. Twin Brother of Thanatos.

Icarus: Son of Daedalus, the talented inventor. Famously wore wings made by his father to escape Crete, but he was so spellbound by the sun that he kept flying higher. He ultimately was killed by the sun's rays because he got too close.

Ichor: Gold Blood of the Gods.

Io: Notorious Lover of Zeus. Turned into a cow by Zeus to hide his adulterous ways from Hera.

Iris: Goddess of Rainbows. Messenger of the Gods. Specifically Works for Hera.

Ixion: The man who tried to seduce Hera. In the Fields of Punishment, eternally spinning on a wheel of fire.

Jason: Greek Hero and Leader of the Argonauts. Retriever of the Golden Fleece.

Khione: Goddess of Snow. Daughter of Boreas and Oreithyia.

Kratos: Personification of Strength. Son of Styx.

Kronos: Titan of Time. Son of Gaia and Uranus. Defeater of Uranus. Fallen Leader of the Titanomachy Wars.

Labyrinth: A maze created by Daedalus in Crete for King Minos. The Minotaur lived and hunted in here.

Lethe: Personification of Oblivion. Has dominion over

the River Lethe, where the deceased souls go when they wish to forget their existence. Daughter of Eris.

Marpessa: Famous Lover of Apollo. Notoriously chose a human male instead of the god.

Megaera: One of the 3 Furies. Resides in the Underworld.

Melpomene: One of the Muses. Goddess of Tragedy.

Metis: Titaness daughter of Oceanus and Tethys. Zeus's first wife. Mother of Athena. Second child was believed to become the most powerful immortal. Killed by Zeus.

Minos: King of Crete. Orchestrator of the Labyrinth. One of the 3 Judges of the Underworld.

Minotaur: Half-man, Half-beast. Son of Queen Pasiphae and a white bull. Slain by Theseus in the Labyrinth.

Mount Olympus: Home of the Gods. Located in the Skies.

Morpheus: God of Dreams. Son of Hypnos.

The Muses: Nine Goddesses who defend the arts. Provide entertainment for the Olympians.

Narcissus: Mortal man, who was so obsessed with his appearance that he could not pull his eyes away from the water's reflection of him.

Nectar: Drink of the Gods.

Nemean Lion: Vicious lion with impenetrable fur. Defeated by Heracles during his 12 Labors.

Nemesis: Goddess of Divine Retribution and Revenge.

Nike: Goddess of Victory.

Nosoi: Personifications Spirts of Plague, Sickness, and Disease. In this story, their form is birds, but their form is ever-changing.

Odysseus: Hailed wisest hero of Greek Mythology. Famous for the Trojan War and his journey home.

Oedipus: The king of Thebes, who unwittingly killed his father and married his mother. Slayer of the Sphinx, which gave him Thebes' crown.

Ogygia: Island where Calypso was exiled. Known as a distant island, most could not find.

Oizys: Goddess of Misery, Anxiety, Grief, Depression, and Misfortune.

Olympians: The 12 major gods of the Greek Pantheon. Olympus Industries: A fictional skyscraper building created for this story. This is where the gods meet when conducting business on earth.

Oneiroi: The gods of dreams in Greek mythology. The innumerable sons of Nyx. (See: Epiales & Hypnos).

Oracle: A person (typically females) considered providing wise, prophetic insight. Another common terminology is a seer.

Paean: Physician of the Gods.

Paris's Judgement: After Eris tossed an apple labeled "to the fairest" around Hera, Aphrodite, and Athena, the women fought to see who was the fairest. They made a Trojan prince, Paris, decide who was the fairest goddess, and each promised him a reward. Paris chose Aphrodite as the fairest; in return, she made a woman named Helen fall in love with him.

Peitho: Personified Goddess of Persuasion, Seduction, and Charming Speech. Daughter of Oceanus and Tethys.

Perseus: Demi-God, son of Zeus and Danae. Slayer of Medusa.

Phobos: God of Fear and Panic. Twin Brother of Deimos. Son of Aphrodite and Ares.

Persephone: Queen of the Underworld. Goddess of Spring. Daughter of Zeus and Demeter. Wife of Hades.

Polymnia: One of the Muses. Goddess of Sacred Poetry and Pantomime.

Pompeii: Once a thriving and sophisticated Roman city, a volcano buried the city under meters of ash and pumice. The catastrophic eruption was Mount Vesuvius in 79 A.D.

Poseidon: God of the Seas. Son of Kronos and Rhea. Husband of Amphitrite. One of the 12 Olympians.

Priapus: Low-level Fertility God.

Psyche: Goddess of Soul. Wife of Eros.

Rhadamanthus: Demi-God, son of Zeus and Europa. Once dead, he became one of the 3 judges of the Underworld.

Seer: See Oracle definition.

Sinope: River Nymph. Daughter of Asopus.

Sisyphus: Man who tried to cheat death twice. Cursed in the Fields of Punishment to eternally push a boulder up a hill, only for it to fall to the bottom again.

Sphynx: Female Monster. Body of a lion, head and breasts of a woman, wings of an eagle, and tail of a snake. Defeated by Oedipus.

Styx: Personification of Hatred. One of the Eldest Immortals. The strongest oaths are to her river.

Terpsichore: One of the Muses. Goddess of Chorus and Dancing.

Thalia: One of the Muses. Goddess of Comedy.

Tisiphone: One of the 3 Furies. Resides in the Underworld.

Titanomachy War: A 10-year war between the Titans and the Olympians.

Typhon: Father of Monsters. Greatest Monster in Greek Mythology Existence.

Urania: Muse of Astronomy. One of the 9 Muses.

Uranus: Father Sky. Husband of Gaia. Father of Kronos. Grandfather of Zeus.

Zagreus: God of Rebirth. Son of Persephone and Zeus.

Zeus: King of the Olympians. The youngest son of Rhea and Kronos. God of Lightning and the Skies. Father to most Gods and Demi-Gods.

ABOUT THE AUTHOR

Trish D.W is a woman with a lifelong dream of being a full-time author. She has dreamed of this moment since she was a little girl at recess writing scripts rather than playing on the play-ground. Each day, her dream becomes a clearer reality, and she is grateful to everybody who has purchased her novel.

FOLLOW TRISH D.W ON THE WEB AT:

trishdw.com

Instagram & TikTok: @authortrishdw

www.ingramcontent.com/pod-product-compliance
Lightning Source LLC
Chambersburg PA
CBHW070833260626
47170CB00007B/2349

9 7 9 8 9 8 6 6 4 3 1 4 4